KEPLER'S CHILDREN

TONY HARMSWORTH

Vinci Books

vinci-books.com

Published by Vinci Books Ltd in 2026

1

A CIP catalogue record for this book is available from the British Library.
Paperback ISBN: 9781036716455
The EU GPSR authorised representative is Logos Europe, 9 rue Nicolas Poussion, 17000 La Rochelle, France contact@logoseurope.eu

By Tony Harmsworth

Mindslip Universe

Supernova

Scorched Earth

Kepler's Children

Mark Noble: Edge of the Void Series

Moonscape

Trappist-1

Replica Paradox

Dark Logic

Hubris Effect

Federation Trilogy

Federation

Federation and Earth

Hidden Federation

Standalones

The Door

The Visitor

By Tony Harrison

3SBY

Chapter One

EXTRA-VEHICULAR ACTIVITY

Caroline Arnold-Pointer, a mixed-race European/Japanese woman, pulled herself hand over hand along the underside of Kepler's C-section. The ship measured eight hundred metres in diameter – a huge disc, a veritable flying saucer. The flat surface of the rear face of the ship stretched on before her into the distance.

'How's the air now?' asked the gruff-sounding male voice of the EVA officer in her helmet's audio system.

Her eyes flashed downward for less than a second. Now was not the time to miss a handhold. The LED display on the upper side of her wrist read zero and blinked red. That was bad. Not only did she have no air remaining, but the reserve was also drained.

'Zero,' she said, panic rising. She didn't want to die out there. Too young for death, she was only twenty-one. She had her whole life ahead of her. All her education and training wasted. Would death be painful? Unlike being exposed to a vacuum, which would cause death in seconds, this would be running out of oxygen. An empty tank. The reserve exhausted. All she had now was the air which existed in her suit and helmet. Any moment she'd be light-headed, disoriented, and her consciousness would fade, never to return. Oxygen starvation featured heavily in her training. She'd already reduced the saturation percentage to the absolute minimum, but that would no longer assist her. The air smelled metallic, as if it was the last dregs of the tank.

Handhold after handhold, she pulled herself along. Don't rush, she said to herself. Haste during an EVA could be even more deadly. Her heart was pounding in her chest, and she could almost hear it beating.

Suddenly she jerked to a halt. Forward motion stopped instantly, and she cried out, 'Argh!' and whispered, 'What the hell now?' to herself. The suit chafed her shoulder as she clung to the handhold.

The essential safety line had reached its maximum length and stopped her. Her handhold almost slipped from her fingers. She was only lightly gripping them as she raced along the hull. Potentially, it was a fatal mistake. Losing her grip would cause her to be yanked back towards the circumference, and she'd spin away from the hull. She'd still be attached, of course, but pulling herself back along the safety cord would leave her where she had been two minutes previously. Critical lost time. She couldn't afford to sacrifice even a few seconds. Her air was gone. It could be the final straw which would kill her.

'Don't take shortcuts,' she warned herself.

Looking around, the vast expanse of the outside of Kepler stretched away from her in all directions. Ahead she saw another twenty to thirty handholds and the safety of the nearest airlock. Her intuition told her to slip the safety catch and risk those last few handholds without a safety line.

The mantra, 'Don't take shortcuts. Don't take shortcuts,' echoed through her mind. She searched the hull again. Two handholds back, a connector poked out of its hole in the hull. She turned, yanked herself back to the hole, connected the clip to her belt, and undid the old one, which slithered back towards its own cubbyhole some forty metres along the way she had come. Secure now, she thought. Quick, quick, turn and pull.

She grabbed the nearest handhold and tugged. Her body had mass, but little weight as it neared the zero-G hub of the hull. Now flying forward, reaching for the next, she almost let the aluminium loop slip through her grasp in her haste. 'More haste, less speed,' she recited to herself. Sweat beaded on her brow. Fog formed on the visor. Was this the end? Was carbon dioxide poisoning her as she used the final dregs of her oxygen? Was it all gone? Did the misting mean she was mainly rebreathing carbon dioxide? Death could arrive in seconds. As it sneaked up on her, her mind would fog too. She looked forward. Hand after hand after hand. Three metres to the hatch. Keep going. Force yourself. 'Come on, Cas. Push yourself,' she murmured. No sign of the predicted headache yet. Grab the hatch!

Both hands gripped a wheel on the outer surface of the airlock. She wrenched at the handle.

Damn, damn, damn, damn! She'd forgotten to anchor herself first and almost went flying off the airlock. Two fingers of the cumbersome gloves kept a hold. She wedged her feet into the closest handhold and turned the wheel again. It was stuck. Was it jammed? If it jammed, her life would end. No time to reach the next nearest airlock.

She heaved with all her might, and she sensed motion. Five spins and she pulled, remembering to secure her feet first. The hatch, about a metre in diameter, swung open.

She let go of the handle, hooked her hand over the edge of the airlock and hurled herself inwards headfirst, the suit's collar cutting into her neck as she concentrated on the essentials.

Still work to do. Still breathing. 'Almost safe,' she said to herself.

While one hand gripped the entrance, the other reached for a safety clip. She connected it to her belt, releasing the previous one simultaneously. She watched the cable wriggling its way towards the hole in the hull.

The moment it cleared the airlock; she twisted around to face the hatch again. Still breathing, she thought again.

She hauled on the inner wheel and pulled. Once more, she'd forgotten to anchor herself, and she crunched into the hatch, wrenching her shoulder. Looking down into the airlock, she hooked her foot through one of the steel hoops and heaved again.

The hoop hurt her instep as the hatch slammed shut. She spun the handle, turned and hit the green button.

All of a sudden, her suit collapsed around her as air flooded inward and the pressure equalised. Frantically, she tore a glove off and fiddled with the helmet clasps, rotating the whole thing until the helmet floated free, the slight pressure difference causing her ears to pop as she returned to normal saturation.

Gasping in a lungful of the loveliest clean air confirmed her safety. She'd survived. 'Made it,' she whispered.

How the hell had it happened? She'd carried out all the safety checks before beginning the EVA. Full tank, full emergency supply, no leaks. Everything secure. The EVA officer himself had checked her clasps. Nothing was amiss. This should not have happened. It should be impossible. Only if something had holed her suit, should she have lost air. That hadn't happened as the air pressure had been standard until she'd deliberately dropped the psi when she'd realised she was in trouble. That was standard safety EVA practice.

So, how, after only being ten minutes into the task, had her tank alarm alerted her to being empty? Or *why* might have been the more relevant question? It shouldn't have happened. She began to feel angry. Annoyed at what system or procedural fault had almost cost her life. The adrenaline was no longer pumping, but her cheeks felt hot with anger. Such things did not occur. It had to be someone's blunder… and it wasn't hers!

The airlock display showed full pressure. She anchored herself and turned the internal wheel. There was a clunk as the seal broke and the inner door opened.

Inside the ship, three grinning faces, including Gerard, the EVA officer, were waiting. Such a shock to see them all there and smiling too. Were they that pleased that she'd made it back to the ship? Of course, they would be. They must have been anxious, but it was odd. Why were they there, waiting for her? Then Gerard laughed.

'What's going on?' she asked, looking around at the three instructors.

'You passed with flying colours,' said Gerard.

What did he mean? Then, like an epiphany, realisation struck her. This had been her emergency response test. She'd been in no danger at all. The instructors had organised the entire event. They'd tampered with her gauge or fitted a radio-controlled one. She'd not been out of oxygen at all.

'You bastards!' she exclaimed at the top of her voice.

'Now, now, Caroline, that's no way to talk to senior officers,' Gerard said and laughed again. They all joined him.

'You sods!' said Caroline, wiping strands of jet-black hair from where the sweat had pasted them upon her forehead and cheeks. 'I'll get you back one day!'

Gerard, still in his own helmetless spacesuit, took a certificate from Helen, one of the other instructors, signed it with a flourish, and handed it to Caroline.

'Congratulations. You still had two minutes to complete the emergency, easily within time. Well done,' the EVA officer said.

Anger still raged within her. She'd believed she was going to die. But she knew it was a necessary part of the training process. So clever. So bloody clever. They'd conned her absolutely. She didn't know that it was her emergency test. She was never in any danger. There'd have been at least two experienced EVA officers outside, hidden in open airlocks in case she'd panicked and lost contact with the ship, but she'd done everything right. Two minutes. That wasn't bad. Most were in the last minute of the allowed time before passing the test. She'd done better than that.

'You said two minutes. What's the record?' she asked.

'Finishing with three minutes eighteen seconds to spare,' said Cardin, a blue-eyed, blond-haired Adonis, she'd once been sweet on and another of the instructors. 'That's mine!' he crowed.

'You had two minutes and forty-one seconds left,' said Gerard. 'The best since Kepler's been underway.'

Now she felt a little better.

'Go get a shower and we'll see you in the Green Bar,' said Cardin.

Caroline headed towards the portside EVA store to remove her suit, then returned to her quarters to get her well-earned shower.

The forceful gush of hot water cascaded through her

hair and over her body as she slowly turned around, soaking up the sheer pleasure of being alive. Quickly lathering, she shampooed, rinsed, then stepped out to grab a towel. Some EVA tests, she'd been told, resulted in more than just sweat having to be washed away. She'd passed with flying colours.

Chapter Two

GREEN BAR

'Damn it all, I thought it was real,' Caroline said, clinking her drink against her husband Graham's, both holding their ceramic vessels at a freakish slant to prevent spillage. The inclination would only have looked odd to visitors who rarely approached the hub. To those in the Green Bar, it was as natural as the strange angle to the floor, which was the bar's version of upright. The bar was so named owing to the walls being entirely covered in images of a tropical forest.

'Well, you passed. Can't have been that bad,' he said.

Gerard, the EVA officer, meandered over to where the couple were standing, looking as if he was walking down a sloping gradient, despite it appearing level. 'She did well. Heart rate only topped two hundred for a few seconds when she shoulder-charged the airlock hatch from the inside!' he said and laughed. 'That probably cost her the all-time record.'

The Green Bar was one of four in the portside of Kepler. On deck five, the curvature of the floor was obvious, and gravity was about a sixth of Earth normal. This was the usual watering hole for most of the portside astronaut corps aboard the starship. Clothing was almost uniform in style, but very individual in colour and accessories. Once the ship was underway, the change in how people dressed was rapid. The relaxed nature of onboard society dictated shorts and tops for men and shorts, skirts or skorts and tops for the ladies. Graham's T-shirt had a faux collar and buttons, very short sleeves and was longer than needed, its hem reaching his groin. Beneath it, he wore Bermuda shorts almost down to his knees and trainers without socks. The T-shirt and shorts were in the gold and dark blue colours of C-sector's basketball team. Caroline's outfit was more delicate; the sleeveless tank top was in a printed design depicting bracken and other forest plants. Her skirt, in a matching print, fell to mid-thigh. As EVA officer, Gerard was still in his uniform of khaki T-shirt with three-quarter sleeves and shorts which reached his knees. Three round, gold, coin-shaped symbols formed a pyramid on the shirt pocket. They proclaimed him to be a senior EVA instructor. An inverted gold crescent underneath them designated him as being in the astronaut corps.

A very good-looking, ebony-haired man in his late teens with designer stubble wandered over to the table with a half-litre ceramic tankard of beer in his hand and a long-legged blonde hanging onto his arm. He too sported the C-sector's team colours, but with an open-necked polo shirt. She was wearing a floral-design T-dress, which clung to her model-like figure.

'Hi, sis,' the man said as he approached. 'Hear congrats are in order. You're a fully-fledged EVA specialist!'

'This is Geoffrey, my brother,' she said to Gerard, who

acknowledged the introduction. 'And this is his girlfriend, Jessica.' She waved a hand towards the blonde teenager.

'Ah, yes, Geoffrey, you're the chess player. You beat my wife in the third round of the portside tournament last week,' Gerard said.

'Was that Mary?' he asked.

'Mhari, but that's close enough. Yes. Do you play chess?' Gerard asked Jessica.

'No,' she replied. 'Tennis is my sport, but not to any great standard. I play for fun. The Coriolis effect makes it extremely challenging.'

'You're training to become a firefighter. Is that right?' asked Gerard, noticing her bronze firefighting badge.

'I am. Should qualify in a few weeks. Fascinating work. A huge amount to learn,' she said, snaking an arm around Geoffrey's waist. He turned and kissed her cheek. There was chemistry there.

'Did Cas pass with flying colours?' Geoffrey asked.

'I was just saying that she did well. Heart rate topped two hundred just once. For some, it hits that level the moment they find they're in danger. She was exceptionally cool, avoided the pitfalls, and had plenty of time to spare.'

'I'm still mad at them,' Caroline said. 'I thought I'd escaped a meaningless death, then found them all laughing at me when I emerged from the airlock.'

'Serves you right for being so confident,' said Gerard.

Four more of the EVA corps came over carrying drinks. Cardin, the EVA test record holder, said, 'My round, what would everyone like?'

'Beer,' said Geoff.

'Same for me,' said Graham.

'Fruit juice for me,' Caroline said.

'Surely something stronger to celebrate,' said Cardin.

Caroline coloured somewhat and replied, 'Well, Gray and I are celebrating another event too. I'm pregnant.'

'Wow,' said Gerard, 'that'll mean you're grounded then.'

'I'm only eight weeks,' Caroline retorted. 'The regs say twelve.'

'Well, I'll make sure you're on light duties if you go outside,' the EVA officer said, giving his charge a kiss on the cheek. 'Congrats again.'

'So, you'll be an uncle,' Cardin said to Geoffrey. 'Few of those on the ship.'

'I believe there's only fourteen sibling pairs onboard,' said Geoffrey. 'They told me a fortnight ago. Thought they might ground her. Didn't know about the regs.'

The celebrations, now twofold, went on for a further hour before the group broke up and headed back towards their quarters for the sleep period.

Graham, Caroline, Jessica, and Geoffrey left the bar together and took the C-sector elevator down from five deck to one hundred deck, the very lowest. It circled the rim of the saucer-shaped starship and was the location where the gravity was almost Earth normal. As the lift descended, they could feel their limbs and bodies becoming heavier and heavier. The centrifugal force prevented the need for zero-g machines of the type used on the international space station. Crew who spent a lot of time at the hub, which was almost zero-g in places, had to spend a substantial time each day running around deck one hundred in order to stop their muscles from atrophying and their bone density from deteriorating. Ship's doctors monitored every resident monthly.

'Glad I decided not to mention my pregnancy earlier. They might have postponed the test,' she whispered, holding Graham's hand tightly as the lift descended.

'Were you thinking of telling them?' he replied, caressing her fingers.

'Well, I'm anxious about it. Was I jeopardising our child by being so gung-ho?'

'No. I don't think so.'

'But radiation outside the ship is so dangerous. It could have damaged our baby.'

'Not on the aft side of the ship. The whole of Kepler itself was protecting you, surely?'

'That's true. If the job had been forward, I might have cried off. Anyway, it's done now. I've got a third scan tomorrow.'

Geoffrey pushed his brother-in-law's arm and asked, 'What are you two whispering about? Another secret? You know twins run in the family.'

Caroline answered, 'No, Geoff. It's just me. I'm a bit anxious about the whole baby thing. God, I hope it's not twins!'

Kepler operated on Greenwich Mean Time, which meant there were twenty-four hours in a day and the entire ship kept the same waking and sleeping times for convenience.

Once out of the lift, they had to walk another hundred metres backled towards their quarters. Backled, of course, did not mean that they faced the wrong way. It was shipboard terminology for walking against the direction of the ship's spin. If you walked with the spin, it was called foreled. It didn't feel any different, but when receiving shipboard directions, it was necessary to be told which way to turn when leaving the elevators, as all elevator doors opened on the same side except on one deck and two deck. Wherever you travelled, the crew always knew that backled was a left turn and foreled a right turn.

On decks thirty to one hundred, the curvature of the outer hull was barely noticeable, and the corridor was little different from any found in an apartment block on the home world.

Geoffrey and Caroline had adjacent apartments on the rim, and they said goodnight. As it was after nine o'clock, the ship's lighting had dimmed to the standard for the sleep period. At seven in the morning, the LEDs would brighten for the new day.

Eight hundred metres in diameter with a circumference of two and a half kilometres, Kepler was a vast ship, built in Earth orbit during the 2040s climate crisis.

One hundred decks stretched from deck one hundred at the rim up to deck one, the bridge. Decks ninety-five to one hundred were where most of the residential apartments were located. Like the spokes of a wheel, the circular ship had six sectors – A, B, C, D, E, and F, and each sector had its own elevators which ran to and from the rim.

Kepler's hub was a cylinder, which protruded forward and aft. The rear section housed the nuclear reactor and the exhaust pipes, expelling the ions which pushed the ship onward. During the first half of the journey, it accelerated at one-tenth of a g. Midway, the hub would detach, rotate and reconnect. Ejected ions would then slow the vessel at the same rate until it reached the destination.

Decks ninety-five to about twenty-five housed many hydroponic farms, which grew all manner of vegetation, from grass to small trees, and chemical quarantine areas separated each deck from the next to prevent any diseases from moving from field to field

Decks from about thirty into the low teens housed production facilities, producing food and ready meals, from tofu to synthetic meats, consumable products from toilet paper to ceramic containers, and much more. Kepler's necessities were all produced somewhere on those twenty decks*.

The Kepler telescope had discovered hundreds of planets before its gyroscopes failed. One planet found was Kepler-452b in the constellation of Cygnus.

More studies followed and, in 2045, the planet became the final destination for the Kepler starship. Owing to time dilation caused when a ship approached the speed of light, the sixteen hundred light-year distance would be covered in about one hundred years. No one setting off on the journey would set foot on the planet.

At the last minute, it was decided to include cats and guinea pigs, so that everyone could at least see what animals looked like and how pets behaved. A whole deck was prepared as a place for chickens to be bred, and another held tanks of water in which tilapia were raised for fish protein.

---

* Anyone having trouble visualising Kepler, can refer to Appendix I for a more detailed description.

Chapter Three

HOME APARTMENT

Graham Hodder and Caroline Arnold-Pointer entered a civil partnership back in 2048 (2SBY). They also had a certificate to try for a baby.

Because of the limited space onboard Kepler, there had to be limits on population growth. Genetics were also important, and all female passengers were required to have two children, fathered by different males. Most conceptions would be by artificial insemination, but if a couple were in a stable relationship, a permit was granted for a love-child.

However, only one love-child was allowed. Each woman's second child must be with a different partner. The reasoning behind this was to avoid the introduction of any genetic problems in the future through inbreeding. The maximum number of children for any woman would be two, unless one died. In those circumstances, a third male would father a third child.

Although stable relationships might exist, the fathers were all entitled to bond with their children.

Slim and beautiful, Caroline stepped out of the shower

and turned left and right, studying herself in the full-length mirror, looking for the telltale bump. Was there a slight swelling? She couldn't be certain. Eight weeks was probably still too early. She still felt fine, apart from occasional morning sickness but anxiety about giving birth was growing even though, for now, it was a long way off.

The apartment bathroom had no tub. There were hot tubs in leisure areas for fun and relaxation, but not in apartments. Instead, she was standing in a wet room, which also housed a wash-hand basin, toilet, and bidet. A full-length mirror filled one wall, with a smaller one above the sink with its shelf for dental equipment and other essentials. A medicine cupboard occupied part of an adjacent wall, and the shower contained a soap holder and dispensers for shower gel and shampoo.

Apartment C-100-42 was a family unit as most were. The wet room was located off the entrance lobby. Caroline and Graham shared the primary bedroom, and they had a single room, which would soon become a nursery. Next to their bedroom was a sitting room with all the expected furniture. To its right was the kitchen with oven, refrigerator, microwave, and dishwasher plus the usual gadgets, cupboards and storage drawers, all in simulated timber. Real wood did not form part of household furniture. It had only been used in ceremonial rooms and the courts owing to the cost of carrying it to orbit.

The most stunning feature of the apartment, however, was one entire wall of the sitting room. It was possible to display a moving image of the countryside or a village scene upon it, but when Graham walked into the lounge with his coffee, the wall was showing the view back towards Earth. Although it gave the appearance of being a window, it wasn't transparent. It was a monitor showing a live feed from a camera on the hub. The view comprised millions of stars but it did not reproduce the astronomical view of the heavens from Earth because Kepler was now moving at a considerable percentage of the speed of light. The Doppler effect red-shifted the stars and galaxies. The stars weren't red yet but had a decidedly pinkish hue. That colour would only become more dominant as speed increased. The view forward could also be displayed live, but the stars were growing increasingly bright in that direction owing to blue-shift which made the wall less than ideal for a relaxing lounge.

As the starship approached the speed of light, time dilation had enormous implications for those on board. To the Earthbound observer, the journey time would be over two thousand years, but the travellers on board the ship would experience just one hundred years or fewer*.

Scientists aboard Kepler had discovered how to use the free hydrogen in space to augment the xenon carried in the storage tanks, and this permitted the acceleration period to be extended. By such means, the journey time could be even shorter, and performance was being carefully monitored.

Geoffrey Arnold-Pointer understood all of this as he was training to become a bridge officer. Relativity was an essential component of his training.

However, as he boarded the same elevator as Graham Hodder, his sister's new husband, he was heading towards

* If you find relativity difficult to understand, there is some extra information in Appendix II.

the hub to visit the communications centre, while Graham was travelling to his engineering project on deck six. After visiting communications, he'd a duty to carry out some fruit picking, then back to the bridge for another training session.

As the elevator rose, citizens entered and left. It was travelling from the rim, where gravity was almost Earth normal, towards the hub where there was just a tenth of a gravity, so when each floor was passed, those who remained in the lift were feeling lighter and lighter.

However, the ship also accelerated forward at one-tenth of a gravity, causing a second effect, which became increasingly obvious. People in the elevator found themselves leaning forward, particularly as they passed the final ten floors. When it reached the hub, the elevator wall opposite the main doors had become the floor, and this resulted in the usual doors now being in the ceiling. The walls joined the floor of the elevator in a gentle curve which allowed the passengers to adjust their standing positions.

The lift stopped at floor zero. Instead of the main doors opening, which would have been of no use to the occupants, a second set opened in what was now the right wall of the elevator, and Geoffrey plus the other passengers exited into a large open area. Down was no longer towards the rim, but towards the rear of the ship. That tenth of a gravity acceleration took precedence.

Geoffrey tentatively walked across the deck, ensuring he did not put too much spring in his step, as he'd have leapt into the air. Weighing 180* pounds on Earth, on this deck, he weighed only eighteen pounds.

He'd been in that section of the ship regularly during his training. Messages used to come directly to individuals, but

* 180lbs = 81.6Kg

now that the contents were becoming scrambled – distance and speed distorting reception – it was necessary to visit the communications centre to retrieve them after they'd been assessed, and to double check that the addressee was correct. They were less frequent now for the same reason.

The corridor was circular. Stairways led down to the reactor section and the workings of the ion drive. Elevators surrounded the hub, leading outwards to the rim in different directions. Each sector had several. Geoffrey walked partway around the hub to stairway four and climbed to the next level forward. The low gravity made the climb quick and easy. Stairway four led to a circular plexiglass room about four metres in diameter. He stood facing a doorway and pressed the green communication button.

'Yes,' said a pleasant man's voice from the speaker.

'Geoffrey Arnold-Pointer here, wanting to check with communications,' he replied.

The door opened into a large open-plan area with a few dozen workstations equipped with screens and computers. He knew where to go. He turned foreled and walked around towards the passenger communications desk. Behind it sat one of the oldest residents, a red-haired woman. Old, of course, was relative. No one on board Kepler was older than thirty-eight at departure, except for a dozen or so senior medical officers and engineers who were essential to the success of the early years of the journey.

She looked up and smiled.

'Geoffrey Arnold-Pointer. I believe you have two messages for me and my sister, Caroline.'

'Let me check,' she said and hit keys while watching her monitor. It took only a minute. 'Yes, there are two. One from Sandra Fletcher and another from Beth Arnold.

Would you like them sent direct to your tablets or on memory cards?'

'Memory cards, please. Two sets. My sister and I try to read all family messages together,' Geoffrey said.

'It's unusual for anyone on board to have a sibling'

'We were both selected for Kepler.'

The woman plugged two cards into the computer and pressed the return key.

'What's the general news from Earth?' Geoffrey asked.

She looked back up at Geoffrey. 'Doesn't get any better. No change in the rate of heating of the atmosphere. Almost nothing living between the tropics. Mass killings on the Mediterranean coastline, through the Middle East and the Stan countries and little news is escaping from Indonesia and the rest of the Far East.'

'What's causing the killings?'

'Countries protecting their borders from migrants escaping the tropics. It's carnage, apparently. That's why there's such a tight control on incoming messages.'

'Oh dear. So tragic. Thanks,' said Geoffrey, with sadness in his heart.

'Here are the cards,' the woman said and handed over the maroon cards. 'Bear in mind that there are lots of errors in the messages these days – primarily letters missing.'

'I will. Thanks.'

Geoffrey returned to the plexiglass stairwell, climbed another two flights, and emerged into a walkway which circled the ship's hub. Turning foreled, he made his way about ten metres until he found a dozen couches, some occupied but most empty. Selecting one, he pressed a button on the arm, and it rotated backwards so that he was looking upwards at an angle of some eighty degrees. The forward view from the ship was now displayed above him. It was spectacular.

Unlike the view from the apartment, this was facing Kepler's direction of travel. These stars were not red; they were blue-shifted and extremely bright. Not only that, but he now faced a large section of the Milky Way galaxy. The view of the entire left side of the galactic lens amazed him. Hundreds of thousands of millions of stars giving the impression of clouds of smoke or dust particles. In addition, he could see nebulae, clusters of stars, star-building clouds and still more galaxies beyond, where there were gaps in the heavens. It was spectacular. Absolutely amazing.

He sat in awe for nearly an hour until his next work duty was almost upon him. He stood up and made his way back to one of the D elevators. His duty that day was at D-80-V1, an orchard.

Leaving the elevator, Geoffrey walked twenty metres foreled along a simple corridor decorated with scenes of jungle and rainforest. He arrived at an airtight door labelled D-80-V1, swiped his identity card, and the door swung open. Inside, although he knew the procedures, the airlock bot studiously notified him of his responsibilities.

'Wear the goggles, hold your nose shut, and when ready, hold your breath and press the amber button.'

He'd already complied. Button pressed, he witnessed a fine spray fall from the ceiling, dampening his clothes and leaving a fine dampness on the floor. He was then hit with a warm blast of air. The entire process took just fifteen seconds.

'You may breathe again,' advised the airlock bot.

The inner door swung open, and he walked into the orchard. This was no earthly orchard with soft grass underfoot and pretty apple trees randomly surrounding him, it was far more regimented. The floor was steel with grills in many places to allow water to fall through to collecting areas where it was processed and recycled. The trees were more like tall bushes growing in tanks though the ceiling height of that deck was almost six metres to allow the trees to grow. Thirty rows of tanks stretched away into the depths of the orchard deck.

Geoffrey looked down at his tablet and pressed a button marked 'arrival'.

The tablet advised, 'Please go to aisle sixteen; a utility bot will meet you. Begin harvesting ripe fruit.'

The aisle Geoffrey was standing beside had the number twenty above it. He turned to his left and made his way along to row sixteen. At the entry to the row, a small cart, about the size of a wheelbarrow but taller, with wheels at each corner, was awaiting him. The interior was lined with a soft material. Geoffrey began picking ripe apples, dropping them into a soft funnel, which fed them into neat rows in the cart's base. As he worked, the robot cart followed him until full, when it shot off into the distance, being replaced by a fresh one.

Geoffrey had a three-hour shift on the orchard deck that day, then an hour for lunch before he would go back to the hub for another three-hour shift learning more about the terminals in the control section of the bridge. After that, he'd take the cards to his sister's apartment and they'd read news from home together.

Fruit picking was therapeutic, but it was the ship's bridge that fired his imagination. He couldn't wait.

Chapter Four

NEWS FROM HOME

After training, Geoffrey rang the doorbell of his sister's apartment, next-door to his own. The door opened, and he waved the two maroon message cards at his older sister. 'News,' he said.

'Come in,' she said, hurriedly making room for him to pass by and they entered the lounge area.

Caroline hit a button on the remote, and the view of the Earthwards stars vanished, replaced with a neutral colour wall which matched the others in the apartment. She didn't want any scenic GIFs running while they read their messages. 'You seen them?' she asked.

'Not yet, Cas. Sat in the gallery for a while, then had a fruit-picking shift and training session to do first,' he said, handing over a memory card.

Caroline plugged it into a cell phone sized console and a 1.5-metre section of the wall brightened. She hit the play button on the console, and the two message headers appeared on the screen. The first was from their parents and headed 'NEWS'. The second was from their stepsister, Sandra, and headed, 'READ BETH'S FIRST'.

'That's an odd thing to say,' said Caroline.

'Just do it,' said Geoffrey, impatiently.

Caroline highlighted the news message and pressed play.

Dear Cas & Geoff,

Not good news, I'm a raid.

There's no easy way to expla this.

You re mber the layout of the wind generator, the refrigerated trail r, the power room and solar panels, I'm sure.

Well, we had a horrendous storm. Lightning struck the genera or and destroyed it. That set fire to the power room and t e chicken house – it incinerated the hens.

Unfortunately, th wind vanes fell onto the roof of the refrigerated trailer which let the heat and rain in, t en toppled onto one bank of solar arrays. The other array was struck by a second bolt.

To make matters worse, the Range Rover was on charge, and the lightning must have passed through the charging cable and set it on fire.

The situation could not have been much worse.

With hav ng no way to get to town to get more cables or supplies, even if any were avail ble, your dad calculated our power, and we had two to three days re ining.

We considered trying to get to Wilson's or Sandra's in Norway but couldn't face several miles on foot i that heat, then a sea-crossing, then being no different to all the other illegal im igrants to Norway. The border force would probably turn us away and, frankly, if we'd got there, tw# more adults could comp mise Wilson and Sandra's chance of survival.

We thought long and hard about our options. With our food spoiling and average temperat res outside over 50°C, we were facing a horrible existence.

Decisi ns taken, we've spent the last two days treating ourselves to our favourite food and wines and, shortly after I've sent this, we'll be taking a couple of tablets the gover ment provided to your father for the end times.

They act in a ma ter of minutes and will be completely painless .

We've had a won erful life, and you are the most incredibly talented children. Wilson and Sandra have lovely families and are in better si ion than us. We hope they'll survive, and we trust to the NASA scientists that you will too.

We're sad we won't ever see your children, but know you'll be devoted to them.

Sorry, but this is the big goodbye.

W love you with all our hearts.

Mum an Dad

Xxxx xx

Geoffrey sat in shock. His sister held his hand. He looked at her and saw tears streaming down her cheeks. He couldn't hold it any longer, and his tears followed a few seconds later.

They sat sobbing for several minutes, both remembering the wonderful time they'd had in Shetland during their last visit.

'You'd have thought they could do something,' said Geoffrey quietly, his words fading away to silence.

'I suppose if the Range Rover were still working, they'd have had possibilities, but without it…' Caroline said through tears.

'They believed remoteness was a benefit.'

'Can't imagine walking all that way in that heat.'

'And what could they have done when they got to Haroldswick? No transport, and the news has been saying that food is in incredibly short supply, and there's gang violence in the streets almost everywhere.'

'Oh God. Imagine being forced to make that choice,' Caroline said and burst into tears again.

'I know, Cas. I know. It's so dreadful. All that planning for nothing.'

'They seem to have been happy, but taking those pills seems awful, Geoff.'

'Indeed.'

They sat in despair again, Geoffrey holding his sister's hand, trying to imagine the lack of possibilities for their parents and their sad end.

'Surprising number of errors in that message. I'd heard that messages were breaking up. It's connected to the time dilation.'

'Better see what Sands has to say,' sniffled Caroline, who pressed the button against the second message.

```
Hi Geoff, Cas,
  You'll have seen mum's message. We
already  new. They copied yours to us
in case it didn't get to you. So, if
it di n't let me know and I'll send it
from Norway.
  We're  ll fine up here in the   ctic
Circle.  e're in good health and the
hea  is bearable. W  still  ope it wi
l get better so  .
  Hope you're both well.
  Lots  f love,
  Sands, Malc and  he girls.
  xxxx
```

'Oh dear,' said Geoffrey, staring at the four kisses.

'That's that then,' said Caroline. She looked at her watch. 'I've got to be in the portside EVA office in thirty minutes. That's my copy of the card in the console, is it?'

Geoffrey nodded, then said, 'Don't think you should do an EVA straight after that news.' He stood.

They hugged and cried again.

Caroline said, 'They thought it through so well; can't believe it all came to nothing just because of a storm.'

'No. Seems so unfair.'

'I'll go and check in, but you're right, I won't be going outside today,' she said, wiping her eyes as she showed him out.

There's nothing worse than losing a parent. To lose both at the same time was devastating.

With a heavy heart, Caroline made her way to the portside EVA headquarters for her evening shift. On each side of the ship, there were always two of the official EVA corps on duty, wearing full EVA spacesuits and alert for any emergencies. It was a somewhat boring part of what was a most exciting job. Being outside the ship was a life-changing experience, with the beauty of the Orion spiral arm behind and the magnificence of the heart of the Milky Way in front. The three-hour standby duty was also in the uncomfortable spacesuit but without the wondrous experience of being outside the ship.

She had long been a qualified EVA astronaut, but this time, newly qualified as a specialist, she would carry out her duty with the gold embossed S on her suit. The chance of being called to do an emergency EVA was extremely slight, so she decided not to let either the bad news about her parents or her still early pregnancy prevent her work.

Inside the ready room, Cardin was already partly into his suit, trying to tidy his curly blond hair.

'Just because you're newly qualified as a specialist doesn't give you the right to be late!' he snapped playfully.

'Sorry. Had some bad news,' she replied.

Cardin immediately realised that something was wrong. 'I was joking,' he said. 'What news?'

'My brother and I just heard that our parents are dead.'

'Oh, how dreadful. I'm so sorry to hear that. How?'

'They'd set up a beautiful refuge on an island north of Scotland. It was lovely.' Suddenly, Caroline found tears flowing again.

Cardin hadn't yet put on the top half of his suit, and he came across to Caroline and encircled her with his right arm. He asked, 'What happened?' then quickly followed that with, 'Don't tell me if you don't feel up to it, though.'

She looked downward, trying to stem the sobs for a few moments.

'No, it's okay. They had this lovely, isolated house, with a bay nearby where they could fish and catch crabs and lobsters. Their refrigerated trailer was stocked with food, and everything was powered by solar and wind. They believed it could be a refuge until the climate returned to normal. If it ever did.'

'What happened?'

Caroline sat and dabbed her eyes with a tissue. 'There was a horrendous storm. Lightning struck the wind turbine, and it fell onto the trailer. More lightning destroyed one of the solar panel arrays, and what remained couldn't create enough power. Their Range Rover caught fire while recharging, so they had no transport, and the nearest town was several miles away, so they had no options left.'

Cardin sat quietly, not prompting or questioning his colleague. If she wanted to continue, she would.

It was nearly three minutes before she did, and her tale was accompanied by racking sobs. 'They realised it was hopeless and took some suicide pills the ministry had given my dad. He was a junior minister in the government.' She paused a while, then stuttered out, 'and that... was... *it!*'

Cardin tightened his arm around her shoulders as Caroline let her tears flow unhindered. He'd have done anything to comfort her. Before she'd met Graham, they'd lived together for a few weeks. She had left him for Graham and Cardin's hurt and longing for her still lived on.

One of the previous shift astronauts, Pierre Damask, came looking for his relief and stumbled upon the scene.

'We'll be through in a couple of minutes,' said Cardin and waved Pierre away with his other hand, making a face to him which cautioned against saying anything. Pierre, still in his full EVA suit, turned and left.

Caroline wiped her eyes and stood up, breaking free from Cardin's arm. She said, 'Must pull myself out of it. Let's get kitted out. Not fair to Pierre and Robert.'

The two EVA specialists continued to climb into their suits, double-checked each other's connections and seals, and went through the door into the standby room, which was adjacent to an airlock ready for an almost instant exit.

The four astronauts touched fists, and Caroline and Cardin's three-hour duty began. While Caroline grabbed the chess set and started to lay out the pieces, Cardin wondered if she had any idea how much he still adored her.

6SBY

Chapter Five

IMPACT

Alarms sounded throughout the ship.

There were procedures to follow and their training cut in immediately. Graham shot out of bed in an instant, and rushed to the hallway, where there was a bank of instruments and a flashing red light. He hit the mute button and studied the information panel, heart racing in fear of there being a leak in the apartment or the rim nearby.

Caroline had been as quick leaving the bedroom and rushing into the nursery where young Gren was sleeping through the noise. It wasn't as loud in the nursery but finding the child hardly stirring surprised her. He was a lovely child, very contented, and slept through anything and everything, so much so that they had his hearing checked. He had perfect hearing but seemed to be able to tune out loud noises naturally.

'Meteor strike!' shouted Graham from the hall, pulling on his dressing gown and casually admiring Caroline's nakedness as she returned to the bedroom to dress. He wondered if it was going to be a critical incident or just one of many dust strikes. 'No drop in pressure near us. Display shows depressurisation on the portside, sector B, deck thirty-five.'

Caroline returned to the nursery, tucked Gren back into his blankets and closed the door. 'I think that's one of the hydroponics labs.'

The phone rang and Caroline grabbed it hurriedly. 'Cas.'

'It's Jane, Cas. One of the labs depressurised. Can you come over, you're on the rota today?'

'Is the whole lab a vacuum?' Caroline answered, clearly concerned about any depressurisation extending farther into the ship.

'No, it's back to full pressure, but we need to check the plants.'

'I'll be there in fifteen,' Caroline said and threw on some working overalls and waterproof footwear. Within a minute she was out of the apartment and running for the sector B elevators, which were about four hundred metres foreled. She'd swiftly regained her fitness after giving birth to Gren and was at the bank of lifts in under three minutes. Graham would keep their child safe until she returned.

She approached the row of doors. One lift was on its way hubwards, one stationary at deck thirty-five and the other on the way rimwards. It would be there any moment.

'Any idea how bad it is?' asked a Black Asian man in his twenties.

Caroline replied, 'Not for sure, Simeon, but Jane said it's repressurised, so can't be too bad. What's in the B-35 labs?'

'Legumes, I think,' said Esther, a White, blonde woman.

'Right, here it is,' said Simeon, as the lift doors opened. They all stepped inside quickly. He swiped his identity card over the reader above an orange button labelled 'EMER-

GENCY', which would prevent anyone else delaying the elevator on its express journey to the scene of the accident. He activated the button and selected floor thirty-five. 'Hold tight,' he said.

They gripped the handholds as the elevator, in emergency mode, rapidly accelerated, covering the two hundred metres to deck thirty-five in just twenty seconds, causing the occupants to experience temporary freefall as it came to a halt.

On that deck, down was still primarily towards the rim, but the ship's acceleration made each of them conscious of the slight tug towards the ship's rear. They left the elevator at a run, went thirty metres foreled and found an assembly of about twenty crew. The leader of Hydro Lab B-35-5 stood at the front of the group. She was a thirty-year-old Chinese woman with a short, boyish hairstyle. Above her left breast, the name tag stated Yafan.

'Thanks for the swift response,' she said, as more people arrived from the other direction. 'An EVA team is in the lab searching out and patching the hole. Darren, the sector B EVA officer, tells me that pressurisation is almost complete, and we'll be able to get in soon.'

'How big was the hole?' a technician asked. 'It will be safe, won't it?'

'About four centimetres,' said one of Yafan's assistants, looking at the technician and assessing whether his natural fear could become a problem for the team.

Lifting her tablet and scrolling through its contents, Yafan continued, 'Keep in mind the priorities. Find any plants that are salvageable and place them in the warmers. Shake soil from anything clearly dead and put it into barrows. Others will collect them later. Although lab B-35-5 is mainly legumes, that represents only half. There are also beds of cruciferous and root vegetables, including onions. While legume plants might not be salvageable if they froze or became desiccated, vegetables could well be edible if it's only damage to their skins. They must be crated and sent to the processing labs.'

Double doors swung open, and the group felt a mass of warm air hitting them. When possible, air was warmed as it refilled depressurised areas. Yafan said, 'Here we go. Get yourselves into teams and remember that time is key. The EVA team told us pressure was down to just five percent, so many plants might have survived.'

Four space-suited individuals, all known to Caroline as members of the EVA corps, emerged from the lab and stood to one side to allow the technicians and volunteers to rush in and begin their work.

Caroline entered the vast laboratory. Beds of vegetables were laid out in rows in metal troughs. The whole place was dull and grey, despite the brilliant overhead lamps which provided the equivalent of sunlight. She looked upwards to the right, where a floor-plan showed produce locations. Her team was to collect vegetables to be sent to the processing labs. The lab occupied twenty-five metres foreled and backled and another thirty metres deep, towards the front of the ship. The ceiling height of this farm was three metres. As decks neared the hub, they were deeper owing to the gradual widening of the ship nearer the centre. At the rim, the ship was quite narrow, a design feature to assist the electromagnetic deflectors to force dust particles to skid off towards the rim. Ideally, none should strike the ship, but as velocity climbed, the system was bound to fail occasionally. Caroline had been outside forward near this location previously, and it was remarkable how scored and pitted the forward hull was. Thousands of microscopic particles had struck the ship and left their mark on the surface though it was mainly the size of the particle which was the most important factor in how much damage it might cause. Usually there was no penetration, but sometimes, as with this one, the particle was large enough to punch a hole in the ship. At close to the speed of light, the kinetic energy of even a dust particle could cause serious damage.

Vegetables in B-35-5 were in raised beds in the central area. Caroline's first task was to look at the closest plants and assess whether the reduced air pressure or cold had killed them. The legumes team would have the hardest task as the plants would almost certainly have died, and they'd need to harvest any seeds which were usable. Immature legumes and the plants themselves would have to be mulched and used for fertiliser.

The first bed Caroline inspected contained cabbages. They were in perfect condition and ready for cropping. She, and a colleague called Ingrid, a White German woman of a similar age, began cutting the cabbages and stacking them in green cases, ready to be transported to the production labs. They dumped the remains of the plants into the brown barrows as waste.

Workers cropped most of the more mature vegetables as the morning progressed. Less mature specimens, if they showed no sign of damage, were left in the beds for a second inspection the following day. They placed damaged plants in the brown recycling barrows.

The shift ended at midday when Yafan called her exhausted team together.

'Thanks for the swift help. We saved some thirty percent of the vegetables either for produce or to be reinspected tomorrow. The rest have gone off for recycling. A normal shift tomorrow should be able to check whether we'll lose any more.'

'That's the third strike this week,' said one helper. 'Is this going to continue as speed increases? We're at little more than half light speed at the moment.'

Caroline, as an EVA specialist, had a good understanding of the hull and the danger it was in. She said, 'I might be able to answer that.'

Yafan waved for her to continue.

'We've been detecting a raised level of interstellar dust this week. We're guessing it's a temporary matter. Perhaps a remnant of a comet tail or something. I know the bridge is monitoring it closely. We transferred extra power to the electromagnetic shield on Tuesday for that reason.'

'So, it won't become a daily problem?' asked Yafan.

'Don't think so unless it's something more common. It's all new to us, of course. Hope not, anyway.'

'How big was the object that hit us?' asked Yafan.

'Just a dust grain,' said Caroline. 'Probably under half a millimetre, but at our speed…'

'What is our speed at the moment?' asked Ingrid.

'About a hundred and ninety thousand kilometres per second, last time I looked at the display.'

'Amazing,' Ingrid said. 'I haven't been keeping track but it barely seems possible.'

'Back on Earth, their days are already four hours longer than ours, and the difference is growing more rapidly now,' said Caroline.

'The strikes are worrying. It makes you realise how vulnerable our environment is. If the hole had been bigger, we'd have lost everything,' said another helper. 'If there had been anyone in the lab when the strike happened, it would likely have killed them, and it could happen to any of us at any time.'

'I know, but that's the very reason we have multiple labs. It would take an enormous strike to wipe out any one crop, and there are seed banks too,' said Yafan.

The helper continued, 'Nevertheless, we're only six years into the journey. There could be a hundred still to come. It's all so fragile. I'm told an impact from a two-metre asteroid would wipe us out. Vacuum is such a horrible way to die.'

'Only if it hit the hub. There's always some danger,' said Caroline. 'Anyway, being thrown into vacuum would be a pretty quick death. You could count it in seconds. You shouldn't worry about it.'

'I suppose,' Ingrid said, retrieving her bag from the floor in the walkway.

Yafan tried to break the morose mood by speaking in a more positive vein. 'Okay, everyone. We did a great job. No serious harm done. Thanks for the quick response. Let's get back to our normal duties.'

The assembly fragmented, walking foreled or backled to find free elevators.

Caroline, still anxious about the journey, returned to the apartment and found Graham playing with Gren on the living room floor with GIFs of rabbits and birds showing on the wall. Gren was giggling and tried to push his furry rabbit toy into the scene. It cheered her up no end.

8SBY

Chapter Six

DIFFICULT DECISIONS

Alain Lavigne, the Black French captain of Kepler, was holding a weekly briefing in his office, off to one side of the bridge. A clear wall allowed him to see the forward view live if he wished. The screens protected the thirty-centimetre-thick transparent aluminium-ceramic-composite glass and that day the view was a display from forward facing cameras. His ultramodern desk faced the view and he sat in a white simulated-leather swivel chair. The office walls bore watercolour paintings of the French countryside, all painted by his wife, Aurélie.

The view forward was extraordinary showing the width of the left and central sections of the Milky Way's heart. This was the home of the Sagittarius black hole and enormous clouds of stars. The word cloud was befitting as the human eye could not distinguish individual stars at this range, yet that is what those clouds were. They were not the nebulae which are common throughout the spiral arms of the galaxy. These stars were so tightly packed as to appear only as smoke. Within the view of the captain, there would be more than fifty thousand million stars.

The Cygnus area of the galaxy was home to Kepler-452, and orbiting it, planet B was the ship's destination. A small monitor on a filing cabinet on the left of the captain's desk showed the star itself, an ordinary sun-like star on the main sequence. It would be decades before its planets would be visible, but being able to see it gave comfort to passengers, proving that it was real and would be reached one day. The live view could be shown on any apartment wall if so desired. Some scientists worried it could be so much larger than Earth that gravity would be excessive; others measured it as only a fraction larger, and humans would have no trouble there. The last data sent to Kepler before communication became problematic indicated that almost all the gases in the atmosphere were present in more or less the right proportions. The planet had water, as proven by the James Webb Telescope, and suitability data was only improving as time went by.

There was, of course, no way that the Kepler starship could *see* the planet. Even the largest telescope on board could not achieve that, but Earth's telescopes gave more positive views as time passed. The real problem was that messages were breaking up because of a combination of Kepler's growing speed and time dilation. Lavigne feared a total communication blackout would not be far away.

What would they do if Kepler-452b wasn't habitable? That was a nightmare no one wanted to contemplate, but the senior crew knew the answer. If Kepler wasn't suitable, they had the locations of several more stars with potentially habitable planets, and the ship's ion drive was more than capable of setting off again in a new direction. How the passengers would deal with such a blow was even less desirable to consider. Some psychologists postulated that the shock of Kepler-452b not being habitable could lead to an onboard revolution. Others said that chaotic scenario wouldn't occur as the bulk of the passengers were sensible enough to know that any lack of suitability was hardly the fault of the captain and crew. Having to start all over again would be the only possible outcome, and most would endure the prognosis. How it would affect the population psychologically was another matter entirely.

Captain Lavigne would not have the problem. It was almost certain that he'd not be alive when they approached Kepler. How to deal with success or failure would be the responsibility of one of his successors. He was now one of the older crew. Kepler had been travelling for eight years, and he was forty-three. Most of his senior officers were nearing the same age apart from the new second officer, Geoffrey Arnold-Pointer, so talented at twenty-four that he might be captain material. He'd spent the last three years learning everything to do with navigation and the ion drive. He'd deserved his swift promotion and often stood in as bridge officer of the day.

Today, Lavigne was concerned about the latest message from Earth. They were becoming increasingly fragmented. If they'd known this was going to happen, they could have got Earth to send each message multiple times, but Kepler was too far away now for any message sent to be received by Earth. The designers had tried to think of everything, but this was something that had been missed.

'Good morning,' Lavigne said as the last officer entered his room. 'Just a brief update. The last message from Earth finally caught up with us and brought news but it's very fragmented.'

Everyone looked expectantly at the captain.

'Sol's behaviour might be changing. The flares have perhaps lessened in frequency, and the excessive heat being produced might be easing. The crisis back home could be improving. However, it is might, maybe, possibly, perhaps. Not easy data from which to draw a conclusion.'

'Seriously?' asked First Officer Cathy Onslow, a White Australian woman of about forty.

'It appears so,' said the captain. 'The question is, how should we disseminate this information?'

'What sort of question is that, Captain?' asked Annette Burgess, the thirty-five-year-old White Californian communications officer.

'Think about it,' said Lavigne.

Geoffrey spoke up. 'Some might want to turn around, Captain.'

'Exactly.'

'Could we?' asked Annette.

'Geoffrey, what would be involved?' asked the captain.

'I'd need to put some time in on it, sir, but we'd need to turn the ship's hub and begin accelerating the opposite way. It would take eight years to kill our forward momentum and then another sixteen years, give or take, to get back to the solar system. That's twenty-four years. It's doable,' said Geoffrey hesitantly as he reassessed his mental arithmetic and reasoning.

'That's roughly my figure, too,' said the captain.

'What? We've come all this way and we're just going to give up and turn around?' asked Cathy. 'We can't do that.'

'Why can't we?' asked Annette. The captain sat back and let the others talk.

Sean O'Hare, an Irish navigation officer, said, 'People on Earth spent a fortune to allow us to set off for a new world. Many gave their lives. This ship cost at least eighty-four lives during construction, plus the hundred who died in that launch disaster. And some of you want to just turn around and throw everything away?'

Sally Roscoe chief engineer, said, 'I'm forty, and will die on this ship, as will almost everyone else except those born onboard. Yes, it's an exciting venture, but I'd like to go home, to walk the green fields of England, to live a real life on a real world and let my children breathe real air. I miss Earth so much.'

'The people of Earth would never forgive us. Our first interstellar voyage and we gave up on it,' said O'Hare. 'It would be a crime, so it would.'

Sally retorted, 'My children were both born on board. One eight and one three. By the time we get to Kepler, they'll be old or dead. If we go back, they'd have a fair chance of setting foot on a planet. They deserve that!'

Geoffrey said, 'Can I speak, sir?'

'Of course,' said the captain, 'you're now one of our bridge officers too.'

'My parents spent the last several years of their lives preparing for my sister and me to be saved in a refuge. A few years ago, we heard they had died during the climate crisis. If we don't go onwards, then their deaths will have been in vain. My mother was very much involved in the Kepler project and was a well-known astrophysicist in her own right. I say we push on; otherwise, we've wasted twenty-four years of our own lives.'

Sally said, 'You want us all to die on this tomb of a ship, and get to the far end and discover planet B is uninhabitable?'

'We're supposed to be pioneers, and you want to throw in the towel?' said Sean. 'If you felt like that, why did you even apply to be in the crew?'

'Things have changed,' said Sally. 'We now know the Earth is safe and we can return there and do so in our lifetimes.'

'Enough!' said the captain. 'I'd like to know the general feeling. Show of hands, please. Who's for going on?'

Geoffrey's, Sean's and Cathy's hands shot up and five more quickly followed.

'Returning?'

Sally and Annette both raised their hands, as did three more.

'That's eight to five in favour of continuing. I still don't know what our way forward is. Should we give everyone on board a vote or should we decide ourselves?' said the captain.

'You've got to give the ship a vote!' exclaimed Sally.

'Do the children get a vote?' asked Sean.

'That's why I'm asking your opinions,' said the captain.

Cathy said, 'We're travelling at a quarter of a million kilometres per second. Time is so dilated we're unlikely to get any more messages from Earth. As time is passing on Earth at nearly twice the onboard rate. By the time we turn and return, almost everyone we knew on Earth will be dead. What will we do, returning to a world that has advanced seventy or eighty years? How would we fit in? Would they welcome us?'

'And how would we feel if we got back to Earth and found the heat had started up again? We've only had one report,' said Geoffrey. 'We should study it in detail. Can we see it, Captain?'

'And what if it was a sick hoax? Can the message be trusted?' asked Sean. 'Captain, can you read the exact communication for us?'

Lavigne picked up a printed sheet and said, 'Unfortunately, the message is fragmented. They've been getting worse this year. This is it.' He passed the copy to Sean, who sat on the right of the group.

```
Mes age R f   e 1  t    epler.     th
 ate: O  ob r 20t  2 5
  U   ate – f ares red  i          fr
ue cy.
   o de   it  d op i  heat, but s
ists optim     c as no    r ase    nce
Ju   . Populat  n s     to      re se
t  d. Pl
     pe        rvi      in Ar   c      e
 n  Ant        a.
   nd.
```

'It's meaningless!' said Sean.

Sally took it from him and studied it. 'No, it's not. Clearly says flares reducing in line three. Scientists or specialists optimistic in lines four and five, and that looks like "drop in heat" in line four. Quite clear to me.'

'That could be "no definite drop in heat," though,' said Geoffrey.

'Oh, come on, Sally,' Sean pleaded. 'We can't even be sure of who sent it or the year, and what the hell are we meant to make of the last sentence? It could be "people surviving in Arctic".'

'Obviously sent by refuge one,' retorted Sally.

Cathy had it by now and said, 'We can't make mission-changing decisions based on this.'

She passed it to Annette, who studied it long and hard. 'I hate to agree, but that is not clear enough to decide to return. We should wait for more messages.'

Captain Lavigne said, 'They've been getting more fragmented for some time. I don't know if we'll get any more at all, let alone more legible.'

Sally asked, 'Is there any way to clean it up?'

'Annette. You're head of communications,' said the captain.

'I'll get my team to go back to the actual transmission and see if they can improve it. We'll put it through AI,' said Annette.

'Okay,' said the captain, 'but until you get results, I want this treated as top secret. Ensure your team knows that too. No leaks, please.'

Chapter Seven

EXCITING PERMISSION

Geoffrey's shift had ended, and he sat, splayed out on the sofa, in the lounge of his apartment watching a shipboard soap opera produced by one of the onboard TV companies. It was remarkable how, often using AI, small video production businesses had sprung up to fill the ship's airwaves with original material to complement the sometimes stale repeats from digital archives. This particular show was interesting as it was set on the ship.

He heard the door click open and looked around. It was Jessica returning from her volunteer work in a hydroponics laboratory. She was also now a fully trained fire officer.

'Hi,' he called, leaving the soap on pause and jumping up to greet his undeniably stunning girlfriend.

'I've got fish and chips,' she called back.

There were some fish bred on board, mainly tilapia and trout, but this wasn't either of those. It was a tofu and mushroom composite which had not just the look of cod but flaked convincingly when cooked, to imitate British fish and chips almost perfectly.

Jessica soon had the plates in the microwave warming, and Geoffrey came up behind her, wrapped his arms around her and pulled her backwards into his grasp. She was so sexy – tall, slim and athletic, with platinum blonde hair. Both in their Bermuda shorts, Geoffrey could feel the warmth of her body through the insubstantial clothing and caressed the backs of her legs with his own. He cupped her breasts tenderly and she leaned into his caresses.

'Later!' she exclaimed, wriggling free as the microwave pinged.

She so loved him and that day she had received some exciting news. She looked forward to breaking it but would wait until *she* was ready, not then with the meal imminent.

Jessica slid two golden battered pieces of the simulated cod and a handful of tasty-looking chips from the cardboard fast-food containers onto the warm plates. Geoffrey drained some peas from a saucepan and added them to the sides.

They both drowned them in vinegar, a little salt, and she added tomato ketchup and he, brown sauce. Salt was one of the essential commodities onboard Kepler. Many ship storage locations held a share of over eight cubic metres so that no single accident would destroy the entire supply. There were, of course, similar caches of other 'unmanufacturables' and 'irreplaceables'. Recycling could not recover one hundred percent of everything either.

While they ate, the soap ended, and they sat together on the couch in their living room, the video wall showing the view from the driver's cab of a train travelling through the Rocky Mountains. Jessica had deliberately positioned herself so that her thigh was tight against Geoffrey's. After her day picking peaches in one of the hydroponic farms, she had in mind to coax some romance and knew it wouldn't need a huge effort to arouse Geoffrey.

'I loved trains,' Geoffrey said between mouthfuls, seemingly ignoring the proximity of Jessica's thigh.

'We never used trains,' Jessica replied. 'I do remember seeing them occasionally as we had a train line visible in the distance. Tanker trains regularly passed by.

'We had a model railway in the attic of our Guildford home. My stepbrother, Wilson, constructed it when he was a teenager. Great fun.'

They continued to devour their meal, then Jessica picked up an envelope she'd placed on the coffee table earlier.

'Notices?' asked Geoffrey.

'Bit more important,' she replied, removing a document.

Geoffrey was still eating, so Jessica began to read, 'It's addressed to me and reminds me I turn twenty-two in six weeks' time.'

'So?'

She poked him in the arm and gave a wicked smile. 'For someone so clever, you're incredibly dense sometimes. I'm a girl.'

He laughed, 'You think I don't know *that*?! I make a point of checking it out almost every day!'

She pushed him again, and he almost spilled some peas he had piled onto his fork. She said, 'So far, you haven't checked it out today! Anyway, what doesn't happen when we have sex?'

'It happens for me… every time!'

'Shut up! And me, but that is not what I mean.'

'What d'you mean then?' he said and looked puzzled.

'Babies, you idiot. This is my clearance to have a baby within the next three years.'

The news dumbfounded him for a moment. 'God, I didn't think about that.'

'We've a decision to make,' she said, her heart full of hope.

'What decision?'

'You're a real prick sometimes!' she said, becoming annoyed. 'As a bridge officer, don't you understand ship's rules?'

'Of course. You can have two children. One by age twenty-five and a second one about eight years later. What's the decision?'

'You're such a moron, Geoffrey Arnold-Pointer. I have to *choose* whether to conceive a child by artificial insemination or we must enter a civil partnership to bear a love-child together.' Suddenly, she was feigning being visibly upset.

'Well, of course we should have one together. Don't you want that?' he said, encircling her shoulders with his arm.

'I thought you didn't care.'

'You thought I didn't want a baby with you?'

'Well, that's what it sounded like,' she said, as genuine tears welled up in her eyes. She grabbed a tissue. She had two great ambitions. One was to become a fire chief one day and the other was to raise a family with Geoffrey. It would make life on board Kepler so much more fulfilling.

Geoffrey tugged her towards him, his lips brushing her cheek and ear, 'And you think I'm stupid? I'd love for us to have a child. I love you.'

They kissed, and put their empty plates onto the carpet. Suddenly his hands were all over her body while hers hooked around his shoulders and neck, pulling the kiss onto her as hard as she could. Soon naked, their couch became a place of intense and emotional lovemaking.

Forty minutes later, they peeled themselves apart and watched clouds skidding over a big sky somewhere in the United States on the wall screen.

'What happens now?' asked Geoffrey.

'Unfortunately, nothing,' she said. 'The implant will take care of your seed, as always, but once we've tied the knot, I'm given an appointment to have the implant removed and a physical check-up, and commit to only allowing you to make love to me until I conceive.'

'And will you commit?' asked Geoffrey with a cheeky grin.

'Moron!' she jibed and pulled his naked body back towards her.

'Hang on!' he protested. 'I'm knackered! Let's get coffee first.'

Later, after coffee and further inspired intimacy, they made the decision to be married instead of having a civil partnership and composed a message to invite their friends and close colleagues to celebrate with them on the day.

Meanwhile, the video wall now portrayed the view from a miniature camera mounted on a golden eagle, which was swooping and soaring around the hills, glens and lochs of the Highlands of Scotland. It made Geoffrey homesick for his parents' ill-fated retreat on Shetland.

Kepler had many meeting rooms for the dozens of clubs which had formed on board. There were fewer official rooms. One was the whole portside half of decks eleven, twelve and thirteen, the grand meeting room, it was called – a huge cinematic space which could seat at least four thousand people, the maximum number of passengers the ship was ever likely to have on board. Every year, so-called council meetings staged by the ship's senior officers reported progress to the residents in that room.

In more regular use were six official assembly rooms, which were available in each of the six sectors, so thirty-six in total. There local administration meetings, official ceremonies such as civil partnerships, weddings, naming events, funerals, plus a multitude of religious services – Baha'i, Buddhist, Chinese, Christian, Druid, Heathen, Hindu, Humanist, Interfaith, Jainism, Jewish, Muslim, Pagan, Rastafarian, Shinto, Sikh, Zoroastrians took place. Even the Flat Earth Society had a Flat Earth Day while hurtling through the universe at close to the speed of light. There weren't many of them, but they still clung to their deluded beliefs. Oddly, of course, their world was now the Kepler, and it could, in all reasonableness, be claimed to be flat! Frisbee-shaped, actually, but flatter than the Earth.

On the fourteenth of December, year eight shipboard time, Geoffrey stood in as near formal wear as anyone had on the Kepler. Black knee-length socks, shiny brogues, black Bermuda shorts to just above his knees, a white shirt with granddad collar and loose-fitting black waistcoat adorned with two medals – one for being a ship's officer of the bridge and another for serving on the first responder service.

He was standing facing the ship's captain, who wore the green officer's uniform, almost identical to Geoffrey's outfit, but in emerald-green with gold-braid on the cuffs and shoulders. Several medals hung on his breast.

Geoffrey's brother-in-law, Graham, stood to Geoffrey's left, equally smart in a blue Bermuda shorts suit. He was best man.

The wedding march played. Geoffrey didn't look behind, but Graham did. With no other living relatives onboard, his civil partner, Geoffrey's sister Caroline, had agreed to give Jessica away, and was walking up the aisle in a yellow minidress with lacy sleeves and matching shoes. Beside her was the bride.

Both women were slim and beautiful, but Jessica had the most stunning model figure, blonde hair, and wore a silver-white shredded dress in the latest disco style. Dozens of ribbons hung down, apparently from her shoulders to her knees, giving the impression that she wore nothing underneath, but it was all held together with a lace underdress, so tightly woven that there was no transparency. Incongruously, a fire service medal swayed over her left breast. She wore a lace veil over her face, crocheted stockings sheathed her undeniably shapely legs, and she wore flat white shoes. Kepler rules did not allow high heels, so Earth's ridiculous stiletto fashion fad had been consigned to history, at least until they reached the new world, when some fool would no doubt revive it.

The traditional wedding march ended as Jessica joined Geoffrey in front of the captain. Caroline took her place a step behind and to one side of Jessica while Graham did likewise on Geoffrey's side. Geoffrey saw his bride for the first time that day. Her beauty brought a lump to his throat. She had to be the most beautiful woman on Kepler. She smiled at him through the veil.

The formalities were brief. They exchanged rings and took the oath to remain loyal to each other for life. Captain Lavigne announced they were now husband and wife and advised the groom that he could kiss the bride, which he did, lifting the veil and applying some considerable gusto, but not for so long that it became embarrassing. Their eyes said it all to each other.

A delighted congregation cheered, applauded and wolf whistled.

Friends had decked out the Buzz Aldrin Recreation Hall with bunting and fairy lights. A romantic ballad sung by Frank Sinatra filled the room as the guests mingled and ate a delicious finger buffet before beginning to dance. What would old blue-eyes have thought about his music being played on an interstellar journey?

Everyone wanted to dance with Jessica, who, they all admitted, although not within the hearing of their own wives, was the most stunning bride who had ever graced the Kepler dance floors. Geoffrey took special care not to drink too much and spent his time in conversations with male colleagues who were constantly ribbing him about his upcoming sexual nuptials.

Eventually, Geoffrey extracted himself from the group of 'lads' and sat down with his sister at a corner table. She gave him her congratulations, of course, and he asked her what life was like with a toddler in tow. Caroline waxed lyrical about the joy toddler Gren gave to her and Graham.

As the evening progressed, some of the senior officers wandered over to say goodbye to the groom, went off to find the bride, and then excused themselves from further festivities.

The food had run out, the cake been demolished, and the drink was having its influence on the die-hards, when the happy couple found each other and discreetly vanished from the Aldrin suite.

Back at their apartment, they discovered balloons and suggestive messages and downright crude slogans tied to or stuck to the entrance. They laughed and kissed, and Geoffrey carried his beautiful bride over the threshold and into a much-anticipated intimate celebration of their matrimony.

9SBY

Chapter Eight

COUNCIL

Despite the captain cautioning the senior officers not to discuss the fragmented message from Earth, rumours began. Perhaps a careless word to a spouse or close friend, who felt compelled to tell their partner, and so on. News of growing unrest on the ship soon found its way back to the ship's junior officers, who were not in the elite senior group but had regular contact with them. Councillors were even more attuned to the dissent.

Those planning Kepler's governance had decided that the captain would be the head of the community. His senior officers handled navigation, communications, hydroponics, food processing, water, irreplaceables, environment, energy, engineering, health, education, legal and policing, ship's services, housing, the arts, archives, and other functions.

In addition, each of the six ship sectors had an elected representative and deputy. From that group of twelve, the entire ship's population elected one of them to be administrator, designated as the president. At that time, Jake Zheng was president of the people. His powers could not overrule the senior officers on the running of the ship, but they knew they had to consider the elected representatives' views.

The resulting general council comprised eleven members plus the president, who held a casting vote on anything which did not affect the actual operation of the ship's systems, on which the captain's decision was final.

Another message arrived, even more fragmented than the last. Captain Lavigne called a senior officers' meeting to discuss it and the rumours.

```
es  ge   fuge   to K   er. E r h
    te: Se    m er 14 h 20 6
  Up    e – t e wa   in  of    e c i  te
h    d    n tel    top  d. Th   e is
 ittl  ata
             ppo  t    h    h    e  t  at
             ur  to norm      els.    m
un  i s w  hin  r  ear
          pol  r  circ        re  liv
 re    vely
      rmal  l     s. Some plant       e
 row  g
  w    n  he  rop cs, but tem      u  s
th r
   t ll  ver  e  ore   an 6 °C. No p
n  o
  d po    te  efug   .
    d
```

Geoffrey said, 'It's even less decipherable than the last one. That temperature is very worrying. It means there are still temperatures of sixty or more degrees.'

Annette, one of those who favoured returning to Earth,

admitted, 'Again, it's not clear enough to decide to return.' She so wanted herself and her children to feel the thrill of life on a real planet. Homesickness had become a significant factor in her life.

Sean said, 'It's much worse than the last one. Totally meaningless, but the temperature is clear. It looks like "normal levels" in the sixth line of the message, but it's impossible to know whether it's saying there are normal levels or there aren't.'

'And "little data to support" in lines four and five shows there's probably nothing definite regarding temperatures dropping,' said Geoffrey.

'You're all so negative,' said Cathy, who was even more homesick than Annette. 'Those two words in the fourth line are almost certainly "definitely stopped". If you add the earlier words as "the warming of the climate," then it becomes clear. Also, it states, "Some plants are growing within the tropics" in lines eight and nine.'

'Yes, but look at the following word, "but" then the sixty-plus temperature reading. We can't go back based on this,' said Sean. 'Would you like to experience sixty degrees C? It can be arranged.'

'Captain Lavigne asked for clarification of the previous one,' said Geoffrey. 'Has that been done? What did it show?'

'Of course,' said Annette.

'And did that last message clean up at all?' asked Cathy.

'No,' Annette said. 'We also put AI to work on it and, frankly, it came up with several versions. None of them helps us decide, but some were promising. This message, when we asked AI to interpret, provided the following, as you can see on your screens.'

Species refuge to [K---?] area. Earliest date: September 14th, 2006.

Update – the warming of the [ecosite/climate/ecosystem] has continued on the upland plateau. There is little data to support the hypothesis that temperatures return to normal levels. The minimum is within polar circulation, relatively normal levels. Some plants are growing well in the tropics, but temperatures there still never drop below 60 (to 69)°C. No permanent refuge identified.

Annette continued, 'Didn't really help. It's guessing at the content. "Species" is obviously wrong, "upland plateau" is nonsense and so is the date. The clearest statement is, "There is little data to support the hypothesis that temperatures return to normal." It's also suggesting plant growth in the tropics, but temperatures never drop below sixty. That is also obviously a guess; it could be sixty-anything! "No permanent refuge identified" again has no meaning.'

'I think we should call a council meeting,' said the captain. 'The rumours are spreading too rapidly for my liking, and people are polarising into return or not return, based on rumour. We need to open up the discussion. Conspiracy theories are becoming increasingly common too. We need to settle everyone down.'

'Exactly!' Cathy said, almost gleefully.

'You could be opening a hornet's nest, sir, you could,' said Sean.

'We have no choice. It's all becoming too public. I want a full officers' meeting tomorrow at ten, and I'll then speak to Jake about an open general council meeting,' said the captain.

President Jake Zheng was a short Chinese man with a characteristic round smiling face and jet-black hair. He met the captain weekly for brief discussions of anything relevant, but it was unusual for the captain to want to see him in the evening. There was a rap on the door. He shouted, 'Enter,' and the captain strode in and sat himself in one of the four visitors' chairs.

'Captain,' said Jake, 'to what do I owe this unexpected pleasure?'

Lavigne always wore his smartest emerald-green uniform for official meetings with the democratically elected head of the ship's population. He crossed his legs when he sat, his knees glossy black between his shorts and socks. He was a fine figure of a man. 'I apologise for this impromptu meeting, but it's about the rumours.'

'To continue or return?' asked the president.

'Exactly. You've seen the second message from Earth?'

'I have. Doesn't add to our knowledge, but it looks like sixty-plus degrees is still being experienced.'

'It seems so. I had a full officers' meeting this morning. All twenty-eight attended, and we took a vote. Nine wanted us to return, three abstained based on insufficient data, and sixteen voted to continue,' said the captain.

'What do you think?'

'I'm for pushing onwards. How about you, Mr President?'

'I'm on the fence, Captain, but I'll support the majority of your officers for consistency.'

'Thank you. I'd like to call an open general council meeting for next Sunday to put the rumour to bed, once and for all.'

'You going to call for a vote?' asked Jake.

'I think we need to. Present all the facts and our officers' recommendation and gauge the reaction.'

'And what if the populace votes to return?'

'I don't think that's likely.'

'Probably not, but what if they do? Strange things can happen in referendums. Have you heard of Brexit?' asked Jake.

'I have indeed. I'm French.'

'I think a show of hands will do at first. If it's really close, then we'd need to go through a long period of debate with advocates for each side being allowed to make their case. Then we'd call for an official secret ballot,' said Jake.

The president pulled out a calculator and entered figures. He said, 'What would you call close? Sixteen out of twenty-eight is only fifty-seven percent wanting to go on.'

'Well, yes, but only nine of the twenty-eight wanted to return.'

Jake entered figures into a calculator. 'That's only thirty-two percent wanting to return. Not so close, really.'

'Hmm,' murmured the captain. 'Okay. Will you introduce matters and then hand over to me to outline the cases?'

'Sounds like a plan.'

The grand meeting room, the whole of decks eleven, twelve, and thirteen, had never seen so many in attendance. The gate count was 1,915 plus children who did not have a vote, but needed to be with their parents, as all nurseries and schools were closed for the assembly. Geoffrey wondered where the remaining adults were. Two senior officers had volunteered to crew the bridge and engineering. Seventeen of the original passengers had died, and none of the children were yet over nine years old. How could anything be more important than the decision over whether to give up their journey? He thought of the old Yorkshire saying, 'There's nowt so queer as folk!'

He, along with the other twenty-six officers with departmental responsibilities plus the twelve councillors, sat on a raised stage on one side of the deck. The captain and president sat in more elaborate seats in the middle of the forty and towards the front. The remaining 1,873 residents sat in rows stretching away towards the far side. With plenty of seats still available, older children with their parents occupied some of them and some parents were battling to control the noise levels and fidgeting of their charges.

President Zheng, wearing a tan-coloured Bermuda shorts suit, stood, and a microphone rose from in front of his seat, at its optimum distance.

He said, 'Good day, everyone. It's wonderful to see so many of the ship's population joining us for this important presentation of the facts of the situation back on Earth. I shall hand over to Captain Lavigne who will outline the current situation and explain why we have called you all here today.'

The captain, smart in his gold-braided, emerald uniform, stood and allowed time for his microphone to rise from the floor.

'Welcome to this meeting of the general council of Kepler. On either side of President Zheng and me are twenty-six of the twenty-eight senior officers who run the ship, plus the elected councillors from the six sectors.'

He took two sheets of paper from an inside pocket of his waistcoat and held them aloft. 'These are the last two messages we have received from Earth. Refuge One in Antarctica has sent them. Both messages are badly scrambled, and they appear on your personal monitors and the large screens on your left and right. AI interpretations of the last two messages are also included.' He folded them and returned them to his pocket.

'The last message prior to these was quite legible, although there were odd letters missing. These two, however, are almost impossible to read.

'Until these messages, news from Earth had shown no let-up in the increasing heat. All life was gone from between the tropics, except for a resistant algae and coarse grass. Temperatures were so high that only specially equipped scientists could visit the region in heat-resistant suits.

'Between the tropics and the polar circles, small communities of people were still surviving, but only barely. In the Arctic and Antarctic Circles, there are towns and other settlements, vastly overcrowded and having great trouble producing enough food to support the increased population, most of whom are migrants from more southerly or northerly countries.

'We understood that the refuges in Antarctica and on the Komsomolets Island were in good condition, but keeping themselves isolated from the general population, as was always the plan. That is still the case.' He pulled a tissue from a pocket and wiped his brow where sweat glistened.

'Senior officers have studied these two messages and applied artificial intelligence to both to see if more sense could be made of them, but it didn't help. Some versions showed that the first message was very positive, but even more contradicted that. Antarctica's latest message contains a very worrying temperature of sixty to sixty-nine degrees Celsius.'

He turned, and his arms showed the senior officers in their emerald uniforms. 'The judgement of the senior officers is that we should ignore these messages. Opinion was split, but after the second message, only two of my officers supported the view that the heat crisis was over.

'President Zheng and ten of the eleven councillors agree with the view of the officers. I should say that those who believed the message was positive were in favour of the Kepler turning around and returning to Earth.' The captain lifted a model of the Kepler, about ten inches in diameter. He held it in front of him.

The hub, of course, would need detaching and reversing for the change of direction, not the entire ship, but the captain didn't want to complicate the demonstration so decided to omit that factor.

'We could return to Earth. First, we would need to reverse the orientation of the ship, thus,' he said and turned the entire ship in front of him. 'We would then need to travel that way for about nine shipboard years. That would make us stationary regarding Earth. We would then need to accelerate in the same orientation for nine more years, which would only bring us back to where we are now, but heading in the opposite direction at the same speed. Once again, we would have to turn the ship,' which he did with the model, 'and decelerate for another nine years, at which point we would be close to Earth.'

Captain Lavigne passed the model to the president, and continued, 'Twenty-seven years would see us back to Earth. If we knew, for certain, that the climate crisis was in reverse, that might become something we would wish to do but just imagine our horror if we got back and found the crisis was still in play or the climate had deteriorated still further.' He paused for dramatic effect.

'What would the people of Earth think of us, having invested so much in our ship? The risk of taking such a decision would be considerable, but it might be worth holding a referendum to see what you all wanted to do.

'However, the view of the senior officers and council, plus me and the president, is that the messages are unreliable, and should be ignored. In this situation, we believe a referendum would be a waste of time.' He sat.

President Zheng stood again.

'Thank you, Captain. We called this meeting to inform you all of our decision to continue onward to Kepler-452. We would like your support. If you agree with our decision, please raise your hands.'

A sea of arms rose into the air, a lot initially, but then it became more as people looked around and saw what others were doing.

'Thank you. Those of you who disagree with our decision, raise your arms now,' the president said.

A few hands shot up, followed by others, but more hesitantly. There were fewer than a hundred in total.

'Thank you, everybody, for giving such support to your senior officers and council members. We will, of course, let you know if any further messages arrive from our home world. Meeting closed.'

There was a lot of talk among the ship's residents and, naturally, it took some time for two thousand people to disperse around the ship, back to their homes and places of work.

Kepler pushed on towards its new home, travelling at over 170,000 miles per second.

Chapter Nine

STUPID OR WHAT?

Policing a spaceship containing over two thousand residents was one duty that came under the captain. He had Chief of Police Melody Armstrong, under whom there were three officers: Cheryl Hart, Jack Head and Enzo Paulini. Melody's blue Bermuda shorts uniform and peaked cap enhanced her athletic body and showed her fitness as she conducted regular daily briefings for her team, but there was often little or nothing to discuss. The police department occupied three cabins on deck thirty-eight. It didn't need more space, and the workload was usually pedestrian.

The general population of the ship comprised all the usual disparate individual views and characters. High intelligence was not a guarantee of common sense. There were the same proportion of fanatics, bigots, radicals, visionaries and plain stupid people as there were on Earth.

Law and order on Kepler was maintained primarily through the goodwill of the passengers. People obeyed signs, alarms were properly reacted to, and general rules observed. Rarely there was petty theft, and there were, of course, more common occasions where behaviour became rowdy, leading to minor violence. People will be people, and even more relevant, some men can't control their carnal desires. There had been eight instances of rape, three of which involved extreme violence. Instances of fighting were dealt with by non-custodial sentences – work details wearing balls and chains – old-fashioned but very embarrassing for the offenders and therefore extremely effective. There had been a single instance of murder and, when cornered, the perpetrator took his own life. It would probably have been classified as a crime of passion. Incarceration was rare. There was a small brig on deck thirty-eight, adjacent to the police department. It comprised thirty prison cells, an exercise room and a catering section. Groups of volunteers looked after the prisoners. They were headed by the prison governor, somewhat appropriately called Doug Blaggard, a well-built thirty-year-old who suffered no nonsense and was not afraid to throw his weight around when needed, and sometimes, even when it wasn't.

All eight rapists occupied cells, plus a couple of individuals whose violence had exceeded simple bad-tempered aggression.

But on the fourth of November 9SBY, law and order was seriously challenged. The only saving grace was that the entire event had been poorly conceived and bungled in its execution. It arose out of the desire of some passengers for the mission to be aborted and the ship returned to Earth.

John Elloway, a muscularly overweight man of about thirty, and his gang of seven henchmen had spent months brooding over the ship's decision to continue to Kepler, even though, in their social media informed opinions, there was a good chance that Earth was coming out of its excessive climate heating. It didn't make sense to them that they should spend the rest of their lives cooped up on Kepler, particularly because there were continual meteor strikes causing stress among the ordinary passengers. It was inevitable there would be some protest movements and the possibility of Earth returning to normal was certainly the trigger in John Elloway's uprising.

Meetings began in groups of three or four in bars. Some left, more joined until there were a dozen core members with similar fanatical views. When Elloway hatched his plan to force the reversing of the ship, some wisely deserted, but a core of die-hards remained. Those recruited more angry and dissatisfied people until the revolt was in the hands of over fifty.

John Elloway and Denver Ellis, a heavily built Black African man, were meeting increasingly frequently and their grumbles to each other were bordering on rants. They became more and more determined to take action.

Ellis ran a sports club where plastic projectiles were fired from compressed-air, shotgun-like weapons and the meetings often took place at his clubhouse. He'd just close the place for a few hours now and then to give Elloway somewhere to express his ideas and encourage support. The room was about forty metres long, and various targets stood on tripod legs. Usually, they were the regular circular bullseye targets, which were also used for archery and javelins, but he provided a few upright figures of men, made of metal, as targets for the compressed-air pellets. He suggested to the group that these could be used as assault weapons.

'Surely, they're nowt but toys,' said Elloway.

'You wouldn't say that if you were fucking hit by one. A headshot could crack yer skull. A shot to the chest would leave you fucking gasping on the floor. Believe me, I've been fucking shot accidentally, and they're no joke!' said Ellis with confidence. 'They're also quickly reloaded and can hold a magazine containing five shots. I wouldn't want to have one pointed at me!' He passed one to Elloway.

The group leader held it, sampling its weight and balance, then fired at one of the bullseye targets. It hit the far right-hand side, and the target spun around and fell over.

'Impressive. Accuracy's rubbish though.'

'You didn't allow for the spin of the fucking ship. Aim twenty-five centimetres left of centre and a little on the high side towards ten o'clock,' said Ellis.

Elloway loaded a second projectile. It snapped into place, and he took careful aim as instructed.

Phut!

'Fucking bullseye! See!' shouted Ellis. 'Got to allow for the Coriolis effect. Fucking nuisance in ball sports too.'

'Hmm, okay, if you're sure,' said Elloway. This seemed ideal for his plan. 'Are you all okay with this weapon?'

There was general agreement, and Elloway added, 'Right, each of you, book in at Ellis Sports and get trained up. We don't want to kill anyone accidentally. Make sure you can shoot straight and compensate for the damned corona effect.'

Ellis stifled a laugh at the *corona* effect. 'Don't worry, John. Give me an hour or two with them and they'll be fucking sharpshooters,' said Ellis. 'Are you fucking sure you can get them to turn the ship? I don't fancy a lengthy jail term if this fails. How much research have you done?'

'I've a mate who was training to become a bridge officer.

He told me what's what. We hold them hostage 'til they do it and then have the turning mechanism and related tech sealed into a secure room under our control. If anyone tries to break in, *boooom* and it's gone!' He was less confident than the impression he gave. The junior officer had only trained for a few months and went on to other things.

'Are you crazy?' said another of the gang, Jason Smith, a weightlifter who'd become a hired yob during the voyage. 'Destroy it and that's us all buggered. The ship will carry on forever. It's as important to us as it is to them.'

'Panic not, Jason. Our guys will duplicate the equipment and keep a second set in a secret location. We'll have tons of time to organise that, and once we're done, we'll keep a skeleton bridge crew. We'll be in charge of navigation.'

'I don't want anyone fucking killed, John,' said Ellis.

'No. They'll do what they're told,' said Elloway.

'Who is going to look after relocating the tech?' asked a more studious individual called Jack Render. 'Sounds a complex bit of organisation.'

'Marina has a couple of tech guys she can call on.'

Marina said in a squeaky voice, 'Piece of cake!' As far as she was concerned, if it involved cabling and monitors then she was perfectly capable of organising it.

'Can't they just rebuild the equipment systems elsewhere and override our change?' asked Smith.

'No, we'll have permanent guards on the bridge,' said Elloway. 'Marina will route everything from the bridge so that we can monitor things.'

'Fucking hell! You do realise we'll have to be in charge for nearly thirty fucking years? Is that even fucking practicable?' asked Ellis.

'Stop worrying,' said Elloway, who turned to the small, nerdy-looking woman. 'Marina, I want you to put together a bomb that'll destroy the contents of a room, say four metres square, and triggered by any break in.'

'I suggest the air pressure is kept below ship's normal, then a rise in pressure would be the trigger,' she said after thinking for a minute.

'It mustn't go off accidentally,' said Elloway.

'Okay,' continued Marina, 'we'll link it to a passive infrared to detect motion. Only if the two both show entry would it explode.'

'Not too fucking powerful; we don't want to breach the hull,' said Ellis.

'No. Obviously. Leave it to me,' Marina said.

'How long will all of this take?' asked Render.

'You allocate me a room, and I'll sort out the environment in a day and move the tech in the next morning,' said Marina. 'How big is the technical equipment?'

'Don't know yet,' answered Elloway. 'Can't be too enormous. It's probably just a console and controls.'

'You sure you've thought of everything?' asked Smith.

'Probably not, but I will by the time we're ready.' Her overconfidence worried Smith, but Elloway seemed to be happy with it.

Six weeks later, eight individuals approached the entrance to the bridge, a wedge-shaped anteroom. Three metres wide at the entrance and five at the door onto the bridge, it was some eight metres long and contained banks of monitors on one side and a couple on the other. Only two of the monitors were being attended to on the right-hand side. A green-uniformed woman was sitting at a desk at the bridge end of the room, working on some papers and entering data into a computer. Next to her stood a ship's officer.

The group entered somewhat clumsily, as they were not familiar with life at such low gravity. The officer on guard duty was taken by surprise, finding so many uninvited people walking into the anteroom. He raised a hand, indicating that they should stop where they were. He knew there were no delegations or educational visits on the agenda for that day. He checked his tablet and said, 'Please wait there. I've had no notification that you were to visit the bridge. Who are you?'

'We're taking over the ship,' said the leading figure, Elloway.

The guard laughed. 'Don't be daft. This isn't the Bounty!'

'Step aside.'

The guard no longer smiled. He unsheathed his taser, but was way too slow. The leading man raised what looked somewhat like a sawn-off shotgun and fired.

It wasn't a loud bang but more of a phut. A projectile left the weapon and struck the guard in the chest. He went down slowly in the low gravity but still like a dropped sack of potatoes. The woman at the word processor fell to her knees to attend to him. He was struggling to breathe; such was the force of the impact. Elloway was pushed backwards by the recoil due to the lack of gravity near the bridge. However, the wall stopped him, and he quickly reloaded.

The projectiles were dull grey, about four centimetres in diameter and fifteen long, and constructed of a plastic material. Now all eight had weapons to hand, and they marched, as best they could in only one-tenth gravity, towards the double doors.

They burst onto the bridge, closing the doors behind them and chaining the handles together.

Sean was first to react, shouting, 'Faith and begorrah! What the hell do you want?'

'Shut up and keep your hands where we can see 'em. The rest of you come here and stand together,' said the leader.

'You can't do this,' said Geoffrey.

'These say we can!' said the leader, raising his gun and waving it in the air.

'You can't fire those in here. You'll puncture the hull,' said Cathy.

Another of the group, Jason Smith, braced himself against a bulkhead and fired his gun at the main window. The projectile struck the glass and rebounded, falling gently back towards the entrance in the low gravity produced by the thrust of the engines. It was almost freefall on the bridge.

'They won't hurt the ship,' said Smith as he reloaded, 'but they *will* hurt you!'

'You idiot!' said Sean, then fell to the floor clutching his abdomen as a pellet hit him in the solar plexus.

'Do nothing stupid. It will be worse for you,' said Elloway.

Cathy dropped to Sean's side and helped him as he struggled to breathe. He was obviously in great discomfort.

Geoffrey asked, 'What do you want?'

'That's more like it. We want some cooperation. Where's the captain? You,' he pointed at Sally, 'go and get him.'

She looked puzzled and stood still.

'*NOW!*' the man screamed, red-faced, and Sally jumped

in fright, recovered her composure, stood her ground and said, 'No.'

'Go get the captain now or this man will get a shot to the head,' he said and moved towards Sean, pointing the gun at his temple. 'And believe me, a shot to the head at close range *will* kill him!'

'Do it, Sally,' said Geoffrey as he watched the officer becoming a bundle of nerves.

'*NOW!*' the man shouted again.

Sally turned and, as fast as the low gravity would allow, headed to the captain's office accompanied by the man called Smith. She returned with Captain Lavigne, looking almost regal in his best uniform. He was calm, upright and defiant, with Smith holding his gun to the captain's back. 'What's this nonsense about?' he asked.

In a calm voice, Elloway asked, 'Which console is used to orientate the ship?'

'Why?'

'I'm asking the questions!'

'How do you mean? Console?' asked the captain.

'There must be a control panel for turning the ship,' said Elloway.

'The engine room carries out minor corrections by varying the ejection of ions from one or more engines,' said the captain. 'We just request the variations.'

'Not minor stuff. *Major* corrections! The bloody turning!'

'There are no major corrections. There's an emergency system in case something large strikes the ship, but that's automatic. We can't control that.'

'How will you turn the ship at the halfway point?' asked Elloway, struggling to talk in a measured manner.

'That's a major operation.'

'Which equipment is used? Stop wasting my time. Show me *now!*'

The captain moved over to the navigation section. 'This is where we would monitor the operation and prepare for the turn. The first thing is to reduce the ship's spin.'

'Why would you reduce the spin?' Elloway was losing his cool once more.

'The ship cannot be turned while it's still rotating. It must be stationary so that the hub can be extracted. What are you planning to do? Why are you here?'

'We want you to turn the ship. We're going home,' Elloway said.

'It's not that simple,' the captain replied.

Ellis stepped forward and almost shouted into the captain's face. 'It's pretty fucking simple from our perspective. Turn the fucking ship! We know you can do it when we get halfway, but we want it done now!'

'I was stating a fact. It's not just a matter of pressing a button!'

'Just do it. No messing about. This man dies if you don't do it,' the leader said, now holding the weapon against Sean's skull.

'Whoa, stop! There's more to it than just turning it. I can explain, but it will take time. Turning the ship will take about twelve hours, maybe more,' said the captain. 'I think you misunderstand the manoeuvre. There's also a lot of planning involved. It can't be done just like that.'

'Don't tell me what I do or don't understand. How can it take twelve hours? Turn the damned ship around now. Right now!' yelled Elloway becoming highly agitated.

'Let me explain,' said the captain. 'It isn't a matter of just pressing a button or twisting some joysticks. Will you let me explain?' Lavigne knew that anything he could do to slow the momentum of the event would work in their favour. It was clear that this Elloway was totally ignorant of the processes needed to turn the hub and reverse direction. Could he make him see sense?

'Why, what's involved?' said Elloway, gradually becoming less confident in his plan, but ensuring he didn't show it in his actions or words. 'But we're not interested in delaying tactics.'

'Firstly, we must stop Kepler's spin. That takes about four or five hours. Then we need two hundred trained volunteers to man all the connections between the hub and the ship. We'll be spending weeks training them when the time comes. We have no one trained to do that now. Then we must stop the main ion motors, take the hub forwards out of the main ship, turn it and then reinsert it with such precision that all the connectors can be joined again.'

'You must be fucking joking!' shouted Ellis.

'I'm deadly serious,' the captain said. 'Once the turn is complete, we start the ship spinning once more and thrust in the opposite direction. It takes days of planning, weeks of training, and has to be undertaken with extreme caution. Everything on the ship must be strapped or tied down, and all the vegetable beds covered to stop soil and hydroponic fluids from floating away. What you ask is impossible with the current readiness of the crew.'

'You're lying!'

Geoffrey spoke, 'The captain is not lying. If you took the time and trouble to study the ship's operational capabilities, you'd know it's true.'

'Don't be condescending to *me*, lacky!' shouted Elloway, reversing his weapon and striking Geoffrey across the arm with it.

Geoffrey was knocked backwards, but steadied himself. Nothing broken.

Then events took a surprising turn. Smith spun around towards Elloway in a rage. 'You fucking prick. Didn't you check any of this out?'

Ellis also turned on their leader. 'You moron. Why the fuck didn't you tell us all of this?'

'I didn't know,' said Elloway almost timidly, then, angrily, he added, 'It's all Marina's fault. She's the tech wizard.'

'Listen,' said the captain, 'you have made a badly considered approach on this. Let's end it before anything worse happens… and take that weapon away from my officer's head.'

'But at the open council meeting, you showed the entire ship turning. You didn't mention any of this hub business,' said another of the group.

'I didn't happen to have a model of the ship which comes apart. I just simplified the procedure,' said the captain.

'You're bloody lying. It can't be that complicated. Why can't you just make a wide swing around?' said Elloway.

'You can't do that at our speed,' said Geoffrey. 'And even if it were possible, the rear of the ship would be facing into the direction of travel. Dust strikes would destroy us.'

Banging came from the bridge doors, and they shook and rattled as others outside tried to gain entry. The insurrectionists turned to look.

Smith and Ellis let their guns fall to the floor. Under his breath, Ellis said, 'You fucking prick, Elloway. How could you *not* know this? It's so fucking basic!'

'Come on,' said Geoffrey. 'No one has been seriously

hurt yet. You'll be in trouble, but surely you don't want to spend the rest of the journey in jail.'

'Give it up now,' said the captain as Sean struggled back to his feet, massaging the centre of his chest. 'Put your weapons down.'

Elloway shook his head, bowed it dejectedly, and let his weapon drift to the floor. The rest of the insurrectionists looked at each other and realised the game was up. They let their weapons fall too. Geoffrey grabbed Elloway's arms and tied his hands behind his back with a cable tie.

'Remove that chain, Sean,' said the captain.

Sean, still rubbing his chest, pushed off towards the door, almost floating as he adopted the graceful flying motion which those experienced in low-G could achieve on the bridge.

Melody Armstrong and two of her officers, armed with tasers, entered the bridge and surveyed the scene.

'They've surrendered,' said Geoffrey.

Within twenty minutes the insurrectionists were cuffed and being led away to temporary holding cells under the watchful care of Prison Governor Blaggard.

'What a bunch of gobshites,' said Sean.

'We need to educate the passengers. I can't believe they're so ignorant of the ship's systems,' said Geoffrey.

So, that was how the ship came to have its first rebellion. What the group had planned was a forced takeover of the ship and, in anyone's language, it was mutiny.

The small courtroom on deck forty-one was packed to the gunwales when the prosecution and defence made their opening arguments. Modelled on archaic courtrooms, it was fitted with polished timber walls, partitions and galleries. Finding actual wood on the ship was a rare treat.

The prosecutor was calling for a life sentence for the leader and ten years for each of his group, while the defence argued that they were an incompetent shower of fools and could never have succeeded and taken control the ship. Their ignorance of the method of changing direction demonstrated that they could never have been an effective force.

The trial lasted four days. The leader was found guilty of mutiny and given ten years in prison. His followers received shorter sentences for insurrection, of two and three years each. The remainder of the group came forward and were given probation.

For the first time, Governor Blaggard's prison was almost full.

Kepler was a complex and technologically advanced spaceship and Jake Zheng, the ship's president, decreed that every passenger be given a comprehensive understanding of operating procedures in the hope that the same sort of situation would never arise again. Captain Lavigne began a review of bridge security.

Kepler ploughed on through the void, ever closer to the speed of light.

Chapter Ten

NEW LIFE

Nine years into the journey, another message from Earth arrived, but even the computers failed to understand a single word. Spaceship Kepler was truly on its own in the void. The course was set, and it would be some forty years before the halfway point was reached and the ship began deceleration. The loneliness of the journey was having its effect on the mental health of some passengers. Those in stable relationships seemed able to cope adequately, as did single individuals with children. It was observed that people were spending longer in the green areas of the ship than previously – a homesickness for the nature and forests of home was growing. The people in no relationship were suffering the most. Some became even more isolated, and the number shunning all group activities was increasing – not excessively, but it was something the health department was keeping an eye upon. Occasionally, it boiled over, and this resulted in the odd suicide attempt, most of which were unsuccessful, and the shrinks could get to work to reintegrate them into society. Nevertheless, loneliness had become a major issue. The civilian elements of the ship's council applied themselves to the problem.

Suicide seemed such a dreadful waste of a life. Everyone selected to be saved from a dying Earth had to go through myriad tests and the chance of joining the exile was hundreds of millions to one, but some slipped through the net, or had been deliberately included to add balance. The passengers should feel privileged. They were the lucky ones. They would be saved, yet many still suffered dark thoughts of being trapped, knowing they were to spend their entire lives in what was a glorified metal cage.

The issue was clear. Two thousand social animals, humans, were hurtling through spacetime at close to the speed of light. The humans on board did not know if their fellow beings, marooned on a heating Earth, even existed any longer. The shipboard years which had passed certainly meant that everyone any passenger had ever met on the home planet was now much older or had died from old age, if not from the climate crisis. Time passing on Earth accelerated as Kepler's velocity approached the speed of light.

Fortunately, only a few had anxiety, suicidal thoughts or depression. Most were well-balanced and children were a great joy to the passengers.

On 14th December, 9SBY, Caroline Arnold-Pointer was sweating profusely in a backless hospital gown on a bed in C-sector's maternity ward. She closed her eyes, screwed up her face and released an anguished cry of pain. Husband Graham stood beside her, holding her hand and whispering comforting words, which she found no comfort whatsoever. Inside, he was in a state of panic, worried about the birth, Cas's health, the pain she was suffering and his inability to do anything about it.

At the foot of the bed, a midwife was keeping an eye on

what was happening beneath the gown, and behind her was a Black African man called Obijuru Njoku. He was the father, not Graham.

No, Caroline had not had an affair with him or even a one-night-stand at a drunken party. Obijuru had been chosen by the ship's computer to father her second child in accordance with the Kepler reproduction rules, and it had all been done using artificial insemination.

It was a condition of shipboard life that the second father could bond with his offspring, hence his standing there, watching the birth with some trepidation. Few liked the second child rule, but most appreciated its importance. Kepler was designed to save humanity. Genetics were a vital component of that objective.

'Here it comes,' said the midwife, her voice rising in excitement as Caroline experienced maximum dilation. 'Push,' she urged. 'You're almost there!'

Caroline cried out again, panted, and pushed. A tightly compressed layer of fuzzy hair appeared.

'It's coming, it's coming,' commented the midwife.

'Push hard, Cas,' said Graham, relieved that the end was almost there.

Obijuru said nothing as his excitement and anticipation gradually increased. He felt like rushing in and helping his child escape but did not. This woman was not his wife. He mustn't interfere, no matter how much he wanted to. His duty was to wait patiently in the wings. But he was sweating and wiping his brow as he watched the tiny body being ejected from its place of comfort into the relatively sterile world of Kepler.

The midwife wrapped the slippery child in a swathe of towels and lifted it up to Caroline, who now breathed heavily after the exertion of three hours' labour. Obijuru moved to the opposite side of the bed to Graham and peered in at the child's face.

'You have a lovely baby boy,' said the midwife.

'He's lovely,' said Obijuru and leaned down to kiss his son's forehead.

'He truly is,' said Caroline, wearing the deepest and happiest smile.

Obijuru squeezed Caroline's shoulder. 'Well done,' he said. 'What a beautiful baby.'

Graham knew he could not father a second child with his wife, Caroline, but his time would come when the computer allocated his seed to some other woman chosen at random and he would then be the man standing like a spare-part at another berthing bedside sometime in the future.

Obijuru was invited to name the child and chose Ezenwa. He was a fit and healthy boy, mixed-race, half Black from the father, one-quarter Japanese from Caroline's mother and one-quarter White from her father. Ezenwa had a rather lovely light-mahogany skin colour. His tight curly hair was inherited from his father, who was an engineer in the atmosphere section. Graham was father to Caroline's first child, Grenville Arnhodder, born in 4SBY and now a fit and playful five-year-old.

Caroline was moved to a general ward for observation, and the visits began. All of her and Graham's friends brought grapes and chocolates and cuddly toys, and Cardin, one of Caroline's closest friends and colleagues in the EVA corps, turned up with the most amazing bouquet of flowers. Flowers were a scarce commodity, most being stored only as seeds, but a few were grown in the hydroponics labs for decoration. Cardin must have pulled strings to get a whole bunch for her. They'd had a brief torrid affair in the early days of the flight, and she knew he still had feelings for her but their friendship remained steadfast.

Caroline's brother, Geoffrey, and sister-in-law, Jessica, had recently had the unexpected delight of twin girls.

The two families had adjacent apartments on the rim. They also had a family history of twins. Having both children in one shot meant Jessica would not have another child with a different father. Twins, Cindy and Roxy, now almost one, completed their family. The girls were only the second set of twins born on Kepler.

16SBY

Chapter Eleven

FIRE

Another message from Earth arrived in 15SB. It was likely to be the last. Only one word was identified – July – but nothing else. This appeared to confirm their messages back to Earth were no longer being received. They'd requested that Earth send all messages at least four times so that AI could try to interpret them from the four fragmented texts.

Now thirty-two years old, Geoffrey Arnold-Pointer's promotion to first officer under Captain Lavigne gave him considerable responsibility. In effect, he was the captain's senior deputy, and it was possible that the captaincy could be his when Lavigne retired in 20SBY. As first officer, he had a second apartment on deck two, adjacent to the bridge. Living in a very low-G environment was great for older people, but not good for any young person's health, so, when he was not deputising for Lavigne, he lived with Jessica and the twins in their rim apartment.

Cindy and Roxy were absolutely identical, their parents only able to tell them apart by a beauty spot on Roxy's behind. Schooling was going well and the little family seemed well adjusted and happy. Jessica was still an outstanding beauty and Geoffrey was the epitome of tall, dark and handsome.

Kepler's velocity reached 299,750 kilometres per second, about as near to the speed of light as it was possible to achieve, meaning every year on board the ship saw sixty years passing on Earth. The number of dust strikes the vessel endured increased with the speed, and weekly hull-breach warning klaxons were not unusual. Most often the damage was slight, but twice there had been serious incidents. The most worrying were always the hydroponic laboratories, and on one occasion in 14SBY, eighteen had died and no crops survived the vacuum. The technicians carted away the frozen remains of dead plants to produce fertiliser, and Lavigne had to preside over eighteen funerals.

Fire caused other regular dangers. One of the worst occurred in 16SBY while Geoffrey was on duty on the bridge. Its interior was brilliantly lit by the forward display of the view in front of the ship. The stars were now mostly an intense blue owing to the Doppler effect from Kepler's velocity. The starship's journey was one-fifth complete. By 40SBY to 50SBY, the time would come to reverse the ship and slow down as Kepler-452b became closer than Earth. Currently, they were continuing the acceleration. Every fraction of a kilometre per second closer to the speed of light would reduce the overall journey time and recent calculations indicated that the one-hundred-year overall journey time could be reduced to eighty. If so, Geoffrey realised that he might actually see the new world during his lifetime if his luck and health stayed good.

On the bridge, a translucent 3D projection of Kepler stood to the left of the captain's station. This remarkable piece of technology showed every enclosed space on the ship, from the smallest single apartments to the largest hydroponic farms. The walls and hull glowed a relatively transparent red. Apartments were misty yellow, hydroponic farms green, production factories blue, and other shades identified rooms which had fewer common functions.

An alarm sounded.

'Fire!' shouted Roger, one of the bridge crew.

A flashing red light immediately indicated the fire's detection and its location. Someone muted the alarm, and Geoffrey hit a button on the console. A computer voice announced, 'Fire in D-34 Hydroponics.'

'Can we dump carbon dioxide?' asked Geoffrey.

'No!' said Roger, checking the occupancy. 'People are working in there! Need to evacuate them first.'

Carbon dioxide could usually kill all fires, but if people were present, they could suffocate before help could arrive. Geoffrey knew to hold the carbon dioxide dump until everyone was evacuated.

Almost instantly, communicators were screaming for attention among the crew on the bridge. Heart rates rose and training kicked in.

Second officer Aarne Larsen called across to Geoffrey, 'Three fire teams despatched!'

'Copy that,' said Geoffrey.

Larsen looked down at his console then wondered if he should tell the first officer what he had seen. He knew the identification of the teams, and it would worry Geoffrey.

He made up his mind. Geoffrey had a right to know. 'Includes team C3,' he said.

Geoffrey's heart rate soared. He did his best not to show his reaction but Jessica, his wife, was second deputy in fire crew C3. She'd be heading into personal danger. It had happened before, and Geoffrey always felt the same gut-wrenching fear. His beautiful wife and the mother of his twin girls was running into danger. He'd often tried to persuade her to take safer duties or maybe work in one of the farms, but she'd always resisted, saying she wanted to contribute to the success of the mission, and her ambition was to become a fire chief. She'd told her worrying husband that his sister was on the EVA squad, even more dangerous, so she wanted to be part of an emergency response team, and anyway, she'd be well protected when the fire was tackled. Working in a farm or production area, if holed, would be far more likely to kill her. Geoffrey was never convinced of that logic and now, as always, when team C3 was in action, he was in a subdued state of panic.

Members of three teams of firefighters were bursting out of the deck thirty-four elevators. One was near the entrance to the fire's source. Jessica and C3 team leader Carlos Moratelli were studying their tablets, waiting for others to connect foam hoses and more firefighters to arrive at the doors.

'It's bad,' said Carlos. 'We'll wait a minute to allow more fighters to arrive and then, Michelle, I want you to drop the fire doors to protect this area of corridor. How many inside?'

A young woman in a D6 team uniform shouted, 'Sir! Three inside when the hit occurred.'

Carlos said, 'We need them out as soon as possible so that we can dump carbon dioxide.'

Partitions between the corridors and the rooms off them were made of steel, used despite the extra weight cost. Aluminium had a lower melting point, and the designers wanted to ensure fire could be delayed from spreading into the ship's core. The entrance to D-34 Hydroponics was already warm. Carlos could feel it on his face. He reached out and touched the wall. It was hot and almost burned his fingertips. This was a severe fire. The workers were probably already dead.

'That's fifteen firefighters present, Carlos,' said Jessica.

'Michelle, drop fire doors now. We're going in! Twelve only. Two remain behind with Michelle. Shut us in to keep this area clear!' shouted the C3 team leader, who had assumed the role of Alpha Fighter.

They all shut their visors and switched on their respirators. Double doors to hydroponics laboratory D-34 slid open, and flames shot out into the passage. Two streams of foam hit the fire, damping it down as twelve firefighters dashed through the flames and into the lab, carrying portable extinguishers.

The piercing wail of alarms inside the lab hit them along with a second wave of flames. Thick, acrid smoke billowed outwards, carrying with it the unmistakable scent of burning chemicals, which stank despite the respirators.

'Listen up, team,' Carlos barked into his radio. 'We've got a serious fire with potentially hazardous chemicals, materials, and gases. Michelle, shut us in, let the other teams into your area and let me know when they're ready to join us. Full gear, no exceptions. Jessica and Rodriguez, you're on point. Rest of you, stay in teams of two. Keep alert, stay safe.'

The firefighters sprang into action with practised efficiency. Jessica and Rodriguez led the way, spraying as they went; the others fanned out behind. Jessica almost tripped, looked down, and saw she'd stumbled across a body, clearly dead and lying on the floor slicked by the sprinkler system.

'One body here,' she called on the radio, pressing the blue button which marked the exact spot on the live laboratory map Michelle was observing outside; two firefighters were sent in to recover the body and check for signs of life. Another call came from somewhere behind her, with the same message.

Carlos saw that the heat signature was off the charts, indicating multiple hotspots throughout the lab.

'Michelle, alert the bridge to evacuate decks thirty-three and thirty-five. This could break through.'

Michelle radioed, 'All crews present outside lab. Fire doors in place foreled and backled. Instructions?'

'Connect to foam hydrants and follow us in. The whole place is ablaze,' said Carlos. 'Bridge. There'll be no one alive in here. Flood the deck with carbon dioxide *now*! Everyone take care. Lots of debris on the floor,' he warned, as the doors opened behind him.

Geoffrey replied to the call for help. 'Looking to flood with carbon dioxide any moment. You're certain there's no living casualties.'

'Certain. This isn't survivable without suits. Sooner rather than later,' said Carlos.

The floor was becoming slick with a mixture of foam, unidentified liquids, and the water from the sprinklers, which was achieving nothing. It made every movement treacherous and the scene inside the lab was chaotic. Fire had engulfed rows of hydroponic beds, their plastic components melting and adding fuel to the inferno. The air was thick with smoke and steam, reducing visibility to near zero.

'Where's that carbon dioxide dump?' shouted Carlos into his communicator.

'Coming,' said Geoffrey.

Jessica and Rodriguez moved deeper into the hydroponics laboratory, sweeping each area for potential victims. Behind them, eight more teams, two dragging foam hoses and others with extinguishers, began the arduous task of extinguishing the blaze.

'Moratelli to bridge. We've got multiple fires throughout the lab. Three dead so far. Visibility severely limited. Where's that carbon dioxide?'

'Imminent,' shouted Geoffrey.

As they progressed, the firefighters encountered a new challenge. The laboratory's ventilation system, still operational despite the fire, was spreading smoke and flames to neighbouring rooms. It was then that the carbon dioxide dump occurred. Flames died instantly. The firefighters double-checked their respirators to ensure they were breathing air, then searched the laboratory, the smoke gradually being washed to the floor by the sprinklers.

In the lab's heart, Jessica and Rodriguez stumbled upon the fire's point of origin. A tangle of electrical wires, likely overheated by the demands of the hydroponics equipment, had ignited nearby flammable materials.

'We need foam here!' Jessica called out. 'This fire's not going down with carbon dioxide alone. There are gas cylinders in its heart, glowing red hot.'

As if on cue, a cylinder which had been lying in the middle of the fire ruptured. It shot into the air as gas escaped, rebounded off the ceiling and hit the firefighters.

Lisa Jupe and Izu Suzuki had been approaching with more foam extinguishers. The cylinder knocked Lisa over, and she landed on her back three metres from the main fire. Izu, protected by being behind a cabinet, rushed out and killed the last of the flames, then switched to water to cool the other cylinders.

'You okay?' he shouted to Lisa.

'I am.' She rubbed her arm. 'Sore arm and chest, but there's another body. It's one of ours. I think it was hit by the cylinder before me.'

Satisfied that he'd damped down the source of the fire, Izu turned and saw the two firefighters. Lisa was lying across Jessica, who was clearly immobile.

Moratelli arrived, helped Lisa to her feet and cradled Jessica's head and shoulders in his arms. 'She's dead,' he said.

'CPR, quick!' shouted Lisa.

'No good. It crushed her chest. Look,' said Carlos, examining the body.

The carbon dioxide was already being purged as the group of firefighters gathered around the body in shock. 'Any more dead?' he asked.

'No, just two laboratory assistants and Jessica. One of the lab assistants might be saveable, and medics are on the job,' said Rodriguez.

Moratelli pulled a communicator out of his jacket. 'Carlos here. The fire's out. Who's officer of the bridge today?'

'Well done,' came the reply. 'I'm officer of the bridge today.'

'That you, Geoff?' asked Carlos, wanting to be sure it really was him.

'It is.'

'Bad news, Geoffrey,' said Carlos. 'We lost three, including one of our own. Brace yourself, don't know how to tell you this, but it's Jessica. Sorry.'

Carlos heard the gasp from Geoffrey. On the bridge, he almost collapsed to the deck, but in the dreadful slow-motion caused by one-tenth of Earth gravity. Michael

Brebner grabbed him and pulled him back to his feet. 'What's wrong?' he asked.

'Jessica.'

All those on the bridge had been listening to the radio chatter of the firefighters, so he didn't need to ask what Geoffrey meant.

'Annette. Take over the bridge. I'm taking Geoff to his cabin.'

'No. *No*,' Geoff said, coming back to his senses. 'I want to go to the lab.' He turned to run to the stairwell, his thoughts in turmoil.

'Right, but I'm coming with you,' said Michael, and the two men dashed down the stairs and round to a sector-D elevator.

In just a minute or two, they emerged onto the foul-smelling walkway outside lab D34. Carlos was standing outside with Michelle. When he saw the first officer arriving, he barred his way.

'Nothing you can do in there, Geoff,' he said.

'I want to see her,' was his retort.

'Can't let you in, sorry. A med team will bring her out any minute. We need to review fire policy. An immediate carbon dioxide dump would have saved Jess.'

'We couldn't,' said Michelle. 'It would have killed the workers.'

'Should have done it anyway,' Carlos replied. 'We were here pretty damned quick; we might have been able to get them out and give first aid.'

Michelle didn't speak again. It had always been a contentious issue. Dumping carbon dioxide was extremely effective, but not when people were in the fire's location. She guessed the argument would rage on at the next fire officers' meeting.

'Was it the fire?' Geoffrey asked, panicking as he imagined his wife burned alive, her hair and body being scorched and blistered.

'It was the fire, but it was an exploding cylinder that killed her. We think it was an oxygen cylinder. It must have ruptured and been jet-propelled at her. We'll find out later. I'm guessing at the moment.'

A med team comprising a doctor and two porters emerged from lab D34 with a stretcher carrying a figure in a firefighter's outfit. It was Jessica.

Geoffrey rushed over to them, and they stopped. He lifted the visor and saw Jessica's lifeless face. Her eyes were closed. 'What caused it… her death, I mean?'

The doctor replied, 'Probably her chest was crushed, but it might have been a broken neck. We'll find out later. She was hit by the cylinder. It would have been instant.'

Geoffrey was struck dumb, unable to speak. He looked around, locking eyes, person by person with each one around him. Dizziness hit him and he staggered against the wall. Michael quickly steadied him. The first officer's eyes were brimming with tears.

'We need to leave here,' said Michael, almost in a whisper.

Geoffrey quickly straightened himself, wiped his eyes with a tissue, but looked devastated.

Suddenly, his whole expression changed and he blurted out, 'The twins, I must get to the twins.' He rushed away to the elevator.

Michael asked, 'Anyone know Caroline's number?'

'Five-five-two-three,' said Carlos.

'I'll call her and break the bad news,' he said, dialling the number on his communicator.

Five days later, over one hundred citizens of Kepler met up in room C-4 on deck ninety-seven.

Geoffrey stood in the same suit he had worn on his wedding day and gripped the hands of the beautiful, blonde six-year-old twins he and Jessica had brought into the world, or rather, the ship. Cindy and Roxy were old enough to be aware of what was taking place. They knew they'd lost their mother to the latest fire, and she lay under a white sheet on a gurney on one side of the room. Geoffrey had wondered whether to not let them attend, but the ship's councillor said it would help him and them grieve in the months to follow.

The captain and all senior crew were present in emerald dress uniforms. Caroline and Graham stood on either side of the twins to offer support, and their own children, Grenville aged twelve and Ezenwa aged six, stood with them.

Fire Chief Edward Stephens stepped up to the microphone and said a few words about Jessica's courage in fighting fires and the fluke explosion of a gas canister, which had taken her life. Geoffrey declined to say anything. He honestly didn't believe he could speak without breaking down. Jessica's favourite song, the cover version of *Forever, Forever* by *Sue Vero*, played over the audio system, and its chorus brought tears to many.

The day we met is burned in my mind,
Handsome, dashing, happy and kind,
Forever, forever 'til the end of time.

A door slid open in the wall. Four firefighters lifted the stretcher off the gurney and carried it into a bare metal compartment, a giant airlock, where they placed it onto a waist-height plinth. The pallbearers stood at attention, saluted, and returned to the main room, closing the door behind them. Geoffrey could see Jessica's body through the observation window.

Captain Lavigne said, 'We commit Jessica to eternity.' He'd have to repeat the announcement for the other fatalities in similar ceremonies over the next couple of hours.

A monitor above the door in the wall came to life and showed the scene behind the Kepler. Countless millions of dull, red-shifted stars.

Geoffrey stepped forward and hit a red button set into the wall before stepping back to enfold the twins' hands again. An alarm sounded twice.

All of a sudden, the monitor showed Jessica accelerating away from the ship at an angle to the ship's wake, a fragile, shrouded human body tumbling and spinning into the distance. Within a minute, she'd vanished from view. She would spend decades travelling through the universe behind her family. One day, when Kepler's deceleration began, Jessica would overtake them and reach the new world long before the ship itself, then speed on for eternity at close to the speed of light towards the brilliant centre of the Milky Way.

There were tears, arms of comfort, hands being shaken, shoulders to cry on, kisses on cheeks, and cuddles for the twins. Family, friends and colleagues left for their sorrowful journeys back to apartments or places of work.

Officers of the watch brought the first of the hydroponics workers' bodies to the C-4 jettison point, and the funerals continued.

39SBY

Chapter Twelve

MANOEUVRE

Now fifty-five years old, this would be Captain Geoffrey Arnold-Pointer's last month in command, and Kepler was about to make its most critical in-flight manoeuvre. His own nephew, Ezenwa or Zen for short was likely to succeed him. He'd grown up following everything his uncle said and did, and had become a mathematical genius as well as a competent officer.

Despite his own training and confidence, Geoffrey's stomach was churning with worry. He'd never had to make such crucial commands and decisions in the past. It had all been leading up to this point in time. There was nothing to compare it to; it had never happened before and was unlikely to be needed ever again. 'Fingers crossed,' Geoff thought, because if their destination were not suitable for colonisation, then a new journey would have to be taken to another likely star system. That, of course, would not be Geoff's problem.

Things had gone well during the thirty-nine years of the journey, and for the last ten years, using free hydrogen molecules collected from the space through which they'd been travelling, the ship had been approaching light speed so closely that the time dilation had become even greater than ever imagined. The LED display showed their speed as 299,770 kilometres per second. They had knocked ten years off the expected time to this point in the journey. After only thirty-nine shipboard years, they had covered half of the 1,642 light-years to Kepler-452. Back on Earth, time had been passing at least eighty times faster than onboard. Calculating the date on Earth was complex, but the navigation officers estimated it would now be roughly 2900AD. Communications officers guessed that there might still be messages from the home world trying to catch up with them and nothing made them more aware of their isolation from home than the fact that the last message had been received twenty-four years previously and just one word within it had been decipherable.

Now, thirty-nine ship years into the journey, the time had arrived to reverse the acceleration. The ship's control hub must be turned to slow Kepler down. The speed achieved meant that they would arrive in orbit around Kepler-452b before 80SBY and some of the original crew could still be alive to see the new world, although they'd never set foot upon it. Human life expectancy onboard increased steadily, but only for those spending more time near the hub and its low gravity. That had the drawback of causing deterioration in muscles and bone density such that returning to normal Earth gravity would be extremely problematic. Any ageing person spending long periods near the hub would never set foot on the new world. Their bones and muscles would find it impossible to cope.

The oldest crew members, who had joined aged thirty-five, were now seventy-four, but some specialist astrophysicists and surgeons had been in their fifties when the journey had begun, and most were still living in good health as they approached and passed ninety. Older residents had apartments close to the hub allocated to them but the vast majority of Kepler's crew spent as much of their off-duty time as possible between decks ninety-five and one hundred. They had to carry out work in lower gravity regions like the hydroponics and food production labs but lived and exercised in the higher numbered decks where gravity was closer to Earth normal.

Orbiting Earthbound telescopes had obtained most of the information available to the crew about Kepler-452b. The James Webb Telescope, and Hubble Telescope had been the main tools though the Hawking Telescope on the far side of the moon, with no interference from Earth gave the best analysis when it came on line around Kepler's departure date.

However, no one could be certain about the planet's size and mass. Earth scientists once believed it to be two or three-times Earth's mass, which might have made life very difficult for the colonists, but the Hawking Telescope yielded more optimistic results soon after departure and the data had been sent on to Kepler. Nevertheless, gravity was likely to be higher than Earth normal.

Under Geoffrey's command, intensive consultations with medical staff and physiotherapists in the crew led the senior officers to make an important decision. When the ship reversed its direction, the rarely used jets that encircled the rim would fire, not just to return the ship to its angular rotation but also to increase the speed at which the ship revolved. Gravity at the rim was to be increased by ten percent per annum until it reached one point five times

Earth normal, the expected maximum gravity on Kepler-452b.

The onboard scientists' thinking was that if the destination planet's gravity was greater than Earth's, at least the passengers and crew would be prepared for it. Those over sixty years of age would have a lower gravity apartment allocated to them so that they would never need to experience the higher G-forces at the rim.

In the weeks leading up to the manoeuvre, many new recruits had been taken on to ensure there was temporarily a much larger number of ship's officers. Then the training began in earnest. Locking and unlocking mechanisms around the hub would be tried and tested, lubricated, tested and tried, all the time with crews communicating with each other on progress. The engineering section left nothing to chance and checked the ion drives to ensure they could be shut down and restarted. All rim jets were fired several times to be sure the buttons and switches worked, and manoeuvring jets on the hub went through a series of simulations ready for the big day.

Turning Kepler meant chaotic gravity throughout the manoeuvre. The tenth of a G acceleration towards the rear would cease. Centrifugal force acting through the rim would be reduced to zero. Everyone would be in free fall, some of whom would never previously have experienced it and would have a taste of the dreaded space sickness. Anything not fixed down would be weightless and could float but when gravity returned, such items would fall.

Four weeks previously, announcements prepared citizens for the manoeuvre. They stored breakables in packing cases and secured them to an appropriate wall or deck with Velcro. Senior officers estimated the hub's rotation taking thirty to forty minutes to stop. In the hydroponics and food production sections, everything was being secured. Workers placed covers over planting troughs to prevent soil, water and fertiliser from getting into the atmospheric filters and the fishponds had tight covers fitted to stop too much water loss. Nothing more could be done. Fortunately, turning the ship was a one-time-only event.

During Kepler's construction in Earth orbit, they practised hub turning flawlessly several times. This time, however, was critical. If there were a problem, the entire vessel would be in danger.

As is always the case, what had seemed way in the future was suddenly upon the crew, and everyone tried to get a good night's sleep.

On the morning of the manoeuvre, Geoffrey and his team took their places on the bridge. The forward view showed the stars of the Milky Way in brilliantly enhanced blue, almost unviewable owing to the brightness, despite the display being dimmed. Geoffrey ordered the shutters to be opened for a final actual view of the Milky Way, and the bridge was flooded with intense light.

A minute was enough. 'Close the shutters,' said Geoffrey, and steel covers closed like a camera diaphragm over the vista. The dimmed display was once again the bridge crew's view forward.

'Shutters closed and sealed,' said Brian Oxley, Geoffrey's first officer, a ginger-haired, White, skinny individual who was one of the very first children born on Kepler. He was desperately keen to be efficient as he hoped for the captaincy one day.

The engineering team in the ion drive compartment, headed by Amrit Benson, a small Asian man, and another of the first-born generation, checked their computers ready for the most important change to the ship's operation until it arrived at the new world. Everyone wore pressure suits in the hub, and a further two hundred citizens, trained over the last three months, waited in the areas of the ship which attached to the hub. They too were in spacesuits as areas connected to the hub would soon be in vacuum.

It was unlikely the hub would suffer depressurisation, but the manoeuvre itself made the control centre vulnerable to dust strikes, hence the caution. The two hundred volunteers in the main body of the ship, who were commanded by the second and third officers, had a simple function, but it involved being exposed to the vacuum of space and considerable danger, even though much of the operation would be automated. Zen was the third officer so was very much involved in the manoeuvre.

Geoffrey spoke into his microphone. 'This is it, crew. We'll begin in five minutes. Everyone, please ensure your feet are strapped to or hooked into the deck.' The captain looked around and saw everyone adjusting buckles on their shoes. He concentrated on giving an air of cool confidence while, inside, his emotions were on fire.

'Engineering?' he asked.

'Ready,' was the response.

'Communications?'

'Ready.'

'Navigation?'

'Ready.'

'Environment?'

'Ready.'

'Control?'

'Ready.'

'EVA?'

'Suited and ready,' said the second officer. He was leading the two hundred trained volunteers positioned around the hub at the points where the ship connected to it.

'Fire control?'

'Ready.'

'Medical?'

'Ready as we can be.'

Geoffrey checked his tablet. He'd missed nothing. It was now or never. 'Engineering, cut the drive.'

'Drive disengaged,' was Amrit's response. Instantly, the bridge officers noticed that the force that pulled them towards the rear of the ship at a tenth of a G was gone. They were truly in freefall. Some had never experienced it – those born onboard – but everyone born on Earth had sampled weightlessness during their launch to join the Kepler, the day they evacuated their home planet.

'Fire outer sector jets,' said Geoffrey.

'Jets firing,' said Brian, carefully monitoring the data on his console.

Geoffrey remembered freefall well. Several on their launch vessel were sick, and the smell of vomit caused many others to suffer the same fate. Fortunately, it didn't affect Geoffrey or his sister who had both been fine.

'Control. Call rim speed reduction, please,' said Geoffrey.

'Ten percent,' said the navigation officer, a woman called Nevaeh Khumala, a tall, slim Black African.

'Twenty percent,' she said.

'Fifty percent.'

'Seventy-five percent.'

'Ninety percent. Reduce power.'

'Jet reduction in progress,' said Brian.

'Ninety-five; ninety-seven; ninety-nine. Rotation stopped,' announced Nevaeh.

'Zero rotation,' confirmed Brian.

'Double check,' said Geoffrey.

Brian studied his instrument panel and called Nevaeh over to check with him. 'Confirmed. Rim stationary,' he said.

'Okay,' said Geoffrey, 'phase two is about to begin. Depressurise connecting areas.'

A few minutes later, the first officer said, 'Depressurising complete.' Now, the corridors and areas connected to the hub were in vacuum. Separation from the ship could begin.

'Begin disconnection,' ordered Geoffrey. So far, so good, he thought.

The two hundred suited individuals, all connected by safety lines to the main ship, unclipped wall sections which joined ship to hub. As they snapped open each numbered clip, they reported to the second and third officers, who kept the first officer and captain apprised of the situation.

Finally, almost five minutes later, everyone had reported in. None had stuck. None had broken. The second and third officers confirmed with each other, and the second officer announced, 'Hub disconnected, Captain.'

'Any shifting?' While disconnected, the hub was still travelling at close to the speed of light but nestled within the disc section of Kepler while it travelled at the same speed. It was important that there be no movement between the two until extraction began.

'No measurable shifting,' said the second officer.

'Begin extraction,' said Geoffrey. 'Easy now. Take care.'

'Minimum ion propulsion started,' said Amrit.

The entire hub of the ship containing the bridge, the engine room and ion drive moved forward along the ship's direction of travel. There were noises of metal on metal as the tight-fitting structure eased its way free of the main ship. Any serious snagging would have to be dealt with. They could not afford to damage any of the outer edges of either the hub or the disc. It was a slow, slow process.

'One metre per second,' said Amrit.

Two minutes later. 'I can see stars looking forward. You're extracted,' said the second officer, seeing the Milky Way through the gap between the hub and disc.

'Continue half a kilometre,' said Geoffrey. 'Count down again, please, Nevaeh.'

'Twenty metres,' she announced, and continued to state how far the hub was in advance of the disc in twenty, then fifty metre intervals. As they closed on half a kilometre, she returned to twenty and ten metre announcements. The extraction was almost complete.

'Five,' she said. 'Two, one, zero!'

'Reverse thrusters off,' said Amrit.

'Is relative motion stopped?' asked Geoffrey.

'Stationary,' said Brian.

Now it had to be rotated through 180 degrees, reinserted, and connected back to the main ship – the difficult bit. Sliding back in would be a slow process. It could not be hurried. Around the front and back of the hub were eight manoeuvring jets, which used nitrogen. One on the portside rear and another on the starboard side forward fired. The bridge crew felt the motion. It was crucial that the rotation was even and directly through the plane of the hub; otherwise, reconnecting would be a nightmare.

'Navigation?' he said.

'Ten degrees.'

'Call each ten, please,' Geoffrey said.

The bridge was experiencing strange gravity effects. Depending upon where they were standing, gravity pulled the crew towards the front or rear.

'Twenty degrees,' said navigation.

Geoffrey was keeping a sharp ear open for any sign of dust strikes as the dust protection system was ineffective during the manoeuvre. They'd had to trust to luck though those with a religion prayed.

'Thirty.'

A schematic showed the hub ship travelling at a bizarre angle.

'Ninety.'

Halfway. The rotational forces were causing the bridge crew to be standing or sitting at a strange angle as the turn continued.

'One twenty.'

This was the most dangerous time. An alarm sounded.

'Rim apartment B-100-101 holed!' came from the EVA officer. 'Team on the way.'

'Anyone inside?' asked medical.

'No. They were on EVA duty,' said EVA.

'Correcting relative motion,' said Brian. 'Negligible effect.'

Geoffrey breathed a sigh of relief. 'Thank goodness it was the main ship, not the hub,' he said. A hole in the hub now could be catastrophic.

'One forty.'

Of course, while the hub was almost side on to the direction of travel, the bridge to ship connectors were extremely vulnerable, and any damage could prevent the hub from being reinserted into the rim section. As the angle increased, the risk reduced.

'One fifty,' said navigation

Thirty degrees to go. Out of sight of the rest of his officers, Geoffrey crossed his fingers. He wasn't superstitious or religious, but it somehow seemed appropriate.

'Begin reverse thrust,' the captain said.

'Reverse firing commenced,' said Brian, and Amrit confirmed.

It was then that a much more serious strike occurred. The entire bridge and engineering crew felt it. A distinct shudder.

'Something hit us near the B connectors,' said Haoyu Guo, the second navigation officer.

'Continue rotation,' said Geoffrey. Not that it could be instantly stopped anyway. He must control his emotions, and he knew he had to maintain a calm demeanour for the sake of everyone else.

'One seventy degrees.'

Almost there, thought Geoffrey. What had hit the ship? How much damage? Would it prevent the crucial reinsertion of the hub?

'One hundred seventy-five,' said Nevaeh.

As the reverse jets completed their task, the last few degrees seemed to take forever. Geoffrey was desperate to see the damage, but he couldn't send a probe until the hub was stationary.

'One eighty.'

'Thrusters off,' said Amrit.

'Send out a probe. Let's see the damage,' said Brian.

Another monitor, to the right of the main screen, came to life and showed the star fields forward of the hub. It rotated slowly and soon showed the B-Sector connectors. There were sheets of jagged metal.

'That's bad. Get the EVA officer for me,' said Geoffrey, his anxiety rising as he tried to imagine reinserting the hub, with lumps of metal sticking out of the rim.

'Sir,' said Brian.

Chapter Thirteen

NIGHTMARE DUTY

The senior EVA officer, in his full spacesuit, floated beside one of the C connectors on the disc part of the ship to which he was tethered. He was, of course, ready to be called into action at any moment to help reconnect the two halves of Kepler. The last thing he expected was a call from Captain Arnold-Pointer.

'Yes, sir. Commander Ken Dupont here, sir,' he said.

'Are you near a monitor?' asked Geoffrey.

'I can be in a few seconds,' he replied.

'Get there.'

Ken looked around. Two volunteers in EVA suits were floating beside him, tethered to the ship and hanging out over the cavernous space where Kepler's hub should be. To their right, they saw the faint red glow of the red-shifted stars behind them. To the left, space glowed brilliantly with the blue-shifted heart of the Milky Way, but a disc blocked off a large section of it. This was the hub. In front of them, the interior doughnut hole of Kepler fell away and then looped back up like a hamster wheel to a position opposite and then over the top of the field of view. It was as if they were standing on the inside edge of a giant wheel.

Around the disc's interior, they observed the other two hundred volunteers, all in spacesuits and all tethered to their own contact points awaiting the hub's reconnection.

Ken pulled himself over to a video monitor near one of the elevator shafts. 'I'm beside monitor sixty-two,' he said, steadying himself, connecting a new tether and releasing the old one.

Geoffrey said, 'Communications. Patch the probe camera through to monitor sixty-two.'

A few tens of seconds later, Ken exclaimed, 'My God, what the hell happened?'

'Something struck us, and it's done enough damage to stop us reconnecting. Every second we don't have the engines running adds even more danger of dust strikes. We've got to repair it, and quickly!' said Geoffrey.

'It looks as if there's a sheet of metal protruding inwards about one metre. Should be relatively easy to cut away to allow us to reconnect, but we'll need to replace it when the ship's reconnected,' said Ken.

'What do you want us to do?' the captain asked.

'Sir,' said Brian, 'we're drifting. Impact knocked us out of position. We're no longer lined up to reconnect.'

Ken didn't hear Brian's information as it was on a different channel. He answered the captain, 'I'd like you to close on the ship so that you're only five or ten metres from us. I can then send a repair squad.'

'Hold on, Ken. We've a bigger problem. I'll get back to you in a moment,' said Geoffrey, who then asked Brian, 'How do we realign the ship?'

Ken was puzzled. There was a *bigger* problem than the

hub having been hit! He waited anxiously all the time the two hundred people in EVA suits were using bottled air.

Amrit, chief engineer, answered the captain's question, 'Easier said than done. The whole point of our care to avoid drifting while turning was because it would be a nightmare to realign.'

'Well, we've no option now. What's involved?' asked Geoffrey, studying the damage on the probe monitor.

'We have sixteen nitrogen jets around the hub, so navigation will need to give us a three-dimensional fix on the line between sectors A and F. We'll need to align the same sectors on the hub to that point. When all three dimensions line up, we'll be able to reconnect, but I can imagine it taking some time,' said Amrit.

'How long?'

The navigation officer, Nevaeh, answered, 'It's a long job, could take hours.'

'What? Hours? Really?' exclaimed Geoffrey. 'That means all the EVA personnel will need their suits charging and air. We'll also be in grave danger of more strikes.'

'It won't help to pressure us; we'll get started immediately. Amrit?' said navigation officer Nevaeh, always cool and proficient.

'Here,' said the chief engineer.

'Patch the controls through to my navigation desk. We'll control it from here,' said Nevaeh.

'Take care. Start us spinning and you'll never get out of it,' Amrit cautioned. 'Seriously!'

'I know,' replied Nevaeh.

'Brian,' said Geoffrey, 'get onto the first and second officers and Ken and get them all to leave the core and wait in the main body of the ship until we get the hub into a position where the repair crew can safely try to repair the damage.'

'No can do, sir!' said Brian.

'What? Why?'

'There are no entry points from the core to the disc. The volunteers are there until we're reconnected. No one expected the operation to take longer than an hour or so,' said Brian.

'Find a way, Brian. There's no way we're losing two hundred volunteers because they can't get to safety.'

'Working on it, sir.'

Where there's a will, there's a way, and the problem was solved, but at the cost of a life.

The solution required all the volunteers moving around the core to sectors A and D. There, they extended fire hoses to act as tethers, and each person made their way to the rear section of Kepler and around onto the main hull. At least on the rear side of the ship they were protected from dust strikes.

Experienced EVA officers, including senior specialist Caroline, the captain's sister, were involved. The fire hoses were attached to loops outside the nearest airlocks, and gradually, over almost fifty minutes, every volunteer but one got back inside the main hull where oxygen and suit power were recharged. The individual who died had vomited in his suit and choked. Not a good way to go and impossible for anyone to perform a rescue. Everyone else, once inside the ship, awaited the return call.

In the meantime, Ken chose his three most proficient EVA specialists, Caroline, Cardin and Derek, to accompany him back to the core with spare oxygen cylinders and power packs. There they waited for the hub to be brought back to a stationary position in relation to the main ship so they could attempt the essential repairs.

Meanwhile, the Kepler was travelling at almost the speed of light with no protection from dust particles or anything larger. It was clear to the EVA specialists that this was an existential problem. Somehow, navigation must return the hub to the correct orientation to be reinserted, then the repair would need to be completed before the hub could be reinserted into the doughnut hole. A huge project.

It took almost two hours to bring the hub into a stationary position in relation to the disc. The meteor strike, probably no larger than a grain of salt, had hit the hub section with such force that it had started the ship spinning in all three directions. It was no longer on the same plane as the disc; it was no longer central over the doughnut core and was still in motion. Okay, the vectors were tiny and could be measured between 0.01 and 0.1 millimetres per second, but that was enough to prevent the hub from docking back into its hole.

'Stationary!' announced Brian. 'We've done it.'

'You sure?' asked Geoffrey.

'Five minutes and no motion in any direction and we're back in position to dock,' said Brian. The entire bridge crew cheered.

'Bring the hub back towards the disc until we're ten metres forward of it,' ordered Geoffrey. 'Ken, do you copy?'

'Copy.'

'You should be ready to go in about eleven minutes,' said Geoffrey, looking over towards Brian, who nodded.

'Copy that, ready to leave the disc section. Give us a go when you want us to start,' said Ken, looking at the rest of his team for confirmation they'd understood too.

Eleven minutes seemed like an hour, then, finally Brian announced, 'Hub is stationary and ten metres from Kepler.'

'You have a go,' said Geoffrey, sending the entire EVA team of four, including his own sister, on a mission which would put them in extreme peril. Much as he would have liked, he couldn't exclude her, having to show no bias as captain, but there was a deep fear within him they might not all return to safety.

The vast doughnut hole in the disc was now in deep shadow as the hub was blocking the brilliance of the hundreds of millions of blue-shifted stars of the centre of the Milky Way. Where there was shade, it was the blackest of blacks. Four space-suited figures, linked to each other by tethers, pushed off into the void, on a slow trajectory towards the B-Sector of the hub.

Cardin made first contact, grasping a recessed handhold and clipping the connector of another tether into the clasp. At least they were now safe. There was no longer even the slightest danger of drifting away from the Kepler.

Caroline and Ken were next to make contact and pushed onwards around the side of the hub, seeing all the connectors which would later be joined with the disc section.

'There's the damage,' said Derek, the fourth member of the team. The others followed him towards a jagged area where part of the hub had been ripped open by the dust strike, an explosive collision at that speed.

Cardin brought up the rear, ensuring they were all

connected by the group tether to the hub. They couldn't take any shortcuts during the operation. One of the few EVA specialists who had qualified before Kepler departed, Cardin was coolly efficient on duty but the life and soul of the group when relaxing.

Ken, a brilliant and strong leader, had long been the chief EVA officer and warned the others, 'Be sure to keep yourselves behind parts of the ship so that you're exposed to minimum radiation and protected from any more dust strikes.' They all acknowledged the message.

Derek reached the distorted section of the hull first. 'Take great care, it has sharp edges,' he cautioned. Derek's expertise was vacuum welding and he would be key to this repair.

Caroline was next. She carefully grasped the side of the steel panel which jutted outwards and tried to bend it back towards the hub. The result, of course, was that Newton's third law pushed her in the opposite direction. Cardin anchored himself to a bracket near the connector and held Caroline's feet. She tried again to bend the panel with limited success. It would move a few centimetres but would still be sticking out of the hub and preventing the two parts of the ship reconnecting. The glowing centre of the Milky Way illuminated the entire area in stark relief. On the bridge, the captain was sweating with the stress of the situation.

'Won't move enough,' said Caroline. 'Think we need to cut it away.'

'Shears?' asked Ken.

'No, nor the grinder,' said Caroline. 'I think it has to be the cutter.'

'Okay. Derek, get the cutter ready,' said Ken.

The team had hoped they could bend the panel back

into position sufficiently to allow the hub to be reinserted in the disc, but the section involved was too substantial. The alternative was to use shears, grinders or a plasma cutter.

Attached to the tail end of their tethers was a plasma cutter the size of a medium suitcase and besides the gas bottles containing argon and nitrogen, there was a container into which they would syphon hot debris. A shroud would protect the astronaut from the arc.

Derek manoeuvred the cutter into position and, with Cardin's help, attached it to the salvageable section of metal sheet.

'Attached,' said Cardin.

'Power up,' said Derek.

'System running,' announced Ken. 'Cas, keep hold of the exhaust container.'

'Will do.'

'Ready to cut,' said Derek.

'Captain,' said Ken.

'Copy you.'

'We're about to cut. There'll be some minor drift of the hub caused by the plasma arc,' said Ken. 'You need to be ready to compensate, or we'll be back in the same situation, having to realign the hub.'

'Okay, Ken. We're aware and ready,' said Geoffrey once Brian had given him the thumbs-up.

'Go to cut,' said Ken.

It was a slow process, with the cutter having to be repositioned and reattached to the panel to cut the next section, but in thirty minutes, the jagged sheet moved.

'Almost through,' said Derek. Cardin held tight to the damaged sheet.

Suddenly, it floated free, and Cardin passed it to Caroline, who strapped it within that section of the hub.

'Will the rest of it fit okay?' asked Ken.

'It will indeed,' said Derek.

'Okay, detach the cutter and hoses and store with the damaged panel,' said Ken.

Caroline undid the cutter clamps, and the cutter pack floated to one side. 'Can you grab that, Cardin?' she said.

'What a catch!' he quipped.

'Always bragging,' she replied and turned to look at the EVA specialist.

That was strange. He didn't respond to her jibe and he looked odd. Was it the sharp shadows within which they were working? Cardin had both hands on the cutter pack, but she couldn't see his face. Freefall played weird tricks on you occasionally. Now he was floating away, still holding the case.

'Cardin?' she asked.

No answer.

She pulled on the tether that joined the two of them, and he jerked and came back towards her, still holding the cutter case. What was wrong with him?

'Cardin?' she asked again.

No answer.

Now it looked as if he was going to bump into her. Cardin had done nothing to stop his movement. He was getting closer, and then she realised why he looked odd. His spacesuit was no longer in shadow. The brilliant glow of the blue-shift stars illuminated the whole of him. She let out a shocked gasp, which morphed almost into a scream, then she needed to stifle rising nausea and looked away. Don't be sick, she told herself, knowing the danger of vomit in a helmet. She looked back towards her former lover and colleague.

Cardin's suit was still carrying the cutter, but the helmet

had no faceplate or sides. It had vanished. His face had a deathly smile upon it. His forehead was gone. Vanished!

'No,' she whispered to herself and then, aloud, '*He's dead*!' A shocked pronouncement, as she tried to accept that Cardin was floating, dead, before her. She couldn't believe it. Only a few seconds previously he'd joked about catching the cutter. Now he was gone. Instantaneous. Caroline was frozen in position, her hand still holding Cardin to stop his movement towards her. He was gone. Dead. Her entire body shivered. She pushed Cardin away, a reaction spawned from her horror, but they were tethered. He'd rebound towards her again.

'Oh, my God!' exclaimed Ken. It was always a commander's worst fear losing one of his team, and he'd also lost one of the volunteers earlier. He'd not forget that day.

'Problem?' asked the captain.

'We've lost Cardin,' said Ken.

'What do you mean?'

'Look at the monitor. You'll see!' said Ken.

'Help me, someone,' said Caroline, almost in tears. 'Get him away from me, please.'

Derek pushed off towards them, swiftly removing Cardin's tether and reconnecting another to him so that he could pull Cardin to one side.

Caroline finally let out a scream of horror and flailed around, trying to grab something which would allow her to turn away from Cardin. A tug turned her. It was Ken, pulling her towards him. 'Take it easy, Caroline. Keep calm. Remember your protocols,' he said. She knew what he meant. Panicking during an EVA could have fatal consequences. She closed her eyes and concentrated on regaining her composure.

In horror, the bridge crew looked at the screen and could see that Cardin no longer had a front or sides to his helmet. Some interstellar debris had struck him, destroying his helmet and killing him with instant decompression.

'Get yourselves and Cardin into a hub airlock pronto,' said the captain. 'Brian, reinsert the hub as quickly as you can safely do it.' His fear was palpable and his fears had been realised. What if it had been his sister? They'd only been a metre apart.

'Going for hub reinsertion,' said Brian, trying to stifle his own horror at seeing Cardin.

'Connection volunteers, back into position immediately,' commanded Geoffrey. 'Let's get this ship back into one piece before there are any more accidents!'

'Volunteers ready,' said the second officer.

Amrit was also worried but knew they needed to keep their cool. He said, 'Keep it slow. Dead slow.' The captain realised his reaction had not been appropriate and tried to settle himself.

The senior officers of the bridge, looking forward, were watching the hole in the centre of the main ship getting closer and closer.

'Easy now,' said Geoffrey. Scraping noises came from the starboard side. He hoped there'd be no serious damage. 'Slower!'

'Any slower and we'd be stationary,' said Nevaeh.

'How much farther?'

'About a metre,' she said, a moment later, adding, 'That's it. Inserted.'

Around the inner rim of the disc, the volunteers were already trying to throw their connectors, but the alignment was off.

'Report. Second officer,' said Geoffrey.

'The clips are about half a metre out of alignment, Captain,' said Ezenwa Arnjoku.

'Control. A tiny thrust and stop,' said Geoffrey.

'Stop!' shouted Ezenwa. 'Back about ten centimetres.'

The hub moved a fraction in the opposite direction and stopped.

'Second officer here, Captain. We're going to connect one. Looks almost perfectly aligned,' said Ezenwa.

'Copy that,' said Geoffrey.

'Locked,' said Ezenwa.

Brian said, 'Okay, start locking the clips foreled and backled. Stop if any do not lock.'

Geoffrey listened intently as more and more of the locks were confirmed secure. Some crew reported having to 'help' the locks by applying hammer blows or crowbar leverage, but after much longer than expected, the first officer reported that all were now secure.

'Test pressure seals,' said Geoffrey.

Almost thirty minutes later, all the pressure tests were verified except for the damaged section. The Kepler was almost complete again.

'Engineering. Fire up the ion drive urgently,' he said. The ion drive would destroy any space dust in front of them. The sooner it was in operation, the better.

'Ion drive firing up with a wide spread,' said engineering.

Geoffrey made a ship-wide announcement, 'Warning. Ion drive firing. Be ready for gravity changes.'

On the bridge, they felt the tenth of a gravity pull towards the rear of the ship once more, only that time, the rear of the hub faced forward. Dim, red-shifted stars filled the view. The manoeuvre was complete. Kepler's near light speed velocity would begin falling.

'EVA, how's the damage?' asked Geoffrey.

'Caroline is sealing the hull over the original damage. Almost done,' said Ken. 'The other damage, the apartment, will need redecorating, but otherwise it's okay, Captain.'

'Well done,' Geoffrey said. 'Well done, everyone. Control, fire up the rotational jets and take it straight up to a hundred and ten percent rotation. Let's start experiencing the higher gravity of our destination world.'

Thirty minutes later, the rotational jets shut down, and Kepler was on its forty-year deceleration period. Over twelve hours had passed during the turning of the ship. The view from the bridge, which had been of the same area of the Milky Way for forty years, was now replaced by the view back towards Earth. In the spiral arm where Earth lay, the stars had become so red and pale that, in places, space seemed almost empty – just a faint red glow reaching their eyes.

Geoffrey freed his feet from their anchor points and wandered off towards his office. Cardin had been a friend of his and Caroline's since before her EVA test nearly forty years previously. How could he prepare a eulogy for such a close friend? He hated shipboard funerals. Cardin was another crewmate who would reach Kepler-452 long before the ship.

He wondered about Caroline, what effect would it have on her? He picked up his communicator and called Graham. Caroline would need all the support she could get.

45SBY

Chapter Fourteen

THE BIG HIT

A benefit of travelling at close to the speed of light was that there was little time to worry about collisions with anything larger than grains of sand. Despite the sensors having been improved upon during the journey, objects in the path of Kepler were unlikely to be detected in time to make any viable course change.

Thirty-six-year-old captain Ezenwa Arnjoku, a grandson descended from Beth and Gren, who had been instrumental in ensuring their family were represented on the journey, stared out at the receding, red-shifted stars which filled the panoramic bridge window. Since the manoeuvre, which turned the ship's hub through one hundred and eighty degrees at the journey's halfway point, things had been going very smoothly indeed. There had been some competition between officers to see who would become the new captain, but second officer Ezenwa Arnjoku had impressed the interview board and had now captained the ship for five years since his uncle, Geoffrey Arnold-Pointer's, retirement. There had only been the odd crisis: a couple of not-very-serious fires and the regular dust strikes which holed the hull and caused the emergency crews to jump into action. Only one had resulted in a fatality. The region of space they were currently traversing seemed devoid of debris. Even the ion gatherers had been underperforming, so much so that he now had a niggling worry that they might not maintain the rate of deceleration which could cause the ship to overshoot Kepler-452. It wasn't critical yet, though, and his advisers hoped that as they approached the outer reaches of the system, they'd see a rise in particles. As that was over thirty years ahead, it would be his successor who would have to worry about it.

He was just about to sign-off for the day and hit the sack when an emergency klaxon sounded on the bridge. Even with very little happening, the bridge was always fully staffed with the captain or first officer, navigation and systems officers and the usual monitoring officers keeping an eye on the environment within the outer reaches of the ship.

This alarm tone was unfamiliar, and rare alarms were generally the most serious. Ezenwa instantly turned to the bridge crew and shouted, 'Report!'

The navigation officer, strapped to a seat behind an impressive array of monitors, looked up at the captain, his eyes widening and colour draining from his face. 'Impact warning! Imminent!' he shouted, his voice trembling just as all hell broke loose.

The impact warning alarm meant that there was a substantial object directly in their path and that there was a danger it would strike immediately. Ship's computers activated evasive manoeuvres simultaneously with the collision. Ezenwa was thrown across the bridge from central to starboard, crashing against the wall, leaving him unconscious.

Kepler's automatic response depended upon which quadrant of the ship was most likely to be struck; maximum thrust was given to all the power on that side to move the Kepler away from the potential impact.

The designers knew that this was unlikely to be of any help whatsoever if an asteroid were going to hit head-on and it was really the equivalent of a Hail Mary. If the object was travelling across the path of the ship or likely to just strike part of the rim, then the response could save many people and there was a slight chance of avoiding any impact at all.

Being struck by anything substantial would have existential implications. If large enough, the ship would be utterly destroyed. The section impacted and the rest of the ship would spin away at such velocity that no one on board would survive the G-forces. If it were even larger, the ship would be vaporised by the energy created. Gone in an instant. Anything smaller could still cause enough damage to kill hundreds as the environment escaped into the void.

It was the impact combined with the Kepler's automatic response that caused the captain to be thrown the width of the bridge. All over the ship, this would have happened to anybody, everybody, and everything not strapped down.

As he flew across the bridge, Ezenwa knew all of this. In his last second of consciousness, he guessed the Kepler was destroyed, and their near fifty-year journey had all been for nothing.

'Zen, can you hear me?' Caroline said, then spoke to another, 'I think I saw his eyes flicker for a moment.'

It was a hospital room with white walls and floral

patterned, pastel-coloured curtains partially surrounding the bed. A blood pressure monitor, an EEG* and other equipment were attached to the patient.

Caroline, now sixty-three years old, but still attractive and distinguished looking, sat in a visitor's chair, holding her son's hand. Beside her, a blue-uniformed doctor said, 'Yes. I think he's waking.' The EEG suddenly increased in activity.

'Zen. Zen. It's Mum,' Caroline said reassuringly.

The man on the bed gave a moan, opened his eyes and tried to focus on his visitor. He squeezed her hand and looked around, as if trying to puzzle out how he had suddenly found himself there.

'We're alive!' he said hoarsely.

'We are indeed,' said Caroline, cheerily. She'd thought she'd lost him.

He squirmed slightly in the bed and asked, 'What happened? Where's Betsy? I should be on the bridge.' He tried to rise but collapsed back onto the mattress.

'You're not going anywhere, Captain,' said the doctor. 'Lie still. Your wife is in the next room but is having a scan at the moment. She had a broken pelvis and will be in to see you as she's mobile now and we want to get her up and about. She was sitting with you until a few minutes ago, and she'll be okay.'

'But what happened? How's the ship?' he asked again. 'Was it a near miss?'

Another voice spoke, and Ezenwa's eyes swivelled to the other side of the room. 'Sadly, not a miss, but we're still roughly on course,' said Ezenwa's uncle, the previous captain, Geoffrey Arnold-Pointer, now also in his sixties.

'Roughly? What does that mean?'

---

* Electroencephalograph

'Not for you to worry about just now. The ship'll be back on trajectory in a couple of weeks,' said Geoffrey.

'We got hit?'

'We did,' said Geoffrey. 'Took out a chunk of sector D up to deck ninety-six.'

'Many dead?'

'Too many. Don't let it concern you. You've been out for nearly a week, and your crew has been dealing with the effects. I've been offering support too, but they've been magnificent.'

'Is someone dealing with the emotional situation? People dead. Dreadful.'

'The psychologists are on it, Zen, and repairs are in hand.'

'What about rotation?'

'It's okay. Took a while, but we're well on the way to correcting the wobble.'

'How, if there's a section missing?'

'We've built a temporary framework across the damage. When it's completed, we'll look at moving mass into the space. The outer deck corridor will be complete again.'

'I can't lie here. I must get up. I must help. Let me see Betsy,' Ezenwa said and tried to lift his body.

The doctor stepped forward and firmly pushed his shoulder back onto the bed. 'Lie still and quietly, or I shall insist your visitors leave. I have tests I need to do shortly, and I don't want you too excited. You had a cracked skull and are lucky to be alive.'

The captain put his hand to his head as if to feel for a crack. It encountered a swathe of bandages. He looked at the doctor rebelliously but then relaxed.

Caroline said, 'Zen, I'll be back later, and I'll bring your deputy to brief you. We're just so relieved that you survived. The impact with the wall could have killed you. Fortunately, it was a smooth section.'

'My head didn't damage it, then?'

'Shut up!' said Caroline, laughing. Zen always had a bizarre sense of humour.

The doctor replied, 'I think you're definitely feeling better.'

'I feel I should do something,' Ezenwa said.

'Your visitors should leave now,' said the doctor. 'I'd like to examine the captain more thoroughly. Don't return before seven.'

'Can I see Betsy?'

'Soon. After I've done some tests.'

Vice-captain Emma Shortwill, a slim, thirty-nine-year-old, mixed-race, Black/Chinese woman with tightly cropped hair, and Caroline Arnold-Pointer entered the captain's cubicle with Dr Anna Tanaka, Ezenwa's physician.

The doctor said, 'Now, I don't want you getting him too excited. He still needs rest, and it will be at least a week before I'll even consider his returning to duty.'

The captain was sitting up in bed, propped up by several pillows and had a better colour that evening than earlier.

'How are you feeling now, Zen?' Caroline asked.

'More myself. Headache's gone, but I still ache all over and feel awfully weak.'

'Not surprised,' said Emma. 'I watched you flying across the bridge. Absolutely spectacular! Superman couldn't have been more impressive. You need to work on your landings, though.'

Zen laughed, 'Bet it gave you all a laugh. So, what's the situation with *my* ship?'

'Well, *Sir*, it's mainly in one piece. We've had probes videoing the damage and the repairs. You can see here that the asteroid took a jagged bite out of the outer rim.' She handed the captain a couple of images.

'My God. How many died?'

'Because it was late in the afternoon, many had not been in their apartments, so we were lucky. We lost sixty-one directly owing to the impact and a further ninety-six indirectly caused by other factors, mainly gravity damage like yours.'

'And that's lucky?'

'Yes, sir. If it had been during the night period, it could have been many more.'

'How's it affected ship's morale?'

'Psychologists are on it, and the president has been giving reassuring speeches. There's naturally a sense of doom, to think that it could have all ended so suddenly. Some have seen it as a challenge to throw themselves into their work. Others have not been so happy and they're being helped as best the mental health doctors can.'

The captain kept switching between the two photographs, amazed at the scale of the damage. He asked, 'How big was it?'

'No one saw it, of course; it came by at close to the speed of light, but the alarm triggered the high-speed recorders, and we got a single image.' Emma passed a large tablet to the captain. 'Press play. It's ultraslow motion.'

Ezenwa looked at the screen and could see two still

frames on the screen. One obviously taken looking forward as the stars were all a brilliant blue, the other showed the dull red glow of stars in the ship's wake. He pressed the play symbol on the first.

Highly luminous stars in front of the ship suddenly had an almost circular black spot hiding those off to the left side.

The spot appeared in just one frame, even though the recording was in ultraslow motion and the view shook violently during the collision. A second video, looking behind the ship, swayed as the ship vainly tried to compensate. There was a large, blurred object, then nothing.

'You need to watch the second video a frame at a time. It's only there for a single frame,' said Emma.

The captain pressed play again but held pause. He then released pause for a moment and pressed again. On the sixth attempt, the object was visible – a blurred lump of rock. The brilliant glow of the Milky Way illuminated its surface, so, although still blurred from the object's motion, enough could be seen to identify it as a typical asteroid, grey and pockmarked with impact craters.

'Size estimate?'

'Twenty metre diameter. We don't know how effective our automatic thrusters were, but we guess that we narrowly avoided an extinction event, sir. It might be that it was crossing our path, not coming directly towards us.'

'No. At our speed it would have seemed stationary and just took out whatever was in its path,' said Zen.

'I suppose so.'

'Was it just an isolated rock? Was there any accompanying material?'

'No further alarms, and radar shows us that nothing has passed nearby since. We were lucky.'

'Very. What reconstruction has been going on?'

'I think you've had enough, Zen,' said Caroline, holding her son's hand. 'Your colour is somewhat raised.'

'No. I need to catch up,' he said and shuffled himself more upright in the bed. Caroline reached behind to plump the pillows.

'The elevator shafts in that quadrant sealed automatically, as did the airtight doors. The impact set the entire ship spinning, and that caused most of the other one hundred deaths from excessive G-forces in the opposite quadrant, plus many, many injuries. The loss of mass in the missing area set up a wobble.'

'Dreadful.'

'We've had engineering crews making permanent repairs, but the ship will forever have a scaffolded area on its rim. The biggest problem is likely to be the loss of three thrusters, which could cause problems if ever we need to turn the ship again. We also lost three landers.'

'Right, yes. Colonist landers or reusable?'

'Colonist.'

'No spare thrusters?'

'We checked all the storage lockers, including those that only hold items required when we land. No replacement thrusters.'

'Seems an oversight. How is the wobble being dealt with?'

Emma replied, 'We thought we might be able to deal with it by adjusting the thrust, but that didn't work so we've built a framework to fill the gap, rebuilt the outer deck, sealed it and moved a lot of mass into the damaged area to compensate.'

'And that's done it?'

'*That* is definitely enough,' said Caroline. 'I don't want you relapsing. We're leaving.'

'We'll survive the week until you come back to the bridge,' said Emma.

'I want a daily update until I'm fit,' the captain said.

'Will do, sir.'

5OSBY

Chapter Fifteen

BLUE SHIFT

Fifty years along the way to Hacienda, the name for Kepler-452b selected by a ship-wide referendum, the number of deaths from old age grew. One surgeon who had joined the crew aged fifty-three was still hanging on to life at one hundred and three, but he was unwell and not likely to last another year.

The next oldest group included those aged thirty-five when Kepler left Earth. Many were now in their eighties. Almost a third of them were still in reasonable health; two-thirds had died. Similarly, some in younger age ranges had lost their lives through ill health or accidents. One dust strike at a food production plant had killed thirty-nine people. The meteor strike five years previously had killed one hundred and fifty and left a similar number seriously injured.

There were, of course, advantages to the deaths. The maximum population Kepler could support was four thousand, so more children could only be born as others died, though the council had allowed the population to grow beyond four thousand in the medium term. They reasoned that no one over the age of sixty would descend to the planet as they would be unable to withstand the gravity after living so long in lower G near the hub, to where all citizens were retired when they reached seventy. The population was also restricted due to there being a finite number of landing ships. When the landing ships left for the planet's surface, Kepler would remain as an orbiting space station. The elderly and the volunteers to look after them would all live out their lives on Kepler, which would then fulfil the function of Earth's international space station for the colonists. It was hoped that the colonists would eventually develop a space industry which might allow regular flights to and from the starship.

Fifty years was also a major celebration. Blue Shift was one of the most prestigious restaurants on Kepler. On deck sixty-seven, gravity there was about Earth normal, and this made it an ideal location for family events which needed to include residents over sixty years of age.

Their table sat fourteen. Geoffrey at one end, now aged sixty-six, and Caroline at the other, sixty-eight. They were the family elders. Graham was there, plus Rosemary, Geoffrey's new wife. The twins, Cindy and Roxy, aged forty, Grenville, aged forty-six, Captain Ezenwa, aged forty, and Cindy, Roxy, Grenville and Ezenwa's partners made up the rest. Geoffrey, Caroline, and Graham's grandchildren were not present. The younger ones were being babysat by the two who were in their late teens.

Cindy and Roxy had applied their identical appearance to becoming proficient in identical jobs, both becoming senior research biologists in the hydroponics section – the largest department on Kepler.

Grenville, Caroline and Graham's oldest son had

followed his mother into the exciting EVA section – dangerous, yes, but exciting too. He had made his way through the ranks to deputy chief EVA specialist.

Captain Ezenwa Arnjoku lifted his fruit juice and made the toast. 'Fifty years since Kepler left Earth. Congratulations everyone, especially Geoff and Cas, who have been on board since the beginning.'

There was a general clinking of ceramic cups and calls of, 'To Kepler'.

Someone shouted, 'And to Earth,' which was also repeated by all.

The captain didn't drink alcohol. Although he wasn't on duty, he oversaw the ship and might be called to the bridge at any time. The others were all enjoying fine wine, particularly a lovely '32 Bordeaux and '38 Chablis. How closely these replicated the wines made in France was a moot point, but they were certainly very popular onboard ship.

Ezenwa sat beside Geoffrey, his uncle and predecessor captain, who couldn't resist asking, 'How's deceleration? Still on target?'

The captain replied in hushed tones, 'We're going to overshoot.'

'By much?'

'We could be approaching at several kilometres per second.'

'How're you going to deal with that?'

'The plan is to use two of the gas giants to slow us down, and there's also a large planet closer in. If we get the calculations right, that should be enough to correct matters.'

'So, not serious?'

'Not really, but we need to get the maths right. If we get it wrong at the first gas planet, then it will be difficult to correct. Might have to overshoot by the best part of a light-year and that would mean having to reverse direction, and you know what's involved in that.'

'I do,' said Geoffrey, 'and a light-year means a great deal of time once velocity is shed.'

'Damn right. Could cost us a decade or two onboard ship. We want to avoid that.'

'I'm sure. It would be very demoralising to fly past Hacienda, view it on the slo-mo cameras and then sail on for another three or four years,' said Geoffrey.

'Might be even more, Uncle,' said the captain.

'How's your recovery going?'

'I still get headaches and my left arm will probably never work properly again, but I'll live.'

The fifty-year celebration continued for another couple of hours, ending with liqueurs, and dancing to a pianist and saxophone player. Similar parties and celebrations took place at many ship locations. The Blue Shift event was not unique.

Later, Geoffrey and Rosemary returned to their low-G apartment on deck fifteen. Caroline and Graham joined them for coffee, and they chatted late into the night.

68SBY

Chapter Sixteen

OUTBREAK

Captain Ezenwa Arnjoku closed his daily log, just a paragraph or two highlighting matters which had arisen and linking them to his files for the day. His head hurt. Most of the time he was okay, but if there was any stress, he'd often end the day with a headache. It was over twenty years since the big hit. He'd been lucky to have been able to continue with his duties. His first officer, Linda Blaney, was excellent and always had his back. She was extremely capable but tended to be somewhat officious. Ezenwa had made it a project to mentor her to become captain following his retirement.

He sat back in his swivel chair, relaxed and faced the view from the ship's hub. Over the last twenty years of his captaincy, he'd watched the stars gradually shifting from a dull red into a slightly more vibrant shade. The deceleration was going well, and it would not be long before Kepler-452 would be visible to the naked eye on the forward viewers. He took some painkillers.

A notification appeared on the screen. 'Routine thaw anomaly in cryo-archive 7. Non-critical. Dr Sen.'

He tapped 'acknowledge' and closed it. Anomalies were the ship's heartbeat; if he stopped to chase each one, he'd never sleep. Still, he marked the message for review. Cryo-archive 7 stored biological samples from Earth plants, microbes, and genetic banks for restoration, if needed, on the destination world. 'Anomaly,' he wondered. What could be meant by that?

He unstrapped himself and stood in the tenth of a gravity, normal for the bridge and his office then switched the monitor to the forward view and looked at the stars ahead. Thousands of millions. So numerous they appeared no more distinct than mist. Somewhere ahead was their destination.

The message had been sent from the medical laboratory on deck forty-five. It smelled of metal and sterility. Ryan Sen floated a hand over the stasis pod's surface. Inside, a row of sample canisters glowed faint blue. One canister's frost seal had melted around the edges – an infinitesimal power fluctuation, perhaps?

He ran diagnostics. Everything read nominal. Yet the biosensor displayed trace metabolic activity, a reading that shouldn't exist for a sealed specimen so he isolated the sample – a soil microbe catalogued as Cryo-Bacillus 316-M that had been shipped up prior to departure and had now been in storage for nearly seventy years.

He made a note: *Possible spontaneous reactivation event. Quarantine initiated.*

It would have ended there if not for a calamitous occurrence.

Technician Leila Ko was twenty-two and restless. Her

rotation duty involved maintaining environmental ducts on deck ninety, which meant long hours alone with humming filters and the low hiss of recycled air. She also carried out courier duties for extra cash. When Dr Sen called for a courier to move a sealed sample to secondary containment, she volunteered – anything to break the monotony. She and her partner were planning a civil partnership so that they could have a first child and every penny she could earn would help to prepare and decorate the nursery when they were allocated a family apartment. Currently, they lived in a single-person unit in A-Sector. They didn't mind having to share a single bed; that was fun, but the unit would be far too small for raising a family.

She hurried through the corridors and took an elevator up fifty decks to forty-five. A hundred metres foreled found her outside cryo-archive 7. No unauthorised people could enter the secure zone, so she rang the doorbell and waited.

A young man in green medical coveralls arrived. 'Yes?' he asked.

'Dr Sen called for a courier,' Leila said.

'This way,' the man said, and led her along a twenty-metre corridor which had two doors on each side and a double door at the end. He pushed on the double door and said, 'Courier, doctor.'

Ryan Sen was a diminutive man in his early sixties, Oriental, perhaps of Malaysian extraction, with a pencil moustache and wispy beard hanging from his chin. He looked up from a spotlessly clean workbench as Leila Ko entered.

'Ah, here you are. Run this case over to cryo-archive one. It's this deck, but in A-Sector. Dr Elise Beauchamp is expecting it,' he said and handed Leila a small transparent case with a handle along the top. It was ten centimetres square and thirty long. 'No stops en route. It's urgent.'

'No problem,' she said, then turned and left.

The containment case was cool in her hand. She didn't notice the micro-fracture along the front seam, no thicker than a human hair. The pressure change as she stepped from lab air to corridor air was enough to vent a trace mist into the passageway.

She sneezed once, thought nothing of it, and continued.

Two days later, Ryan was on the communicator again. 'Captain, I'd like authorisation to wake the micro-analysis drones.' The drones could 'sniff' the air and detect any of a thousand listed chemicals and biohazards. Perfect for checking for anything that should not be in the ship's atmosphere.

'Reason?'

'I'm a little concerned. One of the technicians, Ko, has reported a mild fever and photophobia. Likely nothing, but the correlation with the thaw event bothers me. She carried the sample to cryo-archive one for me. Beauchamp is also showing signs of fever. The container might have been compromised.'

'Immediately quarantine anyone who was anywhere near that case. Act urgently!' Ezenwa replied. 'No general alarms until we know. I'll brief my deputy, First Officer Blaney, and the president, but that's all.' The last thing the passengers needed was the rumour of an escaped virus.

Ryan cut the connection and rubbed his eyes. The medical lab lighting flickered – the LEDs nearing the end of another cycle. He loaded a drop of Leila's blood into the scanner. The spectral display returned something strange: a strand of DNA woven with metallic ions, unlike anything he'd seen before.

It replicated slowly at first, then exponentially once exposed to body temperature.

He whispered, 'What are you?'

Ezenwa didn't sleep well that night. His thoughts continually churned with the actions that might be needed if there was an epidemic. He knew from secret bridge files only accessible by the captains that there was a danger that Kepler had been sabotaged. Could this be it? Why would they have waited so long into the mission? Surely not. He resolved to talk to his uncle, Geoffrey Arnold-Pointer, the previous captain. If an epidemic did begin, he would need to ensure every decision was effective. First Officer Blaney was incredibly efficient. She would be critical in ensuring continuity. Probably, she'd be the captain who oversaw the arrival at the new world. She'd do a good job, he was sure.

The worry was not conducive to restful sleep and he tossed and turned all night, waking with his head thumping again. He breakfasted on painkillers.

Leila awoke that day and couldn't stop coughing. The fever had got worse. She tried to get up and found herself unsteady on her feet. Something was wrong. Then she heard more coughing and, leaning on convenient furniture, made her way out of the bedroom.

In the lounge, her partner Miki Wang was also coughing.

'What is it?' she asked.

'I don't know,' Miki said. 'My throat's sore. Think I'll call in sick.'

'Me too,' she said. 'My watch says my temperature's up. I told Dr Sen, and he told me to stay put and keep him informed.'

'What's your temperature?'

'Forty.'

'Must be an illness,' said Miki, testing his own temperature and finding a similar reading. 'We'd better call him again. Could it be that sample you couriered?'

'Hope not. There was a biohazard label on it.'

By the fifth day, twenty-seven passengers were symptomatic. Ezenwa stared at the numbers scrolling across his command display. The ship's physician had isolated the cases to one rim section, and engineering had turned off the air-circulation system between them until micro-filters could be installed to prevent any airborne spread. How big was the bug? What size filters would be effective?

Ryan's face appeared on the main screen.

'It's a virus, Captain. Possibly a hybrid bacteriophage encoded with metal-binding proteins. I've never seen anything like it. It may have been dormant in the sample since we left Earth.'

'Containment options?' The situation sounded critical. His last ten years as captain had been free of any crises. Until then.

'We can't sterilise the entire atmospheric system. Best I can do is modify the nano filter meshes to trap the viral shells.'

'Do it,' Ezenwa said instantly. 'Do whatever you must.'

He paused before ending the call. 'Doctor… what's the prognosis if this spreads?'

Ryan hesitated. 'It could compromise respiratory function in half the ship within weeks. Mortality uncertain. We may face a full-scale epidemic.'

'Keep me fully in the picture and take whatever action is necessary. I'll speak to the president.' His worst nightmare was becoming a reality.

Ryan was back on the communicator the very next morning. 'Captain, it's spreading rapidly. I think you need to isolate the whole of A-Sector. That's six or seven hundred passengers.'

'What? You haven't already done that?' he asked in amazement.

'No, sir, we've just been quarantining. By isolating the entire sector, we can protect the other five.'

'Do it immediately! I can't believe you haven't already taken that action.'

'It needs your approval, Captain.'

'I told you to do anything necessary. I'm not the doctor, *you are!* Do it right now!' he said and cut the communication. His anger was boiling over and it was important he control it.

A few minutes later, Ryan was back on, 'People within A-Sector will still have access to all of the normal facilities,' he said. 'I suspect it may have been engineered. It doesn't behave like anything I know.'

'What are you prattling on about? Isolation first, speculation later!'

'Sir.'

Engineered? Only one group would want to engineer a virus and hide it in the ship? Could it have been put on board to sabotage the mission? He thought back to the records of some anti-Kepler activists during the years of construction. They'd sabotaged two supply shuttles and might have been responsible for the loss of a mass transport of passengers heading to Kepler. A hundred died in that explosion. How dangerous might the bug be? If someone had planned to sabotage the mission, it might be deadly.

Ryan called back again and said, 'The isolation is being put in place. I'm outside the quarantine chamber where we put Ko and Wang. They're both in a really bad way. I think we're going to lose them.'

'What about a vaccine?'

'It has certain similarities to the HIV* under the microscope. We do have vaccines on board.'

'Have we got enough immunologists?'

'Yes, Captain. I have Doctors Williamson and Ovhatfield already working on it in lab B-64. It'll take time to make any progress.'

'I'm going back to the president,' said Ezenwa.

On the sixth day, Leila Ko died.

Flashing yellow biohazard bands stopped anyone from entering A-Sector or any of the A-Sector elevators. Bridge officers had blocked the power to all doors leading to B- or F-Sectors from the quarantine area.

There were the inevitable protests and pleas to be allowed to go about their daily work, but the captain insisted that once a quarantine had been set, it must not be broken for anyone.

In the rest of the ship, the crew and numerous temporary police deputies were listening for any sign of anyone coughing, and rumours were now rife around the ship.

* human immunodeficiency virus

Panic was setting in, and most people were wearing medical masks. The stock had quickly evaporated, and two machine shops in D- and E-Sectors were producing more as fast as was humanly possible.

Life in A-Sector was becoming increasingly uncomfortable, with passengers not being allowed to leave their apartments after the first week. Deaths were mounting at such a rate that proper funerals could no longer be conducted, and bodies were being taken to the nearest airlocks and jettisoned.

At the beginning of week two, Captain Ezenwa Arnjoku swung through the main corridor between his office and the president's suite, hanging onto handholds in the ceiling. It was easier to move that way than by walking. One-tenth of gravity meant that every step pushed you off the ground and delayed your return. Pulling your weight along handholds was far quicker.

He arrived at President Ingrid Ovmishra's office, knocked, and heard her shout of 'Enter.'

The president had only been in office for a month, so Ezenwa was well aware that he wouldn't receive any great insights from her, but duty required him to pass on what he knew.

'How are things progressing,' she asked, picking up a coffee squeeze pack. She waved it at him and said, 'Want one?'

'Thanks, yes,' he replied. The president pressed a button on her drinks microwave, and after a few seconds, another pouch was ejected. She tossed it towards the captain.

Ezenwa replied, 'Ryan's doing all he can. He sent fifteen doctors and twenty-five nurses into A-Sector. They're wearing full respirators, but, even so, one has already been infected.'

'Can it break out, Zen?' Ingrid asked. She was constantly in fear of the resultant panic if the virus broke out of the quarantined sector.

'Well, we can only hope. I've had the crew sealing every door with impermeable tape to be as sure as we can be that the virus is sealed in,' said Ezenwa.

'Deaths?'

'Already a hundred and fifteen, and many others in a terrible state. Most are staying in their apartments, but the air system can't be shut off, so no one in A-Sector can avoid exposure.'

'So many already. Any recovering?' asked Ingrid.

'There are many, which is promising. More than a hundred have completely recovered. Ryan has arranged for blood samples to be taken, and the immunologists are studying them. There are now fifteen scientists working on the problem.'

'Anywhere near a solution?'

Ezenwa replied, 'One promising possibility. The trouble is that they're trying to do ten years work in ten weeks. Even if they do come up with a vaccine, producing a few thousand doses won't be a quick task.'

Then a glimmer of hope. Doctors Erin Williamson and Adrian Ovhatfield had been re-engineering the HIV vaccine, and early results showed it could stop the virus in its tracks if given within four days of infection.

Ezenwa authorised the vaccine's mass production despite its having only been tested on a handful of cases and Ryan sent teams into A-Sector to treat only those who had recently shown symptoms. If there were side-effects, his decision could be the equivalent of signing death warrants

Naturally, this caused conflict and argument with those who had been carrying the infection for some time, but with survival rates around eighty percent the available vaccine had to be rationed though a mortality rate of one in five was a high price to pay, and extremely frightening.

Immunised medical teams rushed into A-Sector, and there was a three-pronged attack. Recent cases were inoculated and removed to observation areas where the atmosphere could be isolated from the rest of the sector. This included machine shops and hydroponic laboratories. Those who were infected but mobile were taken to the nearest hospitals and quarantined, while nurses and doctors did whatever they could for the more seriously ill and dying passengers.

As with most epidemics, the end arrived almost as fast as it had begun. Christmas 68SBY came and went, and the new year began with the hope that there would soon be an end to it. Few were dying, and there were no new infections. Those who had been caught early were making a full recovery.

The epidemic had been a horrendous shock to everyone on board. That a microscopic virus could wreak such havoc with so many lives was frightening especially as ancient documentaries made on Earth, dealing with smallpox, chickenpox, polio, influenza and covid were being watched by residents, which instilled more fear into the masses.

After three weeks with no new infections, Captain Ezenwa lifted quarantine to the relief of all the families in

A-Sector. He authorised stocks of the vaccine to be kept in readiness and announced a commemorative service in the great meeting room for those who had lost relatives and friends or wanted to show their appreciation to the medical teams.

The council and the president acknowledged that a critical incident had been overcome.

Everyone had been constantly aware of the continual danger to the ship being caused by dust, meteors, and radiation. Breakdowns of equipment were rare, but every passenger knew the protocols if the atmosphere pumps and filters failed and all had fingers crossed that the vital ion drive would maintain its sixty-nine-year faultless operation. No one except the crew and the medical staff had had any inkling that there could be an epidemic. Such matters were under the need-to-know directive.

By the time the virus had been declared defeated, 231 passengers had died, and the rest had received an object lesson on how dangerous it could be to have people living in such proximity on board a starship.

The president set up a medical team to investigate the origin of the infection but the trail went cold when it arrived in cryo-archive 7. There was neither data about its origin on Earth nor the reason for it being in the archive. That certainly added weight to the suspicion that the anti-Kepler activists had engineered it. No information was to be had about any of them who might have come aboard Kepler, so the council and crew became more confident that it was deliberately planted. All the cryo-archives were thoroughly searched for copies of the virus. The containment case was examined in detail, and the hairline fracture which had permitted the virus to escape, looked as if it had been deliberately caused. No one could find any reason the initial anomaly occurred, but Dr Sen retired early, and Dr Ovhatfield became the new head of cryo-archives.

Mud sticks, and Ryan Sen was shunned by many for the rest of the voyage. Did he try to sabotage the mission? Would the passengers ever know for certain?

Kepler-452 was now hundreds of millions of kilometres nearer, and Ezenwa looked forward to his own imminent retirement. It had been a very near thing. The entire human complement could have been wiped out on his watch.

8OSBY

Chapter Seventeen

ARRIVAL

Kepler spent half its journey in reverse, slowing down at the same rate at which it had accelerated during the early part of the trip.

Now, automatic systems guided the enormous spinning starship into a new star system, that of Kepler-452, which visually separated into individual planets and moons, and the computers began their analysis, still more than a year before arrival. Firstly, the ship encountered a region of asteroids and heavy dust, a landmark for the vessel as it meant that they were now in the system which should offer a new home and new hope. Speed by now had fallen, and although there were dust strikes, none were catastrophic in nature, but sector B had one strike that destroyed two entire hydroponic farms. The outside of the vessel was no longer pristine and bore the scars of hundreds of strikes over the eighty shipboard years of travel. They were still travelling too fast to be able to stop at the desired planet so the reverse of a gravitational slingshot would be needed to lose momentum which involved orbiting the giant planets in the opposite direction to their rotations as the ion drive alone could never reduce speed quickly enough.

After the dust clouds, they next encountered the first two gas giants, one of a turquoise hue and another with a ghostly rosy ring, its gaseous atmosphere almost glowing with a welcoming honey tint in the light of the central star. Both were crucial to Kepler's deceleration. The ship swung around the first, then the second, then back to the first, still doing a substantial percentage of the speed of light. Now it could leave the first gas giant and head towards the inner planets at a slower pace. A journey of more than a year.

It then approached the final, inner gas giant planet, not as large as those in the farther reaches of the system, but more massive than Neptune. It bore dozens of gas bands in all the colours of the rainbow, a beautiful but deadly world with a noxious atmosphere. It was used to shed the very last of the huge momentum built up by the starship and needed just the one orbit

The other three worlds were rocky. D was a cold and desert world in an eccentric orbit, which indicated that it might have suffered a collision some aeons previously. Planet A was burned to a crisp. Too close to Kepler-452 ever to have had an atmosphere, and locked in its orbit, one side permanently facing the star and hot enough for lakes of molten metal, while the other side at -241°C was close to absolute zero. It was similar to Mercury in the system of Sol.

The pioneering spaceship was approaching Hacienda. Kepler now travelled at a more sensible speed and began a four-month journey between worlds C and B. It was on final approach.

It automatically entered a stable orbit, almost two hundred miles above the surface of the planet. One of Hacienda's two moons, a little smaller than Earth's, hung in the scene to one side. The other, half the size of the first, was just coming into view in its fast orbit, only fifty thousand miles from the planet.

If anyone had been standing on the deserted bridge, the view of the planet itself would have been mesmerising, but the only signs of life were intermittent clicks, buzzes, and many glowing LEDs showing that systems were operational.

Below, enshrouded in sparse pristine white clouds in formations which all residents of Earth would have immediately recognised, floated Hacienda, the destination planet. A little larger than Earth, jet streams moved weather systems across its surface, one of which had the distinct signature of a hurricane. Electronic sensors measured wind speed and atmospheric temperature, and a small ice cap showed similarities to the Arctic but was in the south. The northern pole, with a similar mass of ice, would come into view as the two-hour orbit progressed.

Beneath the clouds was land. Some appeared brown or ochre, suggesting low precipitation, but other areas were visible through the weather systems, showing many shades of green. This world had life, even if only plant life. If there were plants, it was likely that there would be animals if evolution had progressed as it had on the human home world.

All was well with Hacienda. Temperatures were within tolerances, and wind similarly. The atmosphere was mainly nitrogen, but with sufficient oxygen to support humanity. There were seas and oceans. Rivers implied rain and freshwater in abundance. This could be a perfect replacement world for the exiled population, escaping a possible fiery death on Sol-1 C, better known as Earth.

For two weeks, the starship had been orbiting. Why did the bridge stand empty? No one on duty, no one looking at the stunningly beautiful world beneath, no sounds of civilisation, no voices, mechanical or real. Just the clicks and buzzes of relays opening and closing, circuits cutting in or out, and the odd crinkling metallic sound of equipment casings expanding or contracting as they warmed up or cooled down.

Where were the residents? One could imagine for a moment that there were no souls aboard, however, the double doors to the bridge were suddenly pushed open and Captain Linda Morwenna Ellie Blaney pulled herself into the zero-G environment. Her team of senior officers followed her and manned their workstations.

They'd come from the grand meeting room. For the first time in Kepler's eighty-year existence, the senior officers had called for a mass assembly in the grand meeting room on deck twelve. It was the only time that the entire ship's complement of almost five thousand citizens had been in the same place at one time. With the ship now being in a stable orbit, there had been no need for anyone to be on watch. Many stood because the grand meeting room's design was for four thousand. Hacienda's force of one point four times Earth's gravity would cripple the elderly and infirm so they'd never descend to the surface. There was a benefit. It meant the population could grow by many hundreds. At that point, only three thousand four hundred were fit enough to land on Hacienda. The remainder would forever live on board Kepler, permanently in orbit but at least able to enjoy the stunning views of humankind's new home. They'd also have the satisfaction of knowing they were part of the species' salvation. For all they knew, they could be the only remaining humans in the universe.

During the meeting, the elders sat. The children and young adults stood around the outside for the momentous end of journey celebration. There were several bouts of cheering for the retiring president, Ingrid Ovmishra, and the officers who had steered Kepler through the delicate and critical deceleration manoeuvres. There were also eight raucous hip-hip-hoorahs to end the meeting, which informed everyone that the scientific investigation of Hacienda by the crew was about to begin, despatching sensors and probes being the first order of the day.

It looked habitable, but was it? There appeared to be at least plant life, but would the biology of another world be suitable for species from the planet Earth? No one had ever previously discovered any alien lifeform anywhere in the solar system. Perhaps it would host toxic lifeforms, viruses or predators.

The adventure of exploration was about to begin. Eighty shipboard years had led to that moment in time. The passengers were excited, frightened with the enormity of it all, and inspired by what was to come.

Chapter Eighteen

HACIENDA

Studying the planet's surface with the strongest telescopes on board provided an indication of the most suitable landing spots.

In general, there were two polar continents, some temperate continents and a few drier equatorial continents.

No one wanted to land in mountainous terrain, swamps, floodplains, or desert. Intensive observation of other areas narrowed down the eventual target and a sub-tropical area was chosen.

There seemed to be some woodland, although it wasn't clear whether the plants were trees or more like shrubs or large ferns, but radar seemed to show that the largest stood over ten metres tall. On another continent, they'd found much larger trees, though certainly not as rigid as the tallest trees on Earth as all the plants swung flexibly in the wind. Leaves were green, indicating chlorophyll, but at night there was also a faint luminosity in some areas. Were some plants luminous? Could they be dangerous? Some areas appeared to be blanketed with one particular fern-like tree such that nothing of the ground could be seen and these areas seemed quite unnatural in their uniformity. Distinct patches several kilometres in diameter.

A close-cropped green plant resembling grass covered the most favoured landing site, though details were unclear. Flowers and blossoms were invisible from orbit. Were they present? Flowers would have meant insects or some variation on creatures which assisted with pollination. It was frustrating not having the magnification to be sure from orbit. Higher power telescopes were in storage, but they would likely be too powerful for use from orbit and were solely for astronomical use, perhaps in the search for a new world if Hacienda were unsuitable.

High ground to the east was the source of several rivers which cut their way out of the mountains as tributaries to a larger waterway that meandered its way towards the sea, offering the opportunity to construct a port and fishing enterprise – if, of course, there were fish. Intensive observation of the seas at high magnification had shown occasional objects breaking surface, but were too indistinct to tell what they were or what they were feeding upon.

On the land, there had been some evidence of animal life, but they'd only seen a few trails, not the animals themselves. The observed tracks through the grassland hinted at herds of small creatures. Clusters of objects, apparently alive, had been seen, so herds or flocks of something. It enthralled the biologists on board, who'd handled just guinea pigs, chickens and cats – the only earthly land animals travelling on Kepler.

That day, a probe was to be despatched. Altera Ovindsingh, a slender, dark-haired, mixed-race woman of Asian heritage in her twenties, was to remote pilot it. She sat at a computer console on the bridge, strapped into the chair as the bridge was still an almost weightless environment with a negligible pull towards the rim. Beside her sat Campbell Ovarnold, in his late twenties, another of the trained pilots of not just the probes, but also the landing craft. Neither had done anything like this except in the ship's simulators. Altera and Campbell were the leaders of the backup team to land on the planet, and had the privilege of landing the first probe.

The surname prefix had been adopted on board a couple of decades previously, as combining parents' surnames was becoming too complex. The use of 'Ov' indicated an ancestral name. One of Campbell's ancestors was Beth Arnold and his parents adopted the name Ovarnold.

'You have a go to launch the probe within the next two minutes,' said Marion Ovanders, the navigation officer. 'That should bring you down near location one.'

Altera looked towards Campbell, and he nodded. She pressed the button marked fire. It took a few seconds for the motion of the probe to be reflected in the view on the monitor, but eventually, the orientation to the planet changed. It was drifting away from the ship to a safe distance before firing its main engines to drop out of orbit. Before that however, Altera used manoeuvring jets to turn the probe, and Campbell clicked a button to record the scene. Gradually, it swung around and faced towards Kepler while still drifting away. The entire ship was visible, with the blackness of space surrounding it. It was too bright an object to allow the stars to be visible in the same frame. They could see the huge, scaffolded bite out of the rim caused by the asteroid impact thirty-five years previously. The gap in the outer rim had been filled by a bridge in the outer deck which spoiled Kepler's symmetry.

'Got that,' said Campbell, and Altera continued the swing to point the probe back towards Hacienda's horizon.

The captain was transmitting the video live to the grand meeting room, while the descent was recorded for posterity. On the bridge, several of the ship's officers crowded around the probe console, wanting to be the first to witness a landing while in the vast vaulted auditorium, many hundreds of residents sat in comfortable upholstered cinema seats, watching the video feed. This audience included most of the older population, and there were whoops and cries of wonder as, for the first time, they saw the entire ship in view except for images recorded prior to its departure. The room was still filling when the sequence continued with the probe approaching Hacienda's atmosphere that was somewhat thicker than Earth's.

Altera concentrated on her main screen, allowing the probe's automatic systems to keep it on the correct entry path. Too steep, and it would burn up; too shallow, and it would skip off the atmosphere and be lost in the endless reaches of space.

Some shivers began, causing the scene to vibrate. The leading edge of the frisbee-shaped craft was being buffeted by the thinnest layer of the outer atmosphere. The shaking became more violent. The front and underside of the probe heated rapidly, and the glow became fiery. Sparks and flames wrapped around the entire visible part of the craft. Five seconds later, the screen went blank.

In the grand meeting room, there were cries of dismay, but Captain Blaney's reassuring voice was soon heard. 'Don't be concerned,' she said using the public address system. 'The probe is entering the atmosphere. The extreme heat – more than two thousand degrees Celsius – is causing the area around the probe to ionise and the communications cannot get through. We were expecting this. Our ancestors experienced it many times when landing on Earth after working on our ship. The probe is now autonomous with its onboard computer adjusting its angle of descent to guide it through this critical phase. Speed is also being shed rapidly from forty thousand kilometres per hour down to just a few hundred. We'll see the view again in about two minutes.'

True to her word, the screen on the bridge, followed almost instantly by the screen in the meeting room, flickered back to life. The curve of Hacienda's horizon flattened out as they witnessed the green, brown, and blue features of the planet below.

Residents had often seen videos of the view from altitude of the mother planet with its fields, cities, roads, canals and managed forests, but Hacienda was so, so different. Everything was natural. Mountains ran into woodland and opened out into vast areas of plants and, in some regions, desert. Rivers, lakes and seas filled the scene, sparkling in the hills where the sun caught the cascades, becoming smooth moving masses as they merged into enormous rivers, and the glittering blue of the seas, lakes and oceans, small and large. Studying the surface from the orbiting ship showed no signs of civilisation, and the probe continued to illustrate a world seemingly untouched by any intelligent hand. It looked perfect.

In the meeting room, oohs, aahs, and wows accompanied the video, plus numerous joyful profanities.

Altera couldn't resist a murmur of 'Wow', which Campbell echoed. Hacienda was stunning.

'On trajectory,' said the navigation officer over the speaker on Altera's console.

'Parachutes in two minutes,' said Campbell.

Another critical phase in the descent was approaching. Soon, the probe would eject two large sections. First, the top cover, which would release the pilot chute, a small chute that was attached to the cover and would be yanked from its housing when the cover flew off. It would then soar upwards.

'Cover blown. Drogue chute released,' said Campbell.

The tiny chute rose away from the probe. Immediately afterward, the second part, the heatshield, was released and fell away from the underside. The pilot chute came to the end of its tether and pulled the main canopy out of the probe. Three much larger parachutes now suspended the device as it fell gracefully through the atmosphere towards the target location.

'Heatshield released. Main chutes deployed,' said Campbell, thrilled at the success so far.

'Copy that,' said Altera, workmanlike and efficient. Nothing would go wrong on *her* watch.

In the meeting room, there were more cries of wonder as the view from the probe swung drunkenly from side to side. Several people who had never experienced motion sickness in their entire lives vomited. Others felt equally sick and looked away from the screen to concentrate on something, anything, that was fixed in position. The irony, of course, was that nothing in Kepler was stationary. It was revolving to produce about 1.4 gravities at the rim and was travelling in orbit at forty thousand kph. It was the relative stillness of chairs and people within the meeting room that steadied their eyes and calmed their stomachs. Most soon squinted back at the giant screen.

More sedately now, the view from the probe swung from side to side as the scenery became more like filmed sequences from planes and helicopters on Earth. Individual trees stood out among the woodland areas, and the open plains were a vibrant green. In the distance, a great river was meandering its way towards the coast of a deep azure-hued sea. The excitement was tangible, everyone straining to see if there were any signs of animals or the activity of intelligent life.

'Landing point in view,' said Campbell. They were almost there.

'Ready to jettison parachutes,' replied Altera, her finger hovering over a red button.

She hit it.

Fortunately, neither Altera nor Campbell could hear what was going on in the meeting room. On the ejection of the parachutes, the probe fell like the proverbial stone. Hundreds cried out, thinking that it was going to crash into the ground.

Blaney spoke again. 'Don't panic,' she reassured them. 'The parachutes have been jettisoned and, any second, the jets will control the probe's descent.'

No sooner was it said than the jets took over, steadying the fall and the scene. The designated landing site came into view. More oohs and aahs were released.

'Chutes away,' said Altera. 'Jets fired. Confirm under power.'

'Landing site dead centre,' announced Campbell.

Altera now had eighty seconds of power. The probe was flying at about five hundred metres directly over the river, following a straight section which was fringed with grasses and smaller shrubs.

'Fifty seconds,' said Campbell, as he monitored the fuel.

'Two hundred metres. Ten forward,' said Altera.

'Good sized clearing over to the right,' said Campbell.

The probe banked in that direction, continued to

descend and was now travelling over dry land, easing its way purposefully towards the dead centre of a clear area around one hundred metres in diameter.

'Thirty seconds,' said Campbell.

'Fifty metres. Five forward. Twenty metres. Three forward,' said Altera.

'Twenty seconds.' Time was short, but they both knew that there would be a further twenty seconds of fuel, just in case.

'Two metres. Half forward. Going down.'

'Fifteen seconds.'

'Touchdown!' said Altera.

It was a pity they couldn't hear the noise from the meeting room as the entire assembly cheered, clapped, and whooped with delight.

'Jets cut. We're down. Lavigne Base established,' said Altera.

Campbell leaned towards her and patted her on the shoulder. 'Well done,' he said. 'Lavigne?'

'Our first captain. I thought it would be appropriate,' she replied.

'Great idea,' he said. 'Data collectors operational. Data being received.'

The probe sat dead centre in the designated landing spot. Now they could learn more about their new home.

The television crew was ready. Two cameras were mounted on flimsy tripods, all that was necessary to hold them stationary in the hub, which was under virtually zero gravity, with just a slight pull towards the rim caused by the ship's rotation. The producer, Deborah Ovgreenwood, had operation of the cameras, able to adjust focus, zoom, and control many other features from her tablet. The presenter of the programme, Pedr Ovlarson, read his notes, adding scribbles and deleting others. He was already wired up for the interview. This was to be the last of sixty-one which would become part of the starship and Hacienda's history. The sixty-one were the last humans to have stood on planet Earth and were old enough at the time to describe their feelings.

An assistant held one elbow of the interviewee as they floated into the area of the hub designated for the recordings. A frail old lady with silver hair and bright eyes looked around as they drifted towards the cameras. Her cheeks exhibited that rosy nature, which comes with old age. They were smooth, but the rest of the face was wrinkled and the lips thin and dry-looking, despite the winning smile.

'This way,' said the assistant, and eased the old woman to the designated spot. 'Hold on to this.'

An object the size of a toaster floated in the air. It had handles on each side, and the interviewee grasped one with her ancient, arthritis-riddled fingers. The object, a steadit, controlled its position using tiny jets of compressed air. It would keep the person holding it in the desired position.

'This is Pedr Ovlarson,' said the assistant. 'He'll be conducting the interview.'

'Fine,' said the old woman in a weak but clear voice, commensurate with her age. 'I've seen you on programmes before.'

'I'm so pleased to meet you, Mrs Arnold-Pointer,' Pedr said.

'Please, just call me Caroline, or Cas.'

'Thank you, Caroline. Deborah has explained the nature of the interview?'

'She did.'

'There'll be two cameras, and they will change positions regularly, you can just ignore them. Sometimes they will be showing you and other times me, with various backgrounds including the bridge computers and, of course, the scene through the bridge window.'

'It's spectacular. Never thought I'd live to see it,' she said, releasing a glowing smile.

'I'll be asking you about that shortly. You're comfortable, holding the steadit?'

'Piece of cake,' she said. 'I'm well used to freefall. I was a senior EVA specialist when I was younger.'

'Of course. Okay, now you need to wait a minute while the crew set the right lighting and sound levels.'

'No problem,' she said, and looked towards the front bridge windows.

There was a little fussing around with the producer, ensuring the cameras were in the correct position to continue after adding the opening credits.

'Ready to go, Pedr,' she said after a minute or two.

The production assistant shouted, 'Silence, please! Recording. Five, four.' She held up three fingers, two fingers, then one.

All sound faded. Pedr spoke into the camera. 'Good evening and welcome to the Kepler Legacy Series. Today we're speaking to Caroline Arnold-Pointer who is the sixty-first and last of the Kepler residents who actually stood on our home planet, Earth.'

The camera swivelled around and focused on the old lady's face. She smiled.

'It must be wonderful for you to see Hacienda spread out in front of you from Kepler's bridge.'

'It certainly is. I never imagined that I would see this

day. The journey was supposed to be one hundred years. The crew's good management of the drive saved us twenty years, and that is the only reason I'm seeing Hacienda. I should have been long dead if it had taken the entire century.'

'And how old are you, if that's not too rude a question?'

She laughed. 'At my age it hardly matters. I've just celebrated my ninety-eighth birthday.'

'And you look very well.'

'Let's not be silly – you're filming a decrepit old woman living on borrowed time.' She laughed again.

'What are your best memories of Earth? Just tell us in your own words.'

'We were a happy family. My mother was Beth Arnold, the British Official Astronomer and my father was a British government minister. They were thrown together by Mindslip in 2019. Mum had been a male astrophysicist and my father, Gren Pointer, had been a mother working in retail. Mindslip caused them both to change sex, but they grew to like their new selves and, well, my brother and I came along; to prove they'd adapted well to their new genders.' She chuckled.

'Your brother would be Captain Geoffrey Arnold-Pointer.'

'He was younger than me. We lost him two years ago, so he never saw Hacienda, but he knew we were nearly there. It made me incredibly sad. So near yet so far. My son was also captain.'

'Ezenwa?'

'I'm so proud of him.'

'Continue, please.'

'Well, it was a pretty normal family, but when the climate began to overheat, our parents realised that we needed to be well educated to stand a chance of being selected for one of the refuges. They pushed us, at school and on homework and we both had exceptional results. They were hoping we might be selected for the Antarctica refuge, but it wasn't to be. We were chosen to fly to Kepler-452b – and here I am. Amazing, isn't it?' She laughed again. 'I still can't believe it and the loss of Geoffrey so near to arriving was a tragedy.'

'Take us back to Earth,' said Pedr.

'Our parents realised that the climate warming was becoming a serious threat and bought a croft house in the far north of the Shetland Islands, just north of mainland Britain. They equipped it with wind and solar power, grew vegetables, kept chickens and fished for lobster, crab and various fish in the bay. Our last holiday, all together, was there. Geoff and I were still teenagers, and, some days, the heat was not too much of a problem. We fished and sailed in the sea loch, looked after the chickens and helped grow vegetables. It was all very idyllic.' She paused, took a beaker from the steadit and drank deeply. 'All the time, they were pushing our education and by some miracle, we were both selected for Kepler.'

'Fascinating.'

There were tears in her eyes now. 'I clearly remember our last goodbye. We were in quarantine before leaving for Kepler and could not even touch our parents. I pressed my hand against the glass and remember Mum doing the same. Geoff was very stoic about it all, but when we left the room, he burst into floods of tears and was inconsolable until we blasted off, later that day.'

'Your career on Kepler was impressive.'

The old lady composed herself and smiled. 'Fascinating and so exciting. For the last few years of my working life, I was chief EVA officer for the entire ship and had an exciting time repairing thousands of micrometeor strikes during the journey. It was a good life and, of course, Geoff went on to captain the ship, so we could both take pride in the voyage's success.'

'And how do you feel now, looking down on the new world?'

She let out a beaming smile, dabbed her eyes with a tissue, and directed her gaze to the beautiful planet visible from the bridge. 'Unbelievable. It looks perfect. The odds against it being habitable were actually quite high. We're all so lucky. I wish I could go down there and stand on the grass and experience the breeze, but I guess one point four G would be too much for me.'

She turned and looked at the interviewer. 'Something I've really missed during my life is rain. Real rain. Showers and torrential downpours. I so miss it. I often used to go to deck seventy-two and stand in the rain forest plantation where water regularly drenched the plants and shrubs. That really *did* feel like home.'

Chapter Nineteen

LAVIGNE BASE

Several senior officers were now sitting alongside or standing behind Altera and Campbell, who studied the displays on their two monitors and a further four monitors alongside.

'I have the gas breakdown,' said Altera. 'Nitrogen eighty percent; oxygen eighteen percent. We'll get the trace gases report shortly.'

'Thank goodness that's breathable,' said Greg Stanway, the senior medical officer. He'd been so concerned that the beautiful planet might have a poisonous atmosphere.

'How different is it from Earth?' asked Captain Blaney, more interested in the practicalities.

'Similar. Nitrogen is a couple of percent higher, oxygen the same amount lower. As long as there are no poison trace gases, we should be able to breathe without a problem,' said Greg.

Campbell said, 'Atmospheric pressure higher. About one point three atmospheres.'

'The air will feel thicker,' said Greg. 'We expected that with gravity being higher and the atmosphere deeper.'

'Is that a problem?' asked the captain.

'No. In fact, a lower oxygen percentage at greater pressure is actually likely to be beneficial from what I've read,' said Greg.

'It's very similar to grass,' said the hydroponics officer, Melonie Ovparodi. She was studying one of the camera's viewscreens. 'Maybe waving around a little more as if the leaves are lighter. What wind is there, Campbell?'

'Not much,' he replied, studying a display. 'About five kph.'

'Anything animate?' asked the captain.

'Not so far,' said Altera. 'I've seen no movement whatsoever.'

'The landing jets will have scared any animals away,' said Campbell, offering a partial explanation for the lack of wildlife.

'What's that stuff moving around in the air? Dust?' asked Melonie. Everyone peered at the monitor.

'Can you put it on the big screen, Altera?' asked the captain.

The observers all now gazed at a five-metre screen fixed to the wall above the smaller group of monitors.

'That's odd,' said Altera. 'What is it?'

'How big are the particles?' asked the captain.

'About two millimetres,' replied Altera.

'Too big for dust,' said Melonie.

'And look,' said Campbell. 'They're alive.'

The objects, and there were hundreds of them, moved around erratically like a swarm of midges.

'Brownian motion?' asked Altera, wondering if it were no more than dust particles being buffeted by air molecules.

'Don't think so,' said Campbell, with growing excitement. 'Too large and they seem to move back and forth beside each other. Looks like life to me.'

'How can we make a closer examination?' asked Melonie, eager to get her hands on the bugs.

'We'll need to catch some and take them into the microscope viewer,' said Campbell. 'I'll deploy the second air sampler.'

He hit some keys and a clear tube, about three centimetres in diameter, rose into view at the bottom of the screen. He pressed Z on the keyboard. Several of the objects were sucked into the tube. He hit X, and the suction stopped. He pressed other keys, and his own monitor showed a container. Five or six of the objects were moving about within it. Utilising the up-arrow keys, he enlarged the view.

'They *are* alive! Thought they were. They're flying,' he said. This was a profound discovery. There was animal life on Hacienda, even if only bugs.

As the camera zoomed in, they watched their first known animate alien lifeforms as they passed to and fro through the field of view.

Each was carrot coloured, almost spherical, but with a pointed tail-like structure protruding. Opposite, there was a tiny opening about the size of a woodworm hole and, above it, what appeared to be a single eye. Logically, if the tail was at the rear, the eye was likely to be at the front. Midway down the sides, almost transparent, were the smallest of gossamer wings. Far too small and flimsy to keep the object flying.

'Seem to be about one point five millimetres wide, one point seven long,' said Melonie. 'Those wings seem to only be about nought point two millimetres long and a similar width. How the hell do they keep them in the air?'

'Increased air density?' asked Altera.

'I suppose so, but it can't just be that,' the hydroponics officer said.

'I'm getting some trace gases coming through,' announced Campbell. 'Point zero three percent carbon dioxide, point two five percent argon and, well, that's a surprise, one point seven five percent helium. On Earth we have more argon and almost no free helium. There are also tiny traces of nitrous oxide, xenon and neon.'

'Any of those dangerous?' asked the captain, again keen to accumulate information for practical use. She had a team of astronauts descending soon.

'No,' said Greg. 'Not in those quantities. Helium is unexpected. I'd like to get one of those bugs under the microscope.'

'I'll try to isolate one,' said Campbell. It took him a while, but eventually one flew itself into a minuscule container. 'You won't see much while it's moving. I'll need to kill it. How do I do that?'

'How much control do you have over the atmosphere in that sampler?' asked Greg.

'Quite a lot. What're you thinking?'

'Can you suck out the oxygen?'

'No, not really, but I can replace the air with pure nitrogen. That should kill it,' said Campbell.

'Do that,' said Greg.

Campbell dedicated a monitor to the isolated bug. Using his keyboard, he flushed out the air and replaced it with nitrogen. For a few seconds, there was no effect, then the bug stopped all movement and just hung there in the middle of the tiny flask.

'Think it's dead,' Campbell said. 'It's just floating.'

'Shame that we've just killed the first alien animal we've ever met,' said Altera, with genuine sadness.

'Yes, it's unfortunate but we have to learn about them,' said Greg. 'Can you get it under the microscope lens now?'

'Sure thing,' said Campbell, and he manipulated the flask. 'That's it. See monitor six.'

The bug filled the screen, its colour fading in death from a vibrant carrot colour to a dull carob shade of brown.

'Can you transfer that camera's view to my lab monitor? I'll study it there,' said Greg.

'No problem,' Campbell replied.

'*Look!*' shouted Melonie, agitated and pointing at the screen.

In the zoomed field of view on the main monitor, a large shape travelled rapidly from one side to the other and vanished. It was big enough to more than fill the screen and quickly gone.

'Whoa! What was that?' asked Melonie.

'Pulling back,' said Altera.

The field of view widened, but all they could see was the cloud of bugs.

'Where did it go?' asked Melonie.

'No idea,' said Altera. 'Must have moved quite rapidly.'

Everyone watched the cloud of bugs.

'There! On the right,' said Campbell, his sharp eyes spotting the movement.

A larger spherical object moved through the cloud of bugs a second time and disappeared to the right.

'Can you zoom in on a recording of that?' asked Melonie. 'Looks as if it was feeding on the bugs.'

Altera transferred the recording to another screen, then zoomed in until the larger creature filled the screen. It was about ten centimetres in diameter with a distinct fan-shaped tail and the same tiny wings as had the bugs. This time, there were two eyes. Its mouth was open. Altera advanced the recording frame by frame.

'It's feeding on them,' said Melonie as the video continued.

The larger bug was swallowing the smaller ones as it moved through the cloud.

'Like a whale feeding on krill,' said Campbell. 'Watched it in a historical Earth video once.'

'You're right,' said Melonie, 'but how does it stay up with those tiny wings and tail.'

'Must be lighter than air,' said Altera. 'Greg's bug still floated after it was dead.'

They continued to watch the scene and saw several of the larger bugs sailing through the cloud with their mouths open, vacuuming their prey.

'Fascinating,' said Campbell. 'Wonder if they get any bigger.'

Altera laughed and said, 'What, you think there might be some great white shark thing which swoops around eating the bigger bugs?'

'Could be,' murmured Campbell, accepting that there could be many things lurking in the forests and woodlands.

'As long as they don't eat us!' said the captain.

'To be honest,' Campbell said, 'I'm more concerned about breathing the small ones in.'

'Seriously?' asked the captain.

'I saw a documentary in the archives which mentioned a tiny flying insect called a midge. They were prevalent in the Scottish Highlands and moved around in enormous swarms, like clouds. They also gave a nasty bite, which irritated for days. What if these bugs are like them? My grandmother used to complain about them.'

'We'd better take some sort of head-covering to prevent that. Hopefully, they'll vamoose when we land,' the captain said.

'We can hope,' said Campbell.

'How big are the larger bugs?' asked the captain.

'About eight to ten centimetres,' said Campbell.

'A lot bigger than Earth's hornets, then. Horrible things – they had stings which injected a poison which was very painful to humans according to what I've read,' said the captain.

'Can't see any stings on these,' said Campbell.

A few minutes later, Altera said, 'They've almost gone. Few and far between now.'

'What's changed in the last ten minutes?' asked Melonie.

'Sunshine,' said Campbell.

'They don't like sunshine?' asked the captain.

'Looks like it. The cloud cover has gone, and the landing site is sunny, ma'am.'

'Where did they go?'

Altera rotated the camera view and zoomed in on an area of dense plants. 'There!' she said.

'They've taken cover, then,' said the captain.

At that moment, the radio came to life.

'Greg here. Do you copy?'

'Copy you,' said Altera.

'I know how they float in the atmosphere. They contain a bag which is full of helium. They must absorb it from the atmosphere and then, by expanding or contracting the bag, or taking in more of the gas, they can become more or less buoyant. Fish use a similar mechanism, a swim bladder, which allows them to move up and down a water column except that they use air, not helium,' said Greg.

'Wow,' said Melonie. 'Are they producing the helium we're detecting in the atmosphere?'

'No,' said Greg. 'They don't produce it. Uranium and thorium probably release the helium. There must be more of those elements on Hacienda than on Earth. They can just absorb it through respiration or some other mechanism.'

'Okay,' said the captain. 'Putting the bugs to one side, is there anything which makes the planet uninhabitable? Will it support us?'

'Well,' said Greg. 'There are lots of dangers. Bacteria, viruses and all sorts of potentially lethal plants and animals. We won't know until we get down there.'

'Let's learn what we can from the probe and make that decision only when we're as sure as we can be that we can deal with any curve balls the planet might throw at us,' said the captain, leaving the bridge for her office to prepare a list of items to be added to the landing craft.

Chapter Twenty

PIONEER

Honey Smith-White, a thirty-something Black South African, wriggled her way into the pilot's seat of the Pioneer, one of the descent vehicles which could also be launched back from the planet if necessary. She'd trained for several years to land the ship, but only ever in simulators. Considered the best lander pilot on Kepler, her excitement at the challenge was acute.

The previous day, Campbell and another pilot, Susan Ovkenzie, had sat in the simulator, practising, for the umpteenth time, the landing manoeuvres for one of the fuel-carrying tankers. Never had they had any problems in the simulator, although once, a few weeks ago, the landing had not gone well and the tanker was left sitting at a rakish angle, unable to be relaunched. If it had happened for real, they'd have to deploy a second lander and Kepler only had eight. The tankers were single-use and irreplaceable, so extremely precious.

Altera and another pilot, Olaf Anderson, were landing the other critical part of the mission. An equipment pod. It was thirty metres long, five in diameter, and contained everything the explorers were likely to need in their first few weeks on the surface. That landing had gone without a hitch.

Now, Honey and Olaf sat side by side in the descent ship. These were not the mass transports which would eventually carry Kepler's population to the surface. Those could never return, so would not be sent until the senior officers were absolutely certain that Hacienda was one hundred percent habitable and safe.

Their descent ship was cramped. There was room for only five. Behind the commander and pilot were three scientists – Allan Ovmorgan, Jennifer Ovsilva, and Martin Carter-Bryant – occupying the three passenger seats. Behind them, storage cupboards for all manner of equipment remained sealed. Beyond that were the engines. The ship had power and wings, and they could fly it like a glider once it entered the atmosphere. Then, the jets would fire, and it would behave like an aeroplane, but with vertical landing capability.

If the crew were ever to return to Kepler, the lander could be docked with the fuel tank to blast back into orbit. That was *not* the intention. These five were the spearhead colonists and would never return to the ship unless Hacienda turned out to be unsuitable for humankind.

'One minute,' announced Honey.

They all sat in silence, mulling over their thoughts. The ship was close enough to the rim that there was a comfortable amount of gravity. That would change at launch.

'Ten,' said Honey.

Departure time was calculated to give them the best opportunity of landing close to the fuel-lander, the equipment pod, and the original probe.

'Five.'

This had never been done before. They'd only ever tried descending in the simulator. Seventy-five flights for Honey and forty-one for Olaf. Allan, Jennifer and Michael had also flown the simulator to reenact the freak chance of both commander and pilot becoming incapacitated during the flight. It was most unlikely.

'Zero!'

Pioneer disengaged and was thrown off Kepler at a tangent. Automatic jets cancelled out the force of motion from the mother ship and, within a few seconds, they hung weightless, while the craft fell towards its rendezvous with the atmosphere of an alien world. A world they hoped would become home. Anything less would have been a nightmare, setting off for maybe another hundred years to a random star system which might have no planets at all. There were no Hubble, James Webb or Hawking telescopes to study planets at a distance, and the larger telescopes in storage had nowhere near their power. It would be pot luck, and their fate would be imprisonment in their frisbee-shaped world for the rest of their natural lives.

Vibrations – they were encountering the outer atmosphere. Honey gripped the controls.

Buffeting – thrusters compensated for the impact with the air, which was trying to destroy them. The thrusters had to keep the heatshield pointing forward or they would suffer a fiery death, one of two disasters awaiting any mistake or miscalculation. The other was a crushing impact if they crashed. They knew the risks but had faith in the craft's technology and their own training.

Static filled the cabin. An ionisation field produced by friction enveloped the vessel, preventing communication with Kepler. It would last a few minutes. Suddenly, it ceased. Far too soon. Something was wrong.

Honey and Olaf studied their screens, reading stats to each other like altitude, heading, and power.

'We're too shallow!' said Olaf, the tension causing his voice to crack. 'Turn us, quick!'

Honey pulled on the yoke, and Pioneer appeared to swing and shimmy. 'It's not biting.'

'Harder!' shouted Olaf.

'What's going on?' asked Michael from the rear, all three of them with death-like grips on the armrests.

'Won't turn,' said Honey, still the coolest of the five.

'Firing reverse thrusters,' said Olaf.

'We can hear you guys,' came over the radio from Kepler. 'What's happening?'

'Everyone shut up, we're battling the problem!' said Olaf, with a growing hint of panic in his voice.

'Thrusters not strong enough. Didn't work. We're skipping off the atmosphere,' said Honey.

'We've got to turn her to force us back into the atmosphere.'

'Not enough thruster power to turn. Fire the main engine!'

Olaf hit the fire button, and Pioneer lurched.

'Now cut it,' said Honey.

Silence again.

'Didn't work. Made things worse,' said Olaf.

'What is going on?' said Michael. 'Tell us what's happening.'

'Kepler to Pioneer. Are you able to update us?'

Honey and Olaf sat in silence. They knew what had happened and what it meant.

'Well?' asked Allan. 'What is it?'

Silence.

'Pioneer. Come in please. Do you copy?'

Olaf spoke, 'Pioneer here. We bounced.'

'Pioneer. Say again,' said someone on Kepler.

Honey repeated it. 'Kepler, we bounced.'

'You are joking?' said Jennifer. 'Aren't you.'

'We skipped,' said Olaf flatly.

'You must be able to do something,' exclaimed Martin loudly, with growing panic in his voice.

There was no answering reassurance. All five sat in silence. All sounds outside the ship had ceased. The planet lay beneath them, beautiful and welcoming, but out of reach.

Captain Blaney ordered the feed to the meeting room cut and dashed to the bridge. When she floated into the command centre with its stunning view of Hacienda, she looked at the communications officer and asked, 'What happened?'

'They bounced off,' said the radio operator.

'I know that!' shouted the captain. 'But how?'

The first officer, Rose Russell, said, 'We're looking at the data, but it looks as if the main engine cut off a second early. They were still travelling too fast, hit the atmosphere and skipped off it, ma'am.'

'Pilot error?' asked the captain.

'It doesn't look like it. They managed to fire the engine again so no fault there, but it was too late. That first de-orbiting burn is crucial.'

'They know?'

'They do. We're hearing nothing from them. They must be in shock.'

'Can anything be done?' asked the captain. 'Are we able to help?'

Campbell said, 'No, ma'am. They're already too distant for a rescue mission. We don't have anything which could catch them and turn them around. Even if we did, their velocity is such that both ships would be lost.'

'We all know the dangers,' said Altera. 'They're on a one-way trip. I checked their trajectory; it's an elliptical orbit which will bring them back in eighty-two days.'

'They only have air for sixty,' said Campbell.

'Before that, they'll pass close to Kepler-452. They'll be roasted alive in three weeks.'

Campbell sent Pioneer the data and called them. 'Olaf. Campbell here. I sent you some data. Tell me when you've read it.'

There was silence for a minute or two, then Olaf replied, 'Copy that, Campbell.'

'Sorry.'

'Thanks.'

A message arrived from Pioneer and appeared on Campbell's console. 'Temperature prognosis, please,' it said.

Campbell typed back. 'Ten days.'

Olaf said, 'Copy that last message, Campbell.'

Captain Blaney floated over to the communications console. 'Let me speak to them.'

'Look at this first, Captain,' Campbell said and handed over a tablet showing the orbit data.

'Oh no. Hopeless then?'

'Afraid so, Captain.'

The radio operator passed her a handheld microphone.

'Pioneer. Do you copy?' she said.

'Copy you,' said Olaf.

'This is the captain. You know your situation?'

'We do, ma'am.'

A voice from behind, Martin, asked, 'Is there nothing you can do? Can't Kepler come for us?'

Olaf said, 'No one can help us, Martin. Sorry about that, Captain.'

'We're so sorry this has happened. Make a list of family members you would like to speak with, and we'll set up communications in a side room.'

'Thank you, Captain. We'll do that.'

'You know what you have to do?'

'I do.'

'Our thoughts are with you,' the captain said and returned the microphone to the communications officer. She then said, 'Altera, Campbell put the second team in place. No delays, I want us on the surface as quickly as safely possible. This is going to be awful for morale.'

During the next week, there were many lengthy calls between relatives of the crew and the condemned. Tears flowed freely.

The temperature within Pioneer steadily climbed as the craft fell through its elliptical orbit of Kepler-452. Honey and Olaf knew what had to be done. None wanted to be roasted alive, the fate which awaited them in just a few more days.

The doctor on the crew, Martin, handed out powerful sleeping tablets to each of them. They swallowed them with water, and the commander, Olaf, opened the E-valve. Over the following six hours, atmosphere would gradually seep out of the craft. The pressure reduction would be far too slow to be noticeable. As the crew slumbered, the air pressure would reach critical, and unconsciousness would descend. Death would follow swiftly thereafter.

Advising the Kepler citizens of the tragedy was the hardest thing Captain Blaney might ever need to do.

Several officers, familiar with the landers' systems began an investigation into the problem, but it was a librarian who came up with the probable answer. Gina Lopez asked for a meeting with the captain, saying she had information about the Pioneer disaster. The new president, Anders Petangle, spoke warmly of Gina and advised that the crew take her seriously. The captain called in Campbell and Altera, the backup landing crew and they awaited Gina's arrival.

'Come in,' called the captain when a knock on the door was heard. She sat behind her desk and the two lander pilots were in visitor chairs to one side. The office was in freefall these days, so chairs weren't really necessary but it gave the people a fixed position rather than letting them float around randomly.

Gina was a dark-haired woman in her late forties. Wisps of grey gave away her age. She pulled herself into the office, said hello to the others and steered herself into another of the visitors' chairs.

The captain introduced the others and then said, 'You say you have information about Pioneer. President Ovpetrangle spoke highly of you and your knowledge of Kepler history, which is why we asked you to come. What do you have to tell us?'

'You're aware that there were sabotage attempts against Kepler before departure?'

'I am,' said the captain.

'There were shuttle accidents during construction which could not be explained. There were more than two attempts to bomb Kepler which failed. One was found during the installation of a panel which would have concealed it until it detonated. Each had timers. One of the passenger vessels was also destroyed in strange circumstances and a hundred of the chosen were killed.' She paused and pulled a document from her attaché case.

'This was sent to the first captain of Kepler.' She passed the letter to Captain Blaney.

'In broad terms,' she continued, 'the letter threatens that the landers, including the colonist descent vehicles, would never make it to the surface.'

'We knew about this,' said the captain.

Campbell said, 'Every lander was thoroughly checked at the beginning of the voyage and we inspected Pioneer in great detail before departure. We're making an even more detailed study of our lander, Discovery.'

'I wasn't aware of that,' said Gina.

'It's not the sort of thing you publicise,' said the captain, 'but we really appreciate you bringing it to our attention.'

'I thought that maybe they'd damaged the software or planted a bug in it.'

'You might be right, Gina. We have systems analysts checking every aspect of Discovery's software as we speak. Nothing found so far,' said Altera.

'That's reassuring,' the librarian said.

'Thanks for contacting us,' said the captain. 'We'd rather you didn't talk to others about this. We want to avoid panic when it comes time to release the colonist descent vehicles.'

'I won't repeat any of this,' Gina said and the meeting broke up.

Chapter Twenty-One

DISCOVERY

Altera was the first into the second ship, Discovery. There had been only eight of these reusable landers, and one had now been lost. Altera was determined she would land this one successfully and carried out all the pre-flight checks twice.

Campbell squeezed into the seat designated for the commander and co-pilot. He and Altera were now side by side. Behind them sat Berry Distargon, infectiologist; Martina Kaufman, medic; and Mike Ovfinlay, biologist. They had not been the first-choice crew but were equally well trained and recognised as elite astronauts. Turmoil and anxiety ran through his mind, but he maintained a cool and professional exterior, Campbell was proud that he would be one of the first humans to land on the new world and thought briefly about his family tree, which led all the way back to Beth Arnold and Gren Pointer. Their foresight and determination were the reason he was sitting in that cockpit on such a historic day.

'One minute,' announced Altera, similar turmoil going through her mind.

They all sat in silence, pondering as what had happened to Pioneer preyed heavily on their minds. They were determined not to allow it to happen to them, but space is an inherently dangerous place to work.

'Ten,' said Altera.

They all checked their restraints. Leaving Kepler would not cause much disorientation, but there would be some strange G-forces initially.

'Five.'

Like the other crew, Altera and Campbell had only ever tried descending in the simulator. Sixty flights for Altera and forty-seven for Campbell. Campbell would be ensuring that the full burn took place to slow them enough to enter the atmosphere. The computer had recorded that it had cut the main engine one point two seconds early, and it was that which had caused Pioneer to skip off the atmosphere. Such a tiny error to cause the death of five brave colonists. Why had it made that error? Thoughts returned to sabotage and the Discovery team were prepared for anything similar occurring during their flight.

'Zero!'

Discovery disengaged and was thrown off Kepler at a tangent, the thrusters immediately cutting in to stabilise the flight and point it in the right direction. Altera rotated the ship so that the engines pointed forward ready for the crucial burn.

The anxiety was palpable, despite their trying to conceal it. The error in Pioneer must not recur. Campbell fired the engine. Both he and Altera watched the countdown and, at exactly the right instant, the burn ceased. Campbell had been ready to fire it again if the burn was too short. He breathed a sigh of relief.

The ionisation static filled the cabin.

Six minutes later, 'Discovery. Do you copy?' came over the radio. The captain and bridge officers were worried about them.

'Discovery here. Through the worst,' Campbell said, his heart rate coming back to normal.

'Well done,' said the captain.

Now, Altera was fighting the wind, trying to control the wings and keep a steady descent. This was the most worrying time. Neither she nor Campbell had ever actually flown anything for real! When Kepler was under construction, all the astronauts in the spacecraft were qualified pilots with hundreds of hours of flying experience. This was Altera's maiden flight, and she must get it right first time while experiencing intense pressure. Any error could destroy the lander and kill them all.

'In gliding mode,' said Altera, much calmer than she felt inside. Any minute a crisis could develop, and if it did, she needed it to be one they'd experienced in the simulator.

'What a view,' exclaimed Martina. 'It's all flattening out.'

Mike laughed. 'That's a strange way of describing it.'

'Well, it's not spherical anymore.'

'No. I suppose it isn't,' the biologist retorted with a chuckle.

'Stable glide. Five thousand metres,' said Altera. 'Starting engines in five, four, three, two, one, fire!'

A force kicked them in the back as the lander came back under power, but instead of holding a straight course, the nose dipped, and Discovery plunged towards the planet. There were cries of shock and terror from the crew.

'What the devil?' cried Berry.

'Lost power on the right engine!' said Altera, trying to maintain her cool. 'Trying to correct it.'

'What's happening? What's going on?' asked Mike, his shaky voice indicating extreme terror.

Campbell said, 'Shut up! Essential talk only.' He was as scared as anyone but was determined not to show it.

The lander was now tumbling towards the planet's surface, but it was clear that Altera was trying to recover the situation. Had the fault just been another coincidence? Was the hand of some long-dead saboteur trying to destroy them?

Campbell sat quietly, gripping his armrests, watching and listening to Altera's problems and ready to step in if required. He knew she'd ask if she wanted help and the last thing she needed was unbidden interference.

The violent swinging and plunging came under control.

'Okay,' the pilot said, her voice trembling. 'Think I've got it. Countering the spin.'

Discovery's plunge towards the planet eased as the nose pulled up and level flight reestablished.

'That engine still out?' asked Campbell.

'The others are okay. I've compensated.'

Back on its flight path, the crisis over, fear turned to excitement and awe at the journey.

'I've lost my bearings,' said Altera. 'Where are we?'

'Turn twenty degrees starboard,' said Campbell. 'That should get us back on course.'

'Wow. Amazing,' said Berry, hanging onto her armrests as Altera banked the lander and those on the right side found themselves looking vertically downwards at forests and plains.

'What a view!' exclaimed Martina, thrilling at the scene.

Discovery returned to level flight, but the view was suddenly distorted. The viewport was blurred. Something was hitting the glass and spreading out.

'What the hell is that?' asked Mike. 'You're flying blind.'

'We're in a cloud,' said Altera. 'It's rain hitting the screen. No panic.'

'A cloud! Rain? Real rain?' Mike said.

'Sure is,' said Campbell. 'Never experienced rain.'

'We're coming out of it,' said Altera as the flood of cloud condensation cleared and the land reappeared, isolated drops of water still streaming backwards along the windscreen. 'They never showed us that in the simulator!' she complained and laughed.

'Guess it was too ordinary for pilots flying day in, day out,' said Campbell.

'Beautiful,' said Martina as Discovery levelled out and continued its planned descent. 'The world veritably has become flat. I've seen old films of landings on Earth, but it didn't really seem possible.'

'Hacienda is a lot larger than it appears from Kepler. The horizon is several miles away,' said Campbell, stating the obvious in a reassuring manner.

'Two thousand metres,' said Altera. 'We're okay now.'

'I've pinpointed Lavigne Base,' said Campbell. 'Seven kilometres.'

'Sorry for my outburst,' said Mike nervously.

'No problem,' Campbell said. 'We're all in the I'm-scared-too club.'

'There's the fuel-lander,' said Altera with a whoop of joy as the bright orange fuelled stage stood on the surface in the distance. It was that which would attach to Discovery to take them back to Kepler if ever they were to return.

'And I can see the pod. Don't get too close now,' cautioned Campbell.

'No. Aiming to put down fairly near to the pod, about four hundred metres from the lander and one hundred from the probe. Can see all three clearly now,' she said, her hands and feet caressing the controls to maintain level flight.

'Nice flying,' said Campbell. 'Is it all behaving now?'

'She's handling magnificently. Fully in control. I'm going to get closer to the pod. It'll be more convenient.'

'Okay. No closer than ten metres, though,' said Campbell.

'Altitude two hundred metres. Landing sleds down. Switching to vertical jets. Hovering. One hundred metres. Down at ten. Fifty. Down at five. Twenty metres. Do I have a go to land?'

Campbell scanned all his instruments as a last check. 'Go for landing!'

'Ten, five, two. Touchdown!' said Altera as they felt the undercarriage suspension absorb their weight.

'Whoa! Why's it wobbling?' asked Mike, obviously still anxious about the landing.

'Ground not firm,' said the metallic computer voice, as if it had heard him.

'What's that mean?' asked Martina.

'No panic,' said Campbell. 'It's just spongy.'

'Settled now. Movement within tolerances,' said Altera a few seconds later. 'Purging the jets.'

'Kepler, do you copy?' said Campbell. 'Lavigne Base here. Discovery is on the ground.'

'Copy you loud and clear. Well done, you guys. Massive relief up here,' replied Captain Blaney, then, remembering the words of mission control when Armstrong and Aldrin landed on the moon, she added, 'I think it might be appropriate if I said we were all about to turn blue!'

'We're on a world,' said Altera, enthralled by the view from the cockpit.

'We are indeed,' said Martina. 'Hardly seems real after spending our entire lives on those curved decks.'

There was silence while they all took in the wonder of having landed on another world.

Campbell broke the silence. 'Well, we can't sit here all day. Let's get out and stand on some real ground. Airtight suits on and sealed, please,' he said. 'Have all the fuel gases purged?'

'Confirmed.'

They each pulled a stored backpack from under their seats and opened them, removing spice-coloured outfits. Unselfconsciously, they each stripped down to underwear and climbed into the one-piece suits. Each outfit, made to measure, fitted snugly, boots and gloves being integral to the suits themselves. Once fully outfitted, they pulled life-support backpacks over their shoulders. These contained an air supply, plus pockets for flasks, sampling bags, tools, and minor items of equipment. At last, they lowered their helmets. Shaped like inverted transparent buckets, flanges around the neck attached to a fine Velcro rim which, itself, was secured with a suit flange that sealed the helmet to the suit. They were now on suit air and hermetically protected from any dangers in the atmosphere.

'Check you've got everything you need,' said Altera.

Campbell heard four confirmations that helmets had

been sealed and checked, then he made his way to the rear of the lander. On the wall beside the airlock were several controls.

'Purging our atmosphere with nitrogen,' he said and hit the correct button. An illuminated sign stated 'Oxygen' and the percentage which remained in the ship.

'Oxygen purged,' said the computer. 'Atmosphere now primarily nitrogen.'

Campbell opened the inner airlock. Briefly, the oxygen warning illuminated, but the pumps had soon removed the last traces, and the entire ship and airlock were now on nitrogen to kill any bugs which might have travelled with them. No one wanted to catch anything from the planet, but neither did they want to risk polluting the new world with pathogens from Earth.

The crew awaited a five-minute delay to ensure everything on the ship was dead before they stepped into the airlock.

There was barely enough space for three of them shoulder to shoulder. Mike and Martina would follow. The inner door was closed, and the outer door opened.

In amazement, Altera, Berry, and Campbell found themselves looking out at the surface of an actual planet. Something that had only been a figment of their imaginations for their entire lives. Such excitement.

'It's cold,' said Berry. A lifetime of living at twenty-one degrees C in the ship made encountering a temperature difference an unusual experience. Usually, only emergency workers rushing to seal leaks, and those working with refrigeration felt the cold on the mother ship.

'It is,' said Altera. 'Eighteen Celsius on my gauge.' She shivered. A new experience indeed.

'Hurry up, you lot,' came over the radio from Martina.

'Well, here goes,' said Campbell, who turned to face into the airlock and descended the four rungs of the ladder to the surface.

He stopped at the bottom.

'I name this planet Hacienda. Humankind's first outpost in the vastness of the universe,' he said. 'We dedicate it to the people of Earth who made this day a possibility.'

Cheers came from behind him. He guessed that most people onboard Kepler would watch the scene from his helmet camera and the camera on the equipment pod, which sat just a short walk away.

'Come on down,' said Campbell. Berry and Altera joined him, the outer airlock closed, and Mike and Martina swiftly followed.

The five stood in a group, looking around at their first ever experience of being outside, on a living planet. Each pressed their feet down into the slightly boggy-feeling ground, a unique sensation. Mike turned and closed the outer airlock door.

'The sky's so huge,' said Altera, stumbling onto all fours and shutting her eyes tightly. 'Ooh! Wasn't expecting that.'

Mike crouched to help support her, but as he tried to lift her, she resisted.

'Leave me a minute. I can't open my eyes. My head's swimming. Like I'm drunk!'

'It's incredible,' said Campbell. 'I've heard tell of big skies in America in movies but never understood the term. It's vast!'

'Don't,' said Altera in a tiny voice. 'I can't look.' She covered most of her visor, only peering between her fingers.

'Agoraphobia,' said Martina. 'The vista is too large for her.'

'And clouds. Look at that. Real clouds in the sky,' said

Berry. All except Altera watched clouds changing shapes and moving from one side of the vista to the other.

'That one looks like a cat's head,' said Martina, 'and that's like a blancmange.' They laughed.

'Don't they move fast?' said Campbell. 'That's a surprise. I've seen it in films, but it didn't register really.'

'Can't look,' said Altera, squinting between her fingers.

'Amazing. I thought the clouds would be stationary, but they're moving and changing shape all the time,' said Mike, who knelt down and felt the grasslike plant, running its fronds through his gloved fingers.

'Take care. It isn't sharp, is it?' asked Martina.

'No. Very soft and flexible.'

'Let's open up the equipment pod,' said Campbell. 'I'll feel more comfortable when I have a weapon in case anything unexpected attacks us. Altera, do you need to go back into the ship?'

'No. Just give me time,' the pilot said, opening her fingers a little to see more of the scene. 'I just need to not look at the clouds. They make me feel dizzy. I'm sure it will wear off.'

'Could take a while,' said Martina. 'Keep your eyes on the ground in front of you.'

'Back to dangers. I saw nothing worrying on the remote cameras,' said Berry.

'Maybe not, but the woodland is only a hundred metres away and could contain predators. Our landing jets will have frightened them off. You've seen films of lions and tigers, haven't you? A tiger could cross that distance in seconds. Let's be safe rather than sorry,' Campbell said, and he led the party over to the equipment pod, which was the size of a railway carriage.

'There's some of those bugs,' said Altera, swatting a few which were moving around her helmet.

'Yes, strange things,' said Berry. 'I'm wondering how big these helium-filled animals can get.'

'Gravity's less than shipboard. Only one point three G,' said Mike.

'Glad we've been living in one point four G. It certainly prepared us for this,' said Martina. She punched a four-digit number into the door of the equipment pod, and it swung outward, revealing a large airlock, which occupied the entire end of the pod.

Meanwhile, Mike had walked along the pod and put the same four characters into another keypad and stood back. An entire section of the pod concertinaed outwards from the main body like a portable stage at a rock concert. He pulled on a door handle, and steps cascaded down to the surface, allowing easy access.

'That's the Hacienda atmosphere lab ready for use,' he announced. That section of the pod provided a laboratory which was open to the planet's air for work that did not need to be done in the ship's atmosphere inside.

'There's one of those larger bugs,' said Altera, vaguely waving to her right.

'Oh, yes,' said Martina, 'it's just floating through the swarm with its mouth open.' She reached towards it, but as her fingers approached the creature, it flicked its tail and vamoosed.

'Cool! Quite a turn of speed when it wishes,' she said.

'Here. Take one of these each,' said Campbell, handing out four small handguns to the others.

Altera studied the gun. The shape was broadly similar to a large water pistol. A switch on one side was labelled A and B. If set on A, the gun would give a blast of nitrogen which should be enough to frighten any predator. If not, switching it to B converted the pistol into a deadly weapon, loaded with a dozen 7mm bullets capable of killing any more determined animal. They all set their guns on A. No one wanted to harm anything on their newfound world unless they really had to.

'I'm going to sit in the atmosphere lab until I feel better,' said Altera, who was still having to keep her eyes firmly on the ground.

'Keep alert, though,' said Campbell.

Mike helped Altera up the steps into the open area of the lab where she could sit in an office chair then set to work at the main research bench, studying electronic readouts of the air composition, and the last twenty-four hours of temperature and humidity. Berry had plucked two or three different species of plant and was making microscope samples to study. Campbell and Martina watched while also wandering around the pod, checking for anything untoward. They still did not know whether there were more dangerous predators, but assumed, from reading about carnivores on Earth, that it would take a while before they became curious about the new bipedal lifeform which had arrived in the metal containers.

Martina's duty meant keeping a close eye on her fellow crew members. Her task in those early days was to watch them closely, looking for any signs of illness or disease and she'd confine herself to her airtight suit for several days, even when she gave the others the all-clear to breathe Hacienda's air.

Campbell spoke into his radio. 'Attention. Something bigger over here, approaching the Discovery.'

The quiet, almost whispered message had the desired

effect. Mike and Berry climbed down from the lab, and Martina followed them around to where Campbell was standing. Altera forced herself to overcome her reaction to the large spaces and began scanning the rest of the scene, ensuring nothing was creeping up on them from another direction while the others were distracted.

Chapter Twenty-Two

WRIGGLERS

'Where?' asked Berry.

'Stand still,' Campbell said. 'It's stopped moving. Just to the left of Discovery – it's like a darker patch of the grass, but it definitely moved.'

They all stared at the ground, about fifty metres away. Nothing seemed to happen for almost two minutes, then there was action.

'I see it!' said Berry.

The darker green shape was longer than it was wide and very flat. At the front was a curved scallop-shaped mass, but very compressed. Its entire body was no more than ten centimetres thick. Was the scallop-shape its head? Two raised nodules stood on either side, nearer the front than the sides. Nostrils? Eyes? Ears? There was no way of knowing. Its movement had been just a few centimetres – a sudden forward lurch, then it stopped again. Behind the head, the rest of the body seemed to tail away towards the far end where a fan-shaped object lay flat on the grass.

'What the hell are we seeing?' asked Martina apprehensively.

'Definitely alive,' said Berry.

There was another sudden movement from the creature. It moved forward, almost a metre this time, in a single wriggling motion powered by the fanlike tail and raised itself a tiny amount on flaps to either side of the body, just behind the head. It didn't have any obvious legs and, amazingly, it appeared to float through the air as part of its jerky journey.

'Did it leave the ground then?' asked Berry.

'I think it did, and it's big!' said Mike, concerned in case it turned out to be a predator.

The visitor was almost two metres long and about half a metre wide. A crocodile of that size would be a fearful thing, but this didn't seem to have any jaws or mouth.

'Does it have eyes?' Campbell asked.

'Those two lumps on the head. They're glistening, but tiny, only one or two centimetres across,' said Berry.

'Whoa! Look at that!' said Martina. 'When it moves, it's fast. It just covered more than its own length in less than a second. Where's it going?'

'Heading towards Discovery,' said Berry, who was now filming the animal.

'Can it see us?' asked Mike.

'Don't think so. Seems determined to reach the ship,' said Berry.

'What should we do?' asked Martina.

'Nothing,' said Berry. 'Just observe.'

'Another one, here,' said Altera.

Campbell kept his eyes on the original creature, but the others all turned to look to where Altera was pointing. Another one, lighter, but the same shape and dimensions, was looking directly at the pilot from about ten metres away at the edge of some thicker shrubs. She stood and turned towards it.

'I'm going to take a step towards it,' she said. 'I want to see if it's a threat.'

'Set your gun to B, and take care,' said Campbell.

Altera flicked the switch on her pistol and took two rapid steps towards the animal.

When Altera moved forward, the whole animal seemed to somersault above the ground, turned through one-eighty degrees and the fanlike tail flipped twice, driving it instantly back into the shrubs, half a metre above the ground, where it vanished from view.

'Wow! That was lightning fast!' said Martina.

'Shows they can fly too,' said Berry.

'What's the other one doing? Let's stay alert, guys,' said Altera, backing up to where she'd been standing before the animal vanished. 'They could be dangerous!'

The others turned back towards Discovery.

Mike heard a noise behind him and turned to confront it. A giant eye, the size of a dinner plate was peering out of the shrubs. As it saw him looking, it retreated, and fronds of the bushes whipped back into their normal positions. It made him catch his breath and he immediately set his gun to kill.

'Stop. There's something bigger over there,' he said, pointing his gun towards the spot where the eye appeared.

'What? Where?' asked Berry.

'In the shrubs. A huge eye. Dinner plate size. At least thirty centimetres across.'

'You're daydreaming,' said Martina.

'Honest. Couldn't believe it. It was huge. I promise. It was real,' said Mike, embarrassed that the others might think he'd invented a problem.

'Another of the flat things approaching the lander,' said Berry. All but Mike turned to look.

'It's making its way towards the ship in short, sudden motions. It's close to one of the landing sleds,' said Campbell, who hadn't let the original creature out of his sight.

'Can it hurt the ship?' asked Altera.

'Don't think so. It's almost there,' he replied.

The front of the animal's head was just a few centimetres from one of the four landing sleds which comprised Discovery's undercarriage.

In a single motion, it flipped upwards with a powerful flick of its tail and appeared to stick itself to the shell of the lander, hanging downwards with the tail end draped over the sled.

'What's it doing?' asked Mike.

'Seems to have stuck itself to the ship,' Campbell replied. 'Must have some adhesive mechanism or similar to hold itself to such a smooth surface. Must be sucking it.'

'I think we should chase it off like the other one,' said Berry.

'You want me to air-jet it?' asked Campbell, checking his pistol setting was A.

'Why not?' said Berry.

Stealthily, Campbell crept towards Discovery. 'If those are eyes on its head, it can certainly see me,' he said.

'Careful,' said Mike, flicking his own gun to B… just in case it turned nasty. His gaze was flicking back and forth between the creature and the location where he'd seen the huge eye.

'It seems to be armoured,' Campbell said. 'It looks like it's covered with bony plates.' There was a brief pause in his commentary as he came closer to the animal which was now only a metre or two ahead of him.

'I just saw the eyes swivel towards me,' he said, holding the pistol out towards the creature's head at arm's length.

Suddenly, Campbell cried out and was flat on his back. The creature had dropped off the ship, swung its tail in the human's direction and vanished at incredible speed back towards the woodland.

Martina rushed over to the expedition leader, bent down to him, and helped him sit up. 'You okay? What happened?'

Mike didn't know what to do. Should he help? What if the thing with the giant eye dashed out towards them? Whatever it was, it must have been gigantic – the size of the lander!

'I was just about to fire a jet of air at it when it flipped around and shot off. The force of the tail sent me flying,' he replied, slightly winded by being knocked over.

'You didn't fire, then?' asked Mike, still eyeing the shrubs.

'No. I was just about to when it went off.'

'Where did it hit you? Let me see,' said Martina.

'It didn't. It was the force of the air which knocked my legs from under me. Such power!'

By now, three of the others had gathered around Campbell, helping him up, but also keeping a wary eye open for any return.

'Is he okay?' asked Altera, who was still scanning the rest of their surroundings.

'Phew! I'm fine, just blown over by the force of its tail,' replied Campbell. 'Where's this eye you saw?'

'Gone now,' said Mike, seriously spooked. 'I tell you; it was huge.'

'What did the small one do to the ship?' Altera asked.

Martina peered at the hull where the creature had attached itself. 'Nothing,' she said. 'In fact, there's a clean circular mark where there had previously been some scorching from the atmospheric entry.'

'What? It cleaned it?' asked Altera in surprise.

'Appears so,' said Martina, wiping away some more of the oxidation marks from around the clean area. 'Made a better job of it than I have.' She pointed at the area she'd cleaned, which was smearier.

The flat animals didn't bother them again, but they saw them. Each time one approached any part of the camp; they waved their arms at them and they quickly departed. Of variable sizes, just under two metres seemed to be the largest, but they saw many smaller ones, all of which moved about in the same jerky fashion. Several flipped themselves onto the lander, the pod, and the fuel tank and just hung there, occasionally swishing their tails to allow them to move up or sideways along the vessels. Each time, they cleaned the surface. No one caught sight of Mike's giant eye.

'You just saw the eye, but nothing else?' asked Martina.

'No. Just a giant eye observing me through the fronds of one of the closer trees.'

'No body?'

'Didn't see anything else. No body, no face, and just the one eye. I tell you what, it scared the shit out of me.'

Eventually, Mike became less agitated and a little more relaxed about the eye, and examined one of the clean areas of Discovery in extreme detail to see if there had been any scraping of the metal surface, but there was none. Not only had they cleaned the evidence of atmospheric entry but also areas where soil or plants had been thrown up and adhered to the underside of the pod and lander.

'Are they natural cleaners?' said Mike, as the five of them sat in the pod habitat for some lunch. 'Though I'm more concerned about the eye. That was part of something huge! At least dinosaur size!'

'Shut up, Mike! You're spooking me,' said Martina.

Before they'd entered the living section, they first sprayed themselves with disinfectant and then filled the module with nitrogen to kill any bugs or animals. When it refilled with air, they removed their helmets to eat and drink. Inside the pod, they'd be safe from any natural predator. They discussed Mike's giant eye, but the information was too little to be of any use though Campbell insisted that they take special care when next outside.

Chapter Twenty-Three

SPECIMEN

After lunch, they repeated the quarantine procedure and, as they left the airlock, a couple of dozen of the flat animals hanging onto the pod and Discovery surprised them. As soon as they stepped down though, they all detached themselves and wriggled off into the nearest patches of shrubland and woodland. It had been raining, and the grasslike plant, and the outside of the pod were wet, however, the creatures had left dry patches where they were attached to equipment.

'Good grief!' said Altera. 'What's the attraction for them?'

'I think it's the cleaning procedure itself. They must be getting some nutrients from the remains of the oxidisation of the hulls,' said Martina.

'Must be,' said Berry.

'They're easy enough to chase off, though,' said Altera.

'So far,' said Campbell, 'but what if they lose their fear of us? They could be a real nuisance, especially the bigger ones.'

'We'll worry about that if it happens,' said Mike. 'I've sent a full report up to Kepler with some video sequences.'

Later in the afternoon, there was a shout from Mike. 'I've got one!'

Campbell and Martina rushed over and found Mike with a Perspex container pinning one of the flat creatures down to the ground. About thirty centimetres long, it was dark green and was most unhappy at being constrained – it was thrashing about, trying to free itself.

'Pass me the lid,' he said, and Martina grabbed a rectangular cover with edges which could be snapped shut over the main container.

'Careful,' she said, as Mike eased the lid between the grasslike plant and the underside of the animal.

Eventually, the lid snapped shut, and Mike said, 'Now we can get to see the underside.'

Mike turned the container over, but the animal flipped itself over, so they couldn't get to see the underside, even then. He lifted it and, with Martina in tow, he carried it up the steps into the open laboratory area. The top step seemed to move as he trod on it, and another wriggler shot off through the air, with the force of its tail driving it through midair until it came down on the grass about twenty metres away. He almost fell. 'Damn it!' he said.

'My God,' said Martina, 'they seem to be able to fly as well.'

'But not as far. It's as if they don't have any real buoyancy, unlike the bugs,' said Mike, his curiosity piqued by the event.

'It still covered a fair distance above the ground with the motion of the tail.'

'Yes,' he agreed.

'What are you going to do with this one?'

Mike frowned at her. 'I intend to observe it for a while then euthanise it with nitrogen and dissect it.'

'Such a shame.'

'Regretful, but we need to know what we're up against,' he said dismissively. He didn't like killing things either, but it was a necessary part of scientific procedure.

Mike placed the container on top of another deeper container, which he stood on a mirror. Finally, they could see the underside.

There was a soft underbelly within which they observed a heart beating. The mouth was almost circular. This one was adhering to the bottom of the container. The mouth seemed to provide a seal to hold on to the surface.

Suddenly, its mouth moved forward a centimetre or so. It was rasping against the plastic surface.

'So that's how they clean, sucking and rasping,' said Mike.

'Fascinating,' said Martina.

'At least there are no teeth!' Mike said.

Martina laughed and responded, 'Could still suck you to death!'

Mike photographed the armoured head with its raised eyes and hairy nostrils near the front of the body. Besides the wide flat tail, there were also flaps on each side of the body, just behind the head. Presumably, they helped its motion, but the container was too small to observe them in action.

After finishing the photography, Mike connected two tubes to valves on the top of the container. He fed nitrogen into one, and the other had a pressure valve, which allowed the air to flow outwards. The creature became agitated as the air left but then stopped all motion. Mike shook the container and inverted it. The creature just fell about inside. It appeared to be dead.

'What now?' asked Martina.

'Nothing yet. I want to be sure it's dead.'

'Turn it over again.' Mike did so, and the underside of the animal was exposed. Martina said, 'Look, the heart's no longer pumping.'

'I'm still going to leave it an hour or so before the examination. We could really do with catching some smaller ones so that we can observe behaviour. I have a larger plastic container over there which could house them.'

Berry was working at one of the benches and called for Campbell and Martina to come over. 'The bacteria I've found is killed by penicillin. I think we can release the animals.'

'Let one cat and one guinea pig into the caged compound,' said Martina.

Two cats and four guinea pigs had been shipped down to Hacienda in the pod, and Berry opened two of the sealed containers and lifted a tabby cat and an almost all-brown guinea pig down into the cage, which sat on the surface of the planet next to the steps from the pod.

'We'll observe them for forty-eight hours and see if there are any adverse reactions,' she said. 'We mustn't free them, because they could harm the local wildlife. I read that cats wiped out a population of flightless birds in somewhere called Zealand on Earth.'

'New Zealand,' said Mike.

'The bugs will get through the cage mesh,' pointed out Campbell.

'That's okay, small wrigglers could get in too.'

'I want some small ones to observe, if you can catch any,' said Mike.

'Is the guinea pig eating the grass?' asked Berry, kneeling down to peer at the creature.

'Seems to be. We'll soon know if it's digestible. It's really tucking in to it,' said Mike.

'Did you think any more about your thing with a giant eye?' asked Campbell.

'If you mean by that, did I imagine it, the answer is no. It was real, I assure you,' protested Mike.

'Okay. Calm down. We're all taking care and watching the shrubland,' Campbell said.

That evening, as the sun set, four of the five were working in the atmosphere laboratory, while Campbell was in the pod preparing the evening meal. He rapped on the window to call them in.

Quarantine was carried out in the airlock and, once they were all inside, their helmets came off for the evening as they sat down to a rice dish with synthetic pork and rehydrated vegetables.

'How're the animals?' asked Campbell.

'Both seem fine. The guinea pig is still happily munching on the grasslike plant with no sign of ill effects. I fed the cat and gave them both water,' said Mike.

'You secured their cages?'

'I have. Nothing of any size can get at them in the bio compound outside.'

'What's on the agenda for tomorrow?' Berry asked.

Campbell lifted his tablet and scrolled down the page. 'Berry will be working on bacteria and checking plants for poisons and carcinogens. Mike will continue his work on the atmosphere, airborne pathogens, and the effects of Hacienda's air on the animals. Martina and I will begin planting seeds in the planet's soil and some seedlings. We need to know how Earth plants do in the native soil. Altera will be on guard and monitoring any new animals we encounter.'

'*And* I'll keep a watch out for Mike's cyclops!' said Altera.

'It might have had two,' said Mike becoming niggled. 'It's just that I only saw one.'

'If the animals are okay tomorrow night, I intend to sample the air myself the next day. I take it you've not found anything troublesome so far, Mike?' asked Martina.

'Nothing obvious but the giant eye keeps me somewhat worried about larger native animals. Nothing we've encountered has been any real threat, but there's every possibility that there are great white sharks, buoyed by helium, and looking for a tasty snack. Those wrigglers are armoured. Why are they armoured? Have any of you considered that? That's what I find worrying. What can be such a danger to a two-metre wriggler that it has the need to be covered in armour-plating?'

'Let's do our best to find out soon,' said Campbell. 'Captain Blaney wants to make a general announcement as soon as possible. People on the ship are going stir crazy, especially as they can see us walking around in the open. She'd like to send colonists down within a few weeks or at least set a date to begin the process.'

Chapter Twenty-Four

LEARNING CURVE

With the exception of Martina, who maintained quarantine and always wore an airtight suit and helmet, the others were given the all-clear to breathe Hacienda's air and interact with the plants and animals. Martina was the control.

The tiny bugs were the biggest nuisance as they were sometimes inhaled when they were swarming, and it caused coughing fits, but no long-term danger from ingesting them had been found. The larger bug-eaters kept their distance from the humans, flying off if they were approached. When the smaller bugs were a problem, the humans had some fine-mesh hoods to wear to stop them being breathed in.

Over the next month, dozens more of the native species were discovered within what was being called shrubland because most of the plants were too flexible to be considered woodland. There were trees, but few within a square kilometre of Lavigne Base.

The creatures themselves were fascinating. They all had built-in organs which could extract helium from the atmosphere and could use it to adjust their buoyancy in the slightly denser air of Hacienda. In the case of the wrigglers, the helium sac was tiny which was probably why they tended to move along the ground. The species encountered in the open area of the base were mainly bug-eaters or the wrigglers, which spent most of their time adhering to the lander, pod, probe, and launch fuel tank. Detailed study showed that wrigglers were eating anything organic they found on the surfaces. It hadn't taken long for a kind of green velvet plant, similar to algae, to grow on the metal and glass surfaces, and the wrigglers were useful in that they spent much of their time cleaning it off. Altera counted more than a hundred stuck to various surfaces on one occasion, and they were no longer quite so timid. If they were approached slowly, with no sudden movements, it was possible to run your hand over their skin, which had the texture of shagreen.

One creature that also ate the bugs the team called a green-dart. They averaged some ten to twenty centimetres long, with a laterally compressed tail and tiny wings. The front had a long-pointed spike, about a tenth of the body length, hence the dart part of the name, and their colour was a dull olive green. Campbell was the first to discover they were not as timid as the standard bug-eaters. One was sitting on a set of scales he was using in the atmosphere laboratory. He tried to brush it off with the back of his hand, and it turned and flew at his arm.

'Ouch!' he shouted.

'What is it?' asked Mike, who was working alongside him.

'That damn green-dart stabbed me. God, it stings.'

Martina came at a run. 'Let me see,' she said.

An angry red circle was growing in size on Campbell's arm and his face had a pained expression.

'Describe what it feels like,' said Martina.

'Felt like an injection, but it stings. Really quite a nasty hot burning sensation. A little like a drop of boiling water falling on your skin.'

'Wait there,' she said, and dashed over to her medical kit. She lifted small bottles from the case, reading the labels on each, then returned with a small yellow tube.

'What's that?' asked Campbell.

'Antihistamine,' she said as she squeezed a bead of a yellow cream onto her finger. 'It's one of the medicines the chemists have been producing over the last year or so ready for landing. Supposedly, it treats stings from insects. How's that feel?'

She'd rubbed the cream into the red patch of skin, which had already stopped growing in size.

'Still hurting.'

'How bad? One to ten. Ten being unbearable.'

'Oh. Three. It's sore but not incapacitating. Actually, it's feeling better already.'

'That will be the mild anaesthesia included in the cream. You're not having any other problems?'

'Such as?'

'Palpitations, nausea, feeling faint, balance problems, headache?' She looked deep into his face and slid a blood pressure monitor onto a finger on his other arm, and a thermometer into his ear.

'Nothing like that, no.'

She removed the temperature sensor from his ear and looked at the reading on her tablet.

'Blood pressure okay; pulse normal; temperature normal. You're sure there's no headache. Flex your fingers and test the sensitivity of your touch.'

'No headache. Fingers feel and work okay.'

'Eyesight?'

Campbell looked around the camp and then down at some notes on his tablet. 'All okay.'

'Mike, can you catch one of those things? I want to analyse the poison to see what it does.'

'Right. They tend to sit still so should be easy enough,' he replied and went off with Berry to track one down.

When the crew ventured into the shrubland, they encountered a whole new selection of flying species. The bugs were in greater numbers and fine-mesh hoods had to be worn. The larger bug-eaters, green-darts, and wrigglers were in plentiful numbers, the latter spending much of their time stuck onto leaves and larger stems.

There were more colourful bugs too. Several flying creatures had luminescence, sufficiently bright to be visible in broad daylight. One had a pink stripe, another a glowing red spot like an LED behind the head, another divided down the middle – blue in front and yellow behind. Many had spots, stripes, patterns and many more were just boring muddy-tinted, matt green, blue, black, brown, and grey creatures. Several seemed to change colour like chameleons.

Giving them a general name was not easy. They weren't birds, or insects or any form of Earth flying creatures. If anything, they were more like fish except for the tiny wings and the fact that they could hold absolutely still in midair. Some species seemed to group together, like a murmuration of starlings, a flock of sheep or a shoal of fish and these groupings could be quite spectacular, especially when they emerged from the shrubland and formed groups of hundreds in the open clearings. Berry filmed one beautiful group she called lemon-glow bugs as they flew through the camp, twisting and turning.

'They're like fireflies,' said Mike.

'Fire whats?' asked Altera.

'Fireflies. Flies are a group of insects from Earth. Fireflies were flying insects on Earth, but unlike the lemon-glows, their lights flickered on and off, so they were like, now-you-see-them, now-you-don't. Being nocturnal they came out at night.'

'Sound lovely. Never heard of them.'

'Look up fireflies when you're next at your console. They tended to be restricted to the tropical regions,' Mike said.

Martina said, 'Those small dark blue bugs seem to behave like bees on Earth. They move more smoothly but go in and out of flowers.'

Mike said, 'Bees pollinate. I wonder whether these perform the same function.'

'How do we find out?'

'We'd need to follow them and see if they have a community somewhere, like a beehive. If you grab some specimens, I can check to see if they're carrying pollen.'

'Oh, I think they do,' said Martina. 'When they come out of the red flowers, they definitely have red dust on them.'

'Right. That could mean pollination. We should study it. The hive aspect would be interesting too, to see if they take the pollen back to a nest and do or make something with it.'

'So much to study,' said Campbell, who'd been listening.

'How's that sting?' asked Martina.

'A bit itchy today, and less red.'

'I checked the venom. It's a mild concoction of proteins, enzymes, and peptides. I've done a report. It also contains an anticoagulant. Nearest thing to it on Earth was a black and yellow striped insect called a wasp.'

The crew also encountered larger flying-bugs, the size of geese, but with the same proportionately tiny wings as their smaller companions. Most of these flying creatures ate the bugs or the smaller creatures and the larger animals were not averse to swallowing bugs up to a third of their size, taking their prey into their mouths and, like a snake on Earth, gradually pulling it into their digestive tracts. There were two more sightings of giant eyes which vanished when seen. One by Berry and another by Mike, who was relieved to finally have a second witness. They all continued to be on alert if near or inside the shrubland. By this time, all except Martina had been subjected to a bite or sting from a green-dart.

During day forty-two, Martina shed her suit and helmet, and the advance party determined it was time for the captain to prepare to launch colonist descent vehicles. Hacienda had passed muster and was approved to become humankind's permanent home.

Campbell was preparing the final report to be transmitted to Captain Blaney when he heard a shout from Altera. 'Outside, quick! We've got company and they're *huge!* I think Mike's giant eyes have decided to reveal themselves!'

Chapter Twenty-Five

HACIENDANS

Campbell dashed out to join the others. All five then looked towards the north, where the shrubland became more sparse. Three huge floating beings sat almost stationary, wings running full length along their sides, rippling slowly to hold them in position against the slight breeze. Where had they come from? They were enormous compared to everything the humans had seen so far, over three metres wide and, although they couldn't see their full length as they were facing head-on, they were at least twice as long as their width, possibly eight or even ten metres. Their colour seemed variable with greys of all shades, moving about within their skin, pulsing and waving randomly. Pewter to smoke; slate to charcoal; silver to lead; dove grey to cloud. These were evidently the owners of Mike's giant eye.

In fact, two eyes the size of dinner plates were swivelling from side to side, taking in the Discovery, the pod, and the booster. In front of the leading being was the probe. Hanging down from the animal's forehead area looked like eight tentacles, similar to a giant squid, but all drooping groundward, exhibiting the same rippling greys. The beings were hovering about three metres off the ground.

'Wow! Look at the colours,' whispered Altera in some amazement.

The colour of the lead creature transformed dramatically. The greys were gone. Now they were vibrant yellows, blues, and greens. The effect was stunning, pulsing from back to front and left to right and then the other way. The pulses were moving through the skin, body, and wings like waves, each shade blending seamlessly into the next as it wove its way up, down, left or right. As quickly as the light show started, it ended and the whole beast returned to its mottled greys, each shade pulsating to and fro. The being on the lead animal's left then produced a series of ripples of yellow: pineapple, daffodil, and honey, finishing with a more carroty or tigerish orange which rapidly passed across the entire body before fading back into the original smoky cloud colour.

Number one glided effortlessly forward so that its tentacles overhung the probe.

'Do nothing,' said Campbell in subdued tones. 'Let it investigate.'

'Note how their eyes keep swivelling back towards us. They're waiting for a reaction,' said Mike. 'They know we're significant and we may be considered dangerous or even predators.'

'Just watch and wait,' said Campbell in a loud whisper.

Number one pulsed white in its tentacles, which morphed into a vivid, almost luminescent crimson, then back to greyish white.

It seemed to be waiting.

After a few seconds of inactivity, it tipped itself forward, and the two longest tentacles in the front of the group ran across the probe. Fingerlike extensions seemed to be feeling the antennae's shape. It hardly moved when touched, and the radar array barely flexed as it was stroked. It used two of its finger things to pull an insulated wire towards it, then released it, causing it to spring back into position.

It turned towards the right, and colours wafted across its body once more. Number three pulsed mint, lime, and emerald, with contrasting yellow spots, the spots only moving around the forehead area. Another burst of spectacular colour crossed one's head, and it returned to sensing the probe.

'Shouldn't one of us move towards them to find out if they're hostile or will flee or react in some other way?' asked Altera quietly.

'I suppose it should be me,' said Campbell, a little anxiously. Those tentacles could crush him or drag him into a hidden maw.

'Mike and I have our pistols,' said Berry, the tension clear in her statement.

'Not sure that the bullets will have any effect on these things. We'd probably need a mortar,' said Mike.

'Don't fire on them. Bear with me. Do nothing unless I say or it's obvious they're hurting me,' whispered Campbell.

He took a step forward.

Number one glowed violet briefly. Then it repeated it. Campbell wondered whether that was welcoming or meant as a threat. All three moved backwards about a metre, and the tentacles were now clear of the probe.

He took a step forward again, stood in front of the being and reached forward with his palms upward and open.

One pulsed violet again.

Campbell advanced three more steps. He was now only

ten metres from number one. Number two pulsed a series of magenta, rose and wine, flashing magenta again rapidly, before returning to a shade of graphite. One pulsed red, faded through pink to white then repeated the violet glow. It moved forward two metres and was now directly over the probe again. Could this be a greeting? Did it want to feel the human, perhaps? Campbell could only guess.

'Hello,' he said loudly.

Number one ceased its forward motion and retreated a metre. It pulsed turquoise then rust colours repeatedly, then stopped its colour show and advanced another two metres.

'Can you hear me?' said Campbell, moving forward.

One repeated its retreat and colour patterns then moved another two metres forward. Campbell was now just four metres from the animal and could appreciate its size. If it were dangerous, those tentacles could have him in their grasp in an instant. What was behind them? Did it have a huge set of jaws or a mouth full of teeth that could kill him in a single bite? He remembered seeing video of a lizard which could extend its tongue and drag prey instantly into its mouth. Could these do the same? He could be dead very quickly indeed.

The human stood still, arms still reaching out. Number one reached forward with the central two tentacles. They stopped about a metre short of Campbell but then seemed to stretch and elongate and the fingerlike structures emerged. One brushed his chest. It was cool. Campbell was wearing a synthetic woollen sweater but could feel the coolness through it. He stood stock-still.

The second tentacle touched his shoulder and then followed his arm, taking almost a minute to reach his hand. Finally, it was flesh on flesh. Tentacle to hand. It was indeed cool. It also felt somewhat tacky, like sweaty human skin, but there was no stickiness as it ran over his skin in the softest, gentlest manner.

'No stinging or other sensation?' called Martina, worried about chemicals.

'No. Just cool and tacky,' Campbell replied.

'They might be cold-blooded,' said Mike, 'allowing their body temperature to match their surroundings.'

It seemed to Campbell that it was time for a positive move. He stepped closer and ran his hands over the tentacles. While the undersides were tacky, the upper side was dry and slightly rough. If he'd known what an elephant's skin was like, Campbell would have described the tentacle as being like the pachyderm's trunk. He also noticed a hint of muskiness.

'Altera, Captain here. What the hell is going on?' came over Altera's headset.

'You're watching?'

'And a good hundred or so shipmates.'

'Then you know as much as we do. They suddenly appeared and Campbell's trying to interact.'

'Why not just chase them off?'

'Captain, you can see them. They're huge and seem inquisitive. If we try to chase them and they decide *not* to go it would be a serious problem for us.'

'Maybe. Do you think Campbell's in danger?'

'Your guess is as good as ours. I'd say that the potential for danger is severe, but he's following protocol for dealing with a creature which might have some intelligence.'

'I'll look up the protocols. We're watching closely. Keep me informed.'

'Certainly, ma'am.'

'I know what they remind me of,' said Berry.

'What's that?' asked Mike.

Berry continued hesitantly, 'I saw an undersea programme once and there was a creature called a scuttle-fish or something. It wasn't an actual fish; it was more like a squid. Not scuttle, it was cuttle, a cuttlefish. It changed colours like that.'

'An octopus can do the same,' whispered Mike just loud enough for Berry to hear.

One's tentacle continued to explore Campbell's shape, touching his face, torso, and legs. It extended three very fine fingertips from the tentacle and ran them over the commander's headset, eventually lifting it free and examining it in front of one eye, turning and rotating it. After a minute, it was returned to Campbell. There was an attempt to place it back on his head, but Campbell took it from the being and positioned it correctly.

A series of colours ran over number one and then were seemingly answered by the other two. Number one pulled back behind the probe. They faced each other and appeared to be having a conversation, rapid pulses of colour moving over their bodies. The light show ended, and each of them moved forward. Number two went to Martina and explored her face. She held her cool as its fingerlike digits felt the firmness of her breasts. Another approached Discovery. The third moved towards the pod. Mike and Berry eased to one side to let it through while Altera continued to stand at the end of the pod, farthest from the being. Each flashed an occasional colour sequence.

Number one, once it had examined the exterior of Discovery, pushed itself tight against the lander and placed one of its eyes against the cockpit glass.

'It's looking inside,' said Campbell, who had followed it.

The being backed off, and a tentacle worked its way into the airlock handle. The door opened. It backed off again so that it could look inside then probed the airlock with its main two tentacles. It was trying to open the inner door, but, of course, the system would not allow both doors to be open at the same time.

'It's feeling inside the airlock,' said Campbell.

'Number three is doing the same with the open-air lab,' said Mike. 'It's found the container with the small wrigglers in it.'

Gently and slowly, the animal lifted the transparent container and brought it close to its eye. Suddenly, it displayed a complex series of colours, and the other two animals quickly moved to join it, all peering at the captive wrigglers. Once more, there was a considerable light show in progress between them.

Whatever was taking place quickly turned into a tug-of-war. Number three and number one were each pulling at the container. Three certainly did not want to release it, but number one's body became crimson, suddenly and totally. Number three released the container, and one backed away with it in its tentacles. It turned towards Campbell and laid the container on the ground in front of him.

'What does that mean?' he asked.

'Maybe it wants you to open it,' said Berry.

Campbell reached down and flipped three clasps, opening a doorway at the front. He then closed it and sealed the clasps.

'Now, if it wants to release them, it knows how,' he said.

Number one pulsed a series of colours then stopped. It seemed to be waiting. It pulsed the same colours again then repeated it a third time.

Campbell felt that he was being asked a question. He spread his arms, hands open, which was to show lack of understanding in the protocol manual.

Number one stopped pulsing, reached towards the container, neatly flicked the three clasps and the door flopped downwards. The fingerlike extensions were certainly as sensitive as our own. One of the tentacles then eased into the cage and grasped a wriggler. One at a time, it pulled them out of the container and released them. The wrigglers, once free of their prison, rapidly flapped their tails and half flew, half wriggled back into the shrubland as fast as they could.

'What did all of that mean?' asked the captain over their headsets.

'Maybe it didn't like us keeping them captive,' said Mike.

'Could they be juveniles? Like pupae. A larval stage, maybe,' said Berry. 'Perhaps we had been imprisoning a larval form of the creatures and they didn't like it.'

'Do you think so?' asked the captain.

'No. It's unlikely,' said Berry sharply, then realising the captain might take offence at her tone added, 'though we need to consider all possibilities.'

Number one laid down the empty container then picked up the cage containing the cat and guinea pig. It studied them and creature two joined it, both looking intently at the animals. Suddenly, number one turned towards Campbell and put the cage on the ground in front of him in the same way he had done with the wrigglers' container.

'I think it wants you to release them,' said Berry.

'We can't,' said Mike. 'Biohazard to their wildlife.'

Campbell picked the cage up, turned and placed it on the ground behind him, turned back to number one and waved and crossed his arms.

Number one flashed a number of colours. Two did the

same and then number one backed off. It seemed to understand that the visitors did not want the animals released.

The three beings returned to the place where they'd entered the clearing, faced the humans, and each flashed the same combination of colours. They waited a minute, repeated the colours, then turned and left.

'What was that all about?' asked the captain, pulling herself back and forth on Kepler's bridge.

'I think they were studying us,' said Mike. 'If aliens arrived somewhere on Earth, I'm sure we'd do something similar.'

'What? You think they're intelligent?'

'Captain, you saw it open that container, once I'd shown it how,' said Campbell, running his hand through his shiny black hair. 'It also opened Discovery's airlock. That certainly suggests a considerable intelligence.'

'But why did it release the captured animals?' asked the captain.

'Maybe they have a problem with animals being kept in captivity,' said Berry.

'They must live on something themselves, or do you think they're vegetarian?' asked Captain Blaney.

'Could be,' said Berry. 'They learned more about us during that visit than we did about them. Doesn't anyone else find that a little disconcerting?'

'Of course,' said Altera.

'Did you notice how they spent time studying my facial skin and Mike's beard?' asked Berry.

'I did. They noticed our differences. Your breasts seemed to interest them. Curiosity,' said Mike.

'And, yes, it's *very* worrying,' said Campbell. 'We're the invaders here. Maybe they were an advance party checking us out. They could be back to destroy us.'

'Seriously?' asked the captain.

'It's a possibility,' said Martina, also becoming frustrated at the captain's questions. 'One of them had a good look inside Discovery through the cockpit window. If they're intelligent, they must realise that these are space vehicles.'

'Not necessarily,' said Mike. 'They'd know these are vehicles of some kind but that's all.'

'But where else could we have come from?' asked Martina.

'Another continent,' said Mike. 'Hacienda has more land area than Earth by a considerable margin. It depends how much they travel. How well they've explored their own world.'

'Their examination of the open-air lab was quite thorough, although they didn't try to look through microscopes or switch on monitors,' said Martina.

'Are they a threat?' asked the captain.

'No way of knowing,' said Campbell. 'We need to think about how we'll communicate next time they come. Let's face it, we didn't do anything. I touched its tentacle and showed it how to open the container, but that was it?'

'They did understand that they mustn't release the cat and guinea pig,' said Berry.

'That's right,' said Campbell.

'How do we communicate with a being which only uses colours as a language?' asked the captain.

'Colours are one of the expected communication methods, ma'am. Colours, sound, electromagnetic waves, infrared, harmonics, clicks and taps, radio, facial expressions, ultraviolet, signing or other body-part movements, telepathy. Those are all in the first-contact material,' said Campbell.

'Frankly,' said Altera, 'I think we were shocked by their arrival. They came specifically to check us out so probably had a plan. We had no plan and still don't.'

'We were taken by surprise,' said Berry.

'Then we'd better come up with a plan, and damn quick!' said the captain. 'Let me know what you come up with and, if you need the advice from others up here, just let us know.'

'Yes, Captain,' said Campbell.

'I was hoping to give the go-ahead to start sending colonists, but this changes everything,' said the captain. 'Out.'

The encounter with the – what should they be called? – the Haciendans, shook the crew to its roots. With the captain pressing them to improve the situation, and Berry, wearing a headset, volunteering to stand guard in the atmosphere lab, the rest of the explorers entered the equipment pod. Once much of the equipment had been relocated around the base camp and inside the atmosphere laboratory, enough space had been created for a small sitting room – a personal space where they could chat, drink tea and coffee, and wind down from the perpetual pressure of working outside. Always being prepared for the unknown caused constant anxiety, and now that the Haciendans had appeared, that added to their worries.

Inside, Mike made tea or coffee for each of them, and they sat in the comfortable camp chairs, which had been stored in bags in the atmosphere lab for transportation. It was a cosy environment in which to discuss their options.

'At least we know what the giant eye belonged to,' said Mike.

'Do we think they're intelligent?' asked Campbell to get the ball rolling.

'Certainly,' said Mike. 'They were clearly communicating with each other and possibly trying to communicate with us. Did you notice how they looked through Discovery's cockpit? The main one flashed colours at Campbell several times and waited as if for a reply.'

'That's right. I had no way to answer it,' said Campbell.

'I agree. We must assume that they're thinking creatures. The question is how advanced are they – like apes, dolphins or as intelligent as us?' said Altera.

'Or *more* intelligent than us,' came over the radio from Berry, outside.

'Okay. We'd better come up with some sort of plan. How are we going to communicate?' asked Campbell.

'They seem to use light,' said Altera.

'Not just light,' said Martina. 'The lights ran into each other and there were many shades and patterns. Very sophisticated.'

'They might not return,' Mike said.

'But we must assume they will,' said Campbell. 'Right. First. What do we need to say and how are we going to say it?'

'First of all, we need to consider our communication options,' said Martina. 'Any ideas? Come on, Altera, you're the computer wizard.'

'We must isolate words. We need to build a library of what each of the colours and patterns mean. Our cameras recorded the entire visit, so I have video of all their pulsating colours in conjunction with whatever they were doing at the time. I can analyse the exact wavelengths of the colours used.'

'Is that really necessary?' asked Mike.

'Of course it is. We might see green or blue or turquoise, but if the shades and brightness vary depending on meaning then we need wavelengths. It could be like Chinese, where the word "tang" can mean sugar or soup depending upon the tone used when speaking. Not only that, but translation might not be enough. Human sign language is interpretation and there's a lot more involved than having a sign for each word. I think we could be dealing with something even more complex here.'

'Right. I see,' said Mike, slumping back into his seat.

Altera continued, 'I'll analyse what we already have and build a database with specific brightness, shapes, and colours. When they return—'

'If,' said Berry.

'No. When,' said Altera. 'They *will* return and when they do we need to start to communicate, even if it's one, two, three or yes, no, maybe.'

'Sounds a plan,' said Campbell, well satisfied with how his team was working together to solve the problem.

'We have no idea when they'll return so I'll get on with it immediately,' said Altera. 'It would be good if the rest of you can come up with a structure for the next meeting.'

'Indeed,' said Martina. 'We need to show where we're from, where we are now, and find out their intellectual level and scientific knowledge.'

Chapter Twenty-Six

LANGUAGE

It only took a few hours to set up an area for communication, but it was four days before the Haciendans returned to Lavigne Base. The humans wondered if they should seek them out, but entering such dense shrubland with no sense of direction to follow seemed hopeless. The ship had been asked to look for signs of where they lived, but that had yielded no help either. Maybe they lived underground. The humans were just about to discuss some sort of expedition when there was an excited cry from Berry.

'They're here!'

Everyone wore headsets so that the first sighting could be reported quickly. Campbell rushed down the steps out of the atmosphere laboratory and approached the visitors. Again, there were three. Were they the same three? There was no way of telling as they were of similar size. One had damage to its rightmost tentacle, but Campbell didn't remember whether he'd noticed it last time. He'd check with Altera's video later. Now they were all determined to observe any differences or scars. Knowing they were dealing with the same beings each time would be vital.

The three were close together, within a metre or so of each other. One was closer to him than the other two, who were slightly behind, as if subordinate.

Campbell stood, legs apart, and raised both arms in the air as if beginning a keep-fit exercise. The lead being came closer, giving the impression of curiosity. The humans had temporarily named him or her, Boss.

Campbell swung both arms to the right and said, 'Come,' loudly. He repeated the signal and turned to march purposefully towards the entrance area of the atmosphere lab, where two one-metre monitors were set up on tripods in the shade of the lab's rain canopy. He stopped beside them and turned to face Boss. All three had approached together. That was good. They'd realised that they'd been invited.

Campbell swung his arms again and said, 'Come.' He then pointed at Boss. Nothing. He repeated the action. Boss glowed blue briefly. The left-hand monitor flashed with the identical blue and an AI voice said, 'Come.'

Campbell picked up the remote control, which was on a shelf at the front of the monitor. He held it up and showed it to each of the beings in turn, then pointed it at the screen, which came to life with a single image of Hacienda taken from Kepler. All three came closer to the screen and crowded together, so close that they were each touching the other. They all exhibited multiple colours. Excitement, perhaps? If they'd never seen their world from space, this image would be amazing.

Pressing another button caused Hacienda to zoom out to a globe and rotate on the screen, showing day and night sides. The sequence had been sped up so that the planet revolved every twenty seconds, then it slowed down until it was almost stationary. The camera zoomed out and showed an orbit, with a disc-shaped representation of the starship Kepler travelling around the planet. Campbell caused the ship to flash and said, 'Kepler,' and pointed at himself. He repeated it.

Zooming out farther, the planet's two moons came into view, also orbiting. Zooming out again, Kepler-452 appeared with Hacienda, its moons, and other planets in the Kepler-452 system also appearing as the view expanded. He let them watch it for a minute then hit the advance button. Now, the view twisted away from the local star and showed a constellation of stars known as Puppis. Campbell turned to the monitor and pointed at the centre of the star system and then at himself. He said, 'Humankind.'

The word also appeared on the screen. Boss's head and tentacles turned powder blue, which morphed into a light purple. Was that 'humankind'? Of course not. If anything, it would be more like 'strange animal stuck to ground' or 'alien' or some other reference. Until the humans knew anything to the contrary, the light blue to purple would represent the humans on the database. The monitor repeated the sequence, and the voice said, 'humankind'.

The monitor view now centred on the distant star system and rapidly moved through the cosmos, the impression of speed being achieved by having stars rushing towards the outside of the screen in imitation of Microsoft's early screensaver. After a minute, the solar system came into view with its eight planets. Glorious Saturn with its rings, Jupiter and its stripes. Gradually, Earth became central with the moon in orbit. The camera dived into the atmosphere and showed New York. Zooming continued until Fifth Avenue was on show, with motor vehicles and myriad humans in the streets.

The screen returned to an image of the Earth. Campbell turned back to the visitors and pointed at the planet. He said, 'Earth' with the word Earth also appearing on the screen. Boss repeated his blue/purple combo but added a darker purple spot which grew out of the paler colour. Altera put it into the database as 'Earth'. Altera flashed the colour sequence on the second monitor and followed it with the image of Earth and the word 'Earth'.

All three beings turned to face each other, and the most amazing light show took place between them. They were clearly discussing what they had been seeing and, several times, tentacles indicated the monitor and Campbell too. Within the light show, the humans saw the blue/purple combo several times. There was obviously an exchange taking place about what the beings had just witnessed. It was exciting, and the humans felt real progress was being made.

Once the conversation had died down and they turned back to the screen, Campbell pointed at his chest and said, 'Human.' Altera flashed the relevant colours. The commander then pointed to Boss.

A sunburst of red and yellow spread out from its forehead. After a brief pause, a more complex pattern covered its body, and the other two beings repeated the sunburst pattern.

'Try that, Altera,' said Campbell. 'Just the starburst.'

Altera projected the starburst and showed an image of the three beings. Then she showed the Earth and its colours.

Boss immediately repeated the starburst several times.

Using the remote, Campbell put Hacienda back on the screen and said, 'Hacienda,' also having the word appear beside the globe.

Boss produced a chartreuse glow, which rippled into juniper.

'Got that?' asked Campbell.

'Think so,' said Altera and tried to imitate the colours.

Boss copied the darker green Altera had used and then flashed his juniper colour several times.

Altera projected the chartreuse again, but followed it with a darker green, closer to Boss's juniper.

Boss's entire body glowed cobalt blue. The Haciendans were as excited as the humans, it appeared.

'I think we got it right,' said Altera.

'Show the time sequence,' said Mike.

Campbell checked his remote and pressed a button. The screen filled with Hacienda again. The planet was rotating at a fast speed, moving from day to night every four or five seconds. Then the speed slowed as it had before, and Hacienda came to a stop, the night side showing. It rotated so that a fifth of the orb was in daylight. A white spot showed in the top corner of the screen. Under it appeared the figure one, and Campbell said, 'One.'

Another fifth was daylight. A second spot appeared. The figure one faded and was replaced with a figure two. Campbell said, 'Two.'

They'd argued earlier about whether to break the day into Earth's own twenty-four hours but decided it would be simpler to have a ten-hour day in discussion with the beings, at least until they learned the Haciendan time scale. Campbell completed the ten phases and counted to ten to match them. He then repeated the sequence, stopping at one and waiting. He walked towards the monitor and indicated the figure one and repeated, 'One,' then pointed at Boss.

A bright yellow spot appeared in the centre of its head. Campbell said, 'One.' Boss repeated the yellow spot.

Campbell continued the projection and showed the second phase, saying, 'Two,' and pointing at the figure two. Two yellow spots appeared on its head. The process continued to ten. The team had learned the alien's number system to ten.

One yellow spot; two; three; four; a green spot indicating five; one green, one yellow; and so on until ten was indicated by two green spots.

'Okay,' he said, 'now let's see how bright they are.'

The screen showed a single yellow spot, then blank, then a yellow spot again, then blank, then two spots, then three, then a green spot, then green plus three yellow, then two greens plus three yellows for thirteen. It was the Fibonacci* sequence.

Campbell was surprised when a tentacle extended from Boss and touched his shoulder. He looked around and found Boss showing a blue spot and three yellows.

'Ah, blue is ten,' said Altera. She replaced the two greens and three yellows with one blue and three yellows, held that for a moment and projected two blues and a yellow for twenty-one.

The Haciendans staged another of their light shows to each other, and Boss showed three blue dots and four yellow on his head. Thirty-four – the next number in the sequence.

'Wey-hey!' cried Altera. 'They know it.' She projected five blue spots and one green for fifty-five. Boss followed that with eight blues, a green and four yellows to represent eighty-nine.

Campbell turned to Boss and clapped. This was a prearranged signal in the group, and the others repeated the action. Applause rang out around the base camp. The three

---

* Fibonacci was a 12th Century Italian mathematician.

Haciendans retreated a couple of metres. When the applause stopped, they each produced an identical series of yellow waves along their tentacles. Had humankind learned the Haciendan for clapping?

Learning each other's languages was slow and laborious, but after four lengthy meetings, remarkable progress was being made. The team decided that, as the immigrants, they should use the native language whenever possible. That was difficult because they had no biological way to make the various colours and depended therefore upon showing their hosts words on computer tablets, which they hung around their necks and could control by voice.

Of course, the Haciendans were equally disadvantaged by an inability to make any sounds other than whooshing and whistling through their air inlets. Breathing required air to be taken in through a large orifice under the wings. Their bodies then extracted oxygen (presumption until further tests conducted) and helium before expelling waste air through smaller openings on either side of the tail. The helium was used to maintain their distance from the ground. Burning oxygen produced carbon dioxide in a similar fashion to earthly mammals, and by expelling air, they could accelerate forward rapidly. They could also expel air forwards to retreat. The wings provided direction. It was interesting to see how waves of motion moved back and forth along the wings and the direction of the waves controlled the body's position, holding it steady, turning it or, the team later discovered, producing considerable speed.

Many of the words involved simple multiples of colours, but some required sudden changes of colour and/or dramatic flashes. They noticed that there were often low-level pastel colour waves, and this seemed like whispering and was used between the beings themselves. It was much faster, which made translation impossible. The team guessed these were asides to whatever they were learning or talking about.

The beings quickly and effectively understood concepts and appeared at least as intelligent as humans, but their technology was vastly inferior. They soon understood that humans had come from an alien world many light-years away from Hacienda but did not understand the functioning of the shuttle, the probe, nor the Kepler. They accepted they could perform as described but could not do the mathematics to work out orbits, launch vectors and propulsion systems. As far as the humans understood it, they had not ventured into space, although they knew about stars, constellations, and planets.

As the fourth meeting concluded, Reddo, Boss's name as accurately as the team could make it, asked, 'Time you came to Orangiegreen?'

'Orangiegreen?' Altera asked.

'Home. Our home.'

'We'd love to visit your home.'

Gray and Smoke, the other two beings, approached Campbell and Altera, and their tentacles touched them gently on the front of their bodies. Reddo flashed a wave of turquoise over his entire body, which was understood as, 'follow me.' He turned and went to the edge of the camp. The other two turned and followed. All three turned back, and all three flashed the same turquoise wave.

Reddo said, 'We'll carry. Safest way in forest.' It was, of course, said in their colours, and the human language database converted it into a form of pidgin English.

Campbell walked towards them. The tentacles from Smoke brushed against him and, suddenly, he was hoisted into the air and being held, a couple of metres off the ground. He didn't resist. The grip was gentle but secure with one of the extendable tentacles curled under him to form a seat. Another held him firmly about the waist while two of the larger tentacles supported his back and sides. It was comfortable.

The third being flashed turquoise waves continually.

Campbell said, 'He wants you too, Altera.'

Altera said into her tablet, 'How far going?' and showed the screen to Reddo.

He replied, 'Not far. Tenth time unit.'

What did that mean? A time unit was probably a fifth of a complete day, so a tenth of a unit could mean a journey of an hour or so. Altera wished they had tied down units of time and distance. She tentatively took some steps towards the Haciendans, and the colour flashes stopped. Being three approached her, and she too was soon being firmly held a short distance from the ground.

'What should we do?' shouted Mike.

'Nothing,' said Campbell. 'I think we'll be okay. I'll keep in touch by radio. We have our tablets so can communicate enough to get by.'

A few seconds later, all three, with their guests, turned and vanished into the shrubland.

Chapter Twenty-Seven

HOME

Comfortably encapsulated within the two primary tentacles, the others provided a cage-like shield to protect the humans as the beings sped through the undergrowth, their bodies being flayed by the shrubbery, yet not appearing to receive injury or damage. Their speed was considerable, later estimated by Altera at over twenty miles per hour. Campbell thrilled at the journey, full of anticipation for the beings' home. The sense of danger had eased somewhat and this was more an adventure of discovery.

To Altera and Campbell, it seemed as if they were being taken through a dense jungle, but it was the speed that gave that impression as the shrubbery was not that thick, just being hit at a rate of knots. It was natural to worry about being hit in the face by the plants, but the other tentacles easily fended off the impacts. The Haciendans must have realised that human bodies were more vulnerable than theirs.

On all sides, the variety of flowers mesmerised the humans, and they glimpsed small flying or floating creatures which seemed to be pollinators. The terrain resembled that in the films they had seen of the tropical jungles on Earth.

Over forty-five minutes passed before the Haciendans slowed down and eventually burst out of the jungle of shrubs and into what could only be called a sculptured forest.

These were nothing like the trees the humans had previously encountered. They grew with palm tree-like fronds from their very bases and reached about twenty metres into the sky. At first glance, it was an impenetrable thicket, but the three Haciendans, in single file, entered what gave the impression of being a tunnel of vegetation. The moment they were inside the forest, tunnels of fronds spread out, creating passages which headed in many directions, the group of three following the most substantial, deeper into the greenery. Filtered sunlight gave the Haciendans a pear-coloured complexion.

Light was more subdued within the tunnels, and there was the smell of damp vegetation, which now overcame the musky aroma of their guides. Sounds of the wind outside were softened, almost muted. Inside, there wasn't a breath of air movement.

'Now we know what those even patches of green are spread out around the continent,' said Altera.

'What? Cities?'

'I'd bet.'

Minutes later, they entered a huge green arena. The trees had been trained to form a canopy over a space at least the size of a football pitch. Around the sides, more tunnels led off in different directions, but what immediately caught the eye was a number of what looked to be homes around the fringe. As the party emerged into the space, more Haciendans appeared from the structures and approached with undoubted curiosity, their skins portraying constantly moving colours as they discussed the strange, alien visitors.

The beings lowered Campbell and Altera to the ground. Reddo flashed colours slowly at them. Their tablets interpreted and computer voices said, 'Home. Home to many. People live here.'

They were soon surrounded by over fifty Haciendans, all flashing colours in waves, splashes, spots and other shapes. Some of the canopy's fronds were nearby, and Altera felt them, picked one and passed it to Campbell.

'It's soft, like ferns yet it seems to knit together to produce a tight weave. The texture's similar to handling a chunky cardigan.' She held some to her nose. 'It smells like coriander.'

'You're right. So different to anything we grow on the ship,' said Campbell, looking around at all the colourful conversations being conducted around them. 'I think they're discussing us,' said Campbell.

'Indeed,' said Altera. 'Way too fast for the translators.'

The tablet, which was concentrating on Reddo said, 'Our people welcome you.'

Altera asked, 'Is this a city?' and the tablet produced a coloured sequence.

'Place for many people, yes,' said Reddo.

'How many live here?'

Reddo flashed a complex of dots, which translated into, 'About eight hundred.'

'Do you have many cities?'

'Many. One hundred like this on this land mass within a day's travel.'

'That explains the green areas we saw from orbit,' replied Altera.

Campbell asked, 'What do you do?'

'We think, we teach, we learn, we play.'

'What is your food?'

The answer was a short wave of colours across his tentacles, but there was no translation.

'Don't understand,' said Altera.

'Show you. Come,' said Reddo, and floated towards the rim of the clearing. The humans followed. They entered another tunnel of fronds. 'Danger here,' he added.

About a hundred metres inside they arrived at a huge circular depression in the forest floor, perhaps fifty metres across. Reddo stopped at the edge and held the humans back with his tentacles. A strange sound like maracas beads knocking together, but in huge numbers, emanated from the pit.

'Danger for you,' Reddo said.

There was little light there, and the depths of the bowl seemed in motion. Reddo leaned over the edge, and one of his tentacles extended to the moving mass and lifted something out.

'This food,' he said.

The tentacle held an object the size of a soccer ball. Its outer surface was covered in short, sharp thorns. The humans couldn't make out whether it was animal or vegetable.

Campbell reached out to touch it.

'*No!*' Reddo flashed in crimson, pulling the object away. 'Spikes hurt you perhaps.'

'How food?' asked Altera.

Reddo lifted a second tentacle, and the object was pulled apart into two jagged pieces. Inside, a tangle of meat moved as if alive. It made Altera feel queasy. A proboscis extended from between Reddo's tentacles, dipped into the mass, and it was swiftly vacuumed out of the shell, sounding like sucking the last of a milkshake through a straw, until there was nothing left but a shiny smooth interior surface. He did the same with the other half.

'Was it alive?'

'Alive, yes, but no thoughts. Our people keep them and make them multiply.'

Campbell looked down into the bowl. There were thousands of urchin-like spheres, all moving around, jostling for position, rising and being pushed downwards into the melee.

Reddo said, 'Come to a school with me. We have many want to teach you language for better understanding.' He swung around and returned along the green tunnel. At one point he took a different junction, and they arrived in a small clearing this time, with just a dozen of the beings. All were larger than Reddo. Real giants. None were smaller. Something resembling a circular video monitor was mounted on a stand.

'These elders. Much wisdom. You learn with them.'

'That is good,' said Campbell.

The two humans sat on seats grown out of the soft, dry, plant, facing five of the largest Haciendans. The others retreated to the back of the room. Colours flashed slowly between the elders and meandered across their bodies while images appeared on the screen. Vocabulary was soon being accumulated.

Chapter Twenty-Eight

DIFFICULT REPORT

The team set up remote detectors around the base camp so that they'd know if any Haciendans arrived then entered the habitat module for a meeting to discuss what they'd learned and to find out what the shipboard officers thought about the situation. They settled down in the easy chairs with the monitor showing the captain's office on the orbiting Kepler, where Captain Linda Blaney and people's president, Andy Ovpetrangle could be seen on a split screen. The Kepler leaders were clearly in freefall, the captain floating upright beside her desk.

'You wish to report?' asked the president.

'I do,' said Campbell, lifting his tablet to review some of his notes. He foresaw difficulties.

'Go ahead,' said the captain.

'This might take some time,' Campbell began. 'Altera and I have just spent our sixth session with the elders of the Haciendans, and our vocabulary and understanding of each other has grown exponentially. They're as curious about us as we are about them.

'As we've already reported. The population live in towns or cities which they have grown from a plant called, as near as we can make out, spangledsepiacandy trees. They can control the trees' growth to such a degree that they have built enormous canopies and thousands of tunnels, as we showed you in the video yesterday. There are individual homes within these cities but they also gather in small groups to eat and sleep.

'Their reproduction, we have learned, is by laying eggs in excavated nests. Females lay them and males follow behind fertilising them. The care of the nests and rearing of the young is carried out by adolescent Haciendans who range from about two to four metres in length. Parenting does not seem to be important, but communal care is. Once they exceed four metres, they become fully-fledged members of the commune. That takes about five years. Most of the simple education is imparted before they reach two metres in length and it continues throughout their lives.'

'What do they think about us?' asked the president.

'The Haciendans are curious. They understand that we have come from another star system, that we live around eighty or ninety years and only have one or two children. As far as we can tell, they normally live for well over a hundred years.'

'How many eggs do they lay?' asked the captain.

'Transparent eggs are laid in clutches of five or six and most have three or four clutches when adult. Survival rate is not high. Many of the eggs are never fertilised and die quickly. Hatching occurs several weeks after fertilisation. Some fertilised eggs never hatch owing to defects like fungus attacking them,' said Campbell, projecting a clutch of eggs on another monitor for the group to see. Some were white, viable eggs were transparent. Small, curled-up creatures were stationary or moving around within them.

'What's the reproduction rate?'

'Difficult to be sure, but we think each adult has between one and five offspring during their lives. There are no family groups. The young are always looked after by the adolescents.'

'So not too different from humans, number-wise?' asked the captain.

'No. Broadly similar.'

'What about their intellectual and scientific knowledge?' asked the president.

Campbell swiped across his tablet until he found the relevant page. 'They seem to be as intelligent as us, but they have directed it into the arts and enjoyment of life. There's virtually no industry, and we did not see much advanced technology, although they do have electronics and use radio and video for communication with other local communities. Shortwave is used for communication over greater distances. Their knowledge of their own environment is extensive. They consider anything with a brain to be protected, even if it's a simple creature like the wrigglers.'

Mike broke in and said, 'If you remember, one of the first things they did when we met was to release wrigglers which we were studying in a cage.'

Berry added, 'They don't like us keeping the cats and guinea pigs in compounds either, but we explained how they could be devastating to the native animals if allowed to run free. They accepted it, but reluctantly.'

'Yes,' said Campbell, 'they don't like seeing creatures in captivity and they don't eat anything with a brain. Within their cities, they have pits where they keep a class of creatures we have called urchins. They come in many different types, have protective shells and the inside is primarily muscle for moving around. The Haciendans crack the shells and eat the contents. Urchins are considered to be animals without brains, are easy to keep, and provide ample supplies of food.'

'What about astronomy et cetera?' asked the captain.

'Right,' said Campbell, looking for that section within his notes. 'They're aware of Kepler-452 and call it Hotwhitewave. The system of planets is known to them, and they have and use telescopes. We know they have a two-metre telescope at the city where we're being educated. Stars are believed to be suns like Hotwhitewave, so they have that right and they understand the structure of the Milky Way but were not aware of the trillions of other galaxies. Their astronomical knowledge would seem to be at a level we had in the nineteen-twenties. They understand that we come from Sol and that it's many light-years from here. They consider us to be explorers and are fascinated by video and images of Earth that we've shown them. However, they expressed no desire to visit their moons, nor Kepler. We found that a little strange, but it emphasises their belief that they are at one with the nature on their world.'

Altera added, 'They spend a large amount of time on their own with their equivalent of books – cylinders, ten centimetres in diameter and about forty centimetres long. We've seen many of them holding these devices which produce a kaleidoscope of colours. They also play games.'

'What sort of games?' asked the president, pulling himself back from a rotating position behind his desk.

Altera continued, 'We've observed them wrestling or tussling with each other; also, a team sport with a large spherical object which is tossed to and fro. There seem to be board games too. One, like chess is played by two beings, but some others involve four or five hovering over gameboards up to three metres on a side, with objects which they move around.'

'One-elder told us they'd teach us a couple of games in the next few weeks,' said Campbell.

'So, this learning process is likely to be lengthy?' asked the captain.

'We think so,' answered Campbell.

'Did you get around to discussing why we're here?' asked the captain.

'Not as such,' said Campbell. 'We thought it best to learn as much as possible about them before bringing up something so delicate.'

'They don't know why we left Earth?' asked the president.

'That didn't arise. I didn't want to throw into the conversation something like, "Which part of your world can our thousands of people aboard the ship come and occupy?" in the middle of our trying to create a rapport.'

'We need to know,' said the captain, oblivious to Campbell's sarcasm. 'There's serious unrest beginning among the Kepler population. They're fed up with being imprisoned on the ship when they can see you five enjoying freedom on the planet's surface.'

'We're incredibly busy down here. Learning a language using colours isn't like learning French. It's hard work,' said Altera.

'I understand that but the crew and councillors are now being lobbied regularly about progress,' said the captain. 'Nothing you've told us will ease that situation. It could make it worse.'

'Someone needs to clarify the difficulties for them,' said Mike.

The president broke in. 'We're conscious of not wanting to alarm the general populace.'

'Holding back information will not go down well when it's discovered,' said Altera.

'I think you should keep them updated with all the facts,' said Campbell.

'We will, of course, consider that,' said the captain, becoming even more prickly.

'Frankly,' said Martina, breaking into the discussion, 'we need to find out a lot more about their world. We can't afford to create a situation like the American Indians. We don't have any right to occupy their planet.'

'There's no choice,' said Captain Blaney.

'There is *always* a choice,' said Campbell. 'We must discover what the other continents are like. How much of their world do they occupy? Are there any locations where they don't live, and could we live in those? We need time to find out such information without just blurting out that we're here to stay and which part of their world are they willing to sacrifice for us.'

'The problem,' said the president, 'is that we can't see their colonies from space. They're too well camouflaged the way they manipulate their spangledsepiacandy tree canopies.'

'Are there areas without forests? Any more arid land masses? I seem to remember seeing lots of more arid land before we launched,' Campbell asked.

'We haven't been looking,' said the president.

'Well, it's about time some of you up there took some responsibility and gave us some information to work with,' said Campbell. 'I don't like the way we're the only source of information. Build a bigger telescope or something!'

'*Commander Ovarnold!*' said the captain aggressively. 'Kindly remember who you're talking to.'

'Then give us more to work with, *ma'am!*' he snapped back.

'Settle down now,' interjected the president. 'I'm sure we're all doing our best. Captain, can we build better surveillance equipment?'

'We haven't needed it,' said the captain.

'We have needed it,' said Campbell. 'It's just that nobody has bothered.'

'That is not fair, Ovarnold. I'll progress it now that I know it's needed,' said the captain, more sympathetically.

'Thank you. Please keep us informed,' said Campbell. 'Is there anything else you need from us now?'

'No. I don't think so. We'll set balls rolling up here as soon as we can,' said the president. 'Won't we, Captain?'

'Indeed. Ovarnold, continue to keep us fully informed,' said the captain stiffly, and the signal to the monitor ceased.

'Phew!' said Mike, letting out a long breath. 'Well done. They're expecting too much of us. We're only a first expedition.'

'We could do with some diplomatic help. Should we ask them to send down some people more qualified to deal with intelligent aliens? I feel out of my depth,' said Campbell.

'You've been doing a wonderful job. Think how far we've come already,' said Berry. 'Anyone new they sent down would be at an immediate disadvantage. We're just beginning to understand each other.'

'I'm dreading the question, "Why are you here?" and how to answer it,' said Campbell.

'We're explorers,' said Altera, allowing a cat to get off her lap and head to the galley in search of food.

'We could say that but it's a white lie. We're also

colonists,' said Campbell apprehensively. 'We mustn't be deceitful, or it will certainly lead to a bad outcome.'

'True,' said Martina. 'We must be honest with them when the time comes.'

'Let's call it a night. Altera, Mike and I need to be back in school first thing tomorrow,' said Campbell finishing a container of marginally alcoholic beer Mike had been fermenting from the root of a ginger-like plant he'd been studying.

Chapter Twenty-Nine

CONSPIRATORS

Eric Cho was born in 40SBY to parents who had also been born on Kepler. He was quickly orphaned at the age of five when his parents were both killed during a meteor strike on a production unit in which they were working. An elderly grandparent, born on Earth, stepped in to do her best to raise him but Eric railed against everyone and everything. He believed that the ship had murdered his parents. He became isolated at school and extremely rebellious, many times being found guilty of misdemeanours, fighting, bullying, and just downright disruptive and antisocial behaviour. In his later youth he found himself being punished for crimes he'd made no attempt to conceal. As he reached adulthood, he became increasingly secretive, was an accomplished thief and took great pride in outwitting the authorities.

From time to time, he joined various societies and factions, trying to turn most of them against authority. Most clubs threw him out of their ranks. Those who tolerated him usually found him to be a quiet, but sinister, member.

He didn't want to become an official of any club, and kept his disruption and growing anger under enough control to become a useful, but hardly valued, member of protest groups.

When conspiracy theories indicated that the Haciendans might not accept humans on their planet, Eric Cho sought the company of those who were becoming impatient with progress. A current female partner, Anne, took him along to a meeting of a group she was involved with and Eric seemed to find it the exact match for his personal hatred of imprisonment on the Kepler starship.

The lighting was sufficiently subdued to give the impression immediately that the meeting was clandestine. The room on deck eighty-eight of Kepler was designed as one of dozens of social clubs for the use of the passengers. Double doors opened onto a corridor, which led to the D-sector elevators. Light outside shone so much brighter than inside that its glow framed the doorway, and frosted windows in the doors cast a warm light into the room.

In one corner stood a curved bar with four tall barstools. There were no optics, bottles or other drinks on show, and the draught beer handles had long since pumped the last of their amber liquids. Two three-seater black synthetic leather sofas and four matching armchairs formed a group close to the bar, and a similar set stood on the far side of the room, which measured about fifteen metres square though, it wasn't quite square because the natural segmenting of the ship determined that the walls to the right and left of the entrance diverged to a noticeable degree.

A dark green mottled carpet covered the floor, almost threadbare at the doorway, and the tired wall covering was in subdued shades of the same colour. Even the brass wall lights seemed to be muted, perhaps operating at fifty percent of full power. No one knew why this room had fallen into such neglect, but it was convenient in its anonymity.

Nine people occupied the plush but worn seats nearest the bar. Five men and three women, all in their late forties or early fifties, meaning that they had all been born during the journey and, more importantly, had never set foot on Earth or any other planet.

They were Eric Cho, his partner Anne, Frank, Gus, Harry, Jean, Lionel, Pauline, and Stewart. Pauline and Stewart were Black; Eric was heavily built and part Oriental; and Anne mixed Caucasian and Black. The other four were White, although, to be honest, they all seemed to exhibit some characteristics of mixed heritage, as did the majority of Kepler's youngest passengers. The policy of mixing gene pools was beginning to have an effect.

Eric immediately struck up a friendship with Gus Ovstark, a swarthy but short individual with thinning hair. He'd also been orphaned by a shipboard accident and shared Eric's hatred of life on the starship.

All of the group expressed a hatred of and impatience with the longwinded negotiations being carried out on the planet.

Harry Goodwin, a tall smart-looking individual with a military air, opened proceedings. 'Thank you all for coming. As you know, I'm a bridge officer. I'm going to pass on certain confidences, so I'd appreciate you not letting others know from where the information is coming.'

'No. You're okay, mate, but why are you doing it?' said Jean, keen to be supportive, and others mumbled agreement.

'My half-brother was on Pioneer, the lander which skipped off the atmosphere. They lost their lives because they were one second early cutting off the rocket. Such a stupid way to die. The powers that be just went straight ahead and launched another one without any additional automatic safety systems. It's incompetence and now they're holding back on information about the negotiations.'

'How'd you mean?' asked Gus.

Harry continued, 'Unless you're one of the elite officers, you're being kept in the dark and no one is asking you for ideas or suggestions. It's really begun to rankle.' He crossed his legs and leaned back into the upholstery of one of the chairs. 'You've all been watching the landing team in one or other of the theatres. Did you notice that most of the work seems to be being conducted by just two or three of them. We hardly ever see Commander Campbell Ovarnold or Pilot Altera Ovindsingh.'

'No. Why is that?' asked Pauline.

'Every day, they've been travelling to the city of the Haciendans to learn their language and culture. Apparently, they've become pretty fluent, and the others have been joining them, one at a time, so that they're all becoming proficient,' informed Harry.

'What's it mean for us, then? You got some sort of plan?' asked Eric.

'You may well ask,' said Harry. 'We can all guess that it will lead to negotiations to settle on the planet, but it's becoming problematical.'

'How?' asked Anna.

'Commander Ovarnold and Pilot Ovindsingh are going soft,' said Harry, lowering his voice as if in fear of being overheard. 'And it's being exacerbated by the captain and president being too lenient with them. When I asked about progress at the last bridge meeting, I was shut down curtly. No one is being allowed to make suggestions.'

'Going soft?' asked Eric, leaning forward with his elbows on his knees, and a belligerent look in his eyes.

'At the last meeting with the captain and the president, they were raising significant concerns about withholding the reason for our journey from the aliens,' Harry said. 'They're afraid to tell them.'

'What the hell does that mean?' asked Stewart.

'The captain pushed them on raising the issue and they said they weren't ready and thought that the aliens might refuse to let us land.'

'No!' came from several of the group.

'Yes! They asked the captain to try to find other continents where we could land and where there were no aliens. More arid or frozen or equatorial places perhaps.'

'That'd mean starting all over again to learn about the new areas,' said Lionel, 'and they've wasted fucking months already!'

'Exactly!' said Harry. 'We're stuck here on this flying saucer while they're enjoying the thrill of a new world.'

Gus refilled his glass from a clear bottle of mulberry-coloured liquid and passed it to his right. 'Don't like the sound of this,' he said. 'Spent eighty years getting here and while they gallivant around on the surface, we're stuck on this sodding frisbee.'

'What if the aliens decide we can't live on the planet?' asked Pauline.

'Ovarnold and Ovindsingh are saying we have no right to take away their land. It would be like the Red Indians,' said Harry.

'The what?' asked Gus.

'The politically incorrect name for Native Americans,' said Anne.

'You've lost me, luv,' said Gus.

Anne explained, 'When the Europeans arrived in America, they stole the land from the Native Americans and put them in reservations. They called them Red Indians because, at first, they thought they'd reached the East Indies. North America was a new continent.'

'Why can't we do that with the aliens?' asked Gus. 'That'd solve it.'

'It's reprehensible,' said Anne, shocked at the suggestion. 'No one ever forgave the people of the USA and Canada for doing that.'

'Yeah,' said Gus, 'but they had the whole of Europe to go back to. We've got nowhere. Where the hell could *we* go?'

'Right!' said Jean, who'd been sitting quietly until then. 'We can't be expected to just *leave*!'

The bottle of mulberry-coloured gin was empty, and Eric stood, lumbered over to a bag near the door and fetched another one. He twisted the top and poured himself another glass before passing it around again. 'Nice gin you brought, Gus, this,' he said, sampling the new glassful.

'Aye, very good,' said Stewart.

'Harry, you seem to be telling us this for a reason. What is it? What point are you trying to make?' asked Lionel.

Harry leaned forward, looking left and right to those on either side of him, and lowered his voice still further. 'The aliens are like giant jellyfish. They have very little technology and live in tunnels in the forests. They eat things like raw sea urchins, and their lives are nothing like ours. I reckon we could take a section of their world by force and there'd be nothing they could do to stop us.'

'What? Wipe them out?' asked Stewart.

Frank, who'd said nothing up until then, stood up and said, 'I've heard enough. I'm not getting involved. I'm off!' He marched out of the room.

'No!' shouted Anne at the same moment. 'We can't hurt them. It would be unconscionable.' Eric looked around at her in disgust. Although they slept together occasionally, she riled him with her holier-than-thou attitude.

Anne's attack and Frank walking out took Harry aback, and he sat upright in his chair. 'We don't have to wipe them out. We could just leave them in peace and set up our own colonies, industries and cities around or beside them. Their lives and living requirements would not affect ours,' said Harry, beginning to fear that he had gone too far. He wanted to whip up support, not create a revolution.

'I don't see why a few more of us can't go down,' said Lionel.

'Practicalities,' said Anne. 'The ship only has a limited number of landers which can go both ways. Each needs a tank and booster to get back up to the ship.'

'That's true,' said Harry. 'The colonist landers are one-way only. If things go badly, there'll be no return to the ship. We'd be stuck on the planet, perhaps in the middle of a war.'

'But they've got no weapons,' said Gus, 'or have they?'

'We don't *think* they have any weapons,' said Harry, 'but we can't be sure. We don't have much weaponry either.'

'What do we have?' asked Gus.

'Down there, we have pistols which fire compressed air or projectiles. Those projectiles wouldn't stop the aliens. They're huge, many metres long and wide, like bloody whales,' said Harry. 'The expedition does have a couple of grenade launchers in the habitat store for causing distractions. Those could do damage, but there's little ammunition for them. They are last-resort weapons.'

'There are portable machine guns in one of the storage areas on Kepler. Seen them on the inventory,' said Pauline.

'Didn't know that. They'd be handy. Could we get some?' asked Gus, suddenly quite excited.

'Don't know, I'll check,' she replied.

'We could make more,' said Eric. 'There are plenty of machine shops on the ship. Shouldn't be too difficult to repurpose one to make weapons. We should be making preparations for a war.'

'True,' said Harry, helping himself to a little more mulberry-coloured gin.

'Come on, Harry, why have you gathered us today?' asked Stewart.

'I'm concerned that we could end up in a situation where we have to abandon this world and go on to another star system. I want to set up a group who will fight for us to colonise Hacienda,' said Harry. 'One way or another!'

'Which other star system, where, how far away?' asked Eric.

'We don't have any other star systems that we can be certain have habitable planets. Distance doesn't matter though,' said Harry.

'How can it not matter?' asked Gus, his voice rising in frustration as he realised his own ignorance of scientific matters.

'It's the acceleration and deceleration which takes the bulk of the time. A five light-year journey takes almost the same time as a one thousand light-year journey. When you're close to light speed the distance shrinks remarkably,' said Harry. 'We've just travelled sixteen hundred and forty-two light-years in only eighty years shipboard time.'

'What's the chance of finding another habitable planet?' asked Eric. 'No one ever fucking mentioned that possibility in school.'

'They did,' said Anne. 'You were probably not paying attention.'

'I don't like your attitude, woman,' he retorted.

'I assure you it's mutual!' she said.

'Calm down everyone. The truth is that we really don't know. This one was found by a lot of work done using three enormous space telescopes in Earth orbit. We don't have such tools,' said Harry.

'Well, bugger that!' said Gus. 'We have a perfectly pleasant world here. We should take it. I'm for an invasion.'

'We can't take away someone else's planet,' protested Anne. 'There must be a way of negotiating for some land.'

'We only need part of it,' said Eric, taking another glass of gin. He was becoming inebriated.

'Well, it all must be negotiated. We can't take it by force,' said Anne.

'Damn it all. Why did you even come to this meeting,' asked Gus. 'Whose side are you on?'

'I want us to be settled here, but it must be done fairly. I say give them time,' she replied. 'Also, we may start as only a few thousand people, but on Earth it didn't take a lot of time for the population to grow into the billions. We're a very untrustworthy and greedy species.'

Harry said, 'My plan is that if negotiations fail, we take ten or twenty colonist landers, by force, and head for one of the equatorial continents where it's believed there are no Haciendans living. Once we've landed no one can do anything about it. There's no way to bring us back. Once we're there, we're there permanently.'

The group fell into silence at this, each considering their own needs and desires.

'We must do *something*,' said Eric, becoming angry.

'I think we should pressure them for more action,' said Stewart, who had been pondering it for a while.

'That's why I called this meeting,' said Harry, 'but I'm an officer. I can't pressure the captain, but if the rest of you head away from here and gather more support, you *can* pressure the captain through the council and president.'

Anne said, 'I'm fine with pressing for more action, but not for any use of force against the aliens.'

'It might damn well come to that,' said Gus.

'We must try all other methods first,' she replied.

'Blow them out of the water!' said Eric under his breath. 'I'm for direct action. To hell with people's sensitivity!'

'Anne's right,' said Harry. 'We don't want to overthrow the ship's order – we need to bend it to our will. You need to gather support and numbers, quietly and efficiently then hold a series of huge protests with hundreds of protesters. That *will* force their hand. I'll try to find out more about how to steal the colonist landers.'

'Who's going to coordinate things?' asked Lionel, clenching and unclenching his fists.

Harry said, 'Stewart is very level-headed. I think you should give him the first opportunity.'

Stewart stood up. He wasn't huge but was one of those distinguished-looking people who could command respect. 'I'll give it a go,' he said. 'Will you all follow me.'

'Show of hands,' said Harry.

Six hands rose, all but Gus and Harry himself.

'Gus, what's the problem?' asked Stewart.

'I'd like more action, but I'll follow you for now,' said Gus, his words just slightly slurred from the effects of the gin.

'Okay,' said Harry. 'That's settled. I'll keep in touch with Stewart. I need to ensure the rest of the officers don't suspect that I'm the leak on this. I don't know what security there is on the colonist landers, so I'll work behind the scenes to find out.'

'Right,' said Stewart, 'everyone here on Tuesday. Bring any like-minded colonists, but… and this is important… emphasise that we're a peaceful group. We should be careful not to encourage the wrong sort. Violence will be our very last option and could be our undoing.'

'But it *is* an option,' said Eric, and it was more a statement than a question. Gus nodded in agreement.

'The very *last* option!' Stewart repeated strongly.

Chapter Thirty

A CLOSER LOOK

Kepler was built to contain several vital machine shops and workshops. The designers thoroughly explored all the scenarios the ship might encounter during its interstellar journey and further requirements for when it arrived at its destination. One of these was the possibility that Kepler-452b would be unsuitable for habitation and the ship would need to source a new target planet.

Tucked away on deck thirty-two was an extremely well-protected store. Inside, it was about twenty metres by thirty metres with racking down each side and a double-sided rack down the middle. It smelled musty, was dusty, and looked as if it hadn't been entered for decades. It held the components for several telescopes, including a mirror for a giant two-metre telescope. There were also mirrors for a one-metre and a half-metre telescope.

Two ship's engineers, Barry Heddon and Jacques Duprall, and a navigation officer, Helen Osiro, were carefully unpacking the half-metre mirror. Anything larger would be unlikely to be usable for studying the planet's surface.

The wooden lid, marked in bright red paint, 500MM MIRROR, OPEN WITH CARE, and EXTREMELY FRAGILE, was lifted off and placed to one side, well clear of the open box. Helen began removing layers of felt, folded and protecting the mirror's vital surface. Any marks or scratches would degrade its light-collecting power. Finally, the mirror itself could be seen.

'Wow. Beautiful,' said Helen.

'That's one piece of incredible engineering,' said Barry.

'I think we'd be best repacking it and taking the whole case to the engineering section,' said Jacques.

'It would be safer,' agreed Helen. 'It's too delicate to move unprotected. Where's the rest of the telescope?'

'There,' said Jacques, pointing at a couple of tall crates strapped to the wall of the store. 'I'll call for some help with those. We'll need a trolley for the mirror. That'll be heavy.'

'It says thirty kilograms on the side of the case,' said Helen.

'Yep, we'll need a trolley,' said Jacques. 'What's it needed for?'

'Captain Blaney wants to study some of the other continents, so a large telescope is needed,' said Helen.

'Why?' asked Barry. 'Are things going badly with the aliens?'

'Firstly, they're *not* aliens,' said Helen. 'It's their planet. I think the captain wants to get a better understanding of other continents to save sending expeditions down.'

'Yeah. Suppose so,' Barry said. 'Can't afford to use renewable landers for places we might not colonise.'

'That's probably it,' agreed Helen.

Five days after the confrontational meeting between the exploration crew, the captain and the president, engineering had assembled the 500mm telescope and relocated it to a room off the bridge, which would be used as the observatory.

The room was small, only about four metres square, with the lens mounted within an open framework directed towards a plexiglass window facing the planet. Chairs allowed observers to sit in relative comfort, and a moving image of the surface was rushing by on a two-metre monitor, in front of which was a console bearing controls.

The lighting was subdued to prevent reflections in the plexiglass window; just a small lamp illuminated the monitor controls, and a little light was being cast onto the floors by architectural tubes set low in the walls, to allow people to move around without tripping over obstructions.

'Has it been calibrated?' asked Captain Blaney as she sat down in the most central of the seats. President Ovpetrangle sat beside her.

'It has,' said Helen. 'There are no aberrations in the mirror so excellent magnification. I've had the monitor on the wall set up so that it shows whatever the lens sees.'

'What magnification?' asked President Ovpetrangle, examining the framework that held the telescope in position.

'The engineers have installed three lenses, so we can choose low, medium and high,' said Helen.

'And what's high?' asked the president.

'It would resolve objects at about half a metre in size, so the Haciendans would be revealed, and humans would be just about detectable,' replied Helen.

'That's disappointing,' said the captain.

'We couldn't go to any higher magnification because Kepler is moving too fast over the surface,' said Helen. 'It can track objects for a few seconds only.'

'Track?' asked the president.

'Keep them central in the monitor,' said Helen. 'It would be better using a lower resolution if it's only the Haciendans we're trying to see or if an idea of the general terrain is enough.'

'We're interested in the other continents,' said the captain.

'This giant lens can only see what is within a few degrees of straight ahead. We can't swing it around in here. To do that it would have to be mounted outside. That would need a lot of engineering,' said Helen.

'So, we're not much further forward,' said the president.

'What exactly are you wanting to see?' asked Helen.

'Haciendan communities on the other continents,' said the captain.

'Well, we know there are none on the continents at the poles and two large continents near the equator are mainly arid, so we'd see their plant-cities quite easily and there are none on any of them,' said Helen. 'We can tell that from the scopes we're currently using.'

'Yes, but they'd not be good places for us, either,' said the president.

'Why not ask the Haciendans if there are any continents they're not using?' asked Helen.

'Because it raises issues we're not prepared to discuss yet… and this is all in confidence, Lieutenant Osiro,' said the captain.

'Of course, ma'am,' Helen said. 'I did tell you that the

large telescopes would not really help with observing the surface.'

'That's all, Osiro. You're dismissed,' said the captain, who always became prickly if her knowledge or expertise were questioned.

But Osiro wasn't finished, 'We could rig up a high-speed camera and record the view. Then you could play it back slowly and examine the detail more closely.'

'We'll ask if we need that,' said the captain.

The captain and president watched the monitor for about twenty minutes. Even at low magnification, the ground was flying by far too fast to be useful.

'It's not going to help,' said the president.

'I'll ask Commander Ovarnold to ask some questions about the other continents,' said the captain. 'We need to move things along. What do you think?'

'I agree, but it will need to be done with care,' replied the president, who often felt the captain was a little too gung-ho for his liking.

Chapter Thirty-One

FORCING THE ISSUE

The exploration team enjoyed a leisurely supper in the habitat while discussing the recent information from Kepler and the video which had been provided to help them try to lead the Haciendan elders along the path to discussing other continents. There still had been no questions raised by either party about why the humans were visiting Hacienda. As time went by, Campbell and Altera were becoming increasingly uneasy about the issue and both experienced sleepless nights. They knew that several thousand colonists' hopes and fears rested on their ability to come to a good solution.

It all seemed so unfair to Campbell. The exploration team's duty was to examine the planet and decide whether or not the natural environment would be suitable for a human colony. They had not expected to find intelligent lifeforms. It changed everything. Yes, they'd been trained on first-contact protocols, but there were experts on the ship who could have accompanied them if they'd known about the Haciendans before descending.

The captain, president, and council were obsessed with the fact that there were limited return landers available and were reluctant to send a support team down.

It was all on Campbell and his team's shoulders so he would just have to do his best.

'So,' Campbell began, 'are we all happy with the planned strategy for the next visit to Orangiegreen?'

There was general assent, but Martina said, 'The video is likely to raise the issue of colonisation, no matter how careful you are.'

'Yes, we know,' said Altera.

'We'll play it by ear and try to be noncommittal,' said Campbell.

'Could be easier said than done,' added Mike. 'Just the two of you going today?'

'Fewer chances of getting caught out,' said Campbell.

'I still think that honesty is the best course,' said Berry, collecting the used crockery and cutlery and heading towards the small galley area.

'We're not going to lie to them,' said Campbell defensively.

'No? Does being deceitful count?' shouted Berry from the galley.

'We'll do our best,' said Altera loudly so that her opinion would reach Berry. She didn't like intrigue or politics.

'Right,' said Campbell, jumping up. 'Early night for us two. Want to be fresh in the morning.'

He entered his sleeping cubicle and quickly undressed and set his alarm. The sleeping quarters were only two by three metres with a single bed, and storage facilities for clothes. A small desk with a laptop upon it sat in the corner of the opposite wall. The décor was military with green, khaki, and olive walls, carpet, and bed linen. Minutes later, Altera quietly opened the door and slid into bed with him. Twenty minutes of serious, necessarily silent lovemaking eased their tensions. The others didn't know about their affair, and they wanted to keep it that way. They clung tightly together afterwards, comforted, but anxious about the forthcoming day. Campbell thought he might lie awake pondering possible conversations with the Haciendans, but, in the end, the lovemaking sent him swiftly to sleep. Altera lay still in the warmth of his arms, the combination of the continual two-way education and the anxiety about their making a mistake diplomatically, preying on her mind.

The next morning, one of the Haciendan's floating transports arrived to collect Campbell and Altera. It was some ten metres long and two wide with helium-filled inflated surrounds for protection against the undergrowth. Normally the transports were only a carrying device, so were flat-bottomed and functional, but this one had been specially adapted. It contained three rows of two seats, which could be more easily used by humans.

The Haciendans themselves only ever seemed to travel under their own power, so had no cars, trains or aeroplanes. The explorers learned that any of the beings wanting to travel any great distance would absorb more helium into their bodies and fly at about four to five hundred metres in altitude. They could sleep en route, just floating wherever they were, then continue their journey the next day. However, the humans had learned that journeys of over five hundred kilometres were rarely undertaken.

They climbed aboard and settled into the comfortable

seats for the journey to Orangiegreen, propping a large monitor between the seats. The transports were not autonomous. This one was driven by another creature, which had sufficient intelligence to understand simple orders. It sat at the front of the transport behind a protective screen.

'I wonder why they never built roads,' mused Altera.

'I think travel between their communities is not a priority,' Campbell replied. 'And, anyway, the transports float owing to the helium.'

The driver looked for all the world like a coloured jellyfish. Its dome extended to a metre and, unlike the earthly scyphozoa jellyfish, these had four eyes, one on each side of the domed body. There were also tentacles, which draped over the raised section of the transport where it sat. The controls were simple – up, down, forward and back, and within a few seconds they were travelling at about thirty kilometres per hour and would soon arrive at the Haciendan city.

Entering the meeting room, Campbell set up a tripod and Altera mounted the one-metre monitor, angling it so that both they and the Haciendan elders could see it.

The usual welcoming pleasantries took place, then a being they called Most-Elder, asked about the large monitor.

'We have some video to show you to explain one or two things which still puzzle us,' said Campbell.

More colours covered Most-Elder's foreparts, and Campbell's tablet translated it as, 'Only one or two?' followed by a sequence which represented humour or laughing, then: 'If it were only one or two!'

Both Campbell and Altera repeated the laughing colours on the new monitor.

'What is it which puzzles you so, that you needed to bring this larger device?' asked Two-Elder.

Altera said, 'Our research team on Kepler have been looking at the rest of your world. They have built up a full picture of your continents. This is a video showing your entire planet.'

A globe of Hacienda filled the screen, rotating slowly around its normal vertical axis, but also rotating in a polar orbit so that the whole sphere could be seen.

Most-Elder said, 'That is fascinating. We have produced globes of our world many times, but we have never visited space. This is a unique experience for us.'

All three elders present closed in on the monitor and watched the video for a good ten minutes. They appeared enthralled.

'Beautiful,' said Two-Elder.

'It is, indeed,' said Campbell, who pressed a button on his tablet menu and caused the globe to stop spinning. The camera zoomed in on the continent they were currently on.

'This is where we are now,' said Campbell.

'We do know our land masses,' said Three-Elder.

'Of course,' said Campbell, causing the video to zoom in on one of the arid equatorial continents. 'These areas seem warmer than here with less predictable winds and weather. The entire eastern side of this continent appears to be desert, although conditions don't seem to be as dry on the west.'

'We find that region to be less than pleasant. We rarely cross it,' said Most-Elder. 'When we do, we do so at altitude to keep our temperatures down.

'But you have explored it?' asked Campbell.

'We have. What is it you wish to know? We cannot grow spangledsepiacandy trees there so prefer to live here,' said

Two-Elder, moving closer to the screen to examine the detail.

'We were hoping to contact one of your communities which lives there to see if they could give us scientific data about the region,' said Campbell, following the strategy that the captain's diplomatic team had suggested.

'No one lives there. We just pass through. As Two-Elder said, it is not suitable for our dwellings. Living outside in such heat would not be good for us,' said Most-Elder.

That was a plus, thought Campbell.

'How about this area, which seems to be a number of islands in the southern temperate region?' asked Altera.

'Ah, yes. That region is known generally as Blueyellow-starsland,' said Two-Elder.

'There are many of us living there,' said Most-Elder.

'How do you communicate with them?' asked Campbell – another crucial question he'd been instructed to ask.

'Radio,' said Most-Elder.

'You bounce it off the ionosphere?' asked Campbell.

'We don't know a word for it, but very short radio waves get to the other land masses. What is the ionosphere?' asked Most-Elder.

'There's a layer of charged ions in the upper atmosphere which lets short wavelength signals reflect off it. On Earth we used telecommunication satellites to communicate over vast distances. You've never sent anything to orbit?' asked Campbell.

'We never developed the rockets you have told us about,' said Most-Elder.

'How about this continent?' asked Altera, allowing the camera to zoom in on the southern pole.

'This place is too cold for our species,' said Two-Elder.

'Some brave individuals have tried to reach the southern

axis point, but have never returned,' said Most-Elder. 'The same with the northern axis continent. We did have radio contact with them, but they still died of cold. That was many years ago.'

'I can understand that,' said Campbell.

'We're very sorry to hear of their deaths,' added Altera. 'Many died trying to reach our own South Pole, or axis point, but being warm-blooded, we can protect ourselves from the cold far more easily than you.'

'Warm-blooded?' asked Three-Elder.

'Our bodies regulate our temperature. You can live only within certain temperature ranges,' said Altera.

'That's correct. If we get cold weather, we must huddle down in our forests until it passes,' said Two-Elder. 'It makes us slow and lethargic.'

'Earth's axis has a serious tilt so as we pass around Sol, we have cold and warm seasons. I fear that would be a problem for your species,' said Altera.

'Indeed,' said Two-Elder.

'Thank you for answering those questions for us,' said Campbell. 'It will help us understand you.'

'How much time do you have?' asked Two-Elder.

The ambiguous question hit the humans out of the blue. Campbell and Altera exchanged meaningful glances.

'We have plenty of time,' said Campbell. This noncommittal answer might avoid the real question Campbell suspected the elders had.

'Two-Elder meant to ask when you are returning to Earth,' said Most-Elder.

No such luck. That was it. The question they'd been dreading. The entire exploration team had been working on how to deal with it when it was eventually asked. Now was crunch time.

'We cannot,' said Campbell.

'Why cannot?' asked Most-Elder.

'We don't know if our world still exists,' said Campbell. 'Our sun began to heat up, and it was becoming impossible to live anywhere except the axis points. Our scientists built Kepler and sent us here as they believed your planet might be habitable.'

'So, you are planning to stay here? You are not just visiting explorers?' asked Two-Elder.

'We're hoping you will allow us to settle somewhere on your planet,' said Campbell nervously, his heart in his mouth. Altera sat silently with fingers crossed.

There was no response. No colours to interpret, not even the ultra-rapid colourations which took place when the Haciendans were not worrying about the humans understanding.

How long should they wait, thought Campbell? He knew what he should say next but was hoping for a positive response before committing. He saw Altera's worried glance towards him. Had he waited long enough? It was all a matter of personal judgement.

Deciding he could wait no longer, he spoke. 'We don't have to settle on *this* continent, of course.'

Again, there was no response, although Two-Elder began to answer but a sharp crimson flash all over Most-Elder stopped him. The absence of any colours continued for at least a minute. Campbell felt that Most-Elder had asked for some thinking time.

Suddenly, Most-Elder produced a variety of colours, and then the humans were entertained by one of the Haciendans' rapid flashing communications. All were producing rapid colour swings. The humans' tablets produced just a garbled sequence of unintelligible words.

Campbell wondered if the beings knew that human technology couldn't eavesdrop on their conversations if they were done sufficiently rapidly.

Seconds ran into a minute or more before they stopped communicating. Most-Elder turned back to the humans and said, slowly enough for the tablets to translate, 'We need to discuss this with others. Today's lessons are at an end.'

All the elders turned and left through the green forest tunnel behind them.

'Shall we leave the monitor?' asked Altera.

Campbell switched off the translating software and said, 'Yes, we might need it again. Did that go well, or badly?'

'Difficult to say. Could be okay. Were they angry or just confused?'

'No idea. It looked like anger to me. I hope it wasn't. Let's head back to the transport,' Campbell said. 'We need to report to the ship.'

As if with the weight of the world on their shoulders, they slouched lethargically back to the transport and their otherworldly chauffeur, who had been waiting patiently.

Chapter Thirty-Two

CALL TO ARMS

The call to arms took everyone by surprise.

A chime came over the entire ship's public address system followed by Stewart Ovsmithson's voice. He'd psyched himself up to make the announcement as authoritative as possible.

'Everyone take note! We're all being misled by the captain and the council. Negotiations with the aliens on Hacienda have stalled. Many believe that they're about to turn us away, force us back to the ship and send us off, wandering the galaxy for the rest of our natural lives,' he said, loudly and with passion.

'Don't take my word for it. Go to the great meeting room at eight tonight and make it known that you will not stand for this bunch of jellyfish sending us away from a perfectly suitable planet.

'This announcement might be shut down at any moment. Don't be cheated out of the truth. Go to the great meeting room at eight where action is planned. Everyone should come. Arm yourselves with questions for the crew… if they dare even attend.

'Tell all your friends and…'

The PA was suddenly muted. The entire ship's complement was in shock. Never before had there been such an announcement. Was it true? Had negotiations failed? Were they to be sent packing, drifting through the cosmos for another eighty or ninety years… and what then? The next planet could be barren, or a fiery hell, or with a crushing or poisonous atmosphere, or with immense gravity. Surely some deal could be reached with the aliens.

The questions were many and varied. It seemed that the only way to get answers was to attend the call for the mass meeting.

Captain Blaney was apoplectic with rage. She'd called both bridge crews into her office. There was very little room, with some thirty officers standing shoulder to shoulder.

'Who is leaking information? Tell me now and I'll simply fire you. If you don't, then when I discover who it is, you will face a court-martial and a lengthy incarceration. Well?' she said with considerable anger, looking around the assembly, peering deeply into the eyes of crew members who might be suspect.

No one said anything. No timid arm was raised. No one looked guilty or had a red face. Most looked away when the captain's eyes focused on them. The silence was palpable. Harry stood to one side, looking as if butter wouldn't melt in his mouth. When the captain's gaze fell upon him, he returned it confidently.

First officer, Rose Russell said, 'Are we going to the meeting, Captain?'

'President Ovpetrangle, you're listening in. What's your view?' asked the captain, angry that the culprit hadn't come forward.

A video monitor mounted at head height on the wall of the captain's office, showed the president's head and shoulders. He looked uncharacteristically severe.

'I think we must go. If we don't then rumours will abound and we'll completely lose control,' he said, his voice sounding weak through the monitor's speakers.

'Agreed, but we should meet to discuss strategy, I'll come to your office with my key advisers,' said the captain.

'Now?' asked the president.

'Yes, now! There's no time to waste. Can you get one person from each of the sector councils there too, please?'

'Indeed,' he said.

Captain Blaney, her colour still raised, and wiping her brow, said, 'Is the culprit really going to hide among us? What a despicable individual. Surely you have the guts to admit your treachery.'

There was no reply, and the silence was only broken by shuffling bodies and hands.

'Okay. Dismissed. Senior officers with me to the president's office.'

The crush was quickly relieved as the off-duty officers departed and the others made their way back to their posts. Senior officers joined the captain as she pushed off into the corridor, and they swung from handhold to handhold like Tarzan, in the manner of those who were familiar with moving around in microgravity.

Captain Blaney arrived at the president's office with her deputy Arne Ovlarsen, a slim, blond Caucasian; first officer Rose Russell, a tall, slim, attractive Oriental; navigation officer; Greg Hardcastle, a heavy-set, Caucasian bodybuilder; second officer Ciorstaidh* Ovmacleod, petite and uncompromisingly Scottish; and chief engineer, Ivan Ovpopov, short and dumpy with a round face in tow. All were in full green duty uniforms.

The president was standing in his doorway when they approached along the corridor. He welcomed them and then said, 'I've commandeered meeting room one. Let's head along there. The six senior councillors will be there and the chief of police and his deputy.'

He closed his office door, and they all used the steel handholds to make their way along the corridor. They approached a nondescript doorway which led into a conference room. As it was in zero gravity, the scene inside was quite bizarre. The six councillors, one for each of the ship's sectors, were on short tethers, connected to brackets dotted around the cylindrical meeting room. Chief of police, Marco Andretti, a swarthy man of Eastern European descent; and his deputy, Ellen Ovlester, a grossly overweight Black woman, in blue police uniforms were hanging there too.

'Okay,' said the president. 'Attach yourselves and let's get started. Captain, you have the floor.' The walls of the meeting room gave voices an echoey feel.

'You will all have heard the call for a mass meeting in the great meeting room for eight tonight. We must attend and need a plan to deal with the crowd,' said the captain.

Marco Andretti said, 'We've managed to identify the

---

* Ciorstaidh is the Gaelic spelling of Kirsty

culprit. It's a man called Stewart Ovsmithson. They broke into the communications centre and threatened the staff on duty.'

'That's how they did it,' said the captain. 'Rose managed to cut off the transmission via the bridge override.'

'What is the situation on the ground?' asked the president.

'Not good. Commander Ovarnold and his deputy, Ovindsingh, were left hanging by the Haciendans,' began the captain.

She continued, 'The beings had finally asked about why we had landed, and our people very skilfully dealt with the initial problem. I've listened to the recording and Commander Ovarnold told them we have no planet to go back to, that it might have become uninhabitable, and that they were hoping to stay. There was a long silence, and he added that we didn't have to stay on their continent. The Haciendans went into one of their rapid colour shows, and the speed was such that the tablets couldn't translate. When that ended, the being known as Most-Elder told Ovarnold and Ovindsingh that they needed to retreat to discuss it, probably in some sort of governing council.

'Ovarnold and Ovindsingh left Orangiegreen and returned to Lavigne Base and reported back to me.'

'And there's been nothing further since?' asked one of the councillors.

'No. They're continuing their work at the base and awaiting further communication from the Haciendans,' replied the captain.

'How bad is it, do you think?' asked another councillor.

'That's the problem,' said the captain. 'We really don't

know. They might come back to us and say that everything's fine, but my gut feeling is that they won't.'

'Could we just overpower them?' asked another councillor.

'We think so,' said the president, 'but that is not something we should be considering. Any of you who don't know what happened to the Native Americans and native Australians when Europeans arrived on their continents, should take a lesson in the subject as soon as we finish here.'

'We think the best scenario would be to colonise one of the continents nearer to the equator,' said the captain. 'At least our negotiators have discovered that there are no Haciendans there owing to the heat and lack of the spangledsomething trees they grow their cities from.'

'I suggest,' said the president, clearing his throat, 'that I present the situation in the great meeting room and try to settle the people down, outlining why we cannot just take their planet by force and supporting more negotiation.

'However,' he continued, 'we must be prepared for violence. Chief Andretti, can you deputise a few citizens and be ready to enforce law and order if it gets out of hand?'

'We can try. I can't raise an army though. All I can do in a hurry is call on a dozen reservists, so that will total eighteen. I can arm them, and they all have uniforms,' the chief said, and thought for a moment. 'Eighteen armed police should be capable of discouraging any violence.'

'That sounds like a plan,' said the captain. 'Anything else Mr President?'

'No. That seems the best course of action. Meeting closed.'

After much clinking of tether clips, the assembly broke up and dispersed to their various posts.

Chapter Thirty-Three

REASONED ARGUMENT

Chief Andretti and his team of almost twenty armed police, resplendent in their blue Bermuda shorts uniforms, arrived in the great meeting room half an hour early.

They lined up to the right of the main stage, facing towards the two thousand empty seats. The room had only been full on two occasions, once over seventy years previously when the ship had a momentous meeting to discuss whether to return to Earth. The second occasion had been to celebrate Kepler entering orbit around Hacienda, when there was standing room only.

People were already arriving in dribs and drabs, clusters of curious citizens, unsure whether to sit or to stand. By ten minutes to eight, there were already two hundred seated in the front rows, with more arriving continuously.

Councillors and crew made their way onto the stage from another entrance as eight o'clock approached. Last to enter were the captain, her deputy and the president, who all took their usual seats at the centre of the stage.

At eight precisely, the president struck the table in front

of him with a gavel. Latecomers were still arriving, but the bulk were already seated. The captain estimated the number to be between five and six hundred, and there was an uneasy babble of conversation filling the void. He struck the gavel a second time and a hush developed.

The president laid the gavel on the table and looked out over the throng. He spoke clearly and with authority. 'You will all have heard the announcement which was illegally made over the PA system. We have discovered that the individual concerned is one Stewart Ovsmithson.'

'The council have decided not to prosecute Ovsmithson and now invite him to take the podium and explain himself.' All the councillors, crew and police surveyed the crowd, looking for the man who had so upset the ship's routine.

For the best part of a minute, nothing happened. The president was just about to start speaking again when a tall, well-built, Black man of Afro-Caribbean descent walked down one of the meeting room's aisles towards the front. He climbed the six steps to the stage, stopped for a second, looking as if he'd never noticed the podium before, then mounted its spiral oak steps. One of the few pieces of genuine timber aboard Kepler, it was always polished to perfection, and a relief carving of the United Nations global map filled the front panel.

He spoke nervously and hesitantly, the microphone amplifying his words. 'My name is Stewart Ovsmithson. I'm an electrician and work mainly on domestic sections of the ship. Some of us have become seriously concerned about the negotiations with the aliens. We've heard rumours that they're going to force us to leave Hacienda and find a different world. We'd all be stuck on this ship for the rest of our natural lives so the aliens need to be forced to help us and what we want is the *truth!*' He had become louder throughout and shouted the last word.

Applause rang out spasmodically. Chief Andretti looked around, trying to ascertain which areas of the crowd seemed to support Ovsmithson, but there were no particularly large sections clapping.

Ovsmithson gripped the podium tightly, looked directly at the president and said, '*Well?*'

President Ovpetrangle fiddled with his gavel, shuffled his chair back and stood. He glanced towards the captain, who nodded back.

'Firstly, I must say that the expedition on the surface has been doing an excellent job. When we arrived in orbit, there was no sign of any civilisation on the planet, so, when the Haciendans arrived at Lavigne Base, it was a shock to one and all. The beings communicate using colours and there was a very steep learning curve for Commander Ovarnold and his deputy, Ovindsingh. They're now as fluent as it's possible to be in the Haciendan language, given that they're using tablets to film the colours and software to interpret them into English. The process has to be reversed to make our questions known to them. It's remarkable how well they have done,' said the president, leaning forward on the table.

'The expedition members couldn't just blurt out the reason we were here. Diplomacy was necessary, and the other day, Ovarnold was asking about other continents, hoping to find out exactly where the Haciendans had communities. We now know that the polar continents and those around much of the equator have the wrong conditions for the Haciendans to grow the trees they use to form their cities. That information was needed so that we could determine there were potential areas where we could live without affecting them.' He stood upright again. 'I'm sure few of you realise the care that has been taken in these negotiations. Mr Ovsmithson, your unauthorised rant discredits the fine work our explorers on the surface have been undertaking.'

Waving the gavel in front of him, the president continued, 'Unfortunately, it was at that point that the Haciendans asked why we had come to their planet. Ovarnold did his best to describe the destruction of Earth and this seemed to upset the three elders. We're not sure why. Colonisation had never been raised in previous discussions. The Haciendan elders terminated the meeting and we believe they are now holding their own discussions about how to proceed.'

'Are they going to tell us to leave?' shouted Eric, one of the conspirators, from the crowd. Chief Andretti made a mental note of what he looked like.

The president continued, 'No one should jump to *any* conclusions. So far, all we know is that they're considering the situation. We're awaiting them coming back to Lavigne Base to discuss the matter further.'

'What if they do tell us to leave?' shouted Eric again.

'We think that is unlikely,' said the president, 'but if that were the case, we'd think about occupying one of the other continents, but we're not at that stage yet.'

'Aren't they just deserts?' shouted Eric.

The president calmly answered, 'They are more arid than the Lavigne Base. That has the benefit of meaning there are no intelligent creatures living there for us to bother, and that there's no reason for them to object to our colonising them.'

Eric shouted again, 'Well, I for one don't want to live in a fucking desert!'

'Please, sir. There are children present,' said the president.

Councillor Chen, a small, stocky Oriental woman caught the president's attention and asked, 'Might I answer, Andy?'

The president sat, and Chen got to her feet. 'Good evening,' she said. 'I've been working with Mike Ovfinlay, the biologist with the landing team. He's been sending masses of data to me. I'm also a specialist in Earth agriculture and environments, so I know what I'm talking about.'

She picked up her computer tablet and waved it in front of her, then continued to speak clearly and confidently. 'I have been building up scenarios for all three major continental variations. Yes, where the Haciendans live is probably the most desirable, but the equatorial regions are perfectly suitable for us too. My studies have shown that, using technologies we have brought with us, we can turn desert into the promised land, so to speak. If you haven't read about how Egypt turned arid areas of the Sinai into vibrant crop growing regions, I suggest you visit the library.'

She laid the tablet on the table and continued, 'Even the polar regions can be very pleasant. On Earth, Greenland, the north of Canada, Scandinavia and Russia were all perfectly habitable. It's only the parts of those continents nearest the poles which are permanently frozen. The fringes would be lovely places to live and grow our crops.'

'Thank you, Councillor Chen,' said the president, standing once more. 'Mr Ovsmithson, I appreciate the concerns which led you to fire up this displeasure, but it's most premature. You need to trust us to continue to negotiate in good faith with the Haciendans, but you must also understand that we'll *not* take their land away from them by force. Anyone who thinks we should, would be advised to take a course in Australasian and North American history, not to mention how we dominated and almost wiped-out native populations in South America. Our record in Africa and India make difficult reading too. Do you understand better now?'

All eyes turned to the podium. Stewart Ovsmithson looked from the president down to the left side of the crowd in the meeting room, and back to the president. 'I understand, but we'd like to be better informed of progress.'

'You've been keeping us in the dark deliberately,' shouted Eric.

'There's no reason we'd do that,' said the president, 'but we understand your concerns and will try to keep you all up to date from now on. Now, let's all depart and I promise we'll provide a report on progress each week.'

With the uprising defused in the short term, the captain, the president, the crew, and councillors left through a side entrance while Chief Andretti and half his team stayed behind until the great meeting room was empty. The other half of his team left with the crowd, watching out for any signs of trouble in the corridors.

Bridge officer, Harry Goodwin, who'd begun the rumours, made his way back to his quarters with a sullen expression. He wasn't satisfied with the official situation and was already plotting another conspirators' meeting.

Meanwhile, on the surface of Hacienda, the beings were about to invite the humans to continue their discussions.

The floating transport and other worldly chauffeur arrived in the camp a few days later, relieving much of the anxiety that was keeping Campbell and Altera from sleeping soundly. They'd been concerned that there would be no further contact with the Haciendan elders, with the worrying possibility of some sort of conflict developing. They were as anxious as the population of Kepler, and with better cause. There was a distinct possibility of the elders asking them to leave.

Lavigne Base was, as always, full of activity. Mike was in the open-to-air laboratory, comparing the growth of wheat, barley and other important seeds in the Haciendan soil. Martina was assisting Altera in the study of the germination of plants that were local to the base, and Berry, as always, was concentrating deeply on her microscopes, determining which bugs were likely to cause problems in the medium to long term. She'd already developed a vaccine for a rash which had bothered each of them from time to time. The inoculation had promising results.

'Altera,' Campbell called, having seen the strange vehicle arrive from his location inside Discovery. 'The transport's here. You ready to leave?'

'Sure thing,' she replied. 'Be there in a minute.'

They both grabbed their lunch boxes, flasks and tablets and jumped aboard the alien machine. In seconds, they were heading through the forest, still marvelling at the array of flowers, which seemed to vary on almost every trip. The smells and sounds of the forest filled their senses.

A while later, they entered Orangiegreen, the tightly knit grown walls encompassing them as they plunged deep into the heart of the Haciendans' home city. They arrived in the central park area, where Reddo was awaiting them. How long had he been waiting? Did they communicate with the driver, Campbell wondered? And how?

Reddo gave his welcoming array of colours and led them towards the elders' meeting room. Normally he'd have left them there, but on that occasion, he stayed, and the humans noted that there were a further five Haciendans present. Not for the first time, Campbell wondered what the relationship was between Reddo, who they believed to be the community's overall leader, and the elders, who seemed to be revered for their wisdom. What did this larger contingent of beings mean to the humans' desire to colonise somewhere suitable?

Chapter Thirty-Four

DECEPTION

Once again, the conspirators met in their disused social club. This time, someone had brought finger food, and the booze had more variety.

Harry expressed disappointment that the powers that be had overcome the concerns of the ordinary citizens in the great meeting room. Inside, he was still seething at the fact that he wasn't counted among the elite crew and therefore knew little about the negotiations other than snippets he'd heard on the bridge.

'Well,' said Stewart, 'it seemed to me that the explanation was quite reasonable. I was satisfied.'

'So was I,' said Anne, becoming increasingly unsure why she'd become part of the group. 'I think we need to wait and see what happens.'

'I don't like it,' said Eric. 'There's no way I'm going to permit the captain to take us on another lifetime-long journey, especially with us having no way of knowing if the next star has any planets, let alone any as good as this one.'

'We need to make leaving a fucking impossibility,' said Gus.

'And how exactly would you achieve that?' asked Stewart.

'Simple. We commandeer one of the colonist landers. How many do they hold?' asked Gus, revealing his ignorance about the landers.

'Twelve,' said Harry.

'Right,' continued Gus, 'we pick a dozen people, six male, six female, and send them down to the surface. Those colonist landers are one-way vessels. They can never return. In fact, it would be better to commandeer a dozen. One hundred and forty-four colonists would be committed to staying. There aren't enough reusable landers to ever return the people to the Kepler.'

'Brilliant. That would force the issue,' said Eric.

'Where would you send them to?' asked Lionel. 'The Haciendan's continent or nearer the equator?'

'That's the tricky one to answer,' said Gus.

'And how do you plan to steal the landers?' asked Harry.

'We all know where they are,' said Gus. 'There are five hundred of them around the rim. I've seen the airlocks. Just get in and use them, I don't know, they must have an auto descent mode, surely?'

'They do, actually,' said Harry, 'but they're code protected.'

'So?' said Eric. 'You get us the codes!'

'When are you planning to do this?' asked Stewart, calmly and sceptically.

'Now. Before the aliens can say no to us. Force the issue now!' Eric said.

A period of silence overtook the room with each looking

at the other, trying to work out who was for and who was against.

'Do they all have the same code, Harry?' asked Lionel, who was being swayed by the arguments for action. 'It would be nice to be on the surface, setting up a community.'

'I don't know about the codes. I'll try to find out,' replied Harry.

That afternoon, back on the bridge, Harry Goodwin spotted the captain floating across towards the navigation consoles, and he pushed off to intercept her.

'Captain Blaney. Might I have a word?' he asked.

The captain looked at the bridge officer with one of those expressions that screamed, *If you must!* but said, 'Yes, of course.'

'I was thinking about the course of action if the Haciendans let us colonise,' Harry said.

'In what way?'

'The colonist landers. When were they last inspected? It's so quiet on the bridge now we're in orbit, I was thinking that I could make my way around them, just checking the systems were working properly ready for the descent.'

Captain Blaney thought for a moment, looked Harry straight in the face and said, 'That could be useful. Speak to Ovmacleod. She's been ensuring they have all had a software update from the main navigation computer.'

'Yes, Captain. I'll do that.'

Harry left it for about twenty minutes to give time for the captain to finish what she'd been doing and return to her office, then he pulled himself over to Ciorstaidh Ovmacleod's workstation. He explained his suggestion.

'Have you been in a lander?' Ciorstaidh asked.

'No. Never.'

'I was going down to CDL38 later to check a potentially faulty switch. If you like, we could go down now.'

'Great. That'd be fine.'

'Give me a minute to finish this report and we'll head off to the rim.'

Harry hung onto a ceiling handle for literally two minutes until Ciorstaidh pulled herself over to him and they pushed off towards the exit from the bridge, down one of the stairways using the banisters for support, and waited in the elevator area. With a shush, the doors opened, they entered, and Ciorstaidh pressed the button for deck one hundred, the outer rim of Kepler. The journey took seven and a half minutes and, by the time they reached the rim, they were experiencing Haciendan gravity created by the rotation of the ship.

The change to high gravity seriously bothered many of the older people who lived near the hub to extend their lives, but the crew, including the ion drive engineers, all lived on the rim in order not to become too addicted to freefall. Adapting to having heavy limbs took ten or fifteen minutes. Harry and Ciorstaidh turned foreled and made their way around the E-sector rim.

Apartment entrances were all on the rear side of the corridor, the right. On the left were airlock doors, every five metres. They were numbered. The first they saw bore the numerals CDL17, which stood for colonist descent lander number seventeen. Next was eighteen, and they continued until they came to CDL38.

The corridors at the rim were beautifully decorated with pictures of plants, jungles, forests, lawns, and seascapes. Entrances to apartments were doors that opened inwards from the corridor, while on the other side, the airlocks were rather more functional. The entrance to CDL38 was set into a desert scene, which portrayed sand dunes, brilliant blue skies and camels mounted by Bedouins. Seemingly cut out of the scene was an obround* steel doorway.

At its top, a circular porthole allowed people to look inside. Beneath it to the right, a round, spigot-like handle was the opening device. On the left were three substantial hinges. Around it all was a sturdy frame. The doors were designed to hold the vacuum of space at bay once the CDL had departed, so opened outwards. Beside the handle, a twelve-digit keypad was set into the door.

1 2 3
4 5 6
7 8 9
* 0 #

'Does each door have its own code?' asked Harry.

'They do, but it's a simple combination changed annually. Currently it's eighty for the year and thirty-eight for the lander number,' said Ciorstaidh as she punched in 8038.

'Seriously? Is that it?'

'Well, no one is likely to steal one,' she replied.

Harry was surprised at the lack of security.

He heard a clunk from the door handle, and Ciorstaidh turned it through 360 degrees until there was another click, and the door swung away from them into a short tunnel, no longer than two metres. They were faced by a second door

* An obround is a geometric shape consisting of two semicircles joined by two parallel straight lines.

which had no keypad and also opened inwards, away from them.

Inside, colonist descent lander number thirty-eight opened up before them. It was a cylinder barely high enough for a short person to stand upright. Ciorstaidh was okay, but Harry had to crouch. Four rows of three seats with a pitch of about 700mm were positioned along the opposite side, allowing just 750mm of corridor space as an aisle. The front of the cylinder comprised a mass of controls and a large wraparound window for forward visibility. Nothing could be seen from it until the lander was launched. The room smelled of having been recently cleaned.

'God, it looks complex,' said Harry as Ciorstaidh made her way to the front row and took the farthest seat.

'Looks worse than it is,' she said.

In front of her was a joystick protruding back and upwards so that it sat between her thighs. Above that were a series of small screens.

'First we must boot up the lander by throwing the master switch,' she said and flipped over a red circuit breaker.

The consoles all came to life. Ciorstaidh pointed at each in turn, and said, 'Altitude; artificial horizon; air speed and descent speed.' She then pointed at two further dials. 'This one shows the angle of attack when entering the atmosphere and the other is fuel.'

'How are they launched?' asked Harry, beginning to wonder if Ciorstaidh would get suspicious at his questions.

'The red button in front of the left-hand seat and this one above the artificial horizon screen must be pressed simultaneously,' she said. 'That unlocks the keypad in front of your seat, and the same code must be entered.'

'Eight, zero, three, eight again?' he asked.

'Correct. Then there's a countdown of thirty seconds which can only be aborted by pressing both red buttons simultaneously again, otherwise the CDL is launched.'

'Is it hard to fly?'

'No. Descent is automatic. Controls are for emergencies only. The CDL will pass into the atmosphere, then shed speed down to thirty knots, by which time it will be over the designated map reference preset on the bridge. The parachutes are then jettisoned, the engines fire up, and it descends to the surface.'

'If there are five hundred of them all descending at the same time, won't they crash if they're all heading for the same map reference?' asked Harry, who was worrying about the chaotic situation which this might cause on the ground.

'Ha ha,' Ciorstaidh laughed. 'Each target point is updated live so that they all descend within a few metres of each other. The location will be very carefully selected to ensure there's enough space.'

'Right.'

'This is what I came to do,' said Ciorstaidh, unscrewing a switch and fitting a new one into a hole in the dashboard. Then she ran a cable from her tablet into a nearby slot. There was a rapidly flashing LED above the slot for about two minutes, then it stopped. 'That's it,' she said.

'Many more to do?'

'Still about two hundred with the software update.'

'Can I help?'

'All help welcome,' she said and smiled. 'This was the last lander with a fault. The others are a standard update providing our new fixed orbit. Let's head back to the bridge and I'll feed the regular update into your tablet.'

'I must say that the security on the CDLs is not particularly strong,' said Harry.

'No. I suppose no one is concerned about a passenger stealing a lander. Why would they do that? There's nowhere ready for them down there yet. Also, it takes two to launch a lander. The two red buttons are deliberately two metres apart and they must be pressed by a finger of a living person. It senses the fingerprint, so a long stick wouldn't work.'

'What about the lander's contents.'

'Well, yes,' said Ciorstaidh, 'but the essentials are split between ten landers. If fewer than ten were to land, then it would be difficult to set up the colony.'

Harry had learned a lot. Now, how could he apply it?

The last two years of the journey had been most exciting for ninety-eight-year-old Caroline. The ship had already entered the Kepler star system and she had spent many an hour in the couches behind the bridge where residents could look at a choice of displays: forward, rear and the views outward from the ship's hub. Those starfields swept by quite rapidly but the forward and rear views held relatively steady now that their trajectory had become the outer planets.

She'd had the honour of naming the innermost of the gas giants. It was not as large as Neptune, but had the most wonderful colourful gaseous bands. The pole areas were both a misty grey. Next were pastel yellow bands containing spice-coloured swirls. The division between those and the next was a continually moving narrow area of green gas. It seemed as if the yellow was mixing with the third band, the most ridiculously bright and vivid cornflower blue. The equatorial bands were less distinct, containing pinks, oranges and shades of red.

On this particular day, the ship was on closest approach. Caroline looked at the colourful world which now filled the entire forward view. Magnificent and worthy of the name she chose, Viking.

The journey through the Kepler system was also tinged with a sadness and loneliness brought on by the death of Graham, the love of her life, from a type of leukaemia the doctors were unable to treat. The next month saw her brother, once Captain Arnold-Pointer, finally succumb to a heart condition he'd been battling for a decade. She'd been at both of their bedsides during their last days. Graham had just slipped away in his sleep, but Geoffrey had railed against death. In the last few days he knew the end was coming, but had so wanted to set his eyes on the new home world.

'Do something for me, Cas,' he said.

'Anything.'

'Look upon the new world and raise a glass for me.'

'Of course. If I am able.'

He laughed weakly and said, 'You were always the strong one. I see Mum in your eyes and hair.'

'What? These grey strands,' she said and chuckled.

'No. As you were in the early years.' He grimaced.

'You in pain?' she asked. 'I'll call someone.'

'I think it's time, Cas,' he said, and his grip on her hand relaxed. He'd gone.

'Nurse!' she shouted at the top of her voice.

They arrived in seconds, but Geoffrey was no longer there.

That had been almost two years ago and she was back in the freefall couches behind the bridge, looking at the beautiful new world of Hacienda. How she wished Geoffrey could have been there with her.

She retrieved a pouch from her small handbag. Glasses of liquid were not suitable for a freefall toast.

It contained a golden coloured liquid. She turned the clasp at the top, raised it to the planet above her and drank some single malt whisky to Geoffrey's memory.

Chapter Thirty-Five

THE DECISION

Campbell and Altera entered the meeting room and settled into their comfortable green seats, grown from the spangledsepiacandy trees. The smell of the organic room and its furniture was pleasant and calming though it was rather intimidating to be in a room with so many of these enormous beings, all flashing and waving colours at each other. All of a sudden, they all fell into their equivalent of silence – a shimmering mottled silver-grey colour. They were ready for whatever was coming. Were the humans equally ready? They were full of trepidation after the worrying end of the previous session.

Most-Elder spoke slowly, and the tablet translated into English, 'Welcome, again. We have been thinking about your request to come and live on part of our world. How many of you are there?'

Campbell said, 'Our ship, Kepler, contains around five thousand people, but many can never leave the ship because the gravity down here would kill them.' That caused some rapid colour changes among some of the Haciendans.

'Gravity would kill them. How can that be?' asked Two-Elder.

'I'll try to explain. When I drop something like this communication device, it falls to the ground.' Campbell dropped it from one hand to the other. 'That is caused by the mass of your planet warping space. We refer to it as gravity,' he said.

'We know that force, but why would your people die?' asked Two-Elder.

'They have been living their entire lives in a weaker force of gravity on the ship. As they age, they find life better near the hub of our ship where there's little or no gravity. Living in low gravity causes bones and muscles to deteriorate. If they now came to live here, they would likely die quite soon. Moving around would require extreme exertion, and their hearts would possibly fail.'

'You have low or zero gravity on your ship?' asked Two-Elder.

The humans had never thought about the Haciendans not understanding how gravity on a starship might vary. 'We do,' said Altera. 'Wait a moment.'

She fiddled with her tablet until she found some video taken on Kepler's bridge. She transferred it to the large monitor and said, 'This is the ship's control centre, and you can see the crew floating around the room. We call it freefall.'

'That is surprising,' said One-Elder, moving towards the monitor to study the sequence. 'We float too.'

'You do,' said Campbell, 'but your floating is caused by the sac in your body containing the gas helium. It makes your body buoyant. Objects, however, will fall just like my communication device. Floating using helium is not equivalent to free fall in zero gravity. Notice the computer keyboard floating on the left of the screen.'

One-Elder peered at it then swung back to face Campbell, and said, 'But why is there no gravity in orbit?'

Campbell was shocked at their lack of knowledge of gravity. How on earth could he explain it quickly? It required knowledge of both Newtonian and Einsteinian physics.

Altera saved his anxiety by saying, 'Understanding gravity will take many long lessons. You probably know many of the principles but the physics of the universe which we understand is very complex. We'll be happy to tell and show you more about gravity. When things are in orbit, gravity behaves differently.' She was conscious not to get into any complicated explanations at this point of the meeting. 'A ship in orbit is falling towards the planet, but is travelling too fast to enter into the atmosphere. The people on board are living in zero gravity – in effect, falling forever towards the planet. I can explain in detail some other time.'

Most-Elder said, 'This is all fascinating, but back to your wanting to occupy some of our planet.' He pulled One-Elder back to its original position in the room, using one of his extendable tentacles. One-Elder shook it off and retreated. Most-Elder finished by saying, 'So, it is about two thousand five hundred people?'

'Probably a few more, around three thousand four hundred,' said Campbell. 'They will reproduce so the population will grow over time.'

'Of course,' Most-Elder said.

There was a pregnant pause. Campbell and Altera said nothing, just tried to keep open, interested expressions on their faces.

Most-Elder moved himself closer to the humans, pointed at part of a globe of Hacienda and continued, 'This continent, Starflashfadingblue, has many of our cities, so does Blueyellowstarsland with whom we've been having discussions over the last two days. We do not believe it would be wise for you to colonise either of our two main continents. We think conflict or disharmony could arise. You will be very welcome to have small scientific stations here, so that your people and ours can learn about each other, but not general habitations.'

'We understand,' said Campbell, briefly thinking of apartheid. 'We'd very much like to continue to learn more about you and to tell you more about our science.'

Altera swiftly added, 'Especially astrophysics which is the science of space and gravity.'

'Good,' said Most-Elder, turning the globe and pointing at two equatorial continents. 'Would you be able to live on the equatorial continents of Redrectangleblueedged or Stripesoforangeandgrey? Both have very dry areas and are too hot for us to live and grow our cities.'

'We haven't studied those areas but feel sure they would be suitable. Technology can be utilised to cool our homes and to create freshwater for our crops,' said Campbell.

'We would want rite of passage across your territories and would not want you to interfere with our communications,' said One-Elder. Campbell felt he was the one who was most sceptical about colonisation.

'We can probably help you communicate even better than you do now, with video too,' said Altera.

'Video does not cross those distances,' said Three-Elder.

'No. That is because you're bouncing your signals off the ionosphere,' said Altera. 'Once we're settled, we can give you access to satellites which will provide perfect sound and vision over your whole world.'

Campbell hurriedly added, 'But that will take time. We'll need to get a space industry up and running. It could take many years.'

'Could you take us into space?' asked Two-Elder, who had not spoken until then.

'In time, yes, but you're too large for our current space vessels. We'd need to build special ones.'

At this point, One-Elder turned away from the humans and became a living kaleidoscope with waves of flashing colours all over its body.

Most-Elder replied with a small burst of similar rapidity, and the humans' tablets produced garbled words in translation. Suddenly, the whole assembly of Haciendans was in rapid conversation.

Campbell looked to Altera and whispered, 'What the hell do you think has happened?'

Altera's eyes widened to match Campbell's expression as she shrugged and turned back to watch the colourful display. There was obviously a heated argument taking place. One-Elder had apparently received some extremely dramatic news, and it had upset the entire group.

'Something not good. That's for sure,' she said.

Chapter Thirty-Six

VIOLENCE

Harry spent the next day moving from CDL to CDL, ostensibly checking their readiness and updating software, but in reality ensuring they were all ready for immediate departure. Back on the bridge, keeping his screen turned away from other officers, he compiled a list of the contents of each CDL. Ideally, for any landing, ten CDLs would ensure that there were enough critical resources for a new colony. It could be done with four if the colonists were to rough it. He entered CDL numbers on his tablet.

The next conspirators' meeting comprised the usual faces, but with another thirty who wanted action. It was held in the same disused social club which was now littered with empty bottles and plates. Unfortunately, as dissatisfaction with the actions of the captain and president increased, the desire to stand on the planet's surface grew into an obsession, which was becoming relentless for some.

Harry said, as he handed a list to Stewart, 'These are four CDLs which you will need to take to have a fair chance of establishing a community.'

'Why those four?' asked Gus, whipping the piece of paper away from Stewart's fingers.

'They will provide quality temporary shelters for up to eighty people. You also have the CDLs themselves for radio contact and scientific equipment – different in each of the four. You'll have food for fifty people for four weeks, medical supplies, seeds and tools for planting. One of the landers contains a store of energy bars and drinks to support you for up to six months in case there are no suitable foods where you land. All landers have lists of Haciendan plants you can safely eat.' Harry looked around the room and added, 'Can't some of you give this room a clean. It's beginning to smell of stale beer.'

The individuals looked at each other but no volunteers jumped forward.

'And that's it?' asked Stewart.

'You'll need landing coordinates. I've stored several on this memory card,' Harry said, handing it to Stewart. You'll need to decide which location, and all go to the same one.'

'Thanks. Got it,' said Stewart. 'How are we sure we won't land on top of each other?'

Harry replied, 'They all have a live record of their own landing coordinates, and they communicate with each other and will land nearby, but not too close.'

'Do we have to use four?' asked Gus.

'No. You could use fewer, but you'd be less well prepared to form a colony. The first one on the list contains the emergency rations,' said Harry,

'What do we have to do then?' asked Stewart.

'When we know the Haciendans' decision I'll let you

know which coordinates to use,' said Harry. 'Now, I'm going back to the bridge and will keep myself to myself. Whatever you do is in your own hands. If negotiations go well, I'd suggest you do nothing as the colonisation will proceed properly. This is only for if things go badly. And someone please get this place cleaned up.'

Harry left the dilapidated social club, and the remaining conspirators began drinking. If the Haciendans turned down the colonisation, they would use the CDLs rather than start another interstellar journey.

Within an hour of Harry's departure, arguments began between Gus, Eric, Stewart, and Anne.

Eric said casually, 'Why not go now?'

Stewart replied, 'Don't be daft. What would that achieve?'

'We'd get a head start on the main fleet and choose the best areas of land for ourselves,' said Gus.

'And an action like that, could wreck the negotiations,' said Stewart.

'Well, I'm tempted,' said Gus.

'Me too,' said Lionel, and several others indicated the three of them were not alone.

'I have the memory card with the coordinates and I'm not passing it to anyone else until we know the result on the surface,' said Stewart, holding the card in the air between his fingers.

There was a lot of groaning among the throng as Stewart pushed past Eric to leave the room.

'Hang on,' said Gus. 'Let's talk about this some more. What would be the harm of going down early?'

'You can't,' said Anne. 'As Stewart said, it could muck up the negotiations.'

'Who'd know if we went down to the equatorial continent?' asked Eric.

'We can't go anywhere without the coordinates,' said Lionel.

'I'm not happy about Stewart having the only set,' said Eric. Several agreed.

'Let's meet up, same time tomorrow,' said Gus.

Eric pulled on Gus's arm to hold him back as the others left. 'Hold on mate,' he said.

The two sat together and discussed the options. Gus seemed prepared to wait another few days before taking stronger action but Eric was already planning to move things forward more urgently. He had to get off this ship.

Ellen Ovlester was in a hurry. She'd just been in an apartment on the rim where a crime had been committed. Gravity there was 1.3 times Earth normal, which matched the gravity on Hacienda and Ellen did not find it at all comfortable.

On decks nearer the hub, she moved almost gracefully in the lower gravity where her huge bulk was not such an inconvenience. She knocked and entered Chief Andretti's office on deck thirty-eight, sweating, her heart pounding, and beginning to panic.

Chief Andretti looked up from his desk towards his deputy and immediately sensed her discomfort. He wondered what could have so upset her. 'What's up?' he asked.

'We've got, we've got, got a body,' she spluttered out.

'What do you mean, you've got a body? Calm down and speak more slowly. Sit!'

Ellen collapsed into a visitor's chair. Being on deck thirty-eight, it meant that she fell into it at less than half normal speed. Decks below fifty had a lower level of gravity.

As the springs in the chair gently rebounded to absorb her mass, she wiped her brow, tried to compose herself and said, 'A body has been found in apartment B-100-87. I think, think it's a murder.'

'What makes you think that?'

'His head was a ma-mass of blood. Doc, Doctor Emslie said it was blunt force trauma,' she quoted from her tablet. 'A mass, mass of blood. Never seen anything like it.'

'Where's the body now?'

'Doc took it. B-hospital mortuary.'

'Identification?'

'Don't know. No tablet or ID card. Apartment registered to one Janet Ovanderson. We don't know where she is.'

Chief Andretti turned to his computer and typed in the name. 'She's a fire officer in B-Sector. Have you tried them?'

'No,' Ellen said and burst into tears, 'I can't d-do this any, anymore, sir.'

'Okay. Okay, Ellen, leave it to me,' said the chief and used his communicator to call his second deputy, another woman named Moira Robertson. He barked into the phone, 'Moira, meet me in the B-hospital mortuary. I'll explain there.' He cut the call and said to Ellen, 'Can you do something for me, Ellen? Go to the B-Sector fire office and find out where Ovanderson is and whether she knows the person.'

'But, but she might be the killer,' said Ellen in a blue funk.

Not for the first time, Marco Andretti wondered why he had ever hired Ovlester, but there was no time to worry about it then. 'I'm sure she's not, Ellen. Just go and do it and put her on the phone to me.'

He jumped up and was out of his office before she could protest any further.

Chief Andretti ran backled to a B-Sector elevator and pressed the button for floor sixty-seven, overriding any other stops by swiping his police ID. He emerged into the reception area of B-hospital where several nurses and assistants in blue and green uniforms were on duty, carrying trays, pushing trollies, or sitting at computers. It was clear from his own uniform that he was a senior police officer. He barked, 'Mortuary?'

A receptionist pointed along one of the pastel blue-green corridors and he set off in that direction. Robertson caught up with him en route.

The mortuary was like mortuaries anywhere. Along one side was a wall with thirty cabinets, each one about 750mm square, stacked three high and ten wide. Andretti and Robertson entered and found Dr Emslie at a desk.

'Where is it?' Andretti asked.

'Marco, good morning to you too,' ventured the doctor. He stood and they approached the wall of cabinets.

'This one,' he said, and slid open the drawer. Feet first, the corpse slid outwards, and a support strut with a small wheel fell to the floor to take the weight of the extended drawer.

'Not a pretty sight,' said the doctor as she pulled back the sheet.

The dead man's skull was broken open on one side with

blood and grey matter spilling out but held in place by a strap.

'What a mess,' said Moira Robertson, looking away across the room and stifling nausea. 'Who could have done such a thing?'

'I know that face,' the chief said, slowly. He was the rebel who spoke at the meeting last week. Stewart something.'

The chief's phone rang. It was Ellen who said, much more composed now, 'I found Janet Ovanderson and she tells me her brother was staying with her.'

'Stewart Ovsmithson,' said Andretti.

'How did you know that, sir?' asked Ellen, beginning to panic again.

'No matter. Thank you, Ellen. Take a statement from Ovanderson and take the rest of the day off.' He turned back to look at the corpse and asked the doctor, 'I take it this isn't an accident.'

'No,' said the doctor. 'He was hit several times by a hammer, heavy bar, or something similar.'

'First murder on my watch,' Andretti said. 'I'd better go and talk to the captain and president.'

Chapter Thirty-Seven

HIJACK

Word of the murder had not become public knowledge when Eric, Gus, Lionel, and three other men, plus four female partners, and two more women in it for the hell of it, boarded CDL41. They'd abandoned the plan to take four landers as they couldn't raise forty-eight to take part. Eventually, it had narrowed down to just a dozen protesters. Lander forty-one held provisions and they considered they could live in the lander if they needed to. Lionel had also brought six tents and some weapons for emergencies.

It was claustrophobic with all twelve seats filled, especially with each of them carrying personal possessions as they knew they would never return to Kepler. Gus, Lionel and Eric occupied the front three seats, fired up the main console and Eric pulled the memory card which held the coordinates out of his pocket.

'How did you get Stewart to hand it over?' asked Gus.

'Oh, no problem. He said he'd not want to come, but understood our points of view,' said Eric, who showed not one iota of guilt over the brutal murder he'd committed in apartment B-100-87.

There was no way he was going to tell the others that there had been a violent struggle. He felt nothing for Stewart after he'd bludgeoned him to death with the hammer he'd brought primarily for defence.

He pushed the memory stick into the slot on the dashboard, and a message appeared: 'COORDINATES SET'

'That's odd,' Gus commented. 'I thought there were several, and we were supposed to choose the location we wanted.'

'Yes, I did too,' said Eric, pulling the card out and inspecting it.

'WARNING' flashed up on the console. 'MEMORY CARD DEVICE INCORRECTLY UNMOUNTED'

'Idiot!' said Lionel. 'You could corrupt the data like that. Put it back in.'

Eric examined it again and pushed it home. A tiny red LED flashed for a few seconds, and the console announced: 'DATA POTENTIALLY CORRUPTED. REBOOT CDL'

'How do we do that?' asked Gus.

'I think we need to throw the main switch again and let it all come back online,' said Lionel.

Eric asked, 'Do I take the card out again?'

'Yes, but switch off first,' said Lionel.

Eric flipped the red master switch down. This time, the consoles all changed to black and remained black. He removed the card.

After a few seconds, the lights in the lander dimmed and went out. They were plunged into pitch blackness. One man at the back shouted a question about what the hell was going on, and one of the women screamed.

'Okay, switch it back on,' said Lionel.

Just seconds later, all the lights came on and the consoles on the dashboard lit up as before.

Eric went to slide in the card and Lionel held his arm, and said, 'Wait.'

After another minute, the word 'READY' appeared.

'Now,' said Lionel, 'slide the card in… carefully, man, for God's sake.'

'Okay. I know,' said Eric, who followed the instruction. The console flashed up the same original message, 'COORDINATES SET'. What none of them realised was that the coordinates had been corrupted.

'What do we do?' asked Gus.

'Maybe the choices of coordinates come up after we press the two red buttons,' said Eric.

'What if they don't?' asked Lionel. 'We'll have no idea where the thing is taking us. I think we should postpone until later. I'll find Stewart or Harry and ask what we're meant to do to select the coordinates.'

'No!' shouted Eric, painfully aware of what he'd done. If they didn't leave immediately, Stewart's body would be found. 'We've come this far, let's get on with it.'

'I don't like it,' said Lionel. 'We need to know the coordinates.'

'Let's press the buttons and see what happens,' said Eric. 'It'll probably ask us to choose then.'

Gus and Eric both pressed the red buttons. The keypad flashed red.

'But we still don't know the coordinates are correct,' said Lionel.

'They might be shown after we enter the code or even after we launch,' said Eric.

'I don't like it,' said Lionel, becoming nervous and

worrying about Eric's proximity and size. He didn't want to upset him.

'Enter the code, Gus. Eight zero four one,' said Eric.

Gus punched in the code, and a countdown appeared on one of the console screens.

'Still no coordinates,' said Lionel, becoming agitated. 'I really think we need to postpone.'

'No,' said Eric angrily, grabbing Gus's arm as he reached towards the red button. 'Don't go chicken now. The coordinates will come up when we've launched.'

'I don't think they will,' said Lionel, seriously intimidated by Eric's body language and obvious temper.

'Well, I do, so shut up!' Eric shouted.

The countdown reached zero, there was a dull clunk from the left of the craft, and everyone, restrained by their straps, was thrown towards the inner door as the lander, no longer attached to the ship, flew off the rim at a tangent into space.

There was a communal gasp as the wraparound cockpit window showed stars, the planet and its moons as the lander shot off from the revolving ship. The passengers had been suddenly tossed into free fall; some cried out, one vomited.

The lander's autonomous systems cut in, and the craft stabilised. Now it was facing Hacienda, the beautiful planet filling their field of view. It was mesmerising.

The console stated: 'ORBIT STABILISED. AWAITING OPTIMUM INJECTION BURN'

'What the hell does that mean?' asked Gus.

'It's waiting to fire its deorbiting motors. It won't do that until it knows it's in the right point of its orbit, otherwise it won't arrive at the coordinates,' said Lionel.

'But which coordinates?' asked Gus.

'I don't know. Ask genius here,' he said sarcastically, looking at Eric, who gave him a look that could kill.

'I have a horrible feeling about this,' said Lionel. 'I think we should abort.'

'I don't think we can abort,' said Gus. 'We're already underway.'

'Oh fuck,' said Lionel. 'You'd better not have screwed this up, Eric. Bloody idiot!' Eric remained silent.

All of a sudden, everyone was pushed back into their seats as the lander performed the critical burn to send it down into the atmosphere. They'd passed the point of ever returning. All they could do was try to enjoy the journey, but instead, they were all looking at each other with accusatory expressions. Only the lander knew to where it was headed. Like tourists on a rollercoaster, the passengers couldn't influence the CDL's destination.

First officer, Rose Russell burst into the captain's office, causing Captain Blaney to squeeze her coffee pouch, spraying the liquid into the space above her desk where it orbited in simulation of a spiral galaxy. She shouted, 'What is it?' and grabbed some tissues to scoop the hot liquid from the air.

'A CDL has launched, Captain!' Rose said loudly and nervously. Captain Blaney had been known to be unpleasant to people who delivered bad news.

'What?'

'CDL41 launched without authorisation,' Rose explained.

'You're serious?' Blaney couldn't believe someone would launch without permission.

'I tried to contact it, but the lander is already in radio blackout. It's definitely on its way down.'

'How do we stop more launches?' asked the captain, becoming seriously concerned that the original group of conspirators could be on a quest to get to the surface.

'I don't know?'

'Who would?'

'Greg might.'

The captain grabbed her communicator and called Greg Hardcastle, a navigation officer. 'Hardcastle? Blaney here. How can we stop all CDLs from being launched? Is it possible?'

'Why? What's happened?'

'Questions later damn it! Just tell me, can we stop them?'

'We can change the year designation. That will mean the launch code will not be recognised.'

'Do it. *Now*!'

'What number?'

'Anything. Make it seventy-seven,' said the captain.

'Give me a moment.' On the bridge, Hardcastle opened the settings for the CDL system and changed the year from eighty to seventy-seven. 'Done,' he said.

'How soon?'

'It's done now. No CDL can be launched or even entered without the new seventy-seven prefix. What's happened?'

'We've had an unauthorised launch and it's on its way to the surface,' said the captain. 'I'm going to see the president.'

Chapter Thirty-Eight

DIPLOMACY

The Haciendan mega colour show gradually subsided. They were clearly very agitated and had learned something distressing, like a natural disaster or suchlike. Neither of the humans had ever seen them in such turmoil. There had been much turning and twisting of their hovering positions, and two had appeared to fight, tentacles connecting in a writhing mass before they separated and backed off. It didn't need the tablet translations for the humans to realise that the main elders were trying to bring the group to order. That all the fuss was in virtual silence added even more confusion to the bizarre performance.

Campbell acted. 'What is happening? Can you explain?'

Most-Elder hadn't seen the message on the monitor; it was Two-Elder who drew his attention to it and replayed the human sequence of colours.

One-Elder and Two-Elder turned their bodies a brilliant scarlet, and all the others seemed to calm down, their bodies and tentacles fading back to the neutral grey they exhibited when not communicating. The red, crimson, or scarlet flash was obviously a call of 'Shut up!'

Most-Elder turned through 360 degrees and faced back towards their guests. He said, 'We are very disappointed.'

Campbell decided it was best not to respond until there was an explanation.

Most-Elder continued, 'It appears that a group of your people have attacked part of Stripedbluespots.'

'What is Stripedbluespots?' asked Campbell, wondering how the devil an attack had happened. He whispered to Altera, 'Contact the others and see if they're okay.' Altera busied herself with the communicator.

'A nearby city,' said Most-Elder.

Altera touched Campbell's hand and quietly said, 'Nothing wrong at Lavigne.'

Did this mean some other humans had attacked the neighbouring city? How and why would anyone on Kepler have done such a thing?

He asked, 'How do you mean, they attacked.'

'One of your machines, a big one, larger than your Discovery craft, created a vast hole in part of Stripedbluespots. It made a fire and killed at least a dozen of our people. Others rushed to aid the casualties. Some humans climbed out of the machine, and they killed more of our people with weapons which fire hot projectiles. Why are you doing this?' asked Most-Elder. 'Our people were trying to help.'

'I have no idea,' said Campbell.

'We need to contact the ship to find out,' said Altera. 'This is not normal human behaviour.'

'Have you stopped the fighting?' asked Campbell.

'Seven humans are no more. Three are dead within

your machine which is still burning. Two were restrained and are being held in captivity.'

'I'm so sorry. I cannot imagine why they did this. No one has been authorised to leave the ship. Do you have names?' said Campbell.

'Not human names. One is female and one male,' said Most-Elder.

'Can your transport take us back to our base so that we can contact our ship?' asked Altera.

'You could come with us,' added Campbell in a hurry. 'We have nothing to hide.'

Most-Elder and One-Elder began a rapid colour show for the other Haciendans. It wasn't a one-way conversation. Several of them were producing their own unintelligible patterns and waves. Most-Elder flashed scarlet, and the show stopped.

'Two-Elder will take you back to your base and wait while you speak to your orbiting ship,' said Most-Elder.

'What is the condition of the two you're holding?' asked Campbell. 'So that I can tell the ship.'

Another Haciendan produced some rapid colours for Most-Elder, who said, 'They are not damaged and are being kept in a cage. It is not something we like doing but it was necessary to calm them down, particularly the male who struggled throughout.'

'Come,' said Two-Elder, and he led the humans out of the meeting area to where the transport and its strange chauffeur were waiting.

On the journey back to Lavigne Base, Campbell and Altera opened a channel to Mike, Berry, and Martina, who had just been told about the stolen CDL by the captain, but had been given no specifics.

'What idiots would have screwed up our negotiations like this?' asked Altera.

'There was that group who wanted more action on colonisation. Do you think it was them?' said Campbell.

'Must have been, but I thought that had all been resolved,' came over the communicator from Mike.

'Apparently not,' said Berry. 'What's your arrival time?'

'Five minutes,' said Campbell.

In fact, it was almost ten minutes before the strange transport burst out of the forest and slowed to a halt near the pod, Two-Elder in close pursuit.

'God, he's big,' said Berry, who'd attended few lessons in Orangiegreen and had not met the elders.

'The elders seem to be at least a metre wider and a couple longer than Reddo,' said Campbell as he jumped down from the transport and headed to the open-air section of the pod.

Mike fired up the link with Kepler, and said, 'Lavigne Base here, are you in range?'

There was no answer. The base could only communicate with Kepler for about thirty-five minutes every two hours, when there was direct line of sight to the ship in its orbit.

'It'll be at least another ten minutes,' said Martina.

Campbell turned to Two-Elder and showed his tablet to the being so that he could observe the translated colour patterns. 'Kepler is below the horizon. We've ten minutes to wait until we can speak to them,' he explained.

Two-Elder flashed the colour waves which said that he understood. It looked sullen, hanging there in its smoke grey colour, silently watching the humans.

'We should know more when they're in signal range,' said Mike, repeating his message to the ship.

Finally, almost twelve minutes later, they heard the captain responding, 'Kepler here. What's the situation down there?'

'Ovarnold here, Captain. The lander appears to have crash-landed in a nearby city called Stripedbluespots. It caused the death of Haciendans. Three humans died in the wreck. Nine escaped but opened fire on the Haciendans. They might have assumed they were under attack or panicked.' Campbell's message was also being translated into Haciendan on a second monitor.

Two-Elder responded, 'We did not attack them. It was unprovoked when we approached to see if we could help.'

'Who is that?' asked the captain.

'That is a translation of Two-Elder who returned to Lavigne Base with us,' said Campbell hurriedly. 'He is listening to my report.'

'Thank you for coming, Two-Elder,' said the captain, now realising that this was a more diplomatic situation than she had first imagined. 'Continue, Ovarnold.'

'The nine who escaped the crash opened fire on the Haciendans with, we believe, rapid-fire weapons. Seven of them were killed, but we haven't enquired how. Two are being held captive. The Haciendans can't give us their names as they'd just be meaningless colours,' said Campbell.

Altera added, 'Our negotiations were going well with the elders and an expanded council group. We had almost agreed on us sharing one of their equatorial continents when the news arrived about the crash and attack.'

'How did that happen, Captain?' asked Campbell.

'President Ovpetrangle here. It appears that twelve citizens commandeered a colonist descent lander in order to go to the surface and begin a colony. Two-Elder, I can assure you that this was unauthorised. Another of their number did not go and she reported that coordinates had been provided by a bridge officer…'

'Who has been stripped of command and awaits a court-martial,' added the captain rapidly.

'The list of coordinates,' continued the president, 'was intended to be reviewed and one selected, but the memory card was put into the lander unsorted. Why the onboard computer selected the Haciendan city is unknown. The data may have been corrupted. We are so, so, sorry.'

'I understand what you are saying,' said Two-Elder. 'It is most unfortunate. Life is precious to us, whether our people or humans.'

'We don't want it to damage our relationship with you,' said the president. 'Security has been tightened on all remaining landers. It will not happen again. I promise you.'

'I will report back to the elders,' said Two-Elder.

'What will you do with the prisoners?' asked the captain.

'The elders will decide.'

'If you return them to us, we'll charge and imprison them,' said the president.

'I will tell the elders but imprisonment, by us or you is abhorrent,' Two-Elder said.

Campbell was pleased that there had been no other comment from Kepler. He asked, 'Ma'am, can you send us the full report so that we know exactly what transpired. I take it that it can't happen again?'

'No. It can't,' said the captain. 'Security was not considered important. No one imagined anyone would be stupid enough to steal a CDL. New codes have been issued to the remaining landers.'

'Is Two-Elder still there?' asked the president.

'No, ma'am. It's on its way back to Orangiegreen. It did tell me we can return to continue our discussions tomorrow,' said Altera.

'No harm done, then,' said the captain. 'Can't we get rid of these silly names – Orangiegreen and Striped-bluespots?'

'I'm reluctant to give human names to their cities and continents,' said Altera. 'That is exactly what seventeenth and eighteenth-century colonists did on Earth, and it would be insulting and disrespectful to the Haciendans.'

'And, frankly, Captain, I fear much harm *has* been done,' said Campbell. 'This was a betrayal of trust. Let's hope it doesn't derail our talks. They were going well.'

'All right then,' said the captain. 'Do your best.' And her line cut off. She hated not being in the right.

'Campbell, Altera?' said the president's gentle, educated voice.

'Yes, Mr President,' said Campbell.

'You've done a great job. Thank you.'

'Thank *you*, Mr President,' said Campbell.

Two-Elder returned to Orangiegreen and reported back to Most-Elder and One-Elder. They discussed how they felt about the changed situation.

'So, twelve of the humans didn't want to wait for our permission?' said Most-Elder.

'That's the situation,' said Two-Elder. 'They do appear to be very sorry about it.'

'Sorry won't bring back our lost citizens,' said One-Elder. 'This is what has been worrying me. Can we trust them? If this has happened during important negotiations, what will they do once they are living on our world?'

'We must be sure of their intentions and we must formulate a foolproof agreement,' said Two-Elder.

'They have been travelling for more than their normal lifetimes. That means they are in a desperate situation,' said Most-Elder. 'Can we really tell them to move on?'

Two-Elder changed his position in relation to the others and said, 'I had a conversation with the female and, if I understand correctly, they would be setting off on a journey into the unknown. While most stars have planets, most are not suitable. It is possible they could travel another hundred years and find there is no planet to colonise at all. Can we inflict that upon them? They might be the last of their kind.'

'Their technology and knowledge would be useful to us, I suppose,' said Most-Elder.

'Until they use it against us!' said One-Elder.

'We have no use of the land around our poles, nor the desert areas. What could be the harm?'

'They've proven they can't control their own people,' said One-Elder. 'Some might decide they want our continents. How could we stop them?'

'We must help them. Let's ensure the agreement is as water-tight as we can make it. We should also learn more about their technology so that we are able to protect ourselves if the need arises. They must agree to that condition too,' said Most-Elder.

One-Elder accepted the majority, but they all had concerns. Most-Elder's greatest worry was that if they turned the humans away, that might trigger an aggressive response. A veritable invasion. It was better they negotiated a good agreement first time. Once the human's technology was understood, perhaps they could use that to protect themselves from any infringement.

Chapter Thirty-Nine

AGREEMENT

Once the crashlanding had been smoothed over, the agreement between Haciendans and humans proceeded apace. Within two years, the colonists were given full control of the equatorial and polar continents, areas that could not cultivate spangledsepiacandy trees.

Haciendans could pass freely through the colonist areas, and the humans would have diplomatic locations near the largest Haciendan cities to facilitate understanding and mutual education.

The Haciendans would be given full access to all of the humans' technology and the humans would guarantee that no one would enter Haciendan continents without express permission.

The two mutineers, Eric Cho and Jennifer Santos, were handed over to Campbell and Mike during one of the negotiations. They were chained to heavy stone weights. This presented a distinct problem for the explorers as they had no facilities to keep them captive. One of the transports took the four of them back to Lavigne Base.

For a few minutes there was silence, each with their own thoughts as the transport wound its way from the city of Orangiegreen, through the more common woodland and shrubland towards the base. Floating a metre or so above the ground, the journey was smooth, but branches and leaves sped by, rubbing against the structure. Colourful flying creatures and insect-like fauna added interest.

Finally, the silence was broken. 'What's going to happen to us?' asked Jennifer, a not unattractive woman in her mid-thirties.

Campbell turned to look at her with unconcealed contempt. 'You almost destroyed our negotiations. What the hell were you thinking?'

Eric answered in a calmer than expected manner. 'It all went wrong. We intended to land in one of the drier continents and set up a colony. We ended up in the wrong place.'

'What exactly happened?' asked Mike.

'We couldn't change the coordinates. As we were coming down, Gus tried to gain height to clear an area covered in trees, but the lander banked the opposite way and crashed. The fuel ignited.'

'But why did you kill the Haciendans?' asked Campbell.

'We got out of the lander. It was burning. Some were stuck inside. Once outside we saw those jelly fish things charging us. Some were dead and dying from the crash and fire. The others seemed intent on killing us. We opened fire,' Eric said, casting his eyes downward.

'You idiots,' shouted Mike. 'They were coming to help you.'

'We didn't know.'

'I told them to stop, but they didn't listen,' said Jennifer. 'It was horrible.'

Campbell and Mike didn't speak to them again during the journey.

At Lavigne Base, Campbell and Mike shut the mutineers in the pod, while the five scientists discussed the situation with the president and captain.

Eventually, it was decided to imprison them on the Discovery. Altera set passwords on the controls so that they could not cause any further harm, and they were told to live off the rations on board. Mike rigged a device to hold the inner airlock closed, so that escape was impossible, and the explorers continued with their science. Scientists accompanied the prisoners during daily exercise, although, it was unlikely they'd have any incentive to make a run for it. With no food supplies or shelter, escape was futile.

On board Kepler there were massive celebrations to commemorate the agreement with the Haciendans, then frantic preparations to send down the colonist descent landers.

Firstly, a second reusable lander ferried down a team of senior officers to prepare for the colonists. A location was chosen beside a vast river, which flowed from the mountainous interior of one of the equatorial continents towards what they'd named as the Great Northern Sea.

Considerable plant growth flourished near the river, providing the opportunity to develop farms along the shore and six colonist landers arrived within a few hours containing thirty-six farming specialists to begin the process of cultivation, and a similar number of theoretical builders eager to put their knowledge to practical use.

No one had ever built any buildings on Kepler, of

course, but these individuals had been studying construction methods for several years prior to the ship's arrival at Hacienda.

Four utility pods also descended, carrying small mechanical diggers, bulldozers and other construction equipment. Within two days, foundations were laid for communal buildings, which would act as dormitories until work could begin on actual dwellings.

The excitement was palpable, and more CDLs arrived every day once there were places for people to sleep and eat.

Colonisation proved gradual, yet the excitement of the colonists was spectacular. They revelled in their grounding upon an actual world following decades of existence aboard ship.

On clear nights, people lay on their backs and stared at the sky, often seeing Kepler passing overhead in its two-hour long orbit. They understood that any return to Kepler would require the creation of aerospace industries, a distant prospect, and one that no one was worrying about in the short term. The colonists had also decided that all industries must be as environmentally friendly as possible. No one wanted to pollute the new world in the way that Earth had once been.

85SBY

Chapter Forty

NEW WORLD

Brilliant sunshine piercing cloudless blue skies caused High Street, New Edinburgh, to appear idyllic in its magnificent location beside the River Nile. Wooden fishing boats with brightly coloured sails meandered back and forth on the calm, relentlessly flowing giant waterway as it wound its way towards the Great Northern Sea.

Many structures were charming villas washed in tangerine, yellow, ochre, and spice brown. Three- and four-bedroom homes with precious rear lawns, plunge pools and vegetable patches lined the street in their dozens. The variety of dwellings amused the eyes of the residents. The diversity of the structures was irregular enough not to trouble the sensitive souls who yearned to stamp their marks on the new world.

To one end of High Street there was commerce too. Cobblers, bakers, grocers, hardware stores, seed merchants, and purveyors of tools and machinery. The police station stood there as well, with its cells and its one long-term inmate – Eric Cho.

The town was exactly what would be expected on an emerging frontier. Anything that could be wanted was either brought down from the ship or manufactured locally. Massive glazed hydroponic laboratories located close to the new colony, continued to supply all manner of earthly vegetables, grains, fruits, and legumes. Equipment from Kepler's machine shops had arrived and small factories been built. After five years, there were now surpluses of most foods, and very little was rare in SBY85, though bananas and coconuts were still few and far between and most nut trees were taking their own good time growing to maturity. That week, the first crops of hazelnuts were in the stores so there was the inevitable rush.

One tall, rambling building was the hospital. Much equipment had been brought down with the colonists, but some remained in orbit, where the ageing passengers were becoming more needy as time progressed.

The River Nile was as productive as its namesake in the African desert, and native fish abounded in such quantities that they would almost jump unbidden into the small colourful boats. Other than chickens, brought from Earth, no other land animals were raised for meat, although a type of flying hippopotamus was herded for production of something very similar to milk. The Haciendans were happy with that type of farming as long as the animals were free range and not killed for food. A giant blind-eye was turned towards the chickens. Trade developed in the non-sentient urchin-like creatures the Haciendans ate. Most humans were not impressed, but a continually growing number found the meat a delicacy.

New Edinburgh's population topped four thousand, and a quarter of those were under five. Kepler's children had been born on a new world and had never known outer space, though they would begin to learn about Earth, the great journey, and their new home. As they grew older, special lessons would teach the colourful language of the Haciendans who came to visit and to educate, but AI would forever be needed to maintain two-way communication, for the humans could not change their skin colour and the Haciendans had no ears or vocal cords.

In Orangiegreen and many other large cities of the native beings, humans improved the natives' technical know-how, teaching the findings of eminent scientists whose laboratories had once existed over sixteen hundred light-years distant.

Did Earth itself still exist? Who knew? The planet would almost certainly be there, but would it still host life, or would the relentlessly growing heat have created a final great extinction?

The enormous radio telescopes grown by the Haciendans using foil-lined spangledsepiacandy trees had been trained on the system of Sol, but so far, no signals had been received. Maybe sixteen hundred light-years was too great a distance over which to receive transmitted communications, or, perhaps, the home planet had succumbed to the growing output of what had once been a life-giving sun. Would the exiled humans on this distant new world ever learn Earth's fate? The universe was too vast. Travelling to and from Earth with news would see millennia pass on both worlds. It was meaningless to even contemplate such a project. Dreams of great galactic empires which once enthralled humankind, faded into the past. The universe was so vast, the happenings on individual orbiting specks of dust were insignificant. Humankind's outward urge to explore seemed to have been blunted, on this world at least.

Chapter Forty-One

LOOKING DOWN

Caroline still had a smile on her face after a recent video call with her new great-grandchild, Fetlar, named after her own parents' Shetland retreat. The almost five-year-old child was a joy to behold, and her parents, Campbell and Altera were so in love. It's love which makes the world go around.

When she came aboard Kepler, Caroline Arnold-Pointer had been a highly intelligent, stunningly beautiful, quarter-oriental, slim, eighteen-year-old with long, flowing, jet-black hair, and full of the joys of life. Now, her face was covered in wrinkles, her hair short and grey, and her cheeks a ruddy pink. The endearing and once sexy smile, however, had never changed.

Her parents, Beth Arnold and Gren Pointer, had hoped to get her into the Antarctic or moon refuges but it was not to be. Instead, she was selected for the Kepler refuge and she'd participated in humankind's greatest ever journey on the ship which would head to the stars, hoping to find a habitable new world in the system of Kepler-452. It had done just that.

The journey was to take a century, travelling close to the speed of light, which so distorted time that, back on Earth, over two millennia would have passed. None of the original passengers, who boarded the Kepler, were expected to live to see the destination world, but the scientists had been wrong. They'd underestimated the ingenuity of the engineers on board.

Kepler's innovative crew improved the ion engines en route, and the starship fell into orbit around Kepler-452b after a journey of just eighty shipboard years.

Caroline, now one hundred and three years old, was floating in free fall seeing the planet she'd imagined was forever denied her. She daydreamed about her thrilling career ending up as the chief EVA officer for the whole ship. More specifically, she was remembering the day, aged twenty-one, when she passed her emergency response test and qualified. The bastards had made her believe she was out of air and would die before she could reach an airlock. How much fear spurred her on or inspired the will to live, she didn't know, but she had reached an airlock with nearly three whole minutes to spare – almost a record. She laughed inside at her reaction when she opened the airlock only to find all her colleagues laughing at her panic. What a wonderful day that had been.

Five years previously, her grandson, Campbell Ovarnold became the first human to set foot on the new world – Hacienda, and, now, he was the mayor of New Edinburgh, helping to create and expand Earth's first interstellar colony.

She'd just finished a video conversation with him. Her first great-grandchild meant that the Arnold and Pointer families would live on into the future. A permanent tribute to humankind's determination to survive.

Caroline had one regret. Arriving in orbit around the new world aged ninety-eight meant she could never set foot on the planet. Her bones and muscles would be too fragile. The next best thing was where she was now. That day, one wall of her apartment near the hub was running a slideshow of images of her father's and mother's lives before and after Mindslip. In front of her, however, was something incredibly beautiful. A live display of Hacienda was spread out across the entire wall. The gorgeous planet was in daylight; New Edinburgh had just dropped over the horizon. The atmosphere was milky white and seemed so thin from orbit. All that life on the world within such a small envelope of conditions which made it possible.

Recently, she'd had the great pleasure of video sessions with the Haciendan, One-Elder, who was actually older than her by more than four decades. The main reason for his calls was that the Haciendans wanted to document the history of the few humans who had experienced living on a different planet. Only a couple of dozen remained, and most of those had no adult recollection of living on the home world. That Caroline had been a young adult living on Earth near the end times, made her highly unusual.

One-Elder was fascinated to hear of Caroline's interactions with other animals, particularly of her time on a farm during a school exchange visit she'd had at the age of fourteen. He had her scour the depths of her memories to describe cattle, sheep, pigs, and other livestock which had never been included on the interstellar journey.

Of course, Caroline had turned the last two sessions on their heads, getting One-Elder to open up about her own experiences and life in Orangiegreen. The being had a very gentle nature, and the human regretted she could not reach out and touch the amazing chameleon-coloured tentacles and fly with her through the Haciendan jungles, but it was not to be.

The next day, she had another session planned with One-Elder, which would explore the rising heat on planet Earth. Having Britain's official astronomer as a mother and a government minister as a father meant she was far more knowledgeable about the crisis than other survivors and the elder wanted to hear about life in Guildford before things got too bad, her parents' move to Shetland, and the visits she'd had there.

What inspired One-Elder's fascination with the catastrophe that overtook Earth was Caroline's detailed description of the shocking death of her parents when all possibilities had been exhausted. She hated having to talk about it at first, but soon she found it a relief and comfort to share the pain.

God, she remembered skipping along the beach in the north of the Shetland islands with her brother and rowing out with her father to recover lobster pots and plan barbecue feasts. She'd tell One-Elder all about it.

As it happened, the current image displayed on the wall was of the four of them tucking into just such a lobster dinner. Dad held the camera and was slightly distorted to one side in the selfie. Mum waved a pink lobster claw, and Geoffrey cuddled one of the family's hens. How lovely. Such a beautiful memory.

She became dewy-eyed, they became heavy, gradually closed, and would never reopen.

When One-Elder called Kepler in the morning, the Haciendan would be disappointed and saddened to have missed her.

More by Tony Harmsworth

vinci-books.com/moonscape-mark-noble

Something ancient has awakened on the Moon.

Mark Noble's lunar survey turns deadly when an ancient intelligence begins rewriting the minds of his crew. Cut off from Earth, paranoia spreads as he races to stop it from escaping—because saving humanity may cost its very future.

Turn the page for a free preview…

Moonscape: Chapter One

ROUTINE

The dust returned to the surface as if in slow motion. I'd kicked up a cloud of it as I turned towards Earth which hung in the sky like a Christmas bauble.

The blue and white marbling was extraordinary. I lifted my gloved hand and covered the entire disc with my padded thumb.

With a single digit, I'd hidden all but twenty of the human beings in existence. Assuming my thumb was hiding the location of the ISS, perhaps I'd hidden those eight people too, leaving just the twelve of us on the surface of the moon, including the four in the Chinese habitat.

'Can you straighten it, Mark?' a voice called, intruding into my isolation.

'Two seconds, Roy,' I replied. I straightened the theodolite target pole, lining up the marks on the two gauges. 'Okay.'

I held the pole still and looked across at Roy. Between us was a one-kilometre crater named Timocharis Delta, one of the craters on the fringe of Mare Imbrium. We'd discovered it was relatively new, only a few thousand years old. A previous visit had indicated a magnetic core. Whatever had created Timocharis Delta must have been composed of iron. That wasn't unusual but warranted this closer examination.

In the distance I could see the wall of the main Timocharis crater after which Delta was named. It was far larger, over thirty kilometres wide.

Behind Roy, a kilometre away from me, stood the six-wheel moon-buggy, our home during this multiday expedition. Thirty kilometres to the west, moonbase one awaited our return the day after tomorrow. We'd been carrying out surveys of craters east of moonbase and were now on the homeward arm of the loop.

Back on Earth, our work on the moon's surface had initially been on the news almost every day but was now rarely mentioned. Real science wasn't as exciting as political scandals or soap stars' affairs. Very few of the general public would even know our names.

'Got that, Mark. Give me a few minutes to pack up and I'll drive around and collect you.'

'Roger that.'

That gave me at least thirty minutes to absorb the amazing location. Me, Mark Noble, standing on the surface of the moon, following in the footsteps of Neil Armstrong, metaphorically if not actually. The Apollo 11 landing site, of course, was an internationally protected area. No one was allowed to approach within two hundred metres of it, owing to its historical significance. Neil Armstrong's and Edwin Aldrin's footprints remained as fresh as the day they were made.

I walked ten metres down the slight slope of the outer ring of the crater and turned to watch Roy. I could just make him out, walking towards the buggy. I leaned on the target device. It took little effort to stand on the moon, but there was a tendency to lean forward due to the mass of the backpack. Leaning on the target tripod helped my balance.

'Moonbase, I'm opening the access hatch.' Roy stood on the ladder and swung open the one-metre circular hatch towards the rear of the buggy. His tiny white figure filled the black hole in the buggy for a moment, then he pulled the hatch back into position.

'Copy that,' answered moonbase.

I continued eastwards so that he could collect me en route to our planned overnight camping location.

'I'm in the buggy. Stowing the equipment and sealing the hatch, moonbase.'

'Copy that, Roy,' came the tinny female response.

I plodded eastwards, kicking up dust with each step. 'Moonbase, Mark here. Surprisingly deep dust to the east of Timocharis Delta. At least ten centimetres here. Can't walk without kicking it up.'

'Acknowledge that, Mark,' said Crystal from moonbase.

'On my way,' said Roy.

'Copy that,' said Crystal.

The buggy was on the move, heading eastwards to clear the crater rim. As I walked, I looked down at the deepening dust. I'd not seen dust so thick during my five weeks at moonbase.

'Odd. The dust is now at least twenty centimetres. It's halfway to my knees.'

'Normal here, just the usual couple of centimetres,' said Roy.

'Hi, Mark, Blake here. Looking behind you, is there any change in the surface coloration as it gets deeper?' asked the moonbase commander. I pictured Crystal sitting at the communication centre in the comdome with Blake Smith leaning over her to speak.

I turned. It was becoming more difficult to move my feet. Not seriously, but I felt the resistance. 'No, Blake. Surface looks absolutely normal – the usual darker disturbed dust. You can see my footprints,' I said, sending him a digital image.

'Yes. Odd. Take care. Roy, you listening to this? Any change where you are?'

'I'm kicking up dust with the wheels, but nothing out of the ordinary,' replied Roy.

'Proceed with care,' said Blake.

I walked a few paces farther and stopped. 'Roy, Blake. Dust up to my knees. Copy please.'

Blake cut in. 'Hold your position, Mark. Any deeper with you, Roy?'

'Copy that, Mark. I've eased off to four kph. Can't really see any change here,' replied Roy.

'Proceed with care, Roy. Mark, can you backtrack? I don't want you entering anything deeper.'

'Copy that. Backtracking.'

Soon I was back on the normal surface.

'Would it be better for you to follow my original tracks around the west side of Timocharis Delta, Roy?'

'Well, I'm halfway around now and no change in the surface.'

'Skirt well out into the plain to avoid whatever I've encountered.'

'Watch the speed, Roy. Slow to a crawl,' said Blake.

There was no doubt this was an unusual phenomenon. Before the Apollo missions, there'd been real fears that there might be deep dust, so deep that the Apollo landers might actually disappear into it and be lost forever. None of those fears had materialised.

'Have we encountered anything as deep as this before?' I asked.

'No. Twelve centimetres in an area found by Apollo 14 at Fra Mauro,' said Blake. 'I'll mark the spot for a future investigation.'

The buggy continued its journey eastwards and gradually began to turn south, but well beyond the original planned path. I could see very little dust being thrown up, but Roy was travelling extremely slowly. I looked at my oxygen gauge. Plenty.

'Halfway to Mark,' said Roy. 'Dust still normal.'

'Copy that,' I said. Crystal acknowledged him too.

'I'm walking southwards to save Roy having to approach anywhere near that pool of dust,' I said, trudging slowly away from Timocharis Delta, trying to avoid adopting the bunny-hop gait which was more natural when moving quickly on the surface.

'Copy that, Mark. Roy, skirt farther south to be safe,' said Blake.

I walked a good forty metres southwards. The ground was absolutely solid, with just the usual one or two centimetres of fine, loose regolith. I stopped and turned to watch the buggy's progress.

Roy was now some hundred metres east of Timocharis Delta and almost level with its southernmost tip. 'I'm turning westwards. Should be well south of Mark's dust pit,' he said.

'Roger that, Roy. Proceed with care.'

The buggy was now approaching me head-on. It comprised a single lozenge-shaped cabin about five metres long and three metres wide. Inside there was plenty of headroom. It contained three bunks, cooking facilities, a chemical toilet, and half a dozen seats. The structure sat on a raised chassis with prominent axles and six wheels with chunky tyres. Electric motors powered each axle independently and the hubs of the two front wheels contained additional motors to provide more traction if required. It was now pointing towards me, maybe fifty metres to the east.

'Do you think I'm far enough south of the pit, Mark?'

'Can't be sure, but probably,' I replied.

'Any change in depth?' asked Blake.

'Not so far.'

'Okay. Just stay cautious,' said Blake.

'Copy that.'

The buggy slowed to a crawl.

'Dust's thicker here,' said Roy.

'Okay. Stop,' said Blake.

'Stopped. Left front tyre at least twenty centimetres deep. Right front about ten centimetres. I can see wheels three and four are on normal ground. Think I should turn south again. Blake?' said Roy.

'Right. Turn south,' said Blake.

'Roger that.'

The front wheels turned to the right. The buggy started to move forward to starboard, beginning a turn southward. I watched in horror as the entire cabin began to list to port.

'Oh fuck!' said Roy.

The buggy slid forward and lurched sideways. I saw wheels spinning and dust flying as Roy slammed the drive into reverse.

'I've hit full reverse on all wheels!' shouted Roy.

All that happened was that the starboard wheels started to grip, but that swung the vehicle farther to the south. In dreadful slow motion, the whole vehicle rolled onto its side, half the cabin and all the portside wheels buried in the dust.

'Report!' said Blake.

'Buggy two's on its side. Here's some pics,' I said as I sent a series of images to moonbase.

'On its portside. I'm half buried in dust,' said Roy.

'Stop all drives,' said Blake.

'Drives powered down,' said Roy.

'Seems to be just lying there. Not slipping deeper,' I said. What was most worrying was that the hatch was under the dust. A removable panel on the starboard side would give access, but releasing it involved all sorts of precautions, and even then it was cumbersome and was supposed to fall downwards. If I opened it, how could I lift it onto solid ground?

'No further movement,' said Roy.

I looked at my oxygen gauge. What had seemed plenty before, now seemed far less adequate. We were in trouble.

Moonscape: Chapter Two

BREATHING

I did a quick conversion of my oxygen supply into minutes. A hundred. Not good, given the change of circumstances.

'Just looking at my oxygen, Blake. Nominally a hundred minutes.'

'Right, Mark. We're having a look at your options. Will you head south for another fifty metres, then try to move east and see if that gets you around the dust pit? Great care now and keep the walking to minimum energy. We're checking buggy one right now to give you an ETA,' said Blake.

'Roger. Heading south,' I replied.

The ground remained perfectly solid, so I decided to change my heading to slightly east of south. Still no sign of deep dust.

The radio sprang back into life. 'Moonbase here. Can you tell us how you see your options, Mark?' asked Crystal.

'Well, if I can't get around whatever this dust pit is, then I guess my only option is to go to minimum activity and await your arrival. If I can get to buggy two then I'll assess the situation and discuss with Roy whether to remove the access hatch. An immediate problem comes to mind – the hatch is awkward to manoeuvre, and we wouldn't want it to slide off into the dust.'

'Okay, Mark. I'm relaying that to a moonbase-Earth conference discussing what's happened. Back to you soon,' said Crystal.

'Good job we weren't both inside this thing. That hatch can't be opened from inside,' said Roy.

'Right. We could still get through the back window, but I'd never be able to open that from outside on my own in time,' I said.

I reckoned I was fifty metres farther south now so turned due east, one step at a time.

'Heading due east now. Ground still firm,' I said.

'Roger that,' said Crystal.

Once I was as far east as the buggy, I turned to face it. On its eastern side the three wheels were clear of the dust, as the buggy was resting at about 95° to the horizontal. The inner surface of the centre port-side wheel was just visible.

'Roy. You noticed any further movement since it slipped?'

'No. Nothing.'

'Mark, Roy – Blake here.'

'Go ahead, Blake.'

'Buggy one en route to you now. ETA eighty-two minutes if no obstructions encountered. That's really tight for time for you, Mark. What's your O_2 reading now?'

'Roughly eighty-eight.'

'NASA recommend dropping the psi to 3.8 shortly, but what we need to know first is whether or not you can reach your buggy. Head north towards it but keep east of its position to avoid the pit.'

I took a moment to use the Valsalva device to relieve an infuriating nose itch, then set off. 'Walking north now.'

'Good. If you can reach buggy two it opens up other options, but if you can't, buggy one will have to come south of Timocharis Delta to reach you, to be sure we don't run into the pit. If you can reach it then we can head straight around the north of the crater.'

'Copy that. Ground still firm. Only twenty metres from buggy,' I said.

I walked as economically as I could, keeping a close eye on the depth of dust.

'Still on firm ground. Buggy wheels directly in front of me, about two metres. I've poked the tripod into the dust in front of me and it's still firm. Wondering if there's a sharp ledge.'

'Baby steps, and keep poking,' said Blake.

'Careful, Mark,' said Roy from the buggy.

'Just over half a metre and the tripod is going down into the dust. Pushing. Yes, it's deep very quickly.'

'Great care,' said Blake.

'Can feel the edge with my boot now. There's a drop off, unlike my side of the pit where it deepened gradually. Explains why the buggy tipped so suddenly.'

'Nah. I was careless. Should've reversed away. Turning was crazy,' said Roy.

'O_2, Mark?' asked Blake.

'Seventy-one minutes.'

'We've had Jenny trying to take the panel off buggy three. Took her twelve minutes. So we need to think about the options.'

'Don't really want to open her up unnecessarily,' said Roy.

'No, but if buggy one hits a problem, Mark could soon see his O_2 diving.'

'Why don't I sit quietly for thirty minutes, conserve O_2 and see how buggy one's ETA has changed?' I said. 'If I'm going to open that panel, I've other problems than just the fixings.'

'Explain,' said Blake.

'Well… firstly, I have to step almost half a metre onto the tyre of port wheel one. What if that causes the buggy to roll further? Also, what if the tyre moves? There's nothing to support me unless I lean forward against the underside.'

'I see,' said Blake. 'Roy can lock the wheel so it doesn't move. What's your next move once you're on it?'

'Locked it,' said Roy.

'Thanks, Roy. I'll then have to jump up to grab the starboard side of the chassis. I don't think that will be too difficult given one sixth G, but if I did miss there's no certainty I won't drop into the dust. If I do get up to the chassis, I'll have to climb along it and lie on the side of the buggy to undo the fixings. I don't want to be attempting that on low psi or if I'm running low on O_2. It's now or never, really.'

'I'll go back to NASA on this. Sit quietly, Mark,' said Blake.

Moon suits are not particularly flexible, but I managed to get into a sitting position, facing the Earth. An almost cloudless Australia stared back at me. The gauge read sixty-seven minutes.

Moonscape: Chapter Three

PATIENCE

For a thousand, a million, perhaps even a billion years, it had been lying dormant in the dust of a rocky moon. It had no consciousness because there was no consciousness nearby. It was in deep hibernation. Until now, it had sensed nothing, felt nothing, saw nothing and knew nothing.

But now it had awoken and it could sense a consciousness, just above its resting place. It sent out a tendril and encountered aluminium sheeting. The object was a vessel, lying still and silent in the dust. It became aware of thoughts nearby. It sensed some anxiety, not worry for itself, but for another entity elsewhere.

How could it get closer to the consciousness? It couldn't enter the creature without physical contact. Surrounding it was tightly packed dust. There was no atmosphere. The rocky moon was devoid of gases, but there was atmosphere inside the vessel.

It moved and twisted in the dust, trying to make better contact with the aluminium sheeting of its hollow prey.

Ah, contact. There was warmth. Well, warmer than the

dust. There was something inside the vessel which was most certainly a living creature.

Now it was more fully awake, it sensed a second organism nearby, inactive, breathing shallowly. A long way off, vibrations were approaching.

Self-preservation took over. It needed to ensure it wasn't harmed by these things nor left behind when they passed by. Its primitive, existential need for contact with something alive became all-encompassing.

Tendrils extended, sensing the skin of the vessel, it found a different material. A manufactured metal shaft. Solid. This wasn't hollow like the aluminium. It followed the length of the shaft and reached a much more complex object. The steel entered the centre of an alloy hub which was surrounded by a more pliable substance. It could move the surface of the substance and there was a minute gap between it and the other metallic alloy.

This was somewhere it could conceal itself. Compressing its tendril, it forced itself into the gap, squeezing itself to a thickness of only a micron or two, then straining and thrusting itself through the crevice and into a space between the alloy and the compound of the softer object.

Satisfied it was concealed safely, it waited. The vibrations it had sensed were still a long way off, but rapidly approaching. The two organisms were unmoving. The more distant one was still breathing, but shallowly. The other was behind the aluminium sheeting.

Moonscape: Chapter Four

THE UNFORGIVING MOON

'How's the oxygen now, Mark?' asked Blake.

'Eleven minutes – and I see buggy one on the horizon trailing a cloud of dust,' I said.

'Sounds good.'

'Hi, Mark?' said a female voice over the radio.

'Yes. That you, Linda?'

'Super-heroines to the rescue. I've got Mary with me. We can see you, Timocharis Delta and Roy's wreck. Will be there soon. Mary says she'll teach him to drive later,' said Linda.

Roy choked off a laugh. It was unlike him not to make an instant retort. I figured he was embarrassed.

The rescue buggy was approaching the top of the crater. One helpful aspect of the moon was that the horizon was so close – they'd reach me within a couple of minutes.

Roy's voice cut in. 'Great care as you come around the crater, Linda. We don't know if there are more of these pits.'

'Yes. We must find out about this accumulation. Most unusual,' I said.

'We're taking care, Roy, but we accelerated when we got into your tracks. Coming around the crater now. Still following your tracks. Be there shortly.'

'Stop behind buggy two and I'll come aboard,' I said.

Mary said, 'I've suited up and am driving now, Linda's suiting up as I speak.'

I fought my way to my feet. The difficulty of getting to a standing position was why we normally remained standing when wearing backpacks.

Buggy one came to a halt a couple of metres from buggy two and the dust pit. I made my way around to the door which was being opened for me. Within two minutes I was inside.

'Just for the record, Blake, I've three minutes air remaining. Think we should consider additional supplies mounted outside the buggies in future.'

'Yes, that's a bit tight, Mark.'

Within a few seconds, my backpack was recharged with power and oxygen. Linda and I climbed out of the hatch to assess buggy two.

'We can get a good fixing on the rear strut, Blake. Will it take the strain?' asked Linda.

'Send us an image and I'll forward to NASA,' said Blake.

'Image sent. Taking and sending more,' I said.

The buggy was lying almost on its side with all three starboard wheels in view. The front pair were rotated hard right, which was Roy's last action before it tumbled into the pit.

'If we attach the tow cable to the rear strut, that should

pull it up if you keep a steady reverse drive running, Roy,' said Linda.

'I'm strapped in and ready,' replied Roy.

'Turn the buggy around, Mary, with the rear end towards us, please,' said Linda.

'Will do.'

Linda and I stood still, awaiting NASA's response and taking in the view of Earth hovering in the sky, so near yet so far. Buggy one backed up about forty metres and turned through 180°.

'I'll never tire of this view,' I said, looking at the Earth.

'No. Beautiful. So beautiful, you forget how unforgiving the moon can be,' said Linda. 'Three minutes!'

'I could have extended that by further pressure reductions,' I said.

'Not by much. Suppose we'd broken down en route?'

'I'd have tried to open the emergency panel.'

'An emergency external supply is the answer. I'll do a report when you let me have your notes.'

'Right.'

'Reversing,' said Mary.

We moved to one side of buggy two to keep out of the way. Reversing lights flashed their warning and, if this had been inside the garage dome, we'd have heard loud beeps, once a second. The moon was a world of almost perfect silence, only broken by the odd sound travelling through the spacesuit.

'That's it, Mary. Stop there and power down while we work on attachments,' said Linda.

'Linda?' said Blake.

'Receiving.'

'You've a go on attaching the cable to the rear strut, but NASA says, "no jerking".'

'Roger that, Blake.'

I opened the cubbyhole beneath buggy one and removed a four-metre, multi-strand steel cable about a centimetre thick. At each end it had a simple but heavy-duty snap hook. Linda ran her cable through the tow bar and attached her hook. Cautiously, I made my way towards the rear of our buggy. I felt the edge of the pit with my foot when I was still a metre short of reaching the strut.

'I'm at the pit edge,' I said.

'How about going around via the axle?' asked Linda.

'Your wheels still locked, Roy?'

'Roger that, Mark.'

I skirted the pit until I was adjacent to the rear axle. If I leaned forward, I'd be able to touch the wheel.

'Blake, no real choice here. I'm going to have to jump onto the wheel,' I said.

'No alternative?' asked Blake.

'Don't think so,' said Linda.

'Okay, Mark. Attach your end of the cable to your suit clip, then go for it.'

'Attached.'

I jumped. Pressurised gloves, even with silicon grips, were not the most suitable garments to try and get a grip on metal or the tyre material of the wheel. I began to slip, heard Linda shout out to be careful, and then managed to wedge my hand between the alloy hub of the wheel and the steel shaft.

I heaved myself forward – much easier than it sounds under a sixth of Earth gravity. Now I was secure, lying across the wheel. I could unclip myself and reach across to clip the cable to the strut, but it would leave me untethered.

Linda had anticipated the problem and had already attached another cable to buggy one. She called out, 'Grab this second cable, Mark.'

She threw it. The first attempt sailed over me and the hull of buggy two. 'Coo. Forgot my own strength,' she said and laughed.

I managed to grab it on the second attempt, worked it back through my hand, clipped it to my suit and then unclipped the original cable to attach it to the strut.

Now I sat on the wheel and threw myself forward, Linda taking up the slack. I was safely back on luna firma.

Linda climbed back into her buggy and secured the hatch. I stood away from the action to report on what was happening.

Buggy one eased forward.

'Slack taken up,' I said. 'Begin low-rev reverse drive, Roy.'

He acknowledged the instruction, then the wheels began to spin.

'Okay, Mary. Slowly forward.'

The back end of buggy two began to rise out of the pit and, once the rear wheels were on firm ground, the whole vehicle tipped back to an upright position. In less than five minutes both vehicles were standing on the moon's surface.

I disconnected the cable and stowed it back on buggy one.

'That's your cable returned,' I said. 'I'm going to join Roy, take a rest break and after a meal we'll continue with the survey.'

I made my way around the buggy and found Roy had already opened the hatch. I climbed in gratefully. After we had repressurised it was a delight to slough off my suit.

'There's a no-go on that, Mark. NASA want all four of you back at Moonbase to check out that buggy,' said Blake.

'Looked fine to me,' I said.

'They want it checked,' said Blake.

'Okay, following the girls back,' said Roy.

'We'll try not to lose you,' said Linda.

'Dream on,' said Roy.

Both buggies headed round Timocharis Delta and then west towards base.

Appendix I

Detailed Description of Kepler

I only discovered the existence of aphantasia recently because one of my beta readers is a sufferer. Up to four percent of the population are afflicted. This more detailed description of the ship might help clarify its design for those who have difficulty visualising.

Face On

Imagine facing Kepler as it journeys through space. The front of the ship is the entire eight hundred metre disc. In the centre, about thirty metres in diameter is the hub.

The whole of the front of the ship bows outwards towards you. The back of the ship is flat. Imagine a very shallow bowl with a tight-fitting lid – that is roughly Kepler's shape.

Halfway through the journey, the central hub section

must leave the main ship and turn to face the opposite direction for deceleration.

The reason only the hub turns is because the front of Kepler has various devices to help interstellar dust slide off its convex shape.

The rim of the ship is also the outermost deck, deck one hundred. If you were to draw ninety-nine concentric circles on the ship, that would be the one hundred decks. Apartment decks are just 2.5 metres high, decks cultivating fruit trees have extra height.

Elevators run from the central hub down each of the six sectors – A, B, C, D, E and F. The ship is spinning so the terms portside and starboard side are just terminology for the sectors. A, B and C are considered portside, and D, E and F starboard.

If you are facing the disc of the ship, people are standing on the inside of the rim, their heads towards the hub and feet on the rim. You can walk around the rim like the inside of an enormous hamster wheel. The same applies to all decks.

The Hub

The front of the hub protrudes several metres from the main ship, and this area houses the bridge. You can imagine the hub as being like a can of soft drink sitting within the main disc of the ship. The hub and ship are joined by connectors.

The bridge is the front section. Behind that are admin areas and the captain's and president's offices. Behind them is the engineering section and the ion drives – seventy-two cylinders poking out of the back of the hub like jet nozzles.

During the mid-course manoeuvre, the hub moves

forward out of the main disc, turns through 180 degrees and is reinserted. After this manoeuvre, the bridge is now facing backwards and the ion drives face forward to slow the ship down.

Profile

Now let's look at the ship from the side. Imagine cutting the ship in half so that the contents can be seen.

At the very bottom, the outer deck apartments occupy the space from the rim corridor to the back of the ship – better protection from radiation. At the front are the colonist descent landers, five hundred of them circling the ship. The ship's circumference is about 2,500 metres, so there's a CDL every five metres. Each can hold twelve colonists for descent when Kepler-452b is reached.

In our cutaway of the ship, we can visualise the one hundred decks, averaging just under four metres ceiling height. Because the front of the ship bulges outward, each deck extends farther forward than the one beneath it.

The decks are mirror imaged in the top half of the cutaway.

To visualise a large hydroponics farm, imagine leaving the elevator and entering the farm from a corridor which runs around the entire disc. The farm is wedge shaped, like a slice of cake. The floor will curve from one side to the other as the ship is circular, but inside the deck, you do not feel the curve as gravity is always pulling you downwards. On decks near the rim, the curvature is hardly noticed. Nearer the hub it's visually obvious, but still always feels flat.

I hope this has helped you visualise Kepler.

Tony Harmsworth, 8th January 2026

forward out of the main deck, [illegible] through 180 degrees and is [illegible]. After the [illegible], the bridge is now facing backwards and the [illegible] the ship forward.

Home

Now let's look at the ship from the [illegible] the ship in half so that the [illegible] can be seen.

At the very bottom, the [illegible] the [illegible] from the [illegible] to the back of the ship [illegible]. [illegible] the [illegible] hundred [illegible]. The ship [illegible].

[illegible] of the ship, we [illegible] the [illegible] four [illegible]. Because the [illegible] of the ship [illegible], each [illegible].

[illegible] half of the [illegible].

[illegible] the [illegible] the [illegible] around the [illegible]. The [illegible] the [illegible] to the other [illegible] the [illegible] of the [illegible]. [illegible] the [illegible].

January [illegible] 2024

Appendix Ii

The Speed of Light & Time Dilation

High-speed travel does strange things to the world of the traveller and that of those left behind. In the early twentieth century, Albert Einstein, as a young man, looked at the universe differently from scientists who had come before.

Science considered that there were several universal constants. One of those was time. Surely, time could only pass in one direction and it would always be the same, whether you were on the surface of the Earth, on a distant world, in orbit, or travelling on a speeding comet. The second constant was the speed of light. Experiments took place in the late nineteenth century to discover how Earth was moving in relation to what was believed to be a universal flux, an invented ether through which light waves travelled. If they measured the speed of light in two directions, at ninety degrees to each other, it should be possible to discover Earth's true motion in relation to the rest of the universe. The theory was sound. Michelson and Morley performed an accurate experiment several times, and were staggered to discover that the speed of light was always the same. When Earth was travelling in one direction around its orbit, the speed of light was exactly the same as when the Earth was moving in the opposite direction. It was this discovery that set Einstein on the track of his famous relativity theories. In particular, he imagined the path of a light beam in a fast train and how a stationary observer would measure it.

Light moves at a constant speed, no matter who measures it or how fast they are travelling. Imagine being on a spaceship travelling at half the speed of light. If you measure the speed of light travelling in the same direction, you would expect it to be fifty percent higher than normal, and in the opposite direction, fifty percent slower than normal. In fact, it remains the same irrespective of the speed of the experimenter. How could that be?

Einstein turned it all about-face by considering how observation could fit in with the speed of light being constant. An observer of a person moving at high speed would observe something unexpected. In order for the person in motion to measure the speed of light as being the same as for the observer, the *only* explanation would be that the person in motion was living in an area of slower time. The faster the motion, the slower the time. Einstein's theory flew in the face of scientific logic.

In practical terms, the Kepler starship was accelerating constantly, and therefore its velocity was increasing. In the first few months of the journey from the 2046 launch date, the variance in time was immeasurably small. As velocity increased, an observer on Earth would find that the travellers on Kepler were ageing more slowly. The travellers themselves would not notice any difference onboard their ship, but if they had been able to view the Earth, they would have seen that the observers aged more quickly than they.

About the Author

Tony Harmsworth was born Anthony Geoffrey Harmsworth on 19th March 1948. His father, George, came from Boxmoor, Hertfordshire, and his mother, Williamina Robertson, from Preston Pans in Scotland.

Tony was educated at Welwyn Garden City High School and Bude County Grammar School, where he decisively failed his A and S-level subjects in Pure Maths, Applied Maths and Physics, owing, in part, to severe hay fever, although he admits not working hard enough could have contributed to the failure. His IQ was Mensa tested to 158 in his last year at school. His lifelong interest in science and astronomy has inspired his writing.

As a teenager, Tony developed a deep scepticism of religion, read both the Bible and, later, the Quran, realising that they were nothing but ancient stories without any basis in reality, and became a confirmed atheist. Don't be surprised to find this influencing some of his stories.

Not having a university education, he entered retail and had a talent for shop management. In 1971 he moved into industry, and became an organisation and methods manager at Wella. In 1975 he was head-hunted by British American Cosmetics. Wanting an improved quality of life, he moved to Drumnadrochit in the Highlands of Scotland in 1978.

Here he staged the Loch Ness Exhibition and ran it for ten years, later creating more visitor centres and multimedia presentations on Scotland's history and Macbeth in particular.

After the millennium, he created two successful guided tour companies.

Wanting to set the record straight on Loch Ness, he wrote a very comprehensive sceptical book on the subject, and this gave him the writing bug. He now writes realistic, science fiction in the vein of the late John Wyndham.

After five years of being rejected by publishers and agents, Tony self-published his stories in 2019. Finally, in 2025, Vinci Books acquired his novels and are republishing all his science fiction in new covers and with many translations.

www.ingramcontent.com/pod-product-compliance
Lightning Source LLC
LaVergne TN
LVHW030915080826
845145LV00013B/2906